Judith Lennox was born in Salisbury, Wiltshire, but spent most of her childhood in an isolated part of the Hampshire countryside, living in what had formerly been the gamekeeper's cottage of a large country house. After attending a variety of schools, she read English at Lancaster University, and has since worked as a civil servant, an abstracter of scientific reports, and as a pianist for a ballet school. She met her husband, Iain, at Lancaster, they have three sons and now live in Cambridgeshire. Her two most recent novels, *The Secret Years* and *The Winter House*, are also published by Corgi Books.

Some Old Lover's Ghost

Judith Lennox

CORGI BOOKS

SOME OLD LOVER'S GHOST
A CORGI BOOK : 0 552 14333 2

Originally published in Great Britain by Doubleday,
a division of Transworld Publishers Ltd

PRINTING HISTORY
Doubleday edition published 1997
Corgi edition published 1997

Copyright © Judith Lennox 1997

The right of Judith Lennox to be identified as the
author of this work has been asserted in accordance
with sections 77 and 78 of the Copyright Designs and
Patents Act 1988

Set in 10 on 12 pt Sabon by
Hewer Text Composition Services, Edinburgh

Corgi Books are published by Transworld Publishers Ltd,
61–63 Uxbridge Road, London W5 5SA,
in Australia by Transworld Publishers (Australia) Pty Ltd,
15–25 Helles Avenue, Moorebank, NSW 2170
and in New Zealand by Transworld Publishers (NZ) Ltd,
3 William Pickering Drive, Albany, Auckland

Reproduced, printed and bound in Great Britain by
Mackays of Chatham PLC, Chatham, Kent

To Iain, with love

PART ONE

PROLOGUE

For two days, frost had fringed the reeds and the grass with a silvery filigree. Filaments of ice on every leaf and branch reflected the remains of the dying sun. Ice clung to the walls of the dike. Around the stems of the plants at the water's edge an opaque, whitish glaze hid the rotting vegetation beneath. But where the current ran free a mist rose, small curling wisps like steam from a boiling bath, as though the black heart of the water ran warm.

The dike gouged a channel through the flat East Anglian landscape. To either side of it fields fell away, vast and featureless, their boundaries marked by a pathway of twin ruts or a straggle of stunted bushes. The sun touched the church tower and the bare branches of the trees that surrounded it, and then moved slowly to the empty land beyond, delineating the long ridges left by the plough. All was still: no breeze rustled the frozen grass or flicked aside a swirl of dead leaves to reveal the bare bones of the earth beneath.

As he walked along the bank of the dike, his breath made grey clouds in the chill evening air. It seemed to him that though this land had been stolen from the sea by man, and though the marks of man's stubbornness and ingenuity were visible in the deep scars of the dikes and waterways, yet there was never a sense of ownership, only of borrowing. The low horizon, the vastness of the sky, reduced humanity to small, bustling insignificance. If a god existed, then that god interceded, through flood and tempest, only as a reminder of impotence. When landscape itself was impermanent, then what chance had fragile bones and flesh? Others had believed they had mastery of this place; others had been expelled by the greater armies of water and tide.

Looking ahead, he saw the house that stood by itself a mile or so from the church. As the rays of the setting sun touched them, the panes of glass in the windows flared with red and gold light, and the four-square walls lost their dreariness, so that the house seemed to come alive again. He stood still, remembering, the words *if only* searing his frozen heart just as the dike seared the cold earth. Then the sun sank below the horizon, and the house retreated into the shadows.

He turned back, retracing his footsteps. It was quite dark now, a thin filament of cloud covering the face of the moon, the stars not yet bright. Conscious of the water to one side of him he moved carefully, wishing he had brought a torch or lantern. Just the thought of falling into the dike – a cracking of ice and then no sound at all – made him shudder. Drowning was the worst death: the water in your lungs, your mouth, your nostrils, choking you. Like being buried alive.

The sound of a step, and a gasping breath where he had believed himself to be alone, made him almost lose his footing. His heart lurched against his ribcage, and he looked to left and right, wide-eyed, half expecting the swirls of steam that rose from the water to have acquired shape and substance, to have become small ghosts, the will-o'-the-wisps that haunted the Fen.

But then the cloud thinned, and the moonlight showed him the dog, scrabbling at the sloping wall of the dike. Paws clawing the iron-hard earth, wet nose sniffing for secrets.

Stooping, he gathered pebbles and flung them at the creature until it yelped and ran into the darkness.

CHAPTER ONE

After Toby had gone, I took the bouquet of flowers he had given me and flushed them one by one down the lavatory. Their petals floated on the surface of the water, smooth and pink and perfumed. Then I went to the dreary little room at the end of the corridor, and stared out of the window. It was raining, a dark, thin October drizzle that sheened the streets beyond the hospital. The television was on, but I didn't hear it. I heard only Toby's voice, saying, *I don't think we should see so much of each other, Rebecca.*

I had been unable to stop myself whispering, 'Please, Toby. Not *now*.' I had seen him flinch. Then he had said, 'It just hasn't felt right for a while. But because of the baby—' and he had reddened, and looked away, and I had heard myself say coolly, 'Of course. If that's how you feel.' Anything rather than become an unwanted, burdensome, pitiable thing.

I turned away from the window. *EastEnders* was on the television, and a very young girl in a shabby dressing gown was curled in front of it, smoking. She offered me a cigarette, and I accepted one, though I hadn't smoked since university. On the side of the packet was written a slogan, SMOKING CAN DAMAGE THE HEALTH OF YOUR

UNBORN CHILD, but that didn't matter any more. My poor little half-formed child had been, like the flowers, disposed of. I lit the cigarette, and closed my eyes, and saw petals floating on the water, pink and foetus-shaped.

After I was discharged from hospital I went back to my flat in Teddington. I rent the ground floor of one of the many Victorian villas that line the streets of west London. The rooms – kitchen, bathroom, and bedsitting room – had a dusty, unfamiliar look. There was a heap of letters by the front door, and the answerphone was blinking frantically. I disregarded both, and lay down on the bed, my coat wrapped around me.

I thought of Toby. I had first met Toby Carne eighteen months ago, in South Kensington. There had been a sudden heavy rain shower, I had had no raincoat, and when a gentleman had drawn level with me and offered to share his umbrella, I had thankfully accepted. I say 'gentleman', an old-fashioned term, because Toby had looked, to me, every inch the gentleman – Burberry and black city umbrella; short dark hair just touching his collar; old but expensive leather briefcase. I had guessed him to be around ten years older than me, and I had walked beside him, forgetting to dodge the puddles, hypnotized by his sudden smile and by the unmistakable interest in his eyes. When he suggested going for a drink to escape the rain, I accepted. By the time we parted, he had my name and telephone number. I had not expected him to phone, but he did, a few days later. I'd made him laugh, he explained. I was refreshing, different.

Toby had been my adventure. He had come from another world, and I had believed that our relationship would transform me. And it had, for a while. With

Toby, I had lost weight, had worn smarter clothes, and had my long hair lightened. I had worn high heels and had not tripped over them, and I had bought expensive make-up, the sort that stays where you put it on. I had visited Toby's parents' house in Surrey, and had pretended that I was used to sofas whose cushions did not fray, and bathrooms with matching towels. Together we had visited Amsterdam, Paris, and Brussels; together we had dined in expensive restaurants and been invited to fashionable parties. He introduced me to his lawyer friends as 'Rebecca Bennett, the biographer'; they tended to look blank, which he noticed after a while. He suggested I write a novel; I explained that I needed the solidity of history. He proposed, late and drunk one glorious summer's night, that we try for a baby, but when, a couple of months later, I told him that I was pregnant, he toasted the infant with the best champagne, but did not suggest that we move in together. And when, several weeks after that, I began to lose our baby at a dull but important dinner party, he seemed put out that I had chosen such a time, such a place.

I had considered my remaking, which he had begun and I had colluded with, to be permanent. With one sentence – *I don't think we should see so much of each other* – he had reminded me of what I really was. My 'difference' had become tiresome or, worse, embarrassing. And I hadn't made him laugh for ages.

In the days after I came home from hospital, I did not leave the flat. I drank cups of tea and ate, when I could be bothered to eat, the contents of ancient forgotten tins that gathered dust at the back of the kitchen cupboard. I neither answered the telephone nor opened the post. The dull ache in my belly, a memento of the miscarriage, slowly faded. The panicky feeling, the sense that everything was falling apart, persisted. I slept as much as I could, though my dreams were punctuated by nightmares.

Then Jane turned up. Jane is my elder sister. She has two little boys aged one and three, and a cottage in Berkshire. A mild but persistent mutual envy has always been a part of our relationship. Jane hammered on the door until I opened it, then took one look at the frowsty squalor and at me, and said, 'Honestly, Becca, you are hopeless.' I burst into tears, and we hugged awkwardly, the products of a family not much given to displays of physical affection.

I spent a week with Jane, and then returned to London. You must begin to pick up the threads, she said, as she saw me onto the train. But it did not seem to me that there were any threads left to pick up. The life I had planned had been Toby and the baby and a continuation of the career I had struggled for throughout my twenties. I had lost both Toby and the child and, though I sat dutifully at my desk and stared at my word processor, I was not able to write. I could think of nothing worth writing about. Any sentence I attempted to assemble was clumsy and meaningless. Ideas flickered through my head and I scribbled them down in a notebook, but the next morning they always seemed shallow, empty.

Jane and Steve invited me to stay with them at Christmas. The noise and enthusiasm of the little boys filled in the gaps made by my mother's death, four years ago, and my father's cantankerousness. Back in London, Charles and Lucy Lightman dragged me off to a New Year party. I've known Charles Lightman for years. He and his sister Lucy both have pale green eyes and the sort of fine, light brown hair that keeps to no particular style. Charles and I met at university, but now he has his own production company, Lighthouse Productions, which specializes in television programmes with an archaeological or historical interest. The previous summer we had worked together on a documentary, *Sisters of the Moon*.

At the party, the ritual beginnings of courtship – the *What do you do?* and the *Shall I get you a drink?* – seemed forced. In the bathroom, I caught sight of my reflection in the mirror. Round face, short mousy hair (I'd had it cut a few weeks ago, and could no longer be bothered colouring it), light blue eyes expressing a dazed bewilderment and defencelessness that seemed to me inappropriate to my thirty-one years. I stared in disgust at my inept reflection, and then grabbed my coat and went home. But I thought, as I curled up in bed to escape the sounds of revelry on the street outside, that I was doing better. It was weeks since I had cried myself to sleep, weeks since I had felt a stab of pain at the sight of a dark-haired man, or a baby in a pram. I was teaching myself not to feel. I was teaching myself well.

A fortnight later, I put up in the local shop an advertisement offering tutoring in A level history. I'd taught before, but had thankfully abandoned teaching after the modest success of my biography of Ellen Wilkinson. But every spark of creativity seemed to have died, and I was badly overdrawn at the bank. I had several replies to my advert, yet, as I arranged times in my diary, I felt a qualm of nervousness, a fleeting suspicion that, faced by these unknown students, I would be dull, uninspiring, inaccurate.

In the middle of February, Charles, bearing a Chinese takeaway and a bottle of red wine, called at my flat. *Sisters of the Moon* was to be broadcast at nine o'clock that evening. Looking around with some amazement, he said, 'But you're always so organized, darling,' and I felt fleetingly embarrassed by the heaps of unwashed dishes, the balls of dust gathering in the corners of the room.

Charles and I sat on my bed, watching the television, eating lemon chicken and egg fried rice. My name was on the credits, and I had already seen the preview, of course, but now the programme seemed alien, nothing to do with me. Someone else had interviewed those frail old ladies, someone else had consigned to her tape recorder those sad tales of abandonment and betrayal. *Sisters of the Moon* told the story of a group of women, victims of the Mental Deficiency Act of 1913. The Act had allowed local authorities to certify and incarcerate pregnant women who were destitute or, in the eyes of a judgemental male authority, immoral – unmarried mothers, in other words. The Act was not repealed until the 1950s, and by then the asylum was those women's home, and the outside world a changed, incomprehensible place.

Researching the programme, I had met Ivy Lunn in an old people's home in Nottingham. She had been almost ninety years old, and as bright as a button. I had taken her out to tea, a treat which had evoked in her a mixture of delight and trepidation. When, over scones and jam, she had relaxed a little, she had told me her story. At the age of fourteen, Ivy had obtained a position as a scullery-maid in a house in London, just after the end of the First World War. One morning, the eldest son of the house had come into the bathroom as she was cleaning the tub. She had felt his hands below her waist, pulling up her skirt. She had been afraid to cry out when he had raped her, afraid afterwards to tell anyone. She had understood neither what he had done, nor the possible consequences of it. She had known only that he had hurt and degraded her. When her pregnancy had begun to show, Ivy's mistress dismissed her. When Ivy tried to explain what had happened, it was made clear that all the responsibility was hers. The son was returned to public school, and Ivy was sent to the asylum. Sitting there on the bed, Charles's arm slung around my shoulders, I remembered that I had cried when Ivy had told me her story. I had sat in that chintzy little café and wept tears of pity. Ivy had comforted *me*. And yet now, all these long months later, I felt nothing.

The credits rolled, the closing theme faded, and Charles gave a whoop of delight. His gooseberry-green eyes were bright with exhilaration, and he talked very fast.

'Stunning, don't you think, Becca? Should be some bloody good reviews. I shall go out first thing and buy all the papers. We make a good team, don't we?' And he lunged forward and kissed me.

'Coffee,' I said firmly, disentangling myself.

'I've an idea for another piece—' he yelled, as I ground beans in the kitchen. 'Public schools at the beginning of the century. You know, beating and buggery. I'm going to tie it in with the First World War, loss of Empire, all that—'

He rambled on while I poured boiling water into the cafetière, and put crockery on a tray. After a while, I stopped listening to him. To create a documentary that will make the viewer weep, you have to feel for your subjects. If Ivy Lunn, who had been raped and incarcerated and separated for almost a lifetime from her only child, was no longer able to move me, then I doubted whether anything could.

A week later, I had a telephone call from my agent, Nancy Walker. '*Terrific* news, Rebecca,' she cried. 'I'm *delighted*.' Nancy always speaks in italics. She went on, 'Sophia Jennings from Crawfords has just been on the phone. They'd like to meet up with you, talk through a possible project.' I could almost hear her smile.

Crawfords is a successful and reputable London publisher. Nancy explained, 'They're planning to commission a life of Dame Tilda Franklin.'

Until a few years ago, every newspaper or television investigation concerned with child welfare had necessitated an interview with Dame Tilda. She had devoted her life to the welfare of children – adopting and fostering numerous orphaned infants, setting up psychiatric clinics to care for disturbed children, and organizing charities and helplines and safe houses for those abused or at risk. Loving, yet efficient; gentle, but incisive. When I thought back, I only vaguely remembered Tilda Franklin's face – a fleeting recollection of charismatic beauty and a sense of intelligence and vigour behind the charm.

'They want to talk to *me*?' I said incredulously. 'Are you sure?'

'Apparently Crawfords first contacted Dame Tilda years ago, but she's always refused. And then *she* telephoned *them*, insisting on *you*. She said that she won't consider anyone else.'

There was a pause, as Nancy waited for me to comment. But I said nothing. I was, literally, speechless. I couldn't think why Dame Tilda Franklin should want me to write her biography – and I was still inclined to believe that it was all a mistake – but nevertheless it was as though I had suddenly turned the corner of a very long, dark tunnel, and could see in the distance a pinpoint of light. I knew that I ought to tell Nancy that I couldn't write any more, but for some reason – professional pride, I suppose – I did not.

'*Fascinating* life . . .' added Nancy. 'She did something terribly heroic in the war, I believe. Rebecca?' A note of anxiety had entered her voice. 'You are pleased, aren't you?'

'Delighted,' I mumbled, but remembered too clearly sitting in front of the word processor, unable to write a coherent sentence. I said cautiously, 'I'm not sure, Nancy. All those children . . . Could I do justice to her? And it would be a lot of work . . .'

'That hasn't put you off before,' said Nancy briskly. 'I'm sure you could make a *marvellous* job of it. Think it over, Rebecca. Give me a ring, and I'll arrange a preliminary meeting with Sophia.'

She added a few pleasantries, and then rang off. I sat for a while, staring at the wall. I should have explained, I thought, that I'd lost confidence in my ability even to write a shopping list. And that it really wasn't my sort of thing, to write the biography of a saint. I prefer to show the skull beneath the skin. History only interests me when the glaze cracks, and I glimpse clay.

How could I describe the happy families that Tilda Franklin had created, when that sort of security was something I had never really known? How could I write of the joy of caring for children, when my only attempt to create a new life had ended in miscarriage? I picked up the telephone, ready to dial Nancy's number and tell her that there was really no point in my talking to the people at Crawfords, but I put the receiver back without touching the keypad. There was still that flicker of optimism, that small, muted return of the self-belief I thought I had lost for ever.

I grabbed my car keys and left the house and drove to Twickenham, where I walked, watching the mist rise from the Thames. A wet, yapping dog ran along the bank towards me, and shook himself so that drops of water spun from his fur like sparks from a Catherine wheel. The clouds had thinned at last, and I glimpsed the sun, a dim pearl of pink and orange. The water lapped at the toes of my boots, but I turned away from the river before the clouds could return to blot out the sunshine. And when I reached home, I made myself phone Nancy. I'd go and talk to Crawfords next week, I told her.

Dame Tilda Franklin lived in the village of Woodcott St Martin, in Oxfordshire. Trapped on the M40 between hissing lorries and impatient sales reps, I almost wished I could turn back. But I forced myself to drive on, lurching and pausing with the queues of traffic, peering through the hypnotic sweep of the windscreen wipers.

I'd talked through the project with my prospective editor. She had suggested I speak to Tilda Franklin herself, and, if I was still interested in the commission, rough out some ideas. If Crawfords were happy with my suggestions, they'd pay a reasonable, if not over-generous, advance.

It was a relief to leave the motorway, and to plunge into a countryside of rolling hills and narrow, curling roads, and hollows where mist gathered in pools. I had to stop several times to check the map. I longed for coffee. It was early, not yet nine o'clock, and the world was only half awake. After about half an hour, I reached Woodcott St Martin, a sprawling village with a green, and a duckpond, and a couple of shops. I stopped at the newsagent and asked for directions to Dame Tilda's home, The Red House. 'She's not been well,' said the shopkeeper. 'She often has a touch of bronchitis at this time of year.'

The Red House stood a little apart from the rest of

the village. I saw a gleam of silver river to one side of the building, and playing fields, their untenanted swings ghostly in the greyish light, to the other. The house was large and old, its gables pierced by stone windows. The walls were of dark red brick, and the roof-tiles were discoloured by lichen. Box trees, carved into huge globes and four-sided pyramids, walled the narrow path. The mist faded their dark green leaves, and pearled their fantastic festoon of spiders' webs. Chill and solid, the great topiaried bushes enclosed me between them, cutting me off from the rest of the garden. I shivered: this was not the careful tangle of rose and aster that I had expected. These trees were vast and arcane, their shapes suggesting a symbolism unintelligible to me. I was relieved to escape them for the narrow gravel court in front of the house. When I looked down at myself, and saw the gossamer that clung to my jacket, I brushed it hurriedly away and rang the doorbell.

Inside, I followed Dame Tilda's housekeeper through rooms and passageways. Portraits of children – painted, sketched and photographed – looked back at me from the walls. Children that Dame Tilda Franklin had cared for, I assumed. Infants and adolescents, girls with ribbons in their hair, boys in baggy corduroy shorts and sagging socks. Fading childhood scrawls, a clumsily worked length of cross-stitch, a blurred snapshot of a boy, hair quiffed Fifties-fashion, standing beside a gleaming motor scooter. The gilt frames of the pictures lit the dark oak-panelled interior.

The housekeeper led me to a room at the back of the house and tapped on the door. 'Miss Bennett is here, Tilda.'

The garden room was furnished with shabby, comfortable furniture, and plants – hoya, plumbago, bougainvillaea – crawling up the walls. A woman was standing in a corner of the room, secateurs in hand. She turned towards me.

'Miss Bennett? How good of you to come. I do apologize for suggesting such an unreasonably early hour, but I have a dreadful tendency to fall asleep in the afternoons.'

'Mrs—' But I remembered the damehood, or whatever one calls such things. 'I mean, Dame Matilda—' I floundered.

She put aside the secateurs. 'Call me Tilda, *please*. The "Dame" reminds me of the pantomime. And no-one has ever called me Matilda – so forbidding, don't you think?'

She smiled. Beauty lingers, and though Tilda Franklin was now eighty years old I could see its lineaments still in her high, delicate cheekbones, her straight, narrow nose. Her eyelids were blue-veined, almost transparent, and her light eyes were set deep into her skull. Her face was longish, carefully sculptured, and her spine even in old age was straight. Beside Tilda I felt short, sloppy, troll-featured. She wore a soft tweed skirt, a cashmere cardigan, pearls; I, a long black skirt and suede jacket that I'd always thought possessed a sexily crumpled allure. I should have worn my one good suit.

I asked her to call me Rebecca, and we shook hands. Her fingers were insubstantial and birdlike. I thought that if I gripped too hard the bones would turn to powder.

'You'll join me for coffee, won't you, Rebecca? Such a long journey. So good of you to come.'

She talked about the plants in the garden room until

the housekeeper reappeared with a tray of coffee and home-made biscuits.

'The hoya is in flower already. It has a glorious scent, though only at night-time, of course. I have never understood how a plant can have fragrance at one time of day and not at another. Patrick, my grandson, tried to explain to me once.' She added, 'I am so pleased that you agreed to talk to me, Rebecca. Do you know why I suggested that you write my biography?'

I mumbled cautiously, 'I assumed you'd read my book.'

She shook her head. 'I'm afraid I don't read much these days. My eyesight – such a nuisance. I listen to the television, though. I saw your documentary.'

Everything about her – this house, her appearance, even the coffee cups – proclaimed her to be from another age. I couldn't picture Tilda slumped on the living-room sofa, flicking channels on a remote control.

'You saw *Sisters of the Moon*?'

She nodded. 'Yes. And a few days later, I was in Blackwells, buying a birthday present for my grand-daughter, and I saw your name on a book cover. Providential, don't you think?' She paused. 'I found your television programme very . . . very touching.'

I was horrified to notice that there were tears in her eyes.

'Very touching, and very intelligent. No unnecessary sentiment. No sensationalism. You stood back, and let those women tell their stories. I admire that. It implies a certain wisdom, a sense of your own limited importance in the scheme of things. It implies also a sense of justice. I do believe in justice, you see, Rebecca.' Her expression altered, and her light grey eyes darkened. 'People have forgotten those women, and they have forgotten the power that men like Edward de Paveley possessed. No-one should have such power.'

'Who is – was – Edward de Paveley?'

'Edward de Paveley was my father. He raped my mother, who was a maidservant in his house. When she became pregnant, he had her consigned to the workhouse, and from there she was sent to a mental institution in Peterborough.'

I was aware of a flicker of surprise. Looking at Tilda Franklin now, it was hard to believe that such a proud, elegant woman should have had so ignominious a beginning.

'I am reckoned to have led an interesting life,' Tilda added. 'I have always guarded my privacy, though. But when I watched your programme I thought that could be interpreted as cowardice, rather than a lack of egotism. I have made a bargain with myself – I shall tell the story of my life in order that my mother's story can be told.' Tilda put aside her cup and saucer. 'I would very much like you to consider writing my biography, Rebecca. I don't expect you to give me an answer yet, of course. But you'll think about it, won't you?'

I mumbled something noncommittal. I couldn't bring myself to confess to her that, though I had once been able to write, I was no longer able to do so. That Toby had taken, along with my self-respect, my art.

She seemed to take my silence for assent. 'May I tell you a little more? Both my mother's family – the Greenlees – and the de Paveleys lived in Southam, in the Cambridgeshire Fens. Fen villages were at that time very remote, very rural, little worlds of their own. My mother never travelled further than Ely, and that only occasionally. A wealthy landowner would have great influence in such a place.' Her eyes narrowed. 'My mother's family had lived and worked in Southam for generations. My grandmother died young, and my grandfather – my mother's father – was a labourer for the de Paveleys. They had two children – Sarah was the elder, and Deborah the younger. Their cottage was owned by the de Paveleys, and their renting of it was dependent on my grandfather's continuing to work for the family. So when he died in 1912, the sisters lost their home as well as their father. Deborah, who was sixteen, went into service with the de Paveleys, but Sarah left the village to try her luck elsewhere.'

She paused. Looking outside, I noticed that the sun had broken through the mist. It caught the facets of the crystal chandelier hanging from the ceiling, so that pinpoints of coloured light – blue and orange and violet – danced across the walls.

'I don't know exactly what happened. Only that Edward de Paveley came to my mother's bed and forced himself on her. And that my mother was thrown out of the Hall as soon as her pregnancy became obvious, and that she had nowhere to go but the workhouse. And I guess . . . I guess that my mother pleaded with Mr de Paveley. Told him that the child was his. Asked for his help.'

I imagined a bleak, featureless landscape, striped by narrow bands of water. I saw a young woman, little more than a child, her body distorted by pregnancy. And a man – on horseback, perhaps, or driving one of those boxy turn-of-the-century cars – pausing to speak to her.

'Whatever my mother asked of Edward de Paveley, he refused to help her,' Tilda continued. 'In the May of 1914 she gave birth to me in the workhouse, and then the order was signed confining her to the asylum. I have a copy of that order. Edward de Paveley was a magistrate, and his signature is on the committal certificate.'

She fell silent, and when I glimpsed the terrible sadness in her eyes I could only guess at what it had cost her to lay bare to a stranger the secrets of what she had admitted was a very private soul. Then her expression altered: she seemed mentally to shake herself. 'I was born in the workhouse,' she explained, 'but I spent my infancy in an orphanage. Illegitimate children were taken away from their mothers as soon as they were born, of course. People weren't keen to adopt children such as myself, because it was thought that an illegitimate baby might inherit its mother's immorality.'

The unwanted child, I thought, would salve the horror of her own birth by devoting her life to the rescue of other abandoned children. Such a neat, circular story.

'I lived in the orphanage until I was about a year old. Then Sarah came back.' Tilda smiled. 'My Aunt Sarah. I have a picture.'

She opened the album that lay on the table. I looked down at the photograph. The face that stared back at me had that solemn, slightly uneasy expression common to so many portraits from the early part of the century. Something to do with having to sit still so long for the camera, I suppose. Tilda's Aunt Sarah had a stout, shapeless bosom covered by a high-necked blouse. I could see nothing of Tilda in her plain, strong face, nothing at all.

'Deborah was the pretty sister and Sarah was the clever one,' said Tilda, reading my thoughts. 'I haven't a photograph of Deborah, I'm afraid.'

'You said that Sarah went away after her father died. Where did she go?'

'Oh, anywhere and everywhere, I should imagine,

knowing Sarah. She rarely settled in one place for long. By the time she came back to Cambridgeshire, my mother was dying. The regime was harsh in workhouses and asylums, and Deborah had never been strong.'

Tilda paused, and closed the photograph album. Just for a moment, her thin hand touched mine. 'Sarah knew nothing of what had happened to her sister until she came back to the village. You must understand, Rebecca, how remote East Anglia was in the early part of the century. Very few people had telephones, and my mother had left school when she was ten to look after her father, and was more or less illiterate. Anyway, Sarah travelled to the asylum, and spoke to her sister before she died. Deborah told her what had happened. I imagine . . . I imagine, sometimes, how Sarah must have felt. How it must have eaten away at her, the anger and the guilt.'

'Guilt?'

'At not being there when her sister needed her. Sarah was a strong person, Rebecca. Sarah would have thought of something. Sarah would never have allowed Deborah to go to the workhouse.'

'So Sarah adopted you?'

'Yes. She buried her sister, and adopted her niece. I don't remember the orphanage at all, of course – I was a baby when I left it. But Sarah never tried to pretend that she was my mother. I have always admired her for that honesty. As soon as I was old enough to understand, she told me that I was her younger sister's child. Nothing more than that, naturally.'

Your father raped your mother. I saw the impossibility of explaining such an outrage. 'And you lived . . .?' I prompted.

'All over East Anglia and southern England. Suffolk

... Norfolk ... Kent, mostly. Sarah did seasonal farmwork.'

I smiled. 'Like Tess of the D'Urbervilles?'

'A little like that. In the summer we helped with the harvest and picked hops in Kent. In winter, we'd take in sewing. My Aunt Sarah could sew beautifully. You couldn't see her stitches. She taught me to sew. She taught me everything.'

'Did you go to school?'

'Now and then, if we stayed in a village for more than a few weeks. Sarah taught me to read and to write, and she had a wonderful head for arithmetic. When I did go to school, I was always put in a class years above my age.'

It sounded a colourful, gypsy life, until I remembered that Tilda had been born in 1914, that ominous year, and that she had passed her childhood in the haunted, febrile Twenties. I said tentatively, 'It must have been hard sometimes.'

'Oh yes. I have never since been cold as I remember being cold then. How the frost used to eat into my hands and feet. The clouds that formed in the air when I took my first breath in the morning. And I was teased by other children, of course. For being different.'

Her words were matter-of-fact, untinged by self-pity. She still sat as upright as that woman in the sepia photograph, the aunt who had rescued her from the orphanage.

'I am a little tired,' she said suddenly. 'So tedious to be old.' She turned to me, focusing her flinty grey eyes on me. 'Do you wish to know more, Rebecca? Shall I tell you about Jossy . . .?'

'Jossy?' I repeated.

'Jossy de Paveley. Edward de Paveley's daughter.' Her

expression altered, one of those abrupt changes of mood that I came to realize were characteristic of her. 'She was my half-sister, of course . . .'

When her father was wounded in 1918, Joscelin de Paveley prayed each night that he would not recover. When he returned home, lurching on crutches from the Bentley to the front door, Jossy's infant faith in God faltered, and never quite recovered.

Edward de Paveley's experiences of war, his loss of a leg in the last months of bitter fighting, his near death and eventual recovery, did not, in forcing him to confront his own mortality, soften his autocratic character. To Jossy, the only lasting effect of the war that destroyed for ever Europe's complacency was that her father had become slower, less mobile. He was, simply, easier to run away from.

Through the years of her childhood, Jossy and her father and Uncle Christopher in the steward's house lived separate lives, planets orbiting the necessary sun of Hall and estate, their existences conjoined, but rarely touching. Uncle Christopher's sphere was the fields and dikes and tenant farms, Jossy's was school and the old nursery.

The de Paveleys' house was called the Hall (it may have had another name once, but that had been forgotten centuries ago). The nearest village was called Southam. Both Southam and the Hall were built on small, separate, shallow islands of clay. In wet winters, floodwater licked at the shells and seedlings in Jossy's garden.

Jossy's life was governed by her desire to avoid her father, to escape the contempt in his gaze and the cold sarcasm that brought tears to her eyes. Occasionally, disastrously, their orbits collided. Once he tried to teach her to ride. The lesson lasted less than an hour. Jossy slumped in the saddle as her father shouted at her and beat his riding whip against his false leg. To someone else she might have attempted to explain that though she adored the pony, she was a little afraid of it. To her father, who was never afraid of anything, she knew that would be futile. When she realized that he would sell the pony, whom she had begun to love, Jossy started to weep, which made him angrier. The whip stung her knuckles as they gripped the reins, and Edward de Paveley railed against the fate that had given him only one spineless daughter.

Jossy divided her time between school, where she was reasonably happy, and home, where her happiness was dependent on avoiding her father. She had her own small kingdoms – the nursery, where she taught school to her dolls and gave them tea parties, and the garden, with the old swing. She had her mother's desk in the morning room, where she wrote her stories and drew. She invented companions for herself, sketching pictures of her imaginary family. There were three sisters – Rosalie was the eldest, Claribel the youngest, and Jossy herself was in the middle. Their father was dead, and their mother was a glamorous, shadowy creature.

Jossy realized, when she was eleven or so, that her father would not remarry. Having tea one day with a friend who lived in Ely, she overheard Marjorie's mother say to another lady, 'I told Marjorie to invite poor little Joscelin de Paveley. I knew Alicia, her mother. The father won't marry again – I've heard that his wound won't let him.' Jossy had struggled to hear more, but Mrs Lyons' voice had lowered to a whisper. Jossy was not at all surprised to hear that her father's false leg prevented him from remarrying. It was to her a source of revolted fascination. The echo of his uneven step on the stone flags of the Hall was the sound of fear. She had overheard Cook say to Nana that the master's leg had been blown off at the hip; once, stumbling clumsily in a passageway, she had touched her father's false leg. It had repulsed her, a dead thing attached to a living body.

Jossy had a tendency to be plump, and hair and eyes that she described to herself as mud-coloured. When she was fifteen, she began to rinse her hair with lemon juice and, in the many hours spent gazing into the mirror, almost succeeded in convincing herself that she was becoming fairer.

When she was nineteen, Jossy left school. She'd had two tries at her school certificate, and had failed both, but then most of the girls at her school failed their school certificate. A holding pen for the dim daughters of the rich, her father called it. On the day she left school, Jossy expected something extraordinary to happen, some sort of acknowledgement that she was now a grown woman, a young lady. She would become suddenly beautiful. She would run the Hall with such smooth efficiency that even her father would be impressed. And she would meet, of course, the Gentleman.

She spent hours imagining the Gentleman. He was tall, dark, fleet-footed. He drove a car and rode a horse with fearless competence. He had a mysterious, troubled past, and he cared for Jossy more than for anything in the world. They would meet in romantic circumstances: escaping from the noise and heat of a ball, she would wander into the garden, where he would catch sight of her. He would be momentarily struck off his guard by her beauty. They would dance alone, whirling down paths studded with daisies, the scent of lilies perfuming the air, and the only light the soft gleam of the moon . . .

But nothing changed. Mrs Bradley and Cook continued to run the Hall, and Jossy's hair, in spite of the lemon juice, remained a defiantly muddy brown. She attended dances and parties at her friends' houses, but the boys were gauche and spotty and talked about cricket and motor cars. Nana still made Jossy's dresses, which were not the sinuous clinging satin gowns pictured in the magazines that Jossy bought. Her days were divided between the nursery and the morning room and the garden, but without term-time to break up the tedium. Her outings were to church and to her cousin Kit, in the steward's house. The days seemed very long. She kept her faith, though: she knew that he'd come. Two years after she had left school, Jossy de Paveley still waited for the Gentleman.

I sat back from the word processor. I felt exhausted but exhilarated. Four pages. I had driven home from Oxfordshire and, not even bothering to take off my coat, I had written four pages. And it had been easy. I felt as though someone had slackened the rope around my neck, the rope that had been choking me for months.

It was odd, though, that I had written it as a story. Rebecca Bennett usually wrote dispassionately, objectively, sifting the facts. Yet one can never be sure of the past, it twists and turns like the coloured facets of the crystal chandelier in Tilda Franklin's garden room.

Afterwards I went out to meet Charles Lightman. Over risotto and a bottle of Pinot Grigio, he talked about his latest idea.

'Changing patterns of work – the death of the industrial revolution, darling. Showing how similar the lives of contemporary teleworkers are to their pre-industrial forebears.' Charles gestured with his fork. 'Craftsmen—

they had spinner's elbow or something, and hardly ever travelled more than a few miles from their homes.' The fork stabbed the air again. 'And now people have RSI and can only go anywhere if they can afford to run a car. Neat, eh, Rebecca?'

I said, 'What about the public schools? I thought you were going to—'

'A bit *tired*, don't you think, darling?' Charles shrugged dismissively. 'This would be so much more *relevant*.'

I told him my news, and he frowned, placing Tilda's name.

'Saviour of widows and orphans—'

'Just orphans.'

'Is there enough meat in it for you?'

The waiter poured coffee. I frowned. 'I think so. Though it all seems so long ago . . .'

'Well . . . Ellen Wilkinson . . .' Charles added, rather pompously, 'The task of the biographer is to make his subject relevant to the present day.'

'*Her* subject,' I said automatically. I remembered the urgency with which I had written Jossy's story, how the words had flowed from fingertip to keyboard, but now my relief was tinged with anxiety. Perhaps my recovery was only temporary. Perhaps the next time I tried to write, the paralysis would return.

'And . . .?' Charles coaxed me.

'And I've never written about a living person before. Ellen Wilkinson died in 1947.'

He shrugged. 'Some of the women in *Sisters of the Moon* were still alive.'

'Yes.' I spiralled cream into my coffee. 'It's also that she's *good*.'

Writing the life story of such a pillar of the

community would be time-consuming, and it would also be frustrating. Tilda herself had admitted her fondness for privacy – from what avenues of her life would she shut me off? She had been old and fragile, yet I had sensed the strength beneath the brittle exterior. She had travelled from the workhouse to that weathered, beautiful building that I had visited today. A weak person could not have done that. Her strength both fascinated me and intimidated me.

'The dullness of saints.' Charles's voice interrupted my thoughts. 'Why Satan's the most interesting character in *Paradise Lost*.'

'All those rescued orphans . . . all the blobby little scrawls she's framed and put on her walls . . . they cut her off from me. How could I ever get through to her, Charles?'

I thought that Tilda's goodness and beauty was like an armour. It diminished me, and made her untouchable. I'd look at her, and her armour would shine back, and I'd doubt my own reflection.

'Perhaps,' said Charles lazily, 'you'll discover something juicy. A gorgeously clanking skeleton in the cupboard. Wouldn't that be something?'

I spent the weekend with Jane. On Sunday we wrapped the boys up well, and went for a long walk in the countryside. There were aconites like yellow stars in the hedgerows, and puddles for Jack and Lawrie to splash in. Walking, Jane told me about the tedium of jumble sales and the exhaustion of interrupted nights, and I told her about Tilda. Go and see her again, talk to her a bit more, she said, very sensibly. You've nothing to lose.

So on Monday morning I telephoned Tilda, and on Tuesday I drove again to The Red House. We sat in the upstairs drawing room, by the fire. The room had originally been a solar: a large, semicircular window looked out over the front garden and caught what sun there was. Heat gathered in the room; surreptitiously I slipped off my waistcoat and rolled up my sleeves. The old always feel the cold.

But Tilda's mood had altered since the previous week. She was fractious and difficult, evading my questions or giving incomplete answers. She had become suddenly more frail, so that her skin had the absolute pallor of old age. Outside the wind flung fragments of branch and leaf, remnants of a storm. The howl of the wind, the snap of twig against window pane, seemed to increase her nervousness. I mentioned Jossy's name, and Sarah Greenlees's, but she was monosyllabic, unforthcoming. Tilda's lack of response would, in a person who lacked her uprightness and grace, have been positively rude. I was aware of both anger and frustration. The biography had been her idea, after all, and not mine.

In an attempt to save a wasted day, I persuaded Tilda to let me see the photograph album again. I turned the pages for her and she glanced at them disinterestedly. One photograph in particular caught my eye – a man and a child, both strikingly good-looking. I was about to ask Tilda their names when she started and said, 'Isn't that someone coming up the path? Will you tell me who it is, my dear?'

I rose and looked out of the window, down to where the path was squeezed by the towering box topiaries. 'A man . . . fair hair – tallish. Young.'

I heard Tilda whisper, 'Patrick,' and for the first time that day, she smiled. I remembered that on my previous visit she had mentioned a grandson called Patrick.

'Patrick,' said Tilda, when her visitor opened the door of the solar, 'why didn't you tell me you were coming? You could have had lunch.'

He hugged her. 'It was a spur of the moment thing. I'd a client to see in Oxford.'

Tilda turned to me. 'Let me introduce you to Miss Bennett. Rebecca, this is my grandson, Patrick Franklin.'

We shook hands. 'I had a postcard from Dad this morning,' said Patrick to Tilda. 'From Ulan Bator.'

Tilda sniffed. 'Joshua courts unnecessary danger. He always has.'

'It runs in the family.' Patrick Franklin was wearing a leather jacket and jeans. Not client-visiting clothes, I thought.

'Ask Joan if she will make us tea, won't you, Patrick? Or have you not eaten? I'm sure that Joan would make you an omelette.'

I said quickly, 'I could have a word with your housekeeper on my way out, Tilda.'

She turned to me. 'But you mustn't go yet, Rebecca. We've hardly started.'

I had to stifle my impatience. 'You and Patrick will want to talk—'

'Patrick and I have plenty of time to talk. It would be quite ridiculous for you to rush back to London already. Such a waste of a journey.'

But after tea, Tilda fell asleep, her mouth neatly closed, her eyes flickering behind her lids as she dreamed. Patrick Franklin tucked a rug over her, and turned to me.

'She'll snooze for ten minutes or so. It's so damned

hot in here, I really must escape for a while. Has my grandmother shown you the garden yet, Rebecca?'

The garden of The Red House, which I had glimpsed through the conservatory windows on my previous visit, had been an enticing tangle of paths and overgrown trees. I followed Patrick outside. It had stopped raining, but there was a dampness in the air, and the tug of the wind.

Patrick spoke as we descended the steps of the terrace. 'Tilda told me that you're a writer.'

'I've written a biography of Ellen Wilkinson.'

'Just the one?'

'And a television programme.'

'Oh yes, the mental asylums. Are you a journalist?'

When I shook my head he seemed relieved. 'The Ellen Wilkinson biography was an expansion of my MA thesis,' I explained. 'I've written several articles for *History Today*.' My achievements sounded thin and unimpressive. I didn't mention my A level tutoring: it would have sounded pathetic.

We walked beneath dripping trees, beside crimson and lime-stemmed dogwoods. Crocuses shot purple and gold heads through the soil. The winding brick paths led us to a small circular clearing made of a whorl of moss-covered bricks. A stone nymph, bruised with lichen, stood on a plinth in the centre of the circle.

'Fancy Tilda agreeing that her biography should be written.' Patrick's palm rested on the nymph's head. 'I never thought she would. Various publishers have tried to persuade her over the years, you know. She's sent them all away with fleas in their ears.'

I made my position clear. 'Nothing's definite yet. Tilda would like me to write it, but I'm not sure.'

'Why not?'

'It's a big commitment. I'd have to be certain that I'm the right person to do it.'

Patrick's eyes were bluer than Tilda's. A small smile twisted the corner of his mouth. 'Tilda seems to think you'll do it. Though to be honest, I'd be relieved if you turned her down. I tried to persuade her to give up the idea, but she can be as stubborn as hell.'

Angrily, I wondered if that explained Tilda's altered attitude today. Because of her meddling grandson, she was having second thoughts. 'Why don't you want her to? Because of me? Because I'm not sufficiently illustrious?' I knew I sounded sarcastic.

Again, that lopsided grin. 'Oh no. I should think you're as good as anyone. Better than most, perhaps.'

I wasn't sure what to make of that. I was sure it wasn't a compliment. 'Then . . .?'

'Tilda is old and frail. She thinks she isn't, but she is. I'm afraid that it'll be too much for her. Digging up the past – reliving it. She's had a hard life, in many ways.'

'Is that why you've come today? To warn me off?'

His eyes, as he glanced at me, were cold. 'I came here to check you out.' His bluntness was unnerving. He began to walk back to the house, and I followed him, half running to keep up with his fast, lengthy stride.

'Hell of a hard job, too, I should imagine.' The words were flung over his shoulder, whipped away by the wind. 'My grandmother isn't always the most forthcoming of people.'

'There'll be other sources. Journals . . . newspaper articles . . . family . . .'

He laughed. 'Now there's a challenge.'

'What do you mean?' I scuttled along the path, trying to catch up with him.

'Some of us are rather peripatetic. And we're a big

family, if you include all the adopted and fostered children. And everyone is so . . . opinionated.'

I thought that he was being intentionally irritating. His eyes met mine, challenging me. He was quite disgustingly good-looking. I was aware of his proximity, and of a tingle of excitement – I'd had a similar feeling when I started work on *Sisters of the Moon* . . . a similar feeling when I'd first met Toby. Cross with myself, I pushed through the briars and old man's beard, showering Patrick with raindrops.

Tilda was awake when we returned to the solar. The photograph album was open in front of her.

'Rebecca, this is Daragh,' she said, as though introducing us. She indicated the snapshot I had earlier noticed, of the dark-haired man and the child. Daragh's hair was dark, raggedly cut, and his deep-set, slightly tilted eyes laughed at me through the years. His features were an unusual mix of innocence and rapaciousness.

'You must understand, dear,' said Tilda hesitantly, 'that there are things I don't know. Things I can only guess at. Some of Daragh's story . . . Jossy's . . . But I have had forty years to think of what *might* have happened . . . what *probably* happened . . .'

I said gently, 'All I can do is to gather up the pieces, fit them together, make a pattern. But some of it will inevitably be guesswork.'

Tilda nodded slowly. 'Yes,' she whispered. 'Yes.' And then, more firmly, 'Patrick, you must leave us in peace. The scullery tap drips. There are washers in the cupboard beneath.'

She had become brisk and organizing again, though I noted an air of bravado about her, as if she had resolved some inner battle and come at last to a resolution. I swallowed my annoyance with her grandson, and tried to return myself to the past.

She said, 'I want to tell you how Sarah and I came to live in the Fens. I didn't know then, of course, that I was related to the de Paveleys. Sarah never spoke to me about my father, and I never asked her – one didn't, in those days. One respected one's elders. Anyway, Aunt Sarah told me that she had rented a cottage in Southam.'

Southam, I remembered, was the Fenland village where the de Paveleys lived.

Tilda looked troubled. 'You must remember, Rebecca, that Sarah had two reasons for hating Edward de Paveley. He had taken both her sister and her home.'

'Yet she went back. She went back to a place where she might see him every day.'

'He was ailing by then. Like many men of his generation, Edward de Paveley never really recovered from the war. And the Hall was over a mile away from the village.' Tilda began to leaf through the pages of the photograph album, and then she paused and frowned. 'Sarah changed when we came to live in Southam. She'd always been different – unconventional – but when we moved into Long Cottage she became reclusive. She refused to mix with the other villagers. I know why now, of course, but I didn't then.' She stopped at a page. 'There,' she said, sliding the album along the table to me. 'That's our cottage.'

The black and white photograph showed me a small, low building, brick-built, thatched with reed.

'It was a farmhouse once, but much of the land had been sold off. There was still almost an acre of ground, though. I thought it was wonderful. In the spring, when the blossom blew from the apple trees, it looked like snow.'

I pictured Tilda, light-haired and grey-eyed, her skin clear and unlined, dressed in one of those drop-waisted frocks girls wore between the wars. 'How old were you?'

'I was seventeen. Sarah and I went to Southam towards the end of 1931.'

There was a knock at the door. Patrick peered round the jamb. I looked down at my notebook.

'I've fixed the tap,' he said, 'and Joan's sent up coffee.'

Tilda watched him lovingly as he carried the tray into the room and placed it on the table. When I glanced at my watch I saw that it was already four o'clock. I had arranged to go to a friend's for supper at six.

I refused coffee, and took my leave. Tilda said, 'I shall tell you about Daragh next time.'

I felt Patrick looking at me, but I evaded his eyes. I knew, though, that I had made my decision. Sentences were already forming in my head; I longed to sit and write. Tilda's story had entrapped me, weaving itself around me as finely and invisibly as the chains of gossamer that bound the box trees in The Red House's garden.

When I climbed inside my car, the grey plastic interior, the lights and switches and the jumble of crisp packets and fruit juice cartons, jarred me. They seemed to be from another world, or another time.

CHAPTER TWO

Daragh Canavan left Liverpool for London as soon as he was able. Liverpool was too full of Irish.

He had sailed from Ireland in a hurry, having mixed with the wrong sort of people. It wasn't until he climbed out of the lorry and watched it drive away, leaving him alone amid the rain and lights and traffic noise of a London evening, that he stopped watching his back. Standing on the pavement, Daragh felt a rush of joy that he had left the past behind, so that anything was now possible.

The past was Ma and Da and half a dozen younger brothers and sisters. Daragh's joy diminished a little as he thought of his mother. Shrugging off the ache of homesickness, he gathered up the brown paper parcel containing his belongings, and began to walk. He was cold, and his feet were sore because his boots had worn through at the soles. He had only a few shillings in his pocket. He must find himself something to eat and a bed for the night. Tomorrow he would look for a job. England – London especially – was a land of milk and honey, didn't everyone know that? And he'd been born lucky, his mother had always said so.

Stopping outside a restaurant, he gazed hungrily

through the plate glass. Rain beat down on his shoulders, and when a customer opened the door the smell of the food was dizzying. A waiter looked out and glowered at him, so Daragh moved on. Along the street, he fingered the coins in his pocket as he stared at a menu. The prices shocked him. They wanted four shillings for a bit of fish and a serving of sponge pudding.

Daragh pushed open the door. The waiter approached him, and he felt a tickle of nervousness in his throat as he stood, his damp cap clutched in his hands.

'Yes . . . sir?'

Daragh noticed the pause between the two words, but smiled pleasantly. 'I was wondering whether you'd serve me just a nice pot of tea and a plate of bread and butter.' Hungry though he was, he could not afford the two-course dinner.

The waiter, a little, pasty sort of fellow, twisted his gloved hands together. 'I'm afraid we don't serve tea.'

Daragh waited for the 'sir', but it did not come. 'Just the bread, then.'

The waiter looked him up and down. A condescending smile stretched his thin lips. 'I believe that the church of the Sacred Heart, down the road about half a mile, runs a soup kitchen for men such as yourself.'

Daragh's heart was pounding. Some of the diners were staring at him, and he caught the eye of a beautiful girl, her shoulders and chest indecently bare, her hair as black as the night. She was seated between two foolish-looking men, half choked by their stiff collars, their slicked-back hair gleaming like tar. Daragh turned to leave.

His brown paper parcel, soaked by the rain, chose that moment to tear and spew his belongings over the restaurant floor. As Daragh stooped to gather up his tin mug, his rosary, the green jersey that his favourite sister

Caitlin had knitted for him, and the old underpants that Ma had patched, he heard the black-haired girl's tinkle of laughter. White-faced, Daragh gathered up his things and left the restaurant.

He walked until he reached the big Catholic church at the end of the street. There, the altar, the cross and the pictures of the saints had a familiarity that calmed him. He did not yet look for the soup kitchen, but knelt and prayed. He prayed for his mother and his brothers and sisters and for his old granda who lived out in the country. And he prayed that he would never again, in all his days, make such a fool of himself.

Daragh Canavan discovered that there were two sides to London. There was the entrancing, magical side – the great buildings, the smart theatres and picture houses, the department stores with their glittering window displays – and the other side, the darker side. The hostels, the soup kitchens, the snaking queues at the Labour Exchanges. As the weeks went on and he failed to find work, Daragh's clothes became more ragged, and he hadn't the money for the public baths. Soon, the doormen at the big shops refused to allow him in for a wander round, to take the chill off his bones. He stood outside in the cold March wind, flapping his arms around his body in an attempt to keep warm. Looking in, but shut out, excluded. Cold glass pressed against his fingertips. He was aware of a loneliness and a sense of isolation that he had never previously experienced.

After a month he began to feel desperate. He knew that each day he was becoming less employable. The sight of his reflection in the shop windows offended him. He left London the day after they robbed the tobacconist. He didn't do any thieving himself, he just stood outside in the street as two fellows he'd met at the hostel went through the place. But the scruffy little shop reminded him of old Paddy Meeghan's at home, and he felt a heavy, gnawing shame that his months in England had reduced him to this.

With two pound notes, his reward for keeping watch, in his pocket, Daragh walked to the Great North Road and thumbed a lift. His luck changed at last when a van driver told him that he could put him in the way of a couple of days' farm labouring. Daragh thought of County Clare, where his grandfather lived, where he'd spent many happy summers. He did not, though, discover the gentle rain and rolling hills that he had been expecting. Cutting peat turves, he felt dwarfed by the flat countryside that surrounded him, and by the limitless sky. When a cloud, edged with gold, covered the face of the sun, and the great pale rays of light swept across the earth, Daragh, awed by such a harsh beauty, crossed himself. Paid off after a week, he wandered further into the Fens. The weather had eased and there was a warmth in the air that hinted of spring. Reaching Ely, he walked into the cathedral and sat looking up to where the vaulted stone soared above him. Daragh made a bargain with God: a year's regular attendance at Mass if he found a job that day.

God shook hands on the bargain. When he left the cathedral and walked across the green, Daragh caught sight of a man struggling to roll barrels of ale down the steps to his cellar. He ran across the grass to help lift the heavy barrels from the cart. When they had finished, and the fat, florid publican was wheezing and mopping sweat from his face, Daragh asked about work. He was industrious and honest, and willing to put his hand to anything, he said, as he begged for a few weeks' trial.

Daragh started behind the bar the following morning. He had been employed at the Fox and Hounds for a fortnight when he saw the girl. She was wheeling a bicycle through the cathedral close, talking to a friend. She was tall and slim and straight, her gold-brown hair almost to her waist. Her long eyes were the colour of pebbles washed in a stream. Any other girl that he had ever seen was plain in comparison to her. He felt an odd sense of recognition, a thrill of expectation, as though he had come home.

Tilda cycled the six miles to Ely each weekday. The classes at Miss Clare's Academy of Typewriting and Bookkeeping began at nine o'clock in the morning. When they had first moved to Southam, Tilda had told Aunt Sarah that she wanted to train to be a nurse. Aunt Sarah hadn't exactly said no, but had suggested Tilda wait a year or so and had bought her some hens and found her the place at Miss Clare's Academy.

Each morning she set off for Ely, Aunt Sarah's warnings ringing in her ears. Men and strangers and drink, though not necessarily in that order. Miss Clare's Academy was not as grand as its name suggested. All the lessons took place in the front room of a little house in the back streets of Ely. Miss Clare was tall and angular, and smelt of peppermints. She wore each day a striped cardigan that the girls, her pupils, nicknamed her battledress. She gave her lessons standing, pointing at a blackboard with a wooden stick, peering out into the street as though she was expecting someone – her sweetheart, the girls whispered. Emily Potter, who was Tilda's friend, scribbled wicked cartoons of Miss Clare's supposed lover, and passed them to Tilda in class. The classes were extremely dull. It would have taken imagination and flair to make shorthand interesting, and imagination and flair had long ago passed Miss Clare by. In lessons, Tilda's mind wandered. Her daydreams were frequently interrupted by Miss Clare's studiedly refined tones, or knocked off course by Miss Clare's disconcerting habit of emphasizing the wrong word in a sentence. 'Miss Greenlees, how will you succeed in your future career if you have not *acquired* the habit of giving your employer your complete attention?'

Emily invited Tilda to tea one day. After class, they walked through Ely. It was pleasantly sunny, and Tilda had stuffed her coat into her bicycle basket.

'Do you want to be a typist, Em?'

Emily shrugged. 'Lots of girls are typists, aren't they? And I can't think of anything else to do.'

'You could be an artist.'

'An artist?' Emily was scornful. 'My parents would never let me. Besides' – she took an apple from her pocket and bit it – 'I intend to work for a wonderful man. Tall and dark and handsome and terribly rich. He'll fall madly in love with me and take me away from boring old Ely. Bite, Tilda?'

Tilda took the apple and bit. They walked past a row of shops and a pub.

Emily whispered suddenly, 'I've just seen an absolute dreamboat . . . don't look round yet, Tilda, *please*. Now. Over there.'

Tilda glanced at the young man outside the Fox and Hounds. He was leaning against the wall of the pub, smoking, his dark, slightly curling hair uncovered in the spring sunshine.

'Don't stare,' whispered Emily furiously. 'He's looking at us! Oh, my goodness! *Divine*. Utterly divine!' They both began to giggle as they turned the corner that led to the Potters' house.

Aunt Sarah was in the kitchen, making bread, when Tilda came home. Sarah Greenlees wore a long blue skirt and a white high-necked blouse, covered by a stiff brown apron.

'Your supper's in the stove, Tilda.'

Tilda sat at a corner of the kitchen table to eat her shepherd's pie. The Greenlees didn't have a separate dining room like the Potters, but ate in the kitchen. Over the six months since they had come to Southam, Long Cottage had acquired for Tilda a pleasant familiarity. She had never before lived for so long in the same place. Nothing at Long Cottage was new; the kitchen curtains were a patchwork of dresses that Tilda had worn as a child, the cushions on the settle were made of jumble sale finds and segments of one of Aunt Sarah's vast petticoats. Tilda recalled the Potters' bathroom. Fluffy pink towels and matching soap and talc. The scent of the soap still lingered on Tilda's hands: she sniffed them surreptitiously. She and Aunt Sarah washed using cold water from the jug on their washstands, and bathed in a tin bath in the kitchen.

Tilda poked the shepherd's pie around her plate with her fork, and wriggled in her seat.

'Eat up, child. Waste not, want not.' Sarah Greenlees kneaded the dough.

'Waste not, want not' was Aunt Sarah's favourite saying. Her second favourite was 'Look after the pennies, and the pounds will take care of themselves.' Tilda scraped up the remains of the shepherd's pie, wolfed it down, and rinsed the plate under the tap. Then she ran outside.

She fed the hens and collected the eggs to sell to the shop the following morning. She was allowed to keep half the egg money. Then she weeded between the rows of vegetables, singing to herself as she worked. By the time she had finished, dark, twilit fingers had begun to creep across the sky. Tilda flung off her apron, and ran out of the garden, through the village, along the path by the church that led to the dike. On the bank, she lay on her back in the grass, staring up at the sky. The pink and gold clouds, patterned like a fish's scales, were doubled in the waters of the dike. Tilda closed her eyes, and let herself slowly roll down the bank to the field, gathering speed as she tumbled. Dizzy, laughing, she dug her fingers into the soil to help herself sit up. The tip of her forefinger touched something hard and cold. Scrabbling at the earth, she drew out a small metal disc.

When she scraped away the impacted soil and polished it with the hem of her skirt, she saw that it was a coin. The coin was lumpy and of uneven thickness, and she recognized neither the face impressed on it, nor the battered ancient script. There was a small hole drilled near the rim. Tilda fished in her pocket for a length of string, and threaded it through the coin. As she strung it round her neck, she muttered to herself, 'Grant that no hobgoblins fright me, no hungry devils rise up and bite me,' and crossed her fingers for luck. Then she lay back on the scented grass and thought again of the man outside the Fox and Hounds.

Emily insisted Tilda walk home with her each evening, before cycling to Southam. Three days passed, and they saw only the fat publican, greeting the brewer's dray. Emily was distraught.

'He was probably just passing through, on his way

to London, or somewhere exciting. No-one interesting lives in Ely.'

But on the fourth day, they saw him again.

'Oh Lord,' Emily muttered. 'Oh Lord. Come and stand close to me, Tilda, so I can put my lipstick on without him seeing.' Emily rummaged in her handbag and drew out a lipstick and powder compact. '"Practically Peony",' she whispered to Tilda, between dabs at her mouth. 'Too gorgeous, isn't it? Mummy would kill me. Have some – no—' Emily gave a little scream. 'Too late. He's coming. Oh *Lord*.'

A voice said, 'Can I give you ladies a hand? You look awful laden up,' and Emily whispered, 'Irish. *Divine*.'

He was tall, green-eyed, his curly black hair just touching the collar of his white shirt. 'I don't mean to intrude,' he said 'but I've seen you both once or twice and feel I almost know you already. My name's Daragh Canavan.' He held out his hand. 'Let me help you with that bag, Miss . . .?'

'Potter.' Emily handed him her shopping basket. 'Emily Potter. And this is Miss Greenlees.' Tilda and Daragh shook hands. 'We go to secretarial school. It is terribly dull. I went to London for a weekend in December, and I thought it was absolute heaven.' Emily's face was much the same shade as her lipstick and she was talking too fast.

'I'm more of a country boy myself. Those big cities can be awful lonely places. Where do you live, Miss Greenlees?'

'In a village called Southam, about six miles from here.'

Daragh Canavan walked between them, carrying Emily's shopping bag. When they reached the Potters' home, Tilda climbed on her bicycle, called her farewells, and freewheeled down the slope.

That evening, after tea, Tilda washed clothes, and Aunt Sarah cut wood in the yard. Tilda wrung out the wet stockings, put them in the wicker basket, and opened the scullery door. As she stepped out into the garden, she heard voices.

'I just thought, why not let me chop that wood for you, missus? I could do it in no time.'

Tilda, recognizing Daragh Canavan's voice, almost dropped her basket.

'I can chop my own wood, thank you very much, young man.'

'Ah, sure you can, missus, I just thought to take some of the work from you.'

'And why should you wish to do that?' Aunt Sarah sounded suspicious.

'Because my ma brought me up to be a good, Christian gentleman.'

Tilda heard Aunt Sarah's snort of disbelief, and then the thud as the axe broke into the wood. She left the scullery and crossed the yard.

'Good evening, Mr Canavan.'

Aunt Sarah paused in the act of swinging the axe. 'Do you know this young man, Tilda?'

'We met this afternoon in Ely.'

'I see. Such a good, Christian gentleman.' Aunt Sarah's voice had taken the tone she used with tradesmen who tried to sell her short. The tradesmen tended to wither beneath Aunt Sarah's scorn.

Daragh Canavan looked unabashed. 'And I was just passing through Southam—'

'No-one passes through Southam.' Aunt Sarah raised the axe again. 'Do not take me for a fool.'

'Well then. You have found me out. I admit it. I'm a long way from home, and the young lady was pleasant to me today, and I wanted to see a friendly face. I miss my family – I miss my ma most of all. And my sister, Caitlin. She's a fine girl, like Miss Greenlees. And as it was my evening off, and such a fine night of it, I thought a walk might cheer me up.'

Sarah's eyes had narrowed. 'Where do you work, Mr Canavan?'

'At the Fox and Hounds in Ely.'

The axe crashed down with a disapproving thump, cleaving the log, splitting it in two. Aunt Sarah flung shards of wood into the log basket.

'I was peat-cutting in March, and in the winter I was in London, doing this and that. London's a terrible place, though. I was desperate to leave the city. So I came here to look for farm work.'

'Times have been hard,' Aunt Sarah said, softening a little.

Daragh glanced at the axe. 'And I could cut that great pile of wood in the flick of an eye, if you'd be so good as to allow me, missus. To say thank you for passing the time of day with me.'

Aunt Sarah said austerely, 'I am *Miss* Greenlees, not Mrs, if you please, young man. Tilda is my niece, not my daughter.' Yet she stood aside and handed Daragh the axe.

The metal axehead bit down on the log. Chips of splintered wood flew up in the air. The two women went back into the house. Daragh threw his jacket aside, and rolled up his sleeves. His body arched and his muscles tautened as he swung the axe back and brought it down again.

*　　*　　*

He called once a week, to cut the wood. After three weeks, Aunt Sarah relented and invited him into the house when he had finished. Daragh stood while he drank his tea, and was hurried out of the house the moment his cup was empty. Sarah, shutting the door behind him, turned to Tilda and said, 'He's a rascal. A rascal. You must remember that.' Because Aunt Sarah thought all men were rascals, Tilda didn't take much notice. She was evasive, though, about Daragh Canavan. Occasionally Aunt Sarah asked suspiciously, 'He's not bothering you, is he, Tilda? That young man isn't bothering you?'

Tilda answered, with a degree of honesty, that he wasn't bothering her at all. Daragh Canavan met her and Emily once or twice a week and chatted to them as they walked home. The chats had recently extended into an invitation for a cup of tea in a café, a new experience for Tilda. Aunt Sarah thought cafés were a waste of money.

Daragh made them both laugh, and relieved the boredom and pointlessness of Miss Clare's Academy. One afternoon, they went to the cinema, where they saw *Hindle Wakes*. Emily sobbed into a handkerchief; Tilda, surrounded by gilt and crimson plush as she watched the huge, mouthing figures on the screen, was overwhelmed. When the film finished and they left the picture house, the sun was fiercely bright, the bustle of the street stupefying.

Emily sighed. 'Wasn't it sad? Thank you so much, Daragh.'

A car drew up on the far side of the road. A young man leaned out and called, 'Em! Emily! I've been looking for you everywhere.'

Emily stared and shrieked, '*Roland!* Oh – Roland!' She darted through the traffic. 'Why didn't you tell me you were coming home, you beast? Come and meet my friends.'

Roland was short and plump, like Emily. 'Rollo,' said Emily, after she had hugged him, 'let me introduce you to Tilda Greenlees, my dearest friend. Tilda, this is my big brother, Roland.' Roland shook hands with Tilda.

'And this is Daragh Canavan. We've just been to the cinema.' Roland nodded at Daragh, but did not take his hand.

'Good film?'

'Oh *yes*! Almost as good as *The Constant Nymph*. That's my favourite film.'

'I know.' Roland grimaced. 'I had to take Em to see it three times, Miss Greenlees, when it came to Ely.'

'Tilda's never been to the cinema before,' said Emily.

'You enjoyed it,' said Daragh, looking anxiously at Tilda, 'didn't you?'

Tilda smiled at him. 'It's been one of the best afternoons of my life.'

Daragh's face lit up. 'That's grand, then. We could go again next week, if you like.'

'That would be lovely, Daragh,' she began to say, but Roland interrupted.

'Why don't you girls come for a spin?'

Emily looked at the car. 'Is it yours, Rollo?'

'Bought her with Uncle Jack's money. Let me show you what she can do.' Roland crossed the road and opened the passenger door. Emily bounced after him.

'I'll be getting back to the pub, then.' Daragh was watching the Potters. 'It's almost five o'clock.'

Emily yelled, 'Tilda! Come here!' and Daragh strode off, his hands in his pockets, whistling. Tilda ran across the road. Emily poked her head out of the car window.

'Where's Daragh?'

'He had to go back to work.'

'Oh *blast*. I was going to sit in the back with him.'

The car was soft-topped, the back seat squashed and shallow, barely big enough for two people.

Roland held open the driver's door. 'Sorry it's a bit of a squeeze, Miss Greenlees.'

'Perhaps I should go home.' Tilda had seen the look in Daragh's eyes as he had turned to leave.

'Don't be a goose. Hurry up, Tilda.'

She allowed herself to be persuaded. She had never ridden in a motor car before. As Roland left Ely's winding streets and headed for the open road, he pressed his foot down on the accelerator.

'Where did you meet that chap?' Roland shouted, over the noise of the engine.

'Walking home one day,' Emily screamed back. 'He said that he felt as though he knew us already. Wasn't that romantic?'

'Corny, if you ask me. Probably got the line from some second-rate film.'

'*Roland*. Daragh is absolutely the most gorgeous man I've ever met.'

Roland Potter glanced at his sister, and slowed the car a little. 'Not quite the thing, though, Em. He was wearing *boots*, for heaven's sake. Frightful workmen's things.'

After classes the following week, they picnicked beside the river. Rushes whispered on the banks, and lily pads floated on the surface of the water. Roland told the girls about his job in London, working for a newspaper. 'I'm just a glorified tea boy, actually. I doubt if they'll let me write a sentence for years.'

They dined on egg and lettuce sandwiches, and a blancmange that splayed out as soon as Emily shook it from mould to plate. Roland had brought a portable record-player, and he partnered Tilda and Emily in turn as they danced on the grassy meadow by the river. Afterwards, Tilda sat on the bank, dangling her feet in the water. Mud squeezed through her bare toes, and tiny fishes darted along the shallows. The sun seared her shoulders and the back of her neck.

Emily sat beside her. 'Daragh still hasn't asked me for a date, and I've made it so easy for him. I almost begged him to take me to the fair in Soham.'

Tilda remembered that Roland Potter had not shaken hands with Daragh. She also recalled Roland's comment about Daragh's boots. It worried Tilda to think that Daragh had sensed how quickly Roland Potter had summed him up and dismissed him as not worth bothering with.

'I've a plan. Don't say anything.' Emily raised her voice. 'We could go for a drink, Roland. The Fox and Hounds has a lovely garden.'

Roland looked doubtful. 'I don't know . . . I'm not sure that Mother—'

'Don't be boring. Come on.' Emily stood up, brushing grass from her skirt.

They drove back to Ely, the car bouncing on the uneven road. In the back garden of the Fox and Hounds, Roland found an empty table.

'There he is.' Emily smiled, pleased with herself. In a corner of the garden, Daragh Canavan was loading glasses onto a tray.

'*Em.*' Roland sounded annoyed.

Emily stood up and waved. 'Daragh! Hello, Daragh!'

Daragh crossed the grass towards them. His smile

was fleeting. 'Miss Potter. Miss Greenlees.' He turned to Roland. 'Sir?'

Roland lit a cigarette. 'A pint of best and two lemonades. And' – Daragh had turned to go – 'be quick about it, won't you?'

Tilda noticed the small pause in Daragh's stride, the whitening of his knuckles as his hands gripped the tray.

Emily touched Roland's sleeve. 'Let me have a cigarette, darling Rollo.'

Roland shook his head. 'You're too young, Em. And girls shouldn't smoke in public.'

'*Roland!* So stuffy.' Emily took one from his case. 'I smoked one last Christmas, you know. I tried one of Daddy's.' She placed the cigarette between her lips and struck a match.

'You have to inhale, silly,' said Roland.

Emily persevered. Tilda watched for Daragh. Roland's fingers drummed the edge of the table. 'Where's that fellow? Damned ridiculous—'

Daragh came out of the back door, carrying a tray. As he reached the table, Roland said, 'You took your time.'

Daragh's face whitened. He placed the glasses of lemonade in front of the girls, and took the tankard from the tray. Then he seemed to slip, and the beer spilt over the front of Roland's white shirt.

'So sorry, sir. Terrible clumsy of me.' Daragh walked back into the pub.

Roland, gasping, stood up. Emily dabbed at him with her handkerchief. Tilda, knocking over her chair, ran through the garden.

The bar room was dark and busy, full of farmers, the floor dusty with mud from their boots. She could see no sign of Daragh. Men whistled at her; someone grabbed at her, pulling her towards him. Tilda cursed and shook him off, elbowing through the crowds to the front door. But though she looked frantically up and down the road, she could see no-one, only the purplish shadows of the buildings.

Roland and Emily walked out of the garden, along the street. When they reached the car, Emily said tentatively, 'Rollo . . .?'

'Better walk home. Don't want beer on the seats.' He still dripped. Roland glanced at Emily. 'I behaved like an ass in there. Not sure why. I probably deserved this.' He wrung out his shirt.

'Daragh's not so bad, Rollo. He's kind and he's good fun. And he hasn't tried anything . . . you know.'

Roland nodded slowly. 'All the same, Em, you should keep away.'

'But I *love* him!' she howled.

He shook his head. 'Don't be an ass, Em.'

'But I do! You don't know what it's like, Roland—'

He said, quite kindly, 'Emily, he's just not our sort. And besides, the fellow's madly in love with Tilda.'

She stared at him for a long moment. She could see the truth in his eyes. Painfully, she forced herself to acknowledge it, and, in doing so, understood the ugly little scene in the pub.

'Like you, dearest brother.'

'Yes.' Roland fumbled in his pocket, and drew out his cigarette case. As she accepted the cigarette that Roland handed her, tears trailed down Emily's face, and her shoulders heaved.

Roland passed Emily his handkerchief. 'Mop your face, old girl. Stiff upper lip and all that. He won't make her happy, you know. There isn't the slightest chance that he'll make her happy.'

Tilda found Daragh halfway to Southam, leaning against a bridge, looking down at the water. She braked and called out to him, and slid off her bicycle.

He looked up at her. 'Where are your smart friends, Tilda?'

'I've no idea. Are you all right, Daragh?'

His arms were folded on the parapet. 'I'm great. Just great.'

'In the pub—'

'In the pub, I acted like a complete buffoon. I was jealous.'

'Of Roland?'

He flung out his hands in an angry gesture. 'The car ... the suit ... the cash the fellow has ... even his bloody *socks*, for heaven's sake.'

Tilda giggled. 'His socks?'

The corners of Daragh's mouth twisted in a smile. 'You know, neat little things with diamond patterns on them. Not like these.'

He kicked off his boot. There was a hole the size of a potato in his handknitted sock.

'Oh, *Daragh*.'

'Mary, Mother of God, me feet are as black as night.' He waded into the stream. The water came up past his knees, and he called, 'Come on in, love – it's great.'

Tilda pulled off her boots and, bare-legged, dipped a toe in the water. 'It's freezing, Daragh.'

'Oh, you're a baby, so you are.' He waded back to the bank, and picked her up in his arms. She screamed, but curled her legs around him and laughed.

'You're a witch, so you are, Tilda Greenlees,' he said

softly. Then he bent his head and kissed her. His mouth was firm and hungry, and the clasp of his arms pressed her to him, and she did not want him to let her go. When, eventually, they drew apart, he said again, 'You're a witch, little Tilda, and you have enchanted me,' and slowly let her fall, so that she tumbled, laughing and protesting, into the cool, green water.

On Daragh's half-days, he met Tilda after classes and they cycled back to Southam together. Once, the tyre of her bicycle punctured, and they had to abandon the machine in a ditch. With Tilda perched on his cross-bar, Daragh rode, singing 'The Star of the County Down' and 'Galway Bay' at the top of his voice. The men working in the fields looked up and stared as he zigzagged in tighter and tighter sweeps across the road, so that she shrieked and cried out for him to stop. So he stopped, and she tumbled into his arms, and he kissed her again.

He borrowed a horse – Tilda never knew where from – and she sat on the saddle bow, his arms around her as they rode for miles. When they reached the long barrier of the Hundred Foot Drain, he slowed the animal with a click of his tongue, and leaned forward, his hands encircling Tilda's waist, his mouth caressing her neck. When he stroked her breast, she wanted to forget all Aunt Sarah's warnings and give herself to him, but instead she kicked the horse into a canter, and they flew across the field, Daragh pretending to slide from the saddle, Tilda clinging to the horse's mane.

She had never known anyone like Daragh Canavan. He took her to a posh tea shop one day, ordering cakes and scones in a cut-glass English accent, a monocle (one of the inn's guests had left it in the bar) half masking one mocking green eye. On her eighteenth birthday in

May, she came out of Long Cottage in the morning to find cowslips and ladies' smock in bunches round the front door, and her name spelled out in flowers on the tiny pocket of front lawn. She skipped classes one afternoon, and he took her to a tea dance, guiding her around the floor with careless, easy grace. Then, in front of matrons and shop girls, he kissed her, standing in the middle of the crowded little room, taking the breath away from her. The matrons muttered disapprovingly, but Tilda glimpsed envy in the young girls' eyes.

In the church at Southam, he fiddled with the lock on the little door that led up to the belfry until it gave way, and they scrambled up the narrow, winding stairs. From the tower, they could see for miles across the level fields to the straight line of the dike, and the large, four-square house in the distance.

'Where's that?' asked Daragh, pointing.

'That's the Hall,' Tilda explained. 'The de Paveleys live there. Just the two of them, an old man and his daughter. It must be so strange, only two of you in a big house like that. I can't imagine it, can you?'

Daragh stood behind her. His arms folded around her, touching her breasts. Her head fitted the curve of his neck and chin, but he did not kiss her, because it was a church, and he didn't approve of kissing in churches.

'Oh, I can,' he said. 'I can.'

In July, when the droves were white with dust, Sarah fell ill with a fever, and Edward de Paveley lay on his deathbed. The impending death of the old squire hung like a pall over the village. There was a stillness in the air, a sense of nervous expectation. Though the de Paveleys' property had diminished during the decade and a half since the end of the Great War, Edward de Paveley still owned a row of cottages in Southam and many of the fields that surrounded it. Though to Tilda the squire and his daughter were no more than faces glimpsed in a passing car, she, too, sensed the unease that had become a part of the heat and dust of high summer.

To Daragh, Tilda confided her ambition to be a nurse; and he in turn told her of his plans to buy a little bit of land – his own, no-one else's, not rented, but bought. To Tilda, and only Tilda, he spoke of his last difficult months in Ireland – the mess he had made of his life there, his decision to leave, and to start again.

Aunt Sarah recovered only slowly. Returning to Long Cottage after a stolen half-hour with Daragh, Tilda found her aunt waiting at the door, still in her nightdress, a shawl wrapped around her shoulders.

'Is he gone yet?' said Aunt Sarah.

Tilda stood motionless, her heart pounding. Words darted around her head as she searched for a way to make her aunt understand what Daragh meant to her. Before she could answer, Sarah Greenlees spoke again.

'Have they put the black up?'

A moment's panicking incomprehension, and then Tilda understood, and shook her head.

'There's no mourning in the shop window. Mr de Paveley must still be alive.' Relief mingled with astonishment that Sarah, who had never taken the slightest interest in village affairs, should appear to care about the ailing old squire. Tilda tried to take her aunt's hand and lead her back into the house, but Sarah shook her off. When Tilda went out to the garden to pick beans for their supper, she found that she was trembling, so she lay on the grass, letting the warm sunlight wash over her. The rooms of the cottage had seemed small and dark, and Aunt Sarah had become, for a fraction of a second, someone unfamiliar and disturbing.

When Edward de Paveley died on the last day of July, Sarah Greenlees took the witches' bottle from its hiding place beneath the floorboards, and kissed it. Then she went to bed and slept for twelve consecutive hours, her first uninterrupted night's sleep since she had returned to Southam.

Waking the next day, listening to the church bell tolling fifty-four times – the age of the dead man – Sarah felt as though a heavy load had fallen from her shoulders. She had not realized how much it would hurt her to return to her birthplace. She had come back for Deborah. And for justice. Sarah believed in justice. Not conventionally religious, she nevertheless saw that there was a natural order in the world, an order which, imperilled, could distort the future as well as the past. Once, when she was a little girl, Sarah had knocked over a bottle of elderberry wine on the draining-board, and that bottle had felled its neighbour, and that the one beside it, until half a dozen bottles had crashed to the floor, the child watching aghast. Sarah knew that what Edward de Paveley had done was like that, that its consequences were not yet finished with, they would echo through generations.

Pinning a flat black hat, slightly greenish with age, to her hair the next morning, Sarah called Tilda in from the yard, and told her that they were going to church. To Tilda's amazed protests, she made no response. They were going to church to attend Mr de Paveley's funeral, and that was that.

In church, Sarah led Tilda boldly down the aisle. The villagers stared at them, wide-eyed and foolish, some of them the same people who hadn't lifted a finger to help Deborah all those years ago. Sarah sat three pews from the front, behind the publican and his wife. She disliked churches. God was outside in the skies and the seas and the meadows, not imprisoned in a dark, cold stone building. She sat up straight, oblivious of the curious gaze of the villagers. When the vicar came in, everyone rose. As they placed the coffin in front of the altar, Sarah began to laugh. Tilda tugged at her sleeve; Sarah struggled to change the laugh to a cough.

Glancing across to the adjacent pew, Sarah thought scornfully what a pallid, feeble lot the de Paveleys were. Christopher de Paveley was tall and gaunt, stoop-shouldered at fifty or so, his face cadaverous, his hair thinning. His son was a fairer, shorter version of his father. Wrapped in an ugly black coat, veiled and hatted, most of Joscelin de Paveley was hidden from the congregation.

Later, in the churchyard, Miss de Paveley's veil blew back in the breeze, revealing her features. Round face, brown eyes, crinkly brown hair falling over a black velvet collar. She couldn't hold a candle to Edward de Paveley's other daughter, who stood beside Sarah, wearing a faded cotton dress that had already seen three summers and a cardigan that Sarah herself had knitted. Sarah reminded herself that now that Edward de Paveley was dead, Deborah could at last rest in peace. Which left only the child to be avenged. Sarah imagined the privileged life that Joscelin de Paveley led. Never having to worry where her next meal was coming from, maidservants at her beck and call. As the coffin was lowered into the grave, Sarah felt an anger so intense that it dizzied her.

Then it was over, and the mourners ambled out of

the churchyard into the street. Sarah was a few paces behind Joscelin de Paveley when the girl suddenly stopped walking and stood, frozen.

At first, Sarah couldn't work out what Miss de Paveley was looking at. Her mouth hung open, and her eyes were wide and burning. Then Sarah saw the Irishman. The good-for-nothing was lounging against the gate of Long Cottage. It was his day to cut the wood.

Joscelin de Paveley was staring at Daragh Canavan. Sarah had never seen such naked desire in a woman's eyes. For a fraction of a second Sarah almost pitied her. Then she seized Tilda's arm, and marched her up the street.

Tilda was late home from Ely. Sarah watched for her at the window, twitching the curtain. The whirr of a bicycle released her from anxiety, and she returned to the bread dough, stretching and rolling it, knocking out the air with her strong, square hands. Tilda dumped her shopping basket on the table. Sarah glanced through its contents and said, 'Where is the ink?'

'Ink?'

'I particularly asked you to buy ink, Tilda. I have letters to write.'

'I forgot. Sorry, Aunt Sarah.'

When she looked up, she was shaken by Tilda's expression of dazed happiness. As Tilda crossed the kitchen to take a cup of water from the jug, Sarah watched her. She knew her well; she had brought her up from a baby. Tilda's face, which Sarah knew to be beautiful, was blurred, altered, transformed.

Transformed by love, Sarah guessed with a sudden leap of intuition. Tilda was in love.

Sarah had to lean against the table, the floury palms of

her hands taking her weight. It wasn't hard for Sarah to guess the object of Tilda's love. Though she had always regarded men as at best a nuisance, at worst a curse, Sarah saw how a man like Daragh Canavan, with his seductive looks and honeyed tongue, might charm a girl. Daragh was fit and young, and his hungry green eyes followed Tilda with an expression which reminded Sarah of a mongrel dog she had once rescued from a mantrap. She had been unable to do anything for the dog, its wounds had been too deep, and she had gently helped it from this world. She would have liked to do as much for Daragh Canavan, though less gently. She knew that, unchecked, he would break Tilda's heart.

The thought that Tilda's life might be ruined in the same way as Deborah's had been terrified Sarah. Part of her had always feared for this child, her dead sister's child. All she had done to protect Tilda, all the plans she had made for her niece, could be turned to nothing by a man like Daragh Canavan. Sarah saw through him, saw to the weak and capricious heart of him, and knew that Daragh should not have her. As Tilda left the kitchen to feed the hens, Sarah's hands fisted against her forehead. She could forbid Tilda to see the wretched man, but she saw clearly the dangers in that. She could leave Southam, now that Edward de Paveley was dead. She could confront Daragh, ask his intentions – but if he offered marriage, what should she do?

Sarah remembered the funeral, and the way that Joscelin de Paveley had looked at Daragh Canavan. The beginnings of a wild and freakish idea hovered at the edges of her mind, but could not yet be seized and thrown into view. Then the thought came clear, and Sarah's heart began to pound like a kettle drum. Her fisted hand pressed at the pain in her chest as she sat down again. Joscelin de Paveley is rich, she whispered out loud. Joscelin de Paveley has land aplenty. She stared, her breath tight in her lungs, at the list she had written for Tilda that morning. *Ink*, the final entry said.

And oh, such sweet revenge.

Sarah insisted on accompanying Tilda to Ely next market day. They walked; Sarah refused to cycle and thought the bus a waste of money. Crossing the fields with their seas of ochre corn waved by the wind, Sarah's stout boots tramped purposefully through poppies and pineapple weed; Tilda, behind her, carrying the basket, saw nothing and schemed continually.

In Ely, Sarah bought a reel of thread, harangued the cobbler about the price of shoelaces, and posted her letter. Tilda knew that Daragh would be waiting for her outside the Electric Cinema. When Tilda pleaded for a drink or the lavatory, Sarah went with her to the water fountain and insisted they take turns in the cubicle in the Ladies, to save the penny. Walking home, Tilda's boots scuffed miserably in the dust.

Because of the hot, dry weather, Sarah decided to wash the curtains, rugs and bedlinen. Steam ran down the walls of the scullery, and Tilda's back ached from hauling coal into the stove to boil water. All the rooms in the cottage smelt of household soap and starch, rows of washing hung limply on the line in the windless air, and every moment of the day was busy. When Daragh came to chop the wood, Tilda saw the questions in his eyes. Aunt Sarah watched him, checking that he was doing the job properly, only turning away when he flung off his shirt to wash his face under the pump in the yard.

*　　*　　*

Joscelin de Paveley's overriding emotion on her father's death was one of immense relief. The house seemed suddenly a more pleasant place. She no longer flinched at the sound of a footstep in the corridor, she no longer dreaded dinner-times. Although she wore black, she felt light-hearted.

She sorted through her father's bedroom and study, and made a huge bonfire, burning all his possessions. The false leg, which had lost some of its terror now that it was no longer attached to her father, smouldered in the heart of the flames. Jossy endured a long, dull afternoon while Mr Verney, the solicitor, read out Edward de Paveley's will. 'To my daughter, Joscelin, the Hall and its contents and the residue of the estate. To my brother, Christopher, and his son, the use of the steward's house for their lifetimes.' Small legacies to Nana and Cook and the gardener, and not a word of love or affection. Jossy didn't care. Jossy had seen the Gentleman.

The Gentleman now had a face. And green eyes and black hair. Jossy had glimpsed him in the street after her father's funeral. She had been to Southam several times since in the hope of encountering him again, but had not seen him. He lingered in her memory, though, and in her imagination. She fantasized a dozen times a day about their next meeting. He'd rescue her from robbers or kidnappers; or she'd go to a party, look across a crowded room, and their eyes would meet. Each day she dressed carefully and spent hours doing her hair. Time lengthened and intensified with Jossy's feverish anticipation. She thought of names for him: Charles or Leo or David or Rupert . . .

When she came home from a walk one day, a letter was waiting for her on the hall table. Jossy did not recognize the handwriting. Opening the envelope, she stared, bewildered, at the signature at the foot of the page. Then she began to read.

Since I saw you that day, I have been able to think of no-one else. I long to see you again, to speak to you . . .

Daragh. Such a beautiful and unusual name. He was called Daragh.

He had found a boat nestling in the reeds; he slid the painter from the post and the rowing boat glided slowly into the river. Tilda lay in the prow, one hand trailing in the water. When Daragh knelt beside her, the boat rocked a little. First he kissed her, and then he undid, one by one, the buttons of her blouse. To begin with, she let him kiss her throat and her breasts, but then she wriggled out of his arms and sat up, and the boat lurched wildly, sending up spray.

'You'll have us both in the water, darlin' girl.'

'Give me the oars, Daragh.'

He shook his head. 'No. Sit down, Tilda Greenlees.'

She stood up, so he ran his fingertips from her ankle along her bare calf to her thigh. Her heart was hammering. She could see her reflection in the water: her hair tangled from his caresses, her blouse open.

Daragh lay in the boat, looking up at her. His eyes were narrowed by the sun. 'I've hardly seen you these last few weeks.'

'I haven't been able to get away, Daragh. Aunt Sarah came into town with me again yesterday.'

He searched in his pocket for his cigarettes, flicking open the packet one-handed. 'Do you think she knows about us?'

Tilda looked down at him. 'She'd have said something. And we've been very careful.'

He struck a match on the side of the boat. 'I'll come and see you tonight after work,' he said. 'There's an old ladder in that barn where I cut the wood. I'll throw a few stones at your window—'

'Daragh,' said Tilda. 'Aunt Sarah has ears like a *bat's*.'

He lay back in the boat, smoking. His exploring fingers had reached the elasticated leg of Tilda's bloomers. She stepped over him and seized the oars. The boat swayed, throwing Daragh's matches and cigarettes, balanced on the gunwale, into the river. 'Mary, Mother of God, Tilda!' cried Daragh, and sat up.

'I have to get home.' She turned the boat rapidly, heading back to the bank. 'Aunt Sarah will wonder where I am.' Tilda knew that her face was red, and that a fire burned inside her.

Daragh, too, burned. He had wanted her for months; he had never waited so long for a girl. He had been prepared to wait because she was so young – six years younger than he – and because there was something different, something slightly daunting, about her. If anyone had told him that he would one day be a little in awe of an eighteen-year-old girl, he would have laughed in their face, but it was so.

The landlord of the Fox and Hounds gave Daragh the note as he swept out the cellar the following morning. His mood, already uncertain, worsened as he glanced at the single folded piece of paper and saw that it was an invitation to tea from someone called Joscelin de Paveley. Daragh crumpled up the note and flung it to the floor. He slammed empty bottles into crates, and hurled barrels across the flags. His need for Tilda, which he had thought he could control, had become a torment. It was easier for her; women didn't have the same desires.

As he hacked at the cobwebs, disturbing spiders that had slept peacefully for decades, Daragh knew that he was not being fair. There were, after all, two sorts of women. There were the easy ones, and there were the ones a man could respect. Tilda, like his sister Caitlin, belonged in the second category. He had not wanted Caitlin to give herself to that great lug of a farmhand who courted her back in Ireland. Daragh himself would have murdered the fellow if she had.

There was only one answer to their difficulties, though it was a solution he was loath to accept. He had come to England to make his fortune, and he was well aware that an early marriage would bring with it a trail of bills and babies. A family would tie him to a grindstone he had intended to avoid, and would both curtail his freedom and limit his future. Yet he could not see another way. He needed her so much.

The cellar was tidy, the dust swept into a corner. Daragh's anger too had been swept away, so he picked up the crumpled scrap of paper from the heap of dirt and cobweb, smoothed it out and glanced at it again. He remembered standing next to Tilda in the church tower, and looking out through the window at the Hall. 'The de Paveleys live there,' Tilda had said.

Daragh took the fork in the road that led to the Hall. There, a servant showed him into the drawing room. Daragh stood, cap in his hand, waiting. He couldn't imagine why Miss de Paveley had asked him to tea, but he had nevertheless bought new socks and laboriously patched the elbows of his jacket. When he looked down, his face stared back at him from the polished reddish wood of an occasional table. The furniture was dark and heavy, and a froth of photographs, knick-knacks and ornaments cluttered the mantelpiece and sideboard. Heavy curtains excluded the bright sunlight. Daragh reached out to touch the smooth, silky damask covering of a chair, and then slammed his hand back to his side as he heard a footstep behind him.

A young woman stood in the doorway. 'Mr Canavan?'

'Miss de Paveley?' He'd imagined her a gracious old trout with a lifelong ambition to help young men better themselves. She was not old at all, though. He saw a tall, strapping girl, the ordinariness of her face redeemed by a pair of fine dark eyes.

She didn't smile. She looked terrified. There was a long, awkward silence. At last, Miss de Paveley blurted out, 'That was such a sweet note you wrote me, Mr Canavan.'

He thought she meant his acceptance of her invitation to tea. 'Ah, sure, it was nothing.'

'It was something to *me*.' The vehemence of her tone surprised him. Then she said, 'I'm sorry – I didn't mean—' She looked frightened again.

Daragh felt a mixture of embarrassment and impatience and pity for her. Incongruously, he found himself trying to put her at her ease.

'It's a grand place you have here, Miss de Paveley.' He was going to add, *My ma has a candlestick or two like that*, but was stopped by a caution that his months in England had taught him. He had made a fool of himself too often to court further humiliation.

Conversation died once more. Daragh searched desperately for something more to say. 'My condolences on the death of your father, Miss de Paveley. It must be a sad time for you.'

73

'Oh!' A smile brightened her pale, round face. 'I saw you in Southam after my father's funeral.'

Which explained, at least, how she knew him. Daragh sensed that there was in this odd rendezvous a possibility of advantage. The realization excited him.

'Those people that you were with,' she said. 'Are they relations?'

'Friends, miss. Old friends.'

She seemed to have gained confidence. 'Shall we walk around the grounds before tea, Mr Canavan? I'll just get my hat.'

Miss de Paveley showed him the old motor car in the garage, and her flower garden, and the tennis court. There was no boundary between the kitchen gardens and the fields, just a mingling of decaying brassica stumps and ripe wheat. A dusty track swung out through the fields, parallel to the dike. Daragh could see in the distance a long, low house, its whitewashed walls disappearing into the sky. When she said, 'The estate's mine, now that my father's dead,' he felt a stab of envy that this drab, diffident little thing – younger than he, surely – should have all this. The afternoon seemed to him suddenly irrational and senseless. He wished she'd come to the point – offer him a labouring job, or whatever it was that she intended to do.

Yet when he glanced round at her, he understood, and his heart hammered in his chest. Her great brown eyes burned as she looked up at him. He couldn't think how it had happened, but Daragh Canavan knew that Joscelin de Paveley was in love with him.

He had meant to do it properly, the proposal. Tilda managed to escape the old witch of an aunt, and when Daragh met her in Ely he gave her the single red rose

74

he'd nicked from the garden of the inn, and told her that he'd booked a table in a restaurant. He'd had a bit of luck at cards a few nights past. Tilda looked startled and asked whether it was his birthday, and Daragh shook his head and planted a kiss on her lips. 'Just a treat for you, darlin'.' She fussed a bit about her old dress, but he told her what he knew to be true: that she'd be the most beautiful woman there. So she twisted her long hair into a knot on top of her head (just the movement of her wrists made him ache with longing for her), and then she walked with him to the restaurant.

Daragh caught the waiter glancing at the patched sleeves of his jacket, but he slipped the fellow a half-crown and they were shown to a decent table. Daragh ordered oysters and dressed crab. Tilda had never eaten oysters before, so Daragh showed her how to lift the shell to her lips and let them slide down. 'At home,' he said 'we just pick them out of the rock pools and prise them open with a knife. They're a rare treat.'

Tilda's eyes were enormous. '*Alive?*'

'Still kicking,' said Daragh.

The waiter had served the crab when Daragh told Tilda about the conversation he'd had with the priest. 'He said you could start taking instruction straight away. It'll take a few months, that's all.'

Tilda looked up from trying to pick the meat out of a crab leg. 'Take instruction?'

'So we can get married.' He realized what he had done, and cursed himself. So he pushed back his chair, and knelt on the floor in front of her. 'Will you marry me, Tilda?'

She laughed. He thought, much later, that it would all have been different if she had not laughed. If the other diners, staring, had not also heard her laugh. She took his hand and tried to raise him to his feet, and said, 'Daragh – please – they'll throw us out of here.'

'I'm asking you to marry me, Tilda.' The heat, his frustration, even the unsettling afternoon he'd spent with that peculiar woman, all conspired to shorten his temper. Daragh sat down again. 'We'll marry, won't we, Tilda?'

'Daragh—'

He grasped her hand tightly. 'You'll not say no, will you, sweetheart?'

Her face had become rather pale and rather still. He could feel her distancing herself from him, cutting him off in the imperious way she had. All his doubts had slipped away, and he wanted nothing more at that moment than to be the husband of Tilda Greenless. He felt for the first time a flare of anger that this girl, this *child*, should choose to keep him at arm's length.

She said, 'You're hurting me, Daragh,' and, shamed, he let go of her hand. Then she said, 'You were joking, weren't you?' and his anger returned, doubled.

'Why should I be joking?' Daragh's voice was dangerously low. 'Am I not good enough for you?'

The waiter fussed around the table, refilling their glasses, picking up Daragh's fallen napkin. When he had gone, Daragh said softly, 'You're no better than me, after all, Tilda – less, if anything. At least my granda *owned* the fields I ploughed.'

Her eyes flashed with anger. 'The man's no better and no worse than the master,' she hissed. 'Aunt Sarah taught me that years ago!'

They glared at each other across the table. Anger suited her, brightening her eyes, marking patches of pink on her cheekbones. He found himself pleading with her.

'I've my job at the pub. And I've hopes of something better.' He thought of Joscelin de Paveley, and how he might capitalize on her lust for him by persuading her to help him. 'We could find a couple of rooms in Ely. You're doing that typing course – you could take a little part-time job until the babies come along. That's why you have to take instruction, Tilda. We can't marry until you convert – I'd want my children to be brought up in the Church.'

'I don't want children yet, Daragh.' She was avoiding his eyes. Daragh realized that the diners on the adjacent table – a fat, besuited man and his fancy mistress – were staring at them.

'Of course you do. You like babies. I've seen you cooing over prams.'

'Not yet, though. I don't want babies yet. I'd like them some day, lots of them, but when I'm . . . oh, twenty-one, perhaps.'

Daragh said bitterly, 'You can't plan your life like that, darlin'. You think you're going to do one thing, and you end up doing something else. Babies come along when God tells them to.'

She looked down at her plate. 'I'm eighteen, Daragh. Too young to have children.'

'Plenty of girls have babies at your age.' He shrugged dismissively, and glared at the nosy blonde piece sitting at the next table.

'And are old and poor and exhausted by the time they're twenty.' Tilda had abandoned her crab, and it lay, a jumble of hollow shell and disjointed limb, on the plate in front of her. 'I've seen them, Daragh.'

'My ma had three of us before she was twenty,' he said contemptuously, 'and we always had food in our bellies and shoes on our feet.'

She leaned forward. 'You are rearranging my life, Daragh. Putting it in a different order. Forgetting some of the important bits.'

'Those classes that you hate?' He knew that, little as he could offer Tilda Greenless, it was more than she had now. 'That poky little cottage? The old aunt you're happy enough to deceive – are those the important bits?'

She became very still, her hands curled into fists. 'I've no intention of being a typist all my life,' she said slowly. 'And Long Cottage is better than many of the places I've lived in. And you're right, Daragh, it has been wicked of me to lie to Aunt Sarah. I'll not lie to her any more.'

'So you'll tell her about me?' His voice was scathing. 'Or am I not important enough? Where do I fit into your scheme of things, Tilda? Or was I just to pass the time – just to tease a little – just to string along until something better turns up—'

She stood up then, and folded her napkin and placed it on the table. Then she walked out of the restaurant. Daragh wanted to run after her, but his pride stopped him. Instead he turned to the diners at the adjacent table, and said, with a smile that made them turn back embarrassed to their plates, 'Well then, the show's over, and you can eat your pudding now, can't you?' Then he signalled to the waiter, and ordered a double whisky and swallowed it quickly, tearing the petals from the rose as he drank.

Tilda's eyes were swollen and red. She told Sarah that she had a headache and went upstairs, but Sarah knew that she was crying. Sarah, listening to Tilda's bedroom door closing behind her, smiled to herself. Then she took out the old stocking from beneath the floor brick, drew out several coins, and tucked them into the pocket in her petticoat.

That evening, she lifted the ancient cardboard suitcase down from the tallboy and began to pack.

The unprecedented treat of a train journey and three weeks in a bed and breakfast in Great Yarmouth should have been extraordinarily delightful to Tilda, but was not. All the pleasure she usually took in new places and new experiences was absent. Watching the waves crash down on the pier, walking along the rainswept esplanade, she thought only of Daragh. Locked in the guesthouse's bathroom, the only place where she had any privacy, she tried to write to him. Each time she tore the letter up and flushed it down the lavatory.

Standing on the sea front, watching the waves heave and slap against the pebbles, Tilda knew that she loved Daragh – that her heart ached with loving him – and that she wanted, one day, his children. Tramping for hours with Sarah along the beach, she made a decision. When they went back to Southam, she would tell Daragh that she would marry him when she was twenty-one and no longer required Aunt Sarah's permission. If Daragh loved her, then he would wait for her.

Miss de Paveley invited Daragh to tea for a second time. Together they walked across the fields, where the dry wind rustled the shorn stubble.

'Shall we take the path along the dike, Miss de Paveley?'

She looked up at him. 'Would you call me Joscelin, Mr Canavan?' She had gone pink. 'Or Jossy, if you prefer.'

Daragh let his hand, helping Jossy up the steep

bank, linger just a little longer than necessary on her silk-covered elbow. The humiliation of Tilda's rejection still rankled. There was an element of flirtation in his conversation with Jossy today – clumsy on her part, polished on Daragh's – on which he intended to capitalize.

'Then you must call me Daragh.'

He had the reward of seeing her tremble. If he'd taken her here on the ridge of the bank, he thought suddenly, she would not have objected. He did not touch her, though.

There were no clouds in the sky, and the sun was a bright, hard disc. Heat shimmered on the horizon, making the long, low white house that Daragh had previously noticed seem to shimmer and shift in the windless air. He said, 'That's a bleak-looking place.'

'My Uncle Christopher lives there. He runs the farm.'

Daragh was disappointed. So she didn't need a land agent. He said, hoping to prompt an encouraging response from her, 'I know a fair bit about farm work myself.'

'Are your family farmers, Daragh?'

He nodded, remembering his grandfather's cottage, set in a patch of stony ground.

'You're Irish, aren't you?'

He had smartened up his accent for Joscelin de Paveley, mimicking the clipped, proper English he had learned in London, and was galled that she had nevertheless recognized his origins.

'We had a fine place,' he said mysteriously, 'a grand place, but we fell on hard times. I can't tell you everything, Jossy – there's some things it's better to forget. Let's just say that I won't be going back to Ireland.'

When he saw the sympathy in her eyes, Daragh knew that he had struck just the right note to satisfy her romantic, naive nature. He pressed his advantage. 'So now I'm rather at a loose end. I miss the old country, and I haven't found anything yet to take its place. I've done a bit of this and that, but I'm used to something better. I just need a chance.'

She started to speak, but her words were, to Daragh's chagrin, interrupted by a shout from the field below.

'Jossy! Hello there, Jossy!'

'Kit!' Jossy waved, and ran down the bank. Panting at the exertion, she clumped across the field, Daragh following after her.

A pale, thin young man crossed the field to join them.

'Kit, let me introduce you to my friend, Daragh Canavan.' Daragh noticed with what pride Jossy said 'my friend'. 'Daragh, this is my cousin Kit.'

Kit de Paveley wore filthy corduroys and an old cotton shirt. Even on such a hot day, Daragh was wearing his one good jacket. He knew that a gentleman always wore a jacket. Kit's lank hair was uncovered and needed cutting. As he shook hands, Daragh reflected contemptuously that if he hadn't been told that Kit was Jossy's cousin, then he'd have taken him for a tramp, or a beggar.

'Have you found something interesting, Kit?'

'A couple of coins. Roman.' Animation showed in the light grey eyes. Kit dug in his pocket. 'Beauties, aren't they?' Two small, misshapen black lumps nestled on his palm.

Jossy seemed as unimpressed as Daragh was. 'I thought they'd be shinier.'

'I'll clean them up, of course.'

Jossy's unprepossessing cousin turned away without

a goodbye, heading back to the white house. Daragh thought of taking Jossy's arm again, but something stopped him, a spasm of self-disgust, and a sudden bitter awareness of the unfairness of things. If Tilda had all this. If marriage to the girl he loved would not entail penury. For he did love her: he faced that there and then, as his eyes stung with the heat and the dust.

Daragh had assumed that Tilda would call at the pub, or write to him. That she would apologize, or explain. After a week had passed, and she had done neither, Daragh swallowed his pride and cycled to Long Cottage. To his rap on the front door there was no reply other than the distant rumble of thunder from the clouds which had begun to billow on the horizon. Daragh hopped over the fence, and walked around the little house. All the windows were tightly shut, some curtains drawn. Seizing the handle, Daragh shook the back door, but it refused to open. In spite of the oppressive heat, a cold sensation flowered in his stomach. They never locked the back door.

A girl was whitening the front step of the next door cottage. When she explained that the Greenlees had gone away, Daragh kicked the wicket fence so hard that the stave broke. Then he walked back to the street, seized by the terrible certainty that they had left Southam for ever and returned to the vagrant way of life of Tilda's childhood. As the vast arch of the iron-grey sky pressed down on him, Daragh learned how close love could be to hatred. Tilda had not loved him as he loved her, and his anguish was intensified by the suspicion that she had made a fool of him.

Daragh climbed onto his bicycle and left the village. Crackles of lightning sparked on the horizon, but the air was still dry. As he rode, the countryside was reduced to a streak of dun and ochre, yet the fast slipstream of air could not blank out the words that echoed in his head. *She didn't even say goodbye.* His hair clung to his forehead and the back of his neck with sweat, and there was a bitter taste in his mouth.

A motor car overtook him, rather too close, and then lurched to a halt, sending up dust and pebbles. Daragh, recognizing Jossy as she turned in the driver's seat and waved to him, groaned inwardly.

Her head was uncovered and her coarse brown hair tangled by the wind. 'What luck that we met!' she cried. 'I was driving to Ely – I hoped that I might run into you.'

Her words bubbled and fell over themselves. At another time Daragh might have smiled at her infelicitous choice of phrase. Instead, he raised his cap and said, 'Good afternoon, Miss de Paveley. I hope that you're well.'

She didn't seem to notice his lack of enthusiasm. She said, 'Come for a drive, Daragh,' and he felt angered by the complacent assumption of the rich that he would drop everything, come running.

'Sorry. I've the bike.'

'Leave it in the ditch. See – it's beginning to rain. Or put it in the back of the car.'

He was about to refuse when he realized that now Tilda was gone the only thing to keep him in this damnable place was the hope that Joscelin de Paveley might help him better himself. And besides, Jossy was right, large drops of rain had begun to fall from the darkening sky. Daragh slung the bicycle into the back of the huge, open-top car, and climbed into the passenger seat. Jossy scraped the motor car noisily into gear, rammed her foot on the accelerator, and the Bentley lurched diagonally across the road.

He grabbed the steering wheel, straightening it. 'Do you know how to drive this thing?'

She was hunched over the steering wheel, her tongue between her teeth, her eyes narrowed in concentration. She had to shout because of the noise of the engine. 'No. I'm teaching myself. It was my father's car, but he didn't drive it for years because of his leg. The gardener's boy showed me how to do the gears. I can start and stop, but corners are difficult.'

He felt a fleeting admiration for her, mixed with nausea as they took a bend in the road too fast. He yelled, 'You need to change down a gear.'

She yanked the gearstick again. 'I couldn't get the hood up. You're not getting too wet, are you?'

He shook his head, enjoying the cold shock of the rain on his skin.

'Do you drive, Daragh?'

'A bit.' His uncle, who ran a pub in Dublin, had owned a van.

'Would you teach me properly?'

They were passing the little bridge where he had first kissed Tilda. He was aware of a wave of overwhelming grief, and knew that he wasn't in the right frame of mind to flirt with Joscelin de Paveley. He said, 'I'm a bit busy just now, I'm afraid.'

A herd of goats straggled across the road ahead. Daragh punched the horn and Jossy stamped on the brakes. The goats scattered as the car screeched to a halt.

'Busy?' repeated Jossy, looking across at him.

'My work's at a dead end. I thought I'd look around and try to find something that suits me better.'

He could hardly, he thought, put it plainer than that. Yet the stupid woman just stared at him, her lower lip stuck out.

'Of course,' he added impatiently, 'if I can't find anything here, then I'll have to move on.'

They edged along the road again. Rain drummed on the dry impacted earth. Jossy said, 'You like the Hall, don't you, Daragh?'

She began to talk, as they gathered speed, about wallpaper and distemper. Daragh looked at her almost with dislike. She was, he thought suddenly, one of the dullest women he had ever met.

Then she said, 'I thought, when we are married, we could have the house redecorated.'

Jossy smiled at him, her love blatant in her eyes. Daragh coughed and blenched and reached instinctively into his pocket for his cigarettes. The car veered across the road, and then slid, slowly and gracefully, down the slope into the field below.

CHAPTER THREE

'She changed her religion for him. Joscelin de Paveley, whose family had been Protestant since the sixteenth century, discarded her history and became a Roman Catholic.'

Tilda closed the photograph album with a snap. She looked up, and her eyes met mine. I had always assumed that our feelings become less painful in old age. That in compensation for physical frailties, all those bruising emotions – jealousy, grief, desire – do not trouble us as they used to. I knew, looking at Tilda, that I had been mistaken.

'The news of their engagement was all around the village. All around the county. They were talking about it in the post office when I went to buy stamps. I'd been to Ely the previous day, and the publican had told me that Daragh had given in his notice. I was afraid that he'd left the area. I blamed myself, of course. But when I heard that he was to *marry* . . .' Her voice faltered, fading away.

'You were angry?' I coaxed.

She shook her head. 'No. Not then. Later.' She frowned. 'I felt stunned, literally. The only other time in my life that I can remember feeling like that was when the children were small and we lived in a scruffy little house, and I slipped on the linoleum going downstairs and hit my head on the banister. Not being able to think . . . hardly being able to breathe.' She looked up at me. 'Have you ever felt like that, Rebecca?'

I didn't want to answer. It was not a part of the bargain, to share my secrets with her. But I remembered only too clearly how I had felt when when Toby had said, *I don't think we should see so much of each other.* I had stared at him and at my hospital bed and at my own trembling hands, and they had all seemed unfamiliar.

Tilda did not wait for my reply. 'Most of the other bad things that have happened to me – Holland, and Max, and even poor Erich – I had some sort of warning. But with Daragh . . . nothing.'

I forced myself to speak. 'You must have loved him terribly.'

'Oh, I did. I did.'

I wanted to ask whether that sort of love, dealt so grievous a blow, lingered. Yet I saw an inevitability of pain in her reply. To go on loving when love is futile, or to forget why you loved in the first place – which is worse?

Instead, I gathered my things together and took my leave of her. It was late, and the grey, swollen clouds told me that there was a possibility of snow. I said goodbye and walked downstairs, and took my coat from the peg in the hall. By the time I reached London, small crystals of snow dotted the beams from my car's headlights. At home, I turned up the heating and opened a bottle of wine, and drank it rather quickly. The boiler lurched and grunted, but the radiators gave off only a feeble heat, so I delved in the wardrobe for a warmer sweater. Several garments stuffed in the back of the shelf fell out onto the floor. Just the sight of them filled me with rage. I thought of Tilda, learning of Daragh's betrayal in Southam post office, and I thought of Toby, looking anywhere but at me as he spoke the words that broke my heart. I fetched the kitchen scissors.

I was halfway through cutting a sleeve into neat, half-inch ribbons when there was a knock at the door. Charles Lightman and his sister Lucy stood on the step.

'You haven't returned any of my phone calls,' said Charles, coming in. He had a couple of bottles of wine.

'I told Charles that you were probably working,' said Lucy, 'but he insisted.'

'You shouldn't neglect—' began Charles, and then he stopped as he caught sight of the sweater and the scissors. 'What on earth are you doing, Becca?'

'Cutting it up,' I said. 'Toby gave it to me.'

Charles smiled, but Lucy stared at the label and said, 'But Rebecca, it's Nicole Farhi T!'

I shrugged. 'I wouldn't ever wear it again.'

'But you could give it to Oxfam – or to *me*—' Lucy was horrified.

Charles said, 'That's not the point, is it? It's not the absence of the thing – it's the destruction of it. It's the act of vengeance that's so pleasurable, especially to an obsessive like Rebecca.'

I said, outraged, 'I'm not an obsessive.'

'Of course you are.' Charles had gone into the kitchen to search for wine glasses. 'You were obsessed with Toby Carne, and now you're obsessed with Tilda Franklin. Just look.' The wide sweep of his hand indicated the books and papers that cluttered my desk, the time-line of Tilda's life that I had affixed to the wall, and the old black and white photographs on the pinboard. 'An improvement, of course, but an obsession nevertheless.'

Lucy was cradling the Nicole Farhi jumper in her arms. I said defensively, 'Tilda's a fascinating woman. And it's an interesting job . . . trying to fill in the gaps . . . There's so many things one *can't* know . . . You just have to work out what must have happened as best you can.'

'Perhaps I can cut the other sleeve down. Make it short-sleeved.'

'There's so much you have to assume or infer.'

'Put a little hem around it.'

'It's like a crossword puzzle. Filling in the gaps.'

'Or unpick the shoulder seam.'

'Oh, do shut up about that bloody jumper, Lucy,' said Charles amiably. 'Donald will buy you dozens of Nicole Farhi jumpers, no doubt.' He refilled my wine glass. 'Lu has acquired a new and ghastly boyfriend. He is terribly rich.' He sat down on the floor. 'Anyway, I agree with Rebecca. One shouldn't just let a love affair fizzle out. One should end it with a great, dramatic gesture. So cathartic.'

'Paint his windows black,' said Lucy, bundling up the jumper and putting it in her bag. 'Do it overnight, so he won't know what's happened when he wakes up in the morning.'

'Toby has a third-floor flat.'

'Drain the brake fluid from his car.'

'I don't want to *kill* him, Charles – just humiliate him a bit. Anyway, you know I'm hopeless with cars.'

'I saw a television programme,' said Lucy, 'where an abandoned wife sewed lumps of Stilton into the hem of her ex-husband's curtains. Think of the *smell*. He couldn't work out where it was coming from.'

'Langoustines,' said Charles. 'Langoustines would be better.'

I finished my glass of wine. 'I haven't a key to Toby's flat,' I said regretfully.

But a few days later, Charles appeared again, with an invitation to a Law Society dinner dance. He wouldn't tell me how he'd got it. I argued a bit, but he insisted, and I thought – why not? At worst, I'd find myself in court for petty vandalism. And as Charles pointed out, think of the publicity. So good for book sales.

I changed into something long and floaty, and together – Charles in his ancient dinner suit and me in my Monsoon dress – we stopped en route at Sainsbury's. They hadn't any langoustines, so I bought prawns instead. Then we drove into central London.

I'd been to Law Society functions before, with Toby. I'd always seemed to end up standing on his toe during my inept attempts at the quickstep, or arguing with some right-wing but influential old judge. The chill grandeur of the building, the distant sound of well-bred chatter, were all unpleasantly familiar. With Charles ambling behind me, I scuttled quickly along the corridor to the cloakroom, terrified that Toby might suddenly appear from behind a pillar. The cloakroom was unattended, luckily, and it was easy to find the right Burberry raincoat. Toby still used name-tapes, for heaven's sake. *T. F. Carne*, sewn neatly into the collar of his coat. A hangover from school, I suppose. I wondered whether his mother sewed them for him.

Charles went outside to keep watch. I knelt on the cloakroom floor. My hands trembled so much as I took scissors, needle and cotton from my evening bag that I could hardly thread the needle. Yet there was an awful exhilaration in my task. The pleasure of revenge, as Charles had pointed out. I couldn't stab Toby through the heart, but I could make him ridiculous.

I had nearly finished when I heard a sound behind me. 'Almost done, Charles,' I muttered without looking round.

There was a cough. Not Charles's cough. Suddenly cold, I looked up.

I recognized Patrick Franklin instantly. I remembered walking with him through Tilda Franklin's garden. I remembered how much he had annoyed me. Now he was lounging against the cloakroom counter, his hands in his pockets, looking down at me. I couldn't make out the expression in his eyes.

'I'm just . . . I'm just . . .' I said, floundering. My heart pounded and my mouth was dry.

'You're just . . .' and he peered over my shoulder, 'you're just sewing prawns into the hem of someone's raincoat.'

'There's a very good reason for it,' I said pompously, breaking the thread and bundling my things back into my bag. My face felt hot and pink and I wanted to run. 'Must go,' I said. My voice wasn't working very well. I stood up. 'Bye.'

'Goodbye, Rebecca,' he said. But as I turned to go, Patrick reached out and took my arm, halting me. 'Don't forget these.'

'These' were the leftover prawns, still in their white plastic bag. I shoved them in my pocket, and ran out of the room.

I didn't sleep much that night. I got up early and was working on my book when Jane telephoned at nine o'clock. She had flu and Steve was away on business.

Would I come and help with the boys for a few days? She was apologetic about disturbing my work, but when I suggested that I bring my laptop so that I could get on with things while the boys were asleep, she laughed hollowly, and pointed out that Lawrie hadn't slept through the night since he was born.

My sister's plea for help came as a relief. I was sorry that poor Jane had flu, but delighted to escape London. The events of the previous night – the recollection of the expression in Patrick Franklin's eyes as he had looked down at me, kneeling on the cloakroom floor, prawns in hand – made me squirm with embarrassment. I knew that he must think me mad, and I minded that he should think a madwoman was writing his illustrious grandmother's biography.

So I enjoyed the drive out of London and into the countryside. The sky was a clear, pale blue, and the brown earth in the fields was hazed with green where the new wheat had begun to show. I reached Jane's house by eleven. She lives in a tiny thatched cottage, surrounded by a pretty garden where cabbages nestle beside hollyhocks, and runner beans climb the same trellis as a rambling rose. I can never help but compare her cottage with my drab little flat.

Jane was stuffing grubby cot sheets into the washing machine when I arrived. She looked dreadful, so I sent her to bed. Both Jack and Lawrie had been ill the previous week, and were still runny-nosed and coughing. I made them lunch, most of which ended up on the table or the floor, then I wrapped them up in jackets and woolly hats and gloves and took them out for a walk. On the way home, they both began to complain of hunger, so, with a few guilty pangs about balanced diets, I bought Milky Ways from the shop.

Then I attacked the vast heap of ironing, made up Lawrie's cot, and began to mop up the mud left by the boys' wellies in the hallway. While I was cleaning the floor, Jack decided to help himself to a drink of orange juice from the fridge. I heard the crash and yell as the bottle slipped out of his hands onto the tiles. I dashed into the kitchen, grabbed Jack, who was barefoot, and sat him howling on the kitchen table while I set about picking up fragments of glass. From the doorway, Lawrie told me tearfully that he'd lost Boffy, his toy rabbit. Then the phone rang. I could feel myself breaking out into a hot sweat. I answered the phone (double glazing, of course) before it could wake Jane, carried both weeping boys into the living room, and switched on the TV. *Pingu*, thank God. I wanted to flake out with a stiff gin, but there was still the broken glass and the mud and Boffy to be found, and the boys' tea-time in half an hour. And bath-time, of course. I discovered Boffy stuffed down the back of a radiator, and then I crawled all over the kitchen floor, squinting, terrified I'd overlook a splinter of glass. Then I shoved some fish fingers under the grill and suddenly remembered poor Jane, who hadn't had as much as a cup of tea since eleven o'clock that morning. She was asleep, but by the time I came downstairs smoke was belching from the grill. That set the smoke alarm off, so I had to leap around, flapping open doors and windows. *Pingu* finished, and the boys stood in the doorway, thumbs in mouths, mesmerized by the sight of their aunt standing at the back door in the rain, scraping black gobbets from grill pan to dustbin.

Much, much later, I collapsed on the living-room sofa, a mug of tea in one hand, laptop in the other. I was due to see Tilda again in a couple of days, and I hadn't yet finished writing up my notes from my last visit. I stared at the blank screen, and saw only charred fish fingers and shards of broken glass. Then I heard crying. I dumped my laptop on the floor and ran upstairs.

Lawrie had been sick in his cot; the Milky Way had not been a good idea. I picked him up and tried to comfort him; his howls set off Jack in the next bed, who began to yell in sympathy. I was trying one-handedly to strip the cot whilst cuddling Lawrie and calming Jack, when, to my immense relief, Jane appeared in the doorway. She patted Jack's head and told him firmly to go back to sleep, and then she peeled off Lawrie's sodden sleepsuit and pyjamas while I stripped the cot. Lawrie's clothes, the bedding and, disastrously, Boffy, had all to be washed. Lawrie howled inconsolably as Jane rinsed his rabbit in the sink. He howled throughout the entire cycle of both washing machine and tumble-drier, and he howled and fought as Jane and I changed his nappy and dressed him in clean clothes. All attempts at distraction were rejected – his suck-cup was pushed away, his dummy was batted to the floor. Only when Boffy, untypically clean and fluffy, emerged from the tumble-drier did Lawrie curl up on Jane's lap, and the sobs begin to lessen.

Jane looked down at him, and wearily stroked his curls. 'Poor old boy,' she whispered. 'Poor old boy.' There was no colour to her skin; it seemed transparent. She looked up at me. 'Do you know, Becca,' she said quietly, 'that I'd sell my soul for an uninterrupted night's sleep?'

I didn't doubt her. Lawrie, on Jane's lap, still hiccuped, but his lids had closed.

'Couldn't Steve help more?'

She shook her head. 'We need the overtime. We have negative equity.'

I glanced at her, shocked. 'I hadn't realized.'

'We bought this house at the wrong time. And there's

only two bedrooms, and the boys fight terribly. I don't know when we'll be able to move to a bigger place. I envy you your freedom, sometimes.'

It had been a long time since I had considered myself an object of envy. Not since Toby.

Jane managed a watery smile and, very gently, I scooped Lawrie out of her lap. He didn't stir. I told Jane to go back to bed, and promised to see to Lawrie if he woke in the night.

I carried him upstairs, but did not immediately put him into his cot. Instead, I stood there for a moment, with his warm, velvety head cradled against my shoulder, looking down at the small, perfect curves of his face, at the violet-tinged eyelids, and the fine skin still blotched pink from crying. My own eyes were heavy with tears, but I did not allow them to fall. At last I touched my lips to his forehead and laid him carefully in his cot. He shuffled about a bit, ending up with his knees tucked under his bottom, his rabbit pressed against his face, snoring. I watched him as he slept, and I tried to imagine Toby scrubbing yucky baby clothes in the sink, Toby putting aside his work to run to attend to a sick child. And I couldn't. The images just didn't fit. He would have worried about spoiling his suit. He would have worried about losing a case.

I sat down on the chest of drawers beside the cot and felt, for the first time, a sober regret instead of grief and anger and a need for vengeance. I began to recognize that my relationship with Toby had been based on mutual fantasies. That Toby had been looking for a young, pliant partner to mould into the sort of wife who would be an asset to him in his career. That I had been searching for a family to replace my own flawed, fractured clan. The child had been a part of our fantasy.

My initial disbelief that someone like Toby – handsome, cultured and well-off – might love me had never quite gone away. I had believed, I suppose, that a child might bind us together. As for Toby himself, perhaps he had been attracted to that caring, early-Nineties image of masculinity reinforced by fatherhood: the man in the adverts with the beautiful wife, the adorable child, the fast car. The adverts don't tell the truth, of course: the shiny new car cluttered with carrycots and disposable nappies and baby toys; the brilliant career put on hold by too many sleepless nights.

I stayed another three days with Jane, until she was on her feet again and Steve was back from his conference. Then I drove to Tilda's. As I shut the gate of The Red House behind me and started up the path, I felt a sense of release. The high walls of the box trees, pearled with raindrops, embraced me, and I could smell the heady, hypnotic scents of hyacinth and jonquil. And for a moment, standing there on the pathway, enclosed by the hedges, I closed my eyes, breathing in the perfumed air, elated by the prospect of returning to the sanctuary of the past.

*

They married at the beginning of January, in the Catholic church in Cambridge. Jossy wore white satin, which emphasized her big bust and hips. Daragh, standing at the altar, glancing back over his shoulder, felt a shudder of panic-stricken regret. The ranks of well-dressed strangers, and Jossy herself, plodding up the aisle on the arm of her uncle, seemed nightmarishly unfamiliar. His bride should have had a different face: his bride should have had dark gold hair and cool grey eyes. It was as though he had become caught up in someone else's dream. He had to force himself not to run.

Jossy had wanted a honeymoon. She had proposed six weeks' motoring on the continent, but Daragh had pointed out to her that it was winter. In truth, he had not been able to imagine being stuck for weeks in a motor car with Jossy, in a country where his lack of a foreign language would deprive him even of a conversation with the barman in the evenings. Daragh suggested London and Jossy happily agreed. They were to spend their wedding night at the Savoy Hotel. Daragh, driving down the Great North Road in the sports car that Jossy had bought him as a wedding present, thought that the worst of it was almost over. The horror that had seized him in the church seemed ridiculous out in the cold blue of a fine winter's afternoon. He'd have a drink or two when they got to the hotel – not too many though, he had, after all, a last duty to fulfil. He knew that it hadn't really sunk in, what he had done. He hadn't climbed the ladder a rung or two; he'd leapt to the top. Southam Hall was his, the farm was his, even the steward's house where that peculiar boy and his uncle lived was also legally his. He had rid himself of the last vestiges of his Irish accent; he had devised a less shameful background. His talent for mimicry and invention seemed to have paid off: not one of Jossy's smart friends had refused to shake his hand at the reception. When Daragh remembered his previous arrival in London, less than a year before, he told himself how lucky he had been. Born lucky.

At the Savoy, they dined on caviar and smoked salmon, and drank the best champagne. Whenever Daragh looked up, Jossy's dark eyes were watching him. When that began to grate, he reminded himself that they didn't have to spend the rest of their lives in each other' pockets. He would make something of the estate, and Jossy – well, Jossy would have children. Lots of them The sooner the better.

After dinner, he whirled Jossy a couple of times round the ballroom, and then escorted her upstairs to their suite There, she stood in the bedroom, fiddling awkwardly with the buttons on her gloves, her hair spiralling out of the tidy sculpture her hairdresser had made of it that morning.

Daragh extracted the remainder of Jossy's hairpins, unbuttoned her gloves and peeled them off. Kissing her neck and shoulders, he undid the hooks and eyes at the back of her dress. Her eyes were tightly closed, and he was unsure for a moment whether she was aroused or terrified. When he touched with the tip of his tongue the hollow of her spine, she moaned, so he didn't worry any more. The dress slid to the floor, a pool of spangled black, and Daragh let the straps of Jossy's slip fall over her shoulders.

It was when he began to tackle the complicated boned and laced undergarment that she wore beneath her slip that he found the scrap of paper. It fell to the floor, and he picked it up, and said, 'What on earth is this?'

Jossy's eyes opened and her face went brick red. She mumbled something.

'Pardon?' said Daragh.

'I said, it's your letter.'

He was still confused. She said, 'You remember, dear, the one you wrote to me before we met. I've worn it next to my heart ever since.'

He unfolded the paper, and read, *Since I saw you that day, I have been able to think of no-one else. I long to see you again, to speak to you* . . .

Daragh said, 'I didn't write this.'

'Of course you did, my love. You don't mind me talking about it now that we're married, do you?'

He looked first at Jossy, and then back at the paper. His signature was at the foot of the page. All the clichéd, overblown phrases were written in an approximation of his handwriting. Daragh felt cold inside; cold and rather sick.

He went to the window and forced himself to read the letter all the way through. *The image of your beauty has not left my eyes . . . If I could only hear your voice, touch your hand . . . I know that I am unworthy of you, but love can conquer all . . . Do not speak of this letter again, my love. I crave your pardon for my temerity in writing this. Tear it up, burn it . . .*

Yet Jossy had neither torn up the wretched thing, nor thrown it into the fire. When Daragh glanced back at her, she was still standing in the middle of the room, her corset unlaced, her thighs fat and white above the tops of her stockings.

She whispered, 'Are you cross that I kept it?'

Daragh shook his head. Shoving the letter in his jacket pocket, he muttered, 'Excuse me a moment, won't you? Too much champagne.'

In the bathroom, he rinsed his head under the cold tap and tried not to be sick. He knew that something was terribly wrong, but he could not quite work out what. When he was sure that he was capable, he went back to Jossy, and took her to bed.

But after it was over, Daragh lay awake for a long time in the darkness. Perhaps all this was a mistake, founded on sand. Perhaps he had been meant to take another road entirely. Perhaps someone had deliberately pushed him onto the wrong path, manipulating events to take advantage both of Jossy's gullibility and his own ambition. The fine linen sheets, the down pillow, the silken coverlet seemed just then horrible to him.

Forcing down panic, he tracked the train of events. Someone had written that letter, copying his handwriting, forging his signature. It had been sent to Joscelin de Paveley, purporting to tell her that he loved her. Because of that letter, he had married Jossy and not Tilda. Daragh released himself from Jossy's sleeping embrace, slid out of bed, and from the adjoining chamber rang room service and ordered whisky and cigarettes.

From the garden, throwing frost-rimmed logs into the basket, Tilda heard the loud hammering on the front door. The log slipped out of her grasp, splintering on the icy flags, as she recognized Daragh's voice. Her hands were shaking, and her fingernails were blue with cold. Slowly, she gathered up the scattered fragments of wood, and carried the basket into the scullery.

They were in the kitchen. Sarah's voice first.

'I think you should leave, Mr Canavan.'

Then Daragh. 'I'll not leave until you tell me the truth!'

Tilda opened the kitchen door. Daragh was standing at one side of the table; Aunt Sarah was seated at the other. Sarah looked round. 'Go to your room, Tilda.'

'Oh, come *on*.' Daragh's smile was unpleasant. 'I think Tilda should stay, don't you?'

Tilda shut the door behind her. Yesterday – Daragh's wedding day – she had walked for miles, her head bowed against the wind, following the long line of the dike until Southam and all who lived there were erased from the horizon.

'Why are you here, Daragh?' she said bitterly. 'Shouldn't you be with your wife?'

'I wanted to have a little chat with your Aunt Sarah.' Daragh's face was flushed, his black curls tangled. 'I wanted to ask her about this.' He waved a piece of paper in the air.

'Please go, Daragh.' Tilda's voice was cold. 'Neither of us wishes to speak to you.'

She saw him blench. His gestures were over-large, his voice unnaturally loud. She realized he had been drinking.

'I wanted to explain.' Daragh's finger jabbed in Sarah's direction. '*She* has to explain—'

Sarah sat at the table, her hands folded in front of her, her expression haughty and controlled.

'There's nothing to explain, Daragh.' Tilda opened the scullery door to show him out. 'Go home.'

'Read this.' As he pressed the sheet of paper into her hands, his breathing was audible. 'Read it.'

Tilda looked down. *I know that I am unworthy of you, but love conquers all.* Daragh's name was at the foot of the page, Miss de Paveley's was at its head. Tilda crumpled the note and flung it to the floor.

'I won't read your love letters, Daragh. Get out!'

He seized the letter from where she had dropped it, flattening the paper with one sharp movement of his hand. 'I said, *read* it!' He pushed her forward.

Tilda gasped. Aunt Sarah cried, 'Let her go,' and rose out of the chair. Words and phrases danced in front of Tilda's eyes.

Daragh said, very softly, 'I didn't write it.'

Tilda pointed a shaking finger to his signature.

'I didn't write it. Shall I tell you who wrote it? *She* wrote it. She wrote it so that I wouldn't see you any more.' As he turned to Sarah, Daragh's face was bone white. 'That's true, isn't it?'

Tilda stared at Sarah, waiting for her denial. But Sarah Greenlees remained silent, her body rigid, her features as still as if they had been carved in stone. In the silence, some of Tilda's anger slid away and was replaced by fear.

Daragh's fist struck the table. '*Tell* her, won't you, you old witch? Tell her that it's because of *you* that I married Joscelin de Paveley!'

Sarah spoke at last. 'You married Miss de Paveley because you were greedy.' Her tone was one of quiet satisfaction. 'You married her for her money.'

'I married her because you contrived it!'

Sarah Greenlees whispered, 'You have got what you deserve, Daragh Canavan.'

There was a tight pain behind Tilda's eyes, as though someone was pushing at her sockets with the balls of their thumbs. The room, and Sarah's face, had altered, becoming unfamiliar and strange. The wreath of dried hops and the cut paper shelf liners seemed fragile, lacking in substance. When she looked at the books and crockery on the dresser, their disarray jarred her.

'You've got what you deserve,' repeated Sarah. 'And so has Miss de Paveley.' Then she started to laugh. The sound oscillated around the small room.

'Good God.' All the colour had drained from Daragh's face. 'She's insane. Quite insane.' He stared at Sarah, and then at Tilda. He whispered, 'I loved you. I loved you so much,' and then he turned on his heel and left the house. The car engine roared as he drove away at speed.

Her muscles did not seem to be working properly, but Tilda went to the sink and filled a cup with water and placed it in front of Sarah. Then she sat down at the table, waiting. When Sarah had stopped laughing and had drunk a few mouthfuls of water, Tilda spoke. 'Is it true?'

All the blood seemed to have gone from Sarah's face. Her skin was translucent. She nodded. 'I knew you were in love with him. I found a letter in your room. I copied his handwriting.' The hysteria had gone, and Sarah's tone was flat and exhausted.

'*Why?*'

Sarah looked up from the glass. Her face was ravaged and old. 'Because he isn't good enough for you.'

Part of Tilda seemed to crumble, the confident assumptions of childhood brutally destroyed. Only a small piece of her remained detached, seeing everything with great clarity.

'Why Joscelin de Paveley? Why did Daragh have to marry *her*?'

Sarah shrugged. 'Why not? I knew he'd want her money. I knew the girl desired him.'

Tilda was almost convinced. But then she remembered Sarah's laughter at the squire's funeral, and knew that Sarah, who never went to church, had gone there not to mourn Edward de Paveley's death, but to celebrate it.

'No. That's not enough. You *hate* them. You hate the de Paveleys.'

Sarah's eyes darkened, yet she did not speak.

'*Why?*' whispered Tilda. When Sarah did not answer, she said harshly, 'If you don't tell me the truth, then I shall leave. I'll go, and I'll never come back. I'll live how we used to live, travelling. But without you, this time. *Tell me.*'

There was a long silence. Then Sarah said slowly, 'I hated Edward de Paveley because of what he did to my sister – to your mother.' Her eyes narrowed, and her voice was low and venomous. She whispered, 'I curse the de Paveleys and all their issue.'

Tilda couldn't speak. *Tell me*, she thought.

'Edward de Paveley was your father,' said Sarah. The words were like a sigh.

*

'I didn't believe her at first. I thought that Daragh was right, that she was mad. And perhaps she was, a little – perhaps the sort of powerlessness that Sarah had felt when she discovered what had happened to her sister had unbalanced her. Her need for revenge had become an obsession. She told me how she'd left home when her father died, and how Deborah had gone to work at the Hall. She told me everything. She showed me a copy of my mother's committal certificate. She had a little case of pathetic and dreadful mementoes – a lock of her sister's hair . . . an old doll they'd played with as children . . . a replica of the posy of flowers she'd put in Deborah's coffin.'

I had stopped writing. I knew that I would remember every word Tilda said.

'I still left her, of course. I couldn't bear to stay in that terrible place. I packed a bag and took my egg money and left Southam. I didn't know where to go. I knew only that I had to get away – far away. I walked to Emily Potter's house. I didn't tell her everything, I couldn't bear to. It just hurt and hurt and I had to be away. I had to forget both Sarah and Daragh, and start again. I had to be someone different. I felt . . . oh, I suppose I felt that the past had done me such terrible harm that I wanted to have no past. Of course, you can never escape the past. I learned that eventually. What happened to Deborah, and what I myself did – what I am – all these things were inescapable.'

I refused to believe her. You could change yourself and start again. You could put aside the weak, defenceless creature that you had once been, and grow a shell that covered your heart, your spleen. You had just to keep building up the layers.

'Emily was wonderful,' Tilda added. 'She lent me money and found a train timetable. I decided to go to London. I knew London would be a good place for starting again. It sounded so anonymous.' She smiled, and just then I could picture so clearly the young girl that she had once been: Tilda in her home-made dresses, with her long, beautiful, medieval face, and her grey eyes that made men like Daragh Canavan forget what they had meant to do with their lives.

'Emily gave me one of her nicest hats, and lent me a pair of scissors. Then I ran to the station to catch the London train.'

'Scissors?' I asked, confused.

CHAPTER FOUR

Tilda cut her hair in a third-class compartment of the London train. A woman sitting opposite her said, 'You could get a nice price for that, love, in one of them London hairdresser's,' so she bundled the plait up in a scarf, and shoved it in her bag.

Liverpool Street Station was an inferno of black smoke and hissing steam. Tilda checked Emily's instructions, and searched for the Underground train. Long moving staircases devoured her, a great serpent roared and rushed at her through the darkness. In the carriage, crushed between an enormously fat woman clutching a bag stuffed with newspapers and a city gentleman with a bowler hat, Tilda glanced at her reflection in the window and saw that her hair was two inches longer on one side than the other. She counted the stops: Moorgate, Barbican, Farringdon. Then the train spat her out onto the platform and she ran up the stairs.

Roland Potter's address was 15 Pargeter Street. Tilda asked directions of passers-by. The streets were a cacophony of screaming engines and imperious car horns and news-vendors shouting in an unrecognizable language. The smell of the city – a thick blend of diesel and smoke and rotting vegetation – was new and exciting.

People hurried importantly, their expressions serious and preoccupied.

15 Pargeter Street faced a square patched with sooty plane trees and gnarled hawthorns. Beside the front door were over half a dozen brass bells, with names scribbled on little cards beneath. Tilda found 'Potter', and pressed. There was a distant jangling, and, about five minutes later, footsteps on bare boards. The door opened.

Roland Potter was wearing a vest, trousers and braces. He looked as though he had just got out of bed. His eyelids struggled to prise themselves apart, and he said, gaping at her, '*Tilda.*'

'Roland?' Suddenly, she felt nervous. 'Emily gave me your address. I hope you don't mind.'

'Of course not. Come in. You must be frozen.' Tilda stepped inside, and Roland shut the door behind her. 'I apologize for the togs, but I've been covering the graveyard shift. Literally. Bodies in the mortuary . . . Follow me.' His short, toffee-coloured hair was uncombed and stood up in spikes all over his head.

The house was a warren of winding stairs and dark, narrow passageways studded with doors. Passing one of the doors, Roland yelled, 'A friend of mine, Anna!' and muttered to Tilda, 'Landlady. She likes to know what's going on. I say, give me your bag. There's miles of stairs.'

Roland's room was on the third floor. He pushed open the door. 'Sorry. Bit of a mess.' The floor was littered with discarded socks and shirts, and the table, washstand and fire-surround heaved with dirty dishes. Roland shrugged a jacket over his vest. 'Wasn't expecting company. So sorry—'

'Roland, *please*. It's me who should be apologizing. Turning up like this . . .'

'Oh no. I'm thrilled to see you. Really.' Roland flung open a window, replacing the frowsty air with a cold breeze. 'How's Em?'

'Emily is fine. Well – bored.'

'She'll grow out of it,' said Roland, with elder brotherly lack of interest. He dumped a pile of books and newspapers from a chair to the floor. 'Sit down, Tilda. Tea?'

Tilda nodded and looked out of the window. A milk cart, laden with empty bottles, clanked down the road, and children played tag in the square. She ran her fingers through her thick, bobbed hair, and knew that she had done something irretrievable, that she had changed her life, that she had started again. She had to swallow hard to suppress the sudden rush of grief and excitement.

Roland reappeared with the tea. 'Shopping trip?' he said tentatively, and Tilda shook her head.

'I've come to stay. I've left home,' she added, making it perfectly clear. 'Emily thought you might know where I could find a room.'

His eyes widened. 'I say . . . is it—' He broke off. 'Sorry. None of my business. Um.' He thought for a moment. 'There's a little room on the second floor – a boxroom, really, absolutely minute. Anna keeps her dresses in it. Tell you what – finish your tea and we'll go and see her.'

Tilda followed Roland back to the ground floor, where he tapped at a door. A voice invited them in. At first Tilda could not see anything. The curtains were drawn, and the room was illuminated only by the golden gleam of oil lamps. Then, as her eyes became accustomed to the lack of light, she saw the beaded curtains, the gilt portraits, the embroidered screens and brass candlesticks, and the green parrot in a cage suspended from the ceiling.

Anna was seated in a corner of the room, swathed in shawls and beads. Shadows emphasized the high planes of her cheekbones and her long, slanted black eyes. In the dim light, Tilda could not guess her age.

'Anna,' said Roland, 'let me introduce my friend, Miss Tilda Greenlees. Tilda, this is Anna. She has another name, but none of us can pronounce it. Anna – Tilda's come to live in London, but she has nowhere to stay. I wondered about the boxroom . . . a bit small, I know, but she hasn't a lot of luggage.'

'Come here, child.' Tilda stepped forward. Two thin, gloved palms were laid against her cheeks, tipping her face to the light. 'Let me look at you. Aah—' Anna's cry was echoed by the parrot. 'What have you done to your hair?'

Tilda took the scissors out of her pocket. 'I cut it on the train.'

Anna's tilted eyes narrowed. She looked up. 'Run away, Roland darling – we do not need you. Tilda and I shall talk.'

Roland left the room. Anna said, 'When I left Russia, I threw my rings onto the snow as I rode away. A diamond here, a sapphire there. I do believe in the romantic gesture.' She rolled the r of 'romantic', making it last for an age. 'Don't you?'

Tilda smiled. Anna said, 'Now, I shall tidy up your hair, and then we shall clear my dresses out of the boxroom. It is only a little room, but you are only a little girl. And then you shall tell me why you have run away from home. I suspect a man – a lover – no?'

*   *   *

Cooking supper that evening in the tiny shared kitchen, Roland told Tilda about the other tenants of 15 Pargeter Street.

'There's another Russian on the ground floor. Stefan something. Has a black beard, never says a word except to Anna. And a couple of ballet dancers – Maureen and June – on the first floor.'

A young man in a fraying jersey and corduroy trousers ambled into the kitchen.

'Tilda, this is Michael Harris. He's a chemistry student at Imperial College – makes foul stinks and tries to set the place on fire once in a while.'

'Vile slander,' said Michael amiably. He shook Tilda's hand. 'Are you planning to live in this hell-hole, Tilda, or are you very wisely just passing through?'

'Tilda's taken the boxroom on the second floor.'

'Good grief. Brave girl.'

Roland placed a pan of water on the gas ring. 'How many eggs, Tilda?'

'Two, please, Roland.'

'And there's Fergus—' Roland carefully lowered four eggs into the water. 'Scots. Huge.'

'Drinks a lot.'

'He's homesick, poor old Ferg.'

'And Giles Parker has the room opposite me. He's a poet, knows loads of frightfully famous people. And Celia. Michael is in love with her, aren't you, Michael?'

'Shut up, Roland.' Michael opened a tin of soup.

'Celia sleeps all day and works all night. She is terribly vague about what she does, but she is always stunningly glamorous.' Roland scraped the black bits off the toast, and daubed it with butter. 'That's the lot.'

'Max,' said Michael.

'Of course, Max. He has the attic. Max does some stuff for the paper. He's away at the moment.'

'Came back this morning,' said Michael.

'Oh. I might give him a shout. Then again . . .' Roland dumped boiled eggs and toast on the table. 'Tea's ready, Tilda. Terrific fellow, Max.'

'He's a sarcastic bastard,' said Michael, turning down the gas as his soup boiled over.

Half a dozen of June's friends came round that evening with bottles of beer and cider. As the sleet stuck to the window panes, sliding down in small crystalline trails, they spilled from the kitchen into Michael's room, sitting on stacks of books and papers. Roland brought down his gramophone, and Celia, wearing a chic little hat with a black velvet flower, called farewells as she left the house. The party sprawled through the rooms of the house, becoming noisier, happier, wilder.

Someone pushed a glass of cider into Tilda's hands and she drank it, perched on a window sill, watching one of the ballet dancers' friends mimic the prima ballerina: 'Thirty-two fouettés, darling – Lesley can hardly manage half a dozen.' The dancer was black-haired, dark-eyed, and wore a neat little knitted suit and smoked a cigarette in a holder.

'*So* unkind, Christine,' said June, stuffing her hands in her mouth to stop herself laughing.

The night became for Tilda a series of vignettes: herself and Roland foxtrotting along the corridor; Michael making cocoa in the kitchen with a flask and retort; Fergus, the Scotsman, singing while Stefan played 'Tiptoe Through the Tulips' on the balalaika. Tilda drank cider and smoked a cigarette. Michael wandered off to find her another drink. From the doorway, someone called out, 'Stop this bloody racket, can't you?' and there was a chorus of groans and whistles.

'Too boring, Max.'

'Have a drink, for heaven's sake.'

Max was in his mid to late twenties, Tilda guessed, and he had straight silky dark hair, a quarter-inch of stubble on his chin, and the red-eyed, pale-faced look of a man seriously overdrawn on sleep. He was wearing battered corduroy trousers and a white shirt, unbuttoned, and his chest and feet were bare.

'Max, *darling*,' said the black-haired dancer, pouting. 'You should have told me you were back. I've missed you, sweetie.' Christine ran her fingers through his hair, and planted a kiss on his cheek.

Fergus shouted, 'A drink for the man!' but Max shook his head.

'Michael is making cocoa,' said June, and Max, muttering, shuffled away.

Anna materialized out of the lower reaches of the house, swathed in sparkling shawls and iridescent beads, the parrot cage clasped in her arms. The speed and noise of the party ratcheted up a notch. The hands of the clock showed that it was half past one in the morning. Roland disappeared in search of more beer, leaving Tilda sandwiched between Fergus and one of the dancers. Fergus's hand gripped her waist too tightly, and when he leaned over and kissed her she began to feel suddenly rather sick. Sliding out of the circle, she left the room.

The corridor was dark and cool. Tilda's head spun. Two entwined black figures lounged against the banister, their voices piercing the darkness. She recognized Max and Christine. Christine's back was to her.

'Who's the baby?'

'One of Roland's.' Christine giggled.

Tilda stood, frozen in the passageway. Christine's voice floated back to her through the darkness.

'She looks like a gypsy, doesn't she, Max darling? She must have bought that dress at a Salvation Army jumble sale. And those boots!'

Tilda walked back down the corridor to the kitchen. It was empty now, littered with cocoa powder and milk bottles and fragments of biscuit. Standing at the sink, she watched the tears splash against the dirty cups and slide into the murky water.

A voice said, 'She's a bitch, you know. You shouldn't take any notice.'

She spun round. Max stood in the doorway.

Tilda said stiffly, 'I'm not crying. The cigarette smoke has made my eyes water.'

He was silent for a moment. Then he said, 'As you wish,' and left the kitchen.

He found Roland in Giles's room, playing poker. Bending over, Max whispered in Roland's ear, 'Your little friend's weeping into the kitchen sink,' and then, having done his duty, crawled up the attic stairs, kicked the door shut behind him, and sat on the edge of the bed, his head in his hands, savouring the comparative quiet.

Because he knew that he wouldn't sleep, and because images from the month he had just spent abroad flickered constantly in his head, Max lit himself a cigarette and went to the window. The sleet had chilled to snow, which dissolved as soon as it struck the pavement. The tops of the plane trees, level with his window, shivered in the wind. The attic rooms were always cold, but Max never noticed. They were his sanctuary. None of the parties which ran through the remainder of 15

Pargeter Street like a wildly infectious disease were ever allowed to spread to the attic. The two rooms were tidy, ordered, almost Spartan. Only Anna ever came up here, once every couple of months or so, to share a cup of lemon tea and reminisce about her past. None of the others – not Fergus, nor Michael, nor that idiot Roland Potter who'd let that poor kid get plastered tonight, were ever invited up to the attic. Nor Christine: when Max slept with Christine – something he did every now and then but always slightly regretted – he did so at her rooms in Fulham.

The weather did not look bad enough to prevent him going to Brighton the following day. He had missed Christmas: he felt a mixture of guilt and relief. Max glanced at his watch. It was two o'clock in the morning, and he knew that if he started work now he could finish the article, give it to Roland to hand in to the rag, and catch the seven thirty from Victoria. Then they'd be able to make a day of it.

Lighting himself a second cigarette from the butt of the first, Max sat down at the table and began to type.

The snow cleared overnight, and Brighton sparkled in the clear blue early morning light. Max pressed his finger on the doorbell, and from inside heard yapping.

The door opened. 'Max, darling!'

'Mother.' He hugged her; the dog scrabbled at his legs.

'Brutus,' said his mother feebly to the dog, a little, yelping white-furred creature. She stood back, and Max looked into the flat beyond.

Her eyes followed his gaze. She said quickly, 'I haven't been well, darling—'

'The maid?' he said. 'What about the maid I engaged?'

He walked into the living room, treading through heaps of cast-off clothes, trays of dirty crockery, and piles of cheap paperbacks and magazines.

'She left.'

He thought, looking round him, that he couldn't blame the girl. He began automatically to tidy up, to fling open windows to let out the stale air. His mother stood watching him, her arms clasped around herself, her silk kimono gaping to reveal a greyish nightgown beneath. She looked forlorn.

He went back to her and kissed her cheek. 'It doesn't matter,' he said kindly. 'Why don't you get ready, then I'll take you out for coffee.'

While she bathed, he tried to return some semblance of order to the flat. He found the bills stuffed in the flour jar (*Dear Mrs Franklin, I feel it necessary to inform you that your account is now in arrears to the sum of*), and the empty bottles in her old hiding place under the sink. He put the bills in his pocket to settle later, and stacked the bottles in a cardboard box. Sherry, this time, not gin. She must be more hard up than usual.

In an hour his mother reappeared, wearing a lilac silk costume and a black coat and a little hat at a rakish angle to the side of her head. She said brightly, 'Come on, Max darling, let's go out on the town,' and he took her arm and they left the flat. A sullen sea pounded the stony beach, and in the chill sunlight the fairy-tale roofs and minarets of the Pavilion glinted, a fairy-tale palace.

He took her to the Grand Hotel, her favourite. He ordered coffee, and she glanced at her watch and said, 'Max. Just one teensy sherry?' and squeezed his arm coaxingly. He asked about Christmas.

'Such fun,' she said. 'I gave a little party – just Doris and Heather and the people from next door. We had a lovely time. Doris brought her new lodger. A charming man. A gentleman.'

Max's heart sank.

'And you, darling?' she enquired.

'I was in Germany, as you know.'

'*Germany!*' she said, eyes wide.

'You remember, Mother – I sent you a postcard.'

'How *lovely!* Glühwein . . . and Wiener schnitzel . . . and . . .' Mrs Franklin faltered, her limited and inaccurate knowledge of the Continent letting her down.

'Yes. Well. Something like that.' A collection of different images flickered through Max's memory: Brownshirts interrupting a political meeting in Munich, boots kicking a man's head as he lay curled in the gutter.

'Have you seen your father, dear?' Mrs Franklin's voice was tentative.

'We had a drink together just before I went away.' Max met his father once every six months or so in the bar of the Savoy. They had two drinks and discussed cricket or rugby according to the season. Mr Franklin invariably offered money to Max to cover the most pressing of his ex-wife's bills, which Max equally invariably refused, and then they parted with a handshake.

'How was he?'

'Terrific,' said Max. He lit himself a cigarette. 'You said you hadn't been well, Mother. You look tired.'

'I'm fine, darling.' She patted his hand. 'You mustn't worry about me. But you are looking terribly thin, Max. I shall go to the shops this afternoon and buy steak and I shall cook it for you myself. Would you like that?' She beamed at him.

* * *

Tilda organized her room, arranging her books on the shelves, buying hooks to screw into the back of the door to hang up her dresses. There was a bed and a table and a washstand and a chair and a rug, approximately three foot by two, on the remaining area of floor. The room was tiny, and in the coldest weather ice flowered on the inside of the window panes, but Tilda loved it.

She altered her dresses to make them more like June's and Maureen's, shortening the hems, taking in the waists, replacing large, girlish pink buttons with little pearl ones cut from a cardigan bought in a charity shop. She sold her long plait of hair, and with the money bought herself a pair of silk stockings and a lipstick. She found a pair of second-hand heeled shoes to replace her awful clumpy country boots, and set about getting to know her neighbours. She cooked Michael Welsh rarebit, and spent an evening with Maureen and June, helping them to darn their tights, eating peppermint creams and listening to jazz records. She went to the cinema with Roland one night and Fergus the next, fending off the advances of each. She spent an extraordinary evening at a peculiar nightclub in Hammersmith, watching Giles Parker, dressed in a red velvet tuxedo, read his poems while a pale, etiolated lady mimed. Celia, sorting out her wardrobe, gave Tilda a short black jacket, a white silk blouse and a blue velvet beret so chic she fell in love with it and wore it every day.

After a fortnight, she found a job in an office. Her duties ranged from typing letters to fending off difficult telephone calls when her employer, Mr Palmer, was 'indisposed'. Mr Palmer's in-tray was full of unpaid invoices, and the bottom drawer of the filing cabinet full of empty whisky bottles. The work was dull and tiring, but distracted her, by day at least, from the discoveries that had prompted her escape to London. At night, though, she could not block out the memories. Daragh had married Joscelin de Paveley for her land and money. Daragh's betrayal had changed her, and that, Tilda thought, she resented most of all. She would never love another man as she had loved Daragh. She had given too much of herself to him: it was as though he had torn a layer of skin from her, leaving her raw and exposed.

Aunt Sarah's revelations, too, had scoured away at some essential part of her. Tilda had long ago guessed her birth to be illegitimate – the shame had been there in Sarah's reluctance to talk about her family or about the past, in the disjointed, unrooted life that they had led, and in Sarah's avoidance of all close involvement with other people. But the rape, and the imprisonment of her mother in the asylum – these were horrors that she could hardly bear to contemplate. At first, Tilda had wondered whether Sarah had told her the truth. She had lied, or she had been mad, as Daragh had said. Perhaps madness ran in the family. Yet she could not quite convince herself. If what Sarah had told her was true, then there was a peculiar rationality to what she had done. Sarah had never followed anyone's rules but her own; Sarah's idea of justice was primitive and vengeful. Once, when they had both helped with the harvest at a farm in Norfolk, and the farmer had insisted on serving one dish to his family and another, poorer meal to his labourers, Sarah had spat each day in the silver tureen reserved for the farmer and his wife. Tilda still remembered Sarah's face as she had lifted the silver lid: cold, proud, free of both furtiveness and guilt.

Michael leaned over the banister and yelled down as Tilda climbed the stairs after work one day.

'June has given us tickets for her preview – are you coming?'

Tilda ran to her room and changed her sweater and coat for the white silk blouse and black jacket that Celia had given her. At the theatre she watched with a sense of dazed wonder the silent figures moving on the stage. She was drawn into the tragedy, mesmerized by step and gesture. Afterwards, walking to a pub to wait for the dancers, Roland said, 'Bloody silly, ballet. Can't see the point of it.' Tilda hardly heard him.

Fergus bought drinks; Maureen and June and half a dozen others spilled from the theatre into the saloon bar.

'Awful – simply frightful—'

'Eric turned the wrong way. I had to yell at him. I'm sure that half the audience heard.'

Christine said, 'Where's Max? Is he late? I shall be furious if he's late.'

Tilda drank her cider and settled back in her seat, squashed between Michael and Roland. Roland described, at length, a problem with his motor car. On the opposite side of the table, Christine twitched angrily, glancing at the clock.

Michael told Tilda about his thesis. 'It's taken me two years longer than it was supposed to. My parents are threatening to cut off funds. I haven't enough cash left to pay for a typist.'

'If you can borrow a typewriter, I'll type it for you.'

'Would you really?' Michael beamed. 'That would be splendid. I say, there's Max ... Max!' he shouted. 'Over here!'

Max Franklin, the shoulders of his coat dark with rain, wormed through the crowds to their table.

'A quarter past ten.' Christine's dark eyes were angry. 'It's too bad of you, Max.'

'Sorry, sweetie.'

'I've been waiting for *hours*.'

Max looked tired. He took a couple of pound notes from his pocket. 'Drink, anyone?'

'I suppose you think you're so bloody indispensable – I suppose you assume that I'll just sit here for hours waiting for you—'

Max looked at Christine. Then he said, 'Well, no, actually. I hadn't thought about it, to tell the truth. And, really, I don't care one way or the other.'

Christine's face turned from pink to white. She moved to strike Max, but he caught her wrist, and said softly, '*No.*'

There was a short silence. Christine hissed, 'Bastard – you bastard,' and ran out of the pub. The slam of the door echoed across the bar.

'Drinks, anyone?' said Max again, calmly.

Michael stood up. 'I'll get them – my round.'

Everyone began to talk at once. Roland said, 'Busy, Max?'

'Just trying to finish my piece on the National Socialists' boycott of Jewish businesses.' Max lit himself a cigarette and chucked the packet to Roland.

Tilda leaned across the table. 'Who are the National Socialists?'

Max stared at her. Michael arrived with the drinks. Max said, 'Where are you *from*, Tilda?'

'East Anglia,' said Roland.

'Even East Anglia has newspapers – the wireless—'

'Tilda lived in the middle of nowhere, didn't you, Tilda?'

'You'd have to live on the bloody moon . . . You have heard of Hitler, haven't you?'

'Sort of . . .' She felt angry, suddenly. 'Instead of being so *clever*, Max, why don't you explain to me?'

For a moment, she thought she was going to be subjected to the withering sarcasm he had inflicted on Christine. But Max cradled his Scotch in his hands and explained about the Treaty of Versailles and reparations and the collapse of the American economy in '29, and its repercussions throughout the world, and Adolf Hitler's subsequent rise to power in Germany. Then he stubbed out his cigarette in the ashtray, and added, 'Today, there was a boycott of all Jewish businesses in Germany. In other words, if you patronized your usual butcher, baker or candlestick-maker, and he just happened to be a Jew, then your local policeman was liable to have a quiet word in your ear.'

The bell rang for closing time. Roland glanced at Max. 'Shall we go on to a nightclub?'

Max shook his head. 'I've work to do. I only came here to keep Christine happy.' He smiled. 'She didn't seem to appreciate my efforts, did she?' He picked up his hat and left the pub.

Arriving at work one morning in June, Tilda found a note pinned to the door. 'Mr Palmer ill – office closed.' The cleaner, shuffling downstairs, told Tilda the truth. The business had gone bankrupt, Mr Palmer had had one drink too many and had been knocked over by a black cab on his unsteady way home from the pub. Tilda looked for another job. She tried offices, restaurants and shops. Managers shook their heads at her, explaining that business was bad, or wrote her name and address on a list, promising to get in touch when a place fell vacant. No position ever did fall vacant, or they threw the scrap of paper away as soon as she left the shop. The poverty she saw, walking round London, shocked her. She had seen poverty before, but in the countryside it had seemed somehow less raw, less degrading. Men in cloth caps and elbowless jackets scuffed their heels at street corners. Once she saw a man walking the streets with a sign pinned to his coat: 'Unemployed plumber. Will do anything.' Going home in the evenings after a fruitless search for work, Tilda saw the queues outside hostels. Men – and women – in layers of threadbare, dirty clothes, their hair matted, their faces hollow and hopeless.

She had a couple of days' work delivering flyers to offices in the City, but the press that printed them went bankrupt and disappeared, leaving an empty office and bills – including Tilda's wages – unpaid. She skipped meals, pretending that she was eating in her room. When there was a party, she drank cider and accepted the cigarettes offered to her because they suppressed her appetite. Her inability to find work made her feel useless and unwanted.

One morning, she went up to the kitchen at ten o'clock to make tea. The room was empty except for Max, sitting on the window sill, reading the newspaper. Tilda filled the kettle, and lit the gas. Then she reached up for a cup, and the floor seemed to dissolve and her vision to darken from the circumference, until only a pinpoint of bright light remained in the centre.

When she came to, she was sitting in a chair, her head between her knees. Something heavy pressed on the back of her neck. Tilda wriggled, and a voice boomed, 'Sit still a moment, won't you?'

After a while her sight cleared and the roaring in her

ears went away. Max took his hand from the back of her neck. He said, 'Perhaps you've got flu,' and touched her forehead. 'Though you're not hot.'

Because she was still feeling dizzy, Tilda said feebly, 'I expect I'm just hungry.'

'Hungry?' Max scowled, and stared at her. 'Haven't you been eating?'

She shrugged, and wished he'd go away.

'Are you dieting?'

'Don't be ridiculous.'

He leaned against the wall, hands in pockets, watching her. 'Are you short of cash?'

'Of course not!' Tilda hunched her shoulders and looked away, but he persisted.

'You've work, haven't you?'

'I had a job, but it fell through. I haven't worked for three weeks. I thought I'd be able to find something else quickly, but . . .' Her voice trailed off.

'God. Such optimism. You did know, didn't you, about the other three million unemployed out there?'

She didn't answer. She hadn't known, not really. Things like that hadn't touched the constrained, isolated life that she and Sarah had lived.

Max said, 'Come on, I'll buy you breakfast.'

'There's really no need—'

'Come on,' he repeated impatiently, and she rose to her feet.

They went to a nearby café where Max ordered bacon and eggs and sausage and tomatoes for two. 'Toast or fried bread, sir?' asked the waitress, and Max, glancing at Tilda, answered, 'Both.'

He waited until she was wiping up her egg yolk with a piece of bread, and then he said, 'Where have you looked for work?'

'Oh – everywhere!'

'What can you do?'

'Shorthand and typing. And I can cook . . . and sew . . . and milk cows . . .'

Max's lips twitched as he stirred sugar in his tea. 'People come to London thinking the streets are paved with gold, but they're really just lined with a thousand other poor devils looking for work. You probably ought to go home – go back to wherever it is you came from. You've family there presumably.'

Tilda shook her head. 'I've no-one – no-one at all.'

She had an aunt who had betrayed her, and a half-sister she had never spoken to, who had married the only man she would ever love. Tilda rose and extended her hand.

'Thank you so much, Max, for buying me breakfast. I promise that I'll repay you as soon as possible.' She shook Max's hand, and left the restaurant.

That afternoon Anna visited Max in his attic. She brought with her the parrot, and chocolates wrapped in silver paper, and a box of little black cigars. Max and Anna smoked the cigars; the parrot ate the chocolates. Music issued from Max's wireless.

'Bach – always Bach,' said Anna, disgusted. 'A mathematician's music – there is no passion, Max!'

Max grinned, but said nothing. He was seated at the table, a piece of paper spouting from his typewriter.

'Have I interrupted you, darling?'

He shook his head. 'I've ground to a halt. I've written so much that I've forgotten how to spell.'

'Germany?' enquired Anna, glancing at the heap of typescript.

He nodded. 'Munich and Berlin.'

'Berlin! Berlin is wonderful – I was there in the early Twenties.'

'It's changed, I'm afraid, Anna. They've let loose the wolves.' Max ground his cigar out in a saucer.

'You should not take all the troubles of the world upon your shoulders, Max darling.'

'I don't. I take them in, chew them about, spit them out again. As you said, Anna – I have no passion.'

She smiled, and caressed the parrot's bent neck. Then she said curiously, 'What do you think of our little Tilda?'

He opened the window to let out the cigar smoke, and said, his back to Anna, 'Your little Tilda passed out in the kitchen this morning through hunger, the silly girl.'

'You should be kind to Tilda,' said Anna reprovingly. 'She has a broken heart.'

'Broken heart?' Max looked scathing. 'She doesn't look old enough to break anything more than her dolls. Anyway, she has no work and no money, and refuses to go home. Apparently she can type and do shorthand, and she seems quite – um – *organized*.' He had noticed months ago the transformation of the green dress that Christine had made fun of. 'Apparently,' added Max, 'she's hardly been to school.'

'I never went to school, Max. One didn't. I had a governess, a delightful Frenchwoman.'

Max grinned. 'I think Tilda's education was a little more down to earth. Roland tells me that she and her aunt used to do farm work. I assume the aunt's dead.'

Anna said, 'More tea, darling?' and poured hot water into a pot. 'Are you attracted to her, Max?'

He laughed. 'Of course not. But she's interesting. Rather an oddity.'

'And very pretty.'

'I suppose so. But very young, and unbelievably naive. You know that I prefer sophisticated women, Anna. That's why I adore you.'

She smiled, but did not respond. She said shrewdly, 'You court a certain type of woman, my dear Max, because you know that there is not the slightest danger that you will fall in love with them, or that they will fall in love with you. You know that you can keep them at arms' length – emotionally, if not physically.'

'Perhaps.' Max changed the subject. 'Anyway, I wondered if you could think of anything for Tilda.'

Anna tapped her teeth with a long, painted fingernail, and thought carefully.

Three days later, Tilda started to work for Professor Leonard Hastings. Anna had found her the job. 'Leo is my dear, dear friend, and he is terribly famous and terribly eminent and if I invite him to dine he arrives a week late, and if he did not have the most wonderful cook then he would die of hunger because he would forget to eat. When we last went to a concert, I telephoned him to remind him to catch the train, and at the concert hall, when he took off his coat, I saw that he was wearing his pyjama jacket under his evening dress. He needs a secretary, my dear – someone to tell him what to do, where to go.'

Tilda had each day to travel to Twickenham, where Professor Hastings lived. He was unmarried, his house a treasure cave of books and journals and collections of strange, beautiful things like fossils and volcanic rocks and meteorites. His subject was physics, about which Tilda knew nothing. She was beginning to realize that there were a lot of things she knew nothing about.

She typed Professor Hastings' letters, kept his diary, and persuaded him out of the house when it was time for his lectures and committees. She learned, in a muttered conversation with the cook-housekeeper, that she had had many predecessors, all of whom had given in their notice, or had been fired by the professor. She learned when to hold her tongue, and when discreetly to ignore the professor's less rational requests. She fathomed the system with which he catalogued his books: utterly arcane and hugely complicated, it had reduced several of her predecessors to tears. She touched the books reverently, enjoying the smell of their leather bindings, the look of the closely printed words.

She took the minutes at a meeting of a subcommittee of the Academic Assistance Council, chaired by Professor Hastings. The stories she heard – of penniless refugee students and teachers – horrified her. Their exile dwarfed hers. Some were very young, only sixteen or seventeen. In meetings, Professor Hastings was neither vague nor forgetful. His small, hooded eyes glittered as he issued concise instructions or devastating criticisms of inefficiency or procrastination. Occasionally hollow-eyed young men knocked at his door. Professor Hastings barked questions at them in German, the cook fed them, and Tilda telephoned family after family, looking for someone to take them in. One of the refugees – just a boy – wept tears of relief and loss into his stew and dumplings. Tilda put her arm round him and stroked his hair, and knew that he understood hardly a word that she murmured to him. On the train home that night, she too wept, though she was not sure why.

In September, Professor Hastings went away for three days to give a lecture in Edinburgh. Arriving at work on the second morning, Tilda was greeted by the cook.

'There's a young man and a girl in the parlour,' she hissed. 'Knocked on the door at six o'clock, got me out of my bed. They don't speak a word of English and the professor's not back till tomorrow. And the little girl's a bit odd.'

As soon as Tilda opened the parlour door, the young man rose to his feet and bowed. A child stood beside him, her head bent. The young man spoke, but Tilda understood nothing. Through gesture and writing she found out that the boy was called Gerd Toller, his sister, Liesl. Gerd was eighteen, Liesl only nine. Tilda found an atlas and Gerd indicated the German city from which they had travelled. A small series of scribbled cartoons told Tilda that the Tollers' mother was dead, their father in prison. In spite of her brother's protective arm around her shoulders, the little girl shivered constantly. 'Liesl ist—' said the boy, and tapped his forehead. The cook brought milk and sandwiches, but Liesl would not eat. Tilda coaxed her, tearing off tiny pieces of bread and offering them to her, but the child sat, shuddering, her eyes staring into some terrifying middle distance. When Tilda hugged her, Liesl flinched. Her brother, wolfing down food, launched into a long explanation. Tilda could have wept with fury and frustration at her inability to understand.

That evening, travelling home on the train, she made a decision. Back at 15 Pargeter Street, she dumped her jacket and hat in her room, and then climbed the three flights of stairs to Max's attic. When she knocked on the door, she heard his muttered, 'Come in.'

He was hunched over his typewriter. Without looking round, he growled, 'Just stick Boris in the corner, Anna—'

'It's me. Tilda.'

He swung round. 'God. I thought it was the bloody parrot.'

'I'm very sorry to disturb you, Max, but I wanted to ask you something. Shall I come back later?'

He stood up, stretching out his arms in a huge yawn, and shook his head. 'Uh-uh. Go ahead. Ask. Are you hungry again?'

She was about to be angry with him, when she realized that he was teasing her. She shook her head as he transferred a pile of newspapers from a chair to the floor.

'Sit down. Talk.'

She told him about Gerd and Liesl. When she had finished, he said, 'I'll have a word with the boy, if you want. My German's not so bad.'

'That's very kind of you, Max, but it's just that . . .' She flung out her hands in a gesture of despair. 'I felt so stupid. So useless!'

He said sensibly, 'You did what you could, Tilda.'

'I did nothing. I couldn't do anything, because I couldn't understand what Gerd was telling me. You were right, Max – I am ignorant.'

He said uncomfortably, 'Look – I had no business—' but she interrupted him.

'People think I'm sweet and naive and – oh, *original*.' Tilda's voice was scathing. 'I don't want to be like that. Being sweet and naive doesn't help me, and it doesn't help anyone else. So' – she took a deep breath – 'I'm here to ask you what I should do. Roland only seems to know about motor cars and things, and Michael just tells me about football and chemistry, and the girls talk about their clothes and their boyfriends and ballet. I went to the library, but there are so many books I don't know where to start. So I thought

I'd ask you how I should educate myself. Do you mind?'

He was silent, and she thought that he might refuse her. But then he said, 'No. I don't mind at all. You'll have to tell me what you do know about, and then we can fill in the gaps. Only – not here. I've been incarcerated in this hole for the last forty-eight hours. Let me shave and change and then we'll go for a walk.'

In the evening sunshine, even the dusty little square of planes and hawthorns seemed a small oasis, birdsong and strands of sunlight trapped within it. Max, after he had quizzed Tilda, said wonderingly, 'Good grief – your science is pre-Copernican. You should ask Leo Hastings to talk to you – you don't need to bother with relativity, just to know that the sun doesn't orbit the earth. I'll teach you German and take you to concerts. And I'll pass the newspaper on to you. And you must go to art galleries with Anna – she'd love your company, and she knows a lot about painting.'

The sky had begun to darken a little. They walked slowly back to the lodging house. Max said curiously, 'What happened to the refugees? Gerd and Liesl?'

Tilda sighed. 'I found a bed for the night for the boy, but no-one wanted poor Liesl. I tried everywhere, Max, but once they heard that she wasn't quite right in the head, no-one was interested. I couldn't separate them, so we've put them up in camp beds at the professor's house. I don't know what will become of them. It was awful, Max. There are some children that nobody wants.'

And I was one of them once, a long time ago, she thought, but did not say.

When her stomach upset did not get better of its own accord, Jossy went to see Dr Williams, and learned that she was pregnant. She had mixed feelings about the discovery. On the one hand, her pride that she was to bear Daragh's child was immense; on the other, she had never before felt so unwell. Dr Williams assured her that her morning sickness would pass by the end of the third month of pregnancy. The third month came and went and still Jossy was sick. Her hands and feet were fat and pink; by the sixth month she could no longer feed her sausage-fingers into her gloves. Dr Williams sent for a London specialist. The specialist sniffed and tutted and ordered Jossy to rest. She was supposed to spend the afternoons in bed, but she silently refused to. If she kept to her bedroom she missed Daragh. Instead, she heaved her cumbersome body from drawing room to terrace to garden. In the hottest part of summer she sat with her feet in the fishpond, to keep cool.

Even when the baby moved inside her, she felt none of the joy she was apparently supposed to feel. It was hard to feel joy about something that made her so ill. To Nana (now rather old and wobbly, but proud that her nursery was soon to have another resident), Jossy pretended to long to hold the baby in her arms. She imagined it like her biggest doll: blue-eyed, fair-haired, smiling. She supposed that it would be fun to dress and bathe it, and to take it out in the old perambulator. She imagined walking around the grounds of the Hall, Daragh at her side, the baby laughing.

It was Daragh who told her how the baby would come into the world. She had looked down at the huge globe of her belly one night and admitted complete ignorance. She imagined her stomach splitting open, the baby wriggling out, and everything somehow closing up. If anyone but Daragh had told her otherwise, she would not have believed them. 'Does it hurt?' she asked, appalled by his explanation, and he said, 'A bit, I think,' and patted the top of her head. She seized his hand and covered it in kisses. Because of the baby, they no longer shared a bed, no longer made love. She missed that dreadfully.

At the end of October Jossy fainted, and the specialist was called again. This time she was told to stay in bed until the baby was born. Black spots danced in front of her eyes, and her swollen hands were shiny and red. Daragh caught a cold, and Jossy tiptoed out of bed to make him honey and lemon. The following morning she was woken at five o'clock by an intermittent pain in her back. She lay still, watching the pink clouds slowly lighten the grey sky. The pain was tolerable at first, and then it was not. She knew that it could not be the baby because it was not supposed to be born for another three weeks. When she sat up in bed, something awful happened – a whoosh of liquid between her legs, and a shaming wet patch on the sheets. Weeping, Jossy shuffled out of the room and along the corridor to find Nana.

Marriage to Joscelin de Paveley was not quite what Daragh had expected. After their honeymoon, he had returned to the de Paveley house and estate believing himself to be possessed of unlimited wealth. He could have the motor cars and horses he wanted, the fine clothes, the holidays abroad. He walked around the Hall, glancing at paintings, touching furniture and glassware, knowing that the possession of all this made him worthy of respect. The ability to walk into any shop he chose and buy whatever he wanted distracted him from the memory of the scene with Sarah and Tilda Greenlees. Tilda's coldness, Sarah's laughter, and his own nauseated realization that he had been made a fool of, yet again, haunted him.

Jossy's lawyer, a dull fellow called Verney, called at the Hall to discuss death duties. It had not previously occurred to Daragh that, because of the recent death of Jossy's father, the estate must pay a large sum of money to the government. It seemed iniquitous, somehow. Mr Verney left Daragh with lists of property, rents and income, and a copy of the tax demand. Daragh spent a day and a night in the study with a bottle of Scotch, trying to make sense of it all. The affairs of the rich were unexpectedly complicated. Though the estate's income was large, most of its assets were tied up. Some tenancies were for the incumbent's lifetime, and Daragh, looking at rows of figures, was reminded of the declining profits of agriculture. The de Paveley estate was frozen, committed, bound up in trust funds and endowments.

Swallowing his pride, Daragh went to see Christopher de Paveley, who ran the farm. The steward's house was bleak and damp, the jagged cracks in the walls held together with iron bands, the interior a jumble of disparate pieces of furniture and cluttered bookshelves. Christopher de Paveley was unhelpful and unimaginative. It was obvious to Daragh that though he presumably carried out the day-to-day running of the farm with reasonable competence, Christopher de Paveley had no understanding of and no interest in the wider problems of the estate. The boy Kit skulked in a corner, bent over a book, not even acknowledging Daragh. Daragh gritted his teeth, sensing their resentment.

That night, he tried to discuss the estate with Jossy. She gaped at him adoringly, and offered no useful comments. Daragh was shocked that someone could have so much and just take it for granted. She knew neither what crops the Hall farm grew, nor the extent of their holdings. Jossy wasn't ashamed of her ignorance; she just assumed that he, Daragh, would deal with that side of things, as her father had done.

He could have asked advice of his neighbours, but he did not, because he knew how careful he must be not to betray his origins. He would rather have made wrong decisions than courted humiliation. He told Verney to sell the row of cottages in Southam and a couple of distant fields. There were some dull little paintings of horses in the study; he bundled them up and sent them to an auction house and received back a large sum of money. With the profits from the sales and a sizeable chunk from his bank balance, he was able to pay the death duties.

The baby was due towards the end of November. The specialist's bills were enormous; Daragh questioned them with Dr Williams from Ely. Daragh's mother had, after all, given birth to six children with the minimum of fuss and only a midwife in attendance. Dr Williams pointed out the dangers of Jossy's condition – a danger to both mother and child – and Daragh was obliged to write the cheque. That Jossy could not even manage to do competently the simple female task of having a baby galled him. Her adoration of him, which had in the early, unreal days of their marriage seemed reassuring and a balm to the torment that Sarah Greenlees had inflicted, increasingly confined him. He was used to independence, to freedom of movement. Jossy followed him about like a puppy dog, coming up behind him and nuzzling his neck when he was working in the study, trailing around the estate after him if he was five minutes late for tea. If he so much as looked at another woman she was at his side, all over him, advertising her ownership.

On the morning that they told him that the baby was

coming, Daragh drove to Ely and fetched Dr Williams, and then a peculiar hush descended on the Hall. At midday, Daragh took a horse out from the stables. His mother had had her babies within an hour or two; he could not understand why it was taking Jossy so long. When, after a long and vigorous ride, he returned to the house, he expected to be greeted with the news that he was now the father of a fine son, but instead Dr Williams was waiting for him, a serious expression on his face. Daragh's stomach jolted, and he thought for one terrible moment that the child was dead. Dr Williams explained that Mrs Canavan was still in labour and that Mr Browne, the specialist, was driving up from London to attend her. When Daragh pressed him, Dr Williams admitted that he was concerned for the safety of both mother and child. The doctor went back to Jossy, and Daragh sat down on a sofa, his clasped hands against his forehead, and prayed. He needed a son: he had not realized until this moment just how much he needed a son. A son would justify this marriage, would erase the memory of that madwoman laughing at him. *You have got what you deserve, Daragh Canavan*. The recollection still made him shiver.

The specialist arrived and disappeared upstairs. The housemaid served Daragh a dinner he could not eat. It was dark outside, and the wind battered dead leaves against the panes. Daragh longed to drink, but was seized by a superstitious fear that his self-indulgence would be espied by a critical God, and punished accordingly.

The baby was not born until ten o'clock the following morning. By that time Jossy had been more than twenty-four hours in labour, and Daragh had despaired. When the doctor came to him he knew that it was to tell him of the death of his wife and child. Dr Williams had to repeat twice his invitation that Daragh come to the nursery to see his daughter, before Daragh understood. He felt a stab of disappointment that he had not the son he had longed for, but he followed the doctor upstairs. When he looked into the crib, his disappointment vanished and never returned. His child was beautiful and perfect. She had Jossy's dark eyes, but they were framed by Daragh's own finely drawn face. Though the nanny tutted, he lifted his daughter in his arms and took her to the window. When he kissed her soft, pale brow, tears stung his eyes and he knew that his life had altered for ever. *Caitlin*, he whispered, and he watched her tiny fists open and close like sleepy starfish.

Then the doctor coughed and said, 'Mr Canavan. I must speak to you about your wife . . .' and he had to turn and give the baby back to the old woman, and follow Dr Williams into the privacy of the adjoining dressing room.

Dazed and exhausted, Daragh struggled to concentrate as the doctor told him that Jossy was very ill, that the difficult pregnancy and labour had almost killed her, that though there was now hope that she might recover, she must have no more children. 'You do understand, don't you, Mr Canavan,' said Dr Williams, 'that there must not be another child. You must make sure of that. It is your responsibility.'

CHAPTER FIVE

I could feel myself becoming reclusive, lost in the past, so I accepted an invitation to an old friend's birthday party. By the time I arrived, guests had spilled into every room in the house. My host shrieked at me, pressed a glass into my hand, and then disappeared to welcome more guests. I saw a couple I knew from university and pushed through the crush towards them. They'd just had their first child and the conversation revolved around disposable nappies and organic baby food. I retreated and curled up with a bottle of champagne on the window seat.

I drank, and became more sociable. I talked to a dancer who'd worked with my sister and then to a beautiful actress who knew Charles Lightman. I found myself chatted up by a man in a blue jersey who worked for the National Rivers Authority. With a couple of sticks of celery and a bowl of pistachio nuts, he demonstrated to me how a lock works. The pistachio nuts rolled onto the floor and we scrabbled about, picking them up, and he became quite pink and flirtatious. Then, as I stood up, a hand touched my shoulder and a familiar voice said, 'Rebecca?'

My knees wobbled. I looked round. Toby.

He wore a blue silk suit and his brown hair was cropped closer to his head than I remembered. 'You look well, Toby,' I said. 'Terribly . . . successful.'

During the months since we had parted, I had had time to work out that, to Toby, success is the most important thing. Money and power are part of it, of course, but recognition is paramount.

'You're looking good, Rebecca. I like the hair.'

'You used to prefer long hair.' My voice was sharp. 'You must have changed, Toby.'

He said, 'Perhaps I have,' and I wished I hadn't drunk so much. I wanted to be cool, detached, in control, but it's hard to manage that on half a bottle of Bolly.

He glanced round. 'Hell of a crush in here – shall we go somewhere quieter?'

I mumbled something about needing the loo, detached myself from him and ran upstairs. When I looked down over the banister, Toby was talking to the tall actress who knew Charles. I found my coat on a bed and escaped, ducking through the crowds in the kitchen, stumbling over the dustbins and empty wine bottles that cluttered the back yard. I blew the last notes in my purse on a taxi to take me home, falling drunkenly out of the cab just after one o'clock.

I didn't even attempt to go to sleep. Instead I heaved out a cardboard box that Tilda had given me the previous day and began to go through the contents. It was mostly press cuttings, in no particular order, the paper yellowed and torn at the edges. Recognition was obviously of little importance to Tilda. I wondered, as I flattened out strips of newsprint and stuck Scotch tape along the fragile folds of magazine pages, what it was that she most cared about. Family, perhaps. Words and phrases from the cuttings seized my attention. 'Dame Tilda Franklin attends the opening ceremony of a hostel for the young homeless in London . . .' 'A lifetime devoted to children . . .' 'You cannot learn before you have loved, and you cannot love until you know that you yourself are lovable . . .'

I felt safe again. The distant past was controllable and unthreatening. With the exaggerated care of the rather drunk, I sorted the cuttings and photographs, trying to establish a chronological order. By half past two I had reached the late Seventies, when Tilda had supposedly retired. I had the beginnings of a headache, but I felt rather pleased with myself.

I searched in the box again to check that I had not missed anything and discovered an envelope wedged between the overlapping slats of cardboard. I drew it out and glanced at the address. Daragh Canavan Esq., it said, in round, loopy handwriting. It was addressed to the Savoy Hotel. For the second time that night my heart began to beat very fast. There was that strangely exciting sense of the past – which in spite of everything always seems more closely allied to fiction than to reality – touching the present. The envelope was already slit open; I took out the single sheet of paper.

It was not from Tilda, but from Jossy. *My darling*, I read, *You have been away four days, and it seems like four years. I miss you so much – everything is dull and pointless when you are not here.* More in the same vein, and then, as if an afterthought, *Caitlin misses you too.*

There was no date on the letter. What a tiresome man you were, Daragh Cavanan, I thought. Beautiful, but tiresome. And what a slavish, degrading letter to write. Had Jossy realized by the time she had written that letter that Daragh did not love her, had never loved her? Did she believe that her devotion would ultimately secure his love when, of course, that sort of unreturned passion is more likely to repel? Did she write that last, desperate 'Caitlin misses you', guessing that it was the child who brought her errant husband home?

I shut the letter away in a drawer in my desk. When finally I slept that night, I dreamed of Toby, but he had Daragh Canavan's face.

I spent Sunday nursing my hangover, finishing organizing the cuttings and listing by date the achievements and incidents described in them. I was aware of the telephone lurking ominously in the corner of the room, but it did not ring. On Monday morning, I telephoned Oxfordshire to speak to Tilda about a gap of a few years I had discovered in the press cuttings. Was there another box, or had she disappeared from public life for a while?

A voice I did not recognize answered the telephone. 'Melissa Parker,' it said briskly. 'Can I help you?'

'I'd like to speak to Tilda Franklin,' I began. 'I've the wrong number, perhaps—'

'I'm afraid Tilda isn't well. She's in hospital, actually. I'm her daughter. Can I help you?'

The shameful thing was that my first emotion was one of disappointment and frustration. I'd wanted to find out what happened next. But almost immediately following came concern, and a measure of guilt.

I explained who I was, and Melissa Parker told me that Tilda had angina, but was not thought to be in any danger. She gave me the name of the hospital and the ward number, and when I put the phone down, I stood uncertainly, staring at the heaps of notes and files I had amassed over the weeks. Then I grabbed my jacket and my bag and left the house.

I bought narcissi, tulips and freesias from the florist

at the corner, and put the bouquet in the back of my car. The poor thing didn't want to start, which should have warned me. Although it was April, the temperature had plummeted, and the roads that were in shadow were still glazed with frost. I made it most of the way along the motorway before the Fiesta's engine began to stutter and cough. I cursed and begged, but it made no difference, and I just managed to swing onto the hard shoulder before it died completely. I'd given up my AA membership a few months ago, in a ruthless economy drive, and though I opened the bonnet and peered inside, the blackish mass of tubes and wires told me nothing. Trying not to think of maniacs attacking lone women drivers, I walked the quarter mile to the nearest telephone. Then I waited for what seemed like hours, becoming colder and colder, for the breakdown truck. Eventually it came, and the mechanic muttered about blocked fuel lines and towed me away. At the garage, peering in my purse, I discovered that I had two pounds and fourteen pence. The mechanic looked at the car and sucked his teeth and directed me to the bus stop. The bus lurched and rumbled along country lanes, so by the time I reached Oxford I felt sick as well as frozen. I found a cash machine and drew out some money, but I was so cold it was a struggle to punch in the buttons of my pin number. I stuffed the cash into my purse, and went to the tourist office to ask directions to the Radcliffe Infirmary. It was only then that I remembered I'd left Tilda's bouquet on the back seat of the Fiesta.

It was four o'clock when I reached the hospital. The place was huge and confusing, like all hospitals. My brain, still numbed by cold, lost me three times on the way to Tilda's ward. When I got out of the lift, carrying the rather pathetic bunch of daffodils I'd bought in the market in Oxford, I saw a middle-aged woman standing beside the drinks machine. Patrick Franklin stood beside her. I remembered sewing the prawns into the hem of Toby's coat, and my heart plummeted and I knew that my face was fiery red.

I wanted to go straight back into the lift, but it was too late, Patrick had already seen me. A small, mocking smile played around the corners of his mouth. I ignored him, and held out my hand to the middle-aged woman.

'Mrs Parker?'

Melissa Parker was in her late fifties, smartly dressed, her greying hair smoothly waved. 'Yes?'

'I'm Rebecca Bennett. We spoke on the phone this morning.'

'Miss Bennett! How good of you to come.' Melissa's voice was Home Counties, with none of Tilda's gentle East Anglian lilt. She shook my hand.

I took a deep breath. 'Patrick,' I said, and he nodded to me. I had been mistaken about the smile, I thought; he was glowering.

'How is Tilda?'

'A little better. My daughter's with her.' Melissa glanced at her watch. 'I must go – we really should try to contact Josh, though no doubt he will be maddeningly unavailable, as usual.' She looked flustered.

It clicked, then. Patrick's father – Tilda's son – was Josh Franklin, the travel writer. Every now and then one sees an article by him in a colour supplement, accompanied by a photograph in which he is pounding across salt flats or squatting in a tent, surrounded by nomads in exotic rags.

'Matty!' called Melissa suddenly. 'Matty! Over here!'

I looked around but could see only a couple of nurses, bustling purposefully down the corridor, and a girl in black leggings, black top, and DMs. She had a nose-ring and little purple plaits in her chestnut hair, and couldn't possibly be related to smart, conventional Melissa Parker. Yet she strode across the lino towards us.

'Grandma's asleep,' said the girl with the nose-ring. 'Can I have a Coke, Mum?'

Matty Parker looked about sixteen. She was several inches taller than her mother, and she had, beneath the thick kohl and mascara, clear grey pellucid eyes, just like Tilda's.

'We haven't time,' said Melissa. 'Your father will be home.'

'I'll drink it in the car. Go on, Mum.'

'Have you an address for Josh, Patrick?'

'There's a twenty pence in your coat pocket. Can I have that?'

'I'll phone Laura, in Delhi.'

'I only need another fifteen.'

'She should be able to get a message to him.'

'So thirsty—'

'Mother will not be sensible. She is eighty, Patrick. She really – oh, Matty, do be quiet! And why you had to wear that – that *thing* . . .!' Melissa's voice wobbled.

I said, 'Here you are,' and fished in my pocket and found some change. Melissa said tearfully, 'There's really no need,' and Patrick explained to me that he'd used up all his change in the car park. The coins clanked inside the drinks machine. Matty said, 'Mum doesn't like my nose-ring, Patrick. Or my tattoo. Have I showed you my tattoo?' She pulled aside several layers of black T-shirt to reveal a skinny arm ornamented from shoulder to elbow with a jade-green Celtic knot.

'Delightful,' said Patrick.

'I'm going to sue.' Melissa dragged Matty to the lift. 'She isn't eighteen. It's against the law, isn't it, Patrick?'

I heard Matty's, 'Grandma likes it,' and Melissa's final despairing, 'Just *too* bad—' as the doors closed, swallowing them. Then I was alone with Patrick.

I waved the daffodils at him and said quickly, 'I'll leave these with the nurse,' and headed up the corridor. Tilda was asleep behind green flowered curtains; I left her to what peace and privacy can be had in a hospital, and deposited the wilting flowers and a scribbled note with the sister. I'd hoped that Patrick would be gone by the time I came back, but he was standing opposite the lift, lolling against the window sill, hands in pockets.

He asked me whether I was driving home straight away, and I had to explain what had happened to my car. 'Pig of a day to break down,' he said. 'I'll give you a lift. I must go back to London tonight.'

I couldn't think of a polite way of refusing him. We left the hospital and walked to his car. I'd expected something macho in British Racing Green, but Patrick drove an oldish Renault. He drove fast and skilfully, though, and the silence was deafening. He still seemed cross and brooding, and dark shadows were smudged under his eyes. I was aware of his hands, resting lightly on the steering wheel, and the small golden hairs on the backs of his wrists. The silence was intolerable: I had to speak.

'About the prawns – you must think me mad—'

Again, that twist to the corners of his mouth. 'Not at all. It brightened a very dull evening.'

'I don't usually do things like that—'

'No?' He glanced sideways at me. 'How disappointing.'

I could think of nothing to say to that. I gave up attempting to explain, and voiced my other worry. 'I hope I didn't upset Tilda. I mean – I hope that it wasn't what we talked about that made her ill.'

Patrick changed down a gear to take a tight corner, and shook his head. 'It was to do with you, but only very indirectly. She was sorting out material to give you, and she came across some pictures – sketches, watercolours, that sort of thing. So she went into Oxford to buy frames – at least she didn't drive, thank God, she took the bus – and then she got out the stepladder and hung the pictures.' His voice was grimly amused. It was dark outside, and the treetops linked together overhead, their branches briefly golden as the headlamps lit them. 'She was taken ill overnight. Just wore herself out, the doctor thinks.'

Silence seized us again as he drove onto the motorway. I was exhausted; it had been a long, tiresome day, and I could have fallen asleep. He'd offered me a lift, though, and I felt that I should make an effort.

'I thought that Melissa's daughter was rather . . . surprising.'

Patrick gave a crack of laughter. 'Aunt Melissa had everything just right until Matty came along. Married the right husband, lived in the right house, had two daughters who were credits to her. Then – wham – Matty, the troublesome late baby. Tilda adores her, of course.'

Very late, I thought. Melissa must have been well into her forties when Matty was born.

I wanted to ask him about his father, the illustrious Josh Franklin, but the humour had gone from his eyes and his mouth had settled back into grim lines. I didn't even attempt conversation for the remainder of my journey. I let my eyes close, wishing I could sleep yet unable to relax because of his nearness. I wandered into that state between wakefulness and sleep, where the bleep of the indicator whenever Patrick changed lanes mingled with a patchwork of random and disjointed thoughts. When we reached my flat, I asked, certain that he would refuse, whether he would like coffee.

He glanced at his watch. 'Yes. Thank you.'

Hell, I thought, as I unlocked the door of the flat. I realized how hungry I was. I'd had a cup of tea at the garage and a Mars bar in Oxford, that was all. I peered in the fridge.

'Would you like an omelette?'

He blinked. 'I don't want to put you to any trouble—'

'It's no more trouble to make two than one. And I'm starving.'

I beat eggs in the kitchen while he prowled around my front room. The egg mixture bubbled pleasingly in the pan – one of my better efforts – and I took the plates and cutlery through.

'You don't mind eating here, do you? Only the kitchen's rather cold.' I put his plate on the arm of my one comfortable chair.

'I'd eat on the pavement if someone else cooked for me.'

I put on a CD, as a precaution against silences. I guessed that Patrick, like Max, would like Bach. He sat down at last, and seemed to relax a little.

'Tilda's illness must have been very worrying for you.'

He tore his chunk of bread in half. 'Aunt Melissa phoned in the middle of the night.'

'It's what might have happened,' I said.

'Quite. I was working late anyway, so I just drove

down to Oxford straight away.' He grinned, and the smile lightened his face, making him look more approachable. 'God – when I was twenty I used to be able to miss a night's sleep and hardly feel the worse for it. I must be getting old.' He finished his last piece of omelette and stood up. 'Thank you, Rebecca, that was just what I needed. I must go, I have to be in court tomorrow.'

After he had gone, I could not, to my surprise, settle to anything. I'd thought to have a hot bath and collapse quickly into bed, but though I soaked for half an hour in the Chanel bubble bath that Lucy Lightman had given me for Christmas, I no longer felt sleepy. So I cleaned the kitchen with untypical thoroughness, handwashed some clothes and flung them over the rack in the bath, and looked through bank statements and cheque stubs to make sure I had enough cash in my current account to pay for the repair to my car. And all the time I thought not of Toby, but of Patrick. I couldn't work out why I was thinking of Patrick – he was, after all, morose, unwelcoming, and sarcastic, and I still couldn't recall the episode with the prawns without doubling up with embarrassment. He was physically attractive, it was true, but though it was six months since Toby and I had split up, I did not yet feel ready for another relationship. I had no idea what Patrick thought of me, but I guessed that he had been reasonably pleasant tonight because of my professional relationship with Tilda. Yet whenever I closed my eyes I saw his face, and I struggled to find a comfortable position for my hot, aching limbs.

I fell asleep eventually in the early hours of the morning. I was woken by the sound of a footstep on the stairs. I opened my eyes. The room was a complete, velvety black. I wanted to reach out and light the candle on my chest of drawers, but I was unable to move. A creak as the door opened, and then a rustle of fabric told me that *he* was in the room. I wanted to scream, but could not. I lay very still, eyes shut, praying that if he believed me asleep he would go away.

I felt the bedclothes peeled off me, one by one. The coverlet, the scratchy blankets. Outside in the night, an owl hooted. I was shivering violently, and though I tried to whisper *No*, no sound came out. He lifted my nightgown, bared my body. Then he lay on me. His weight suffocated me; I tried to struggle, to scream, to push him away, but I was paralysed. He was forcing the breath from my lungs. I tried to move my head from side to side, to make even the small movement of opening my eyes, and as I found my lids and prised them apart, I felt tears slide from my face. My sobs repeated the rhythmic movement of his body. I gasped for breath.

When I awoke, he still lingered. There was still the weight of his body on mine, an incubus. I didn't know whether I had cried aloud, but I reached up my hand and touched the tears that beaded my lashes. It was only when I fumbled for and found the light switch, rather than a candle, that I convinced myself that it had only been a dream. Light flooded the room, extinguishing the ghost of Edward de Paveley, who belonged, after all, to another time. Yet the image of the servant's attic remained with me, and I focused on the television, the laptop, the CD player, as if to reassure myself that it really was 1995, and not 1913.

I went into the kitchen to make myself a cup of tea. My hand shook as I filled the kettle, and tea leaves scattered from the spoon to the work surface. But I took my mug and sat down at my desk, and switched on my laptop. I had left Tilda in the London of the early 1930s, trying to forget Daragh Canavan. Though

Tilda's ghosts might now haunt me, they compelled me too, drawing me into their story.

*

The train lurched into Liverpool Street Station. Out of the clouds of white steam a small figure appeared, screamed, dropped her suitcases and ran down the platform.

'Roland! Tilda!'

Tilda hugged Emily as Roland dashed up the platform to collect his sister's cases. 'Em, you look marvellous. It's been so *long*. I moved into the new room yesterday.'

Celia had married, and Emily's letter telling Tilda that Mrs Potter had at last agreed to let her work in London had arrived the day that Anna had offered Tilda Celia's old room. It was a large, spacious room, easily big enough for two, at the front of the house.

Roland hailed a taxi to take them back to Pargeter Street. After he had hauled his sister's suitcases upstairs, he glanced at his watch.

'I've to work this evening, I'm afraid, Em. The theatre critic has appendicitis.' He stooped and kissed Emily. 'Tilda has something organized, haven't you, Tilda?'

'Max is taking us to the theatre and to supper.'

'Terrific. I'll be off then.'

Tilda helped Emily unpack. 'I've simply masses to tell you,' said Emily, flinging stockings into a drawer. 'Oh heavens, what shall I wear tonight? You look so *chic*, Tilda. I've my old blue thing or my old red thing. I'm going to buy a black dress – Mummy won't let me buy black. And I'm going to sign up at a secretarial agency, and find a boyfriend. Who's Max, Tilda?'

'I wrote to you about Max.' Tilda arranged Emily's

dresses on hangers, suspended them from the picture rail, and considered them. 'The red, I think, Em. The navy blue is rather—'

'It makes me look like a parlourmaid,' said Emily glumly. 'A rather fat parlourmaid.'

There was a knock at the door. When Tilda opened it, Max, outside, tapped his watch.

'We ought to go.'

'Roland can't make it. He has to review a play.'

Max grinned. 'I know. A left-wing prose-poem in a church hall in Brompton, poor blighter.'

They went to a musical and then to supper afterwards. Emily howled through the play, Max slept. Since the previous September, Max and Tilda had been to a play or concert almost every week. Max chose the programmes: part of Tilda's education, he explained. He took her to Shakespeare and Shaw, Bach and Mozart. She discovered that the more you educated yourself, the more you realized you didn't know. Max made her book lists, which she ploughed through, abandoning the dullest with a howl of rage but entranced by the best, turning page after page, falling asleep over the book in the early hours of the morning. At first, Tilda's discussions with Max had sometimes degenerated into argument: Max exasperated by what he saw as her contrariness, Tilda provoked by his lack of patience. But almost imperceptibly their quarrels had lessened, animosity replaced by mutual respect, and then by friendship. Occasionally when the weather was fine they went for walks in the countryside, taking the train and hiking over field and coast. Max was good company and utterly unforthcoming, which suited Tilda. She did not enquire about his family because she did not want him to enquire about hers. There was a skin of pain and shame that she could not slough off.

After supper, Max escorted Tilda and Emily back to their room and disappeared up to his attic. Tilda made cocoa in the kitchen and she and Emily drank it in bed, huddled in sweaters and dressing gowns because it was January, and the room was cold.

Emily said, 'Are you in love with Max?'

Tilda laughed. 'Of course not.'

'I don't see why not. He's rather good-looking and frightfully intelligent.'

Tilda dipped a biscuit in her cocoa. 'Then you may fall in love with Max, Em.'

Emily shook her head. 'I don't think so. He's just the teeniest bit terrifying. And he thinks I'm trivial – no, Tilda, he does, I can tell. Some men do. I don't care, they're probably right. I'm looking for a man who'll worship me. Could you recommend anyone?'

'Well . . .' Tilda considered the other occupants of 15 Pargeter Street. 'There's Michael. He's great fun. And Fergus – sweet, but a bit – well, *passionate*.'

'Yum,' said Emily. 'I like Fergus already.'

'And Stefan, though he's rather odd. And Giles, but he prefers men. I think, to be realistic, Fergus and Michael are your best bet.'

'And you?' Emily clutched her hot-water bottle. 'How many lovers have you had, Tilda?'

Tilda shrugged. 'None.' She wrapped her eiderdown around herself. The window panes were opaque with frost, though it was not yet midnight.

'Because of Daragh?'

Tilda did not reply. She was friendly with all the male residents of 15 Pargeter Street, but she wasn't in love with any of them. She would never again experience the same exhilarating delight that she had known with Daragh. She simply wasn't capable of it. If she married, then she must settle for less.

'I saw him,' said Emily, 'in Ely. I was walking home from my awful job. Daragh was coming out of the draper's.'

'Did you speak to him?' Tilda's voice was a whisper.

Emily nodded. 'I was going to tear him off a strip, tell him how awful he'd made you feel, but somehow . . .' She shrugged. 'You know what Daragh's like, Tilda. You just look at him and you *melt*, somehow. All your good intentions go. I told him that you were in London staying near my brother, and having a terrific time. I didn't want him to think you were pining for him.'

'I'm not,' said Tilda sharply.

'Of course not. Anyway, he told me that he has a baby daughter – Kathleen or something – so I suppose he's a respectable family man now.' She frowned. 'He seemed different. I can't quite . . . Smarter, of course . . . and more sure of himself. But – well, *colder*, and rather . . .'

'What?'

'Rather unhappy,' said Emily.

Tilda had not only worked longer for Professor Hastings than any of her predecessors had, she had also taken on new responsibilities. As Professor Hastings' work with the Academic Assistance Council had increased, so had Tilda's. She spent much of her time on the telephone or writing letters, finding homes and funding for exiled students. She had one day charmed a crabby acquaintance of Professor Hastings' into providing books and stationery for one of the refugees. The professor, impressed, had called her into his study the following day, given her a battered address book and a box of scribbled notes, and told her that she would now be responsible for fund-raising. The job involved everything from organizing jumble sales to accompanying Professor Hastings to the occasional college dinner – all to further the cause of academic refugees in Britain.

Tilda discovered that she was good at persuading people to donate money, time or help. To the maternal she described the loneliness of the young people who arrived penniless in Britain; to the practical she emphasized the skills and talents that the refugees could offer to their adoptive country. In February, she visited Liesl Toller in the children's home in Oxford in which she was living. The institution had agreed to take Liesl if funds were provided. There had been no other solution. Tilda herself raised the money by a combination of coaxing and nagging. The institution, which housed over a hundred physically and mentally handicapped children, appalled Tilda. None of the children were addressed by the staff by name, only by the number assigned to them. Though they were fed and bathed and kept reasonably warm, they were given no affection and were allowed no toys. Tilda brought with her a teddy bear for Liesl, but it was confiscated by the matron. Friends and relatives were allowed to visit only twice a year, so although Gerd Toller lived in a college only a few miles away, his sister rarely saw him. On the journey back to London, Tilda stared out of the carriage window, seized by a mixture of anger and grief. *There are some children that nobody wants.*

And for the first time in a year she found herself thinking of Aunt Sarah without anger and bitterness. Aunt Sarah had taken her from the orphanage when no-one else had claimed her. Without Sarah Greenlees,

Tilda knew that she too might have become one of those silent creatures she had seen in the institution, rocking herself back and forth, banging her head rhythmically against the wall, twisting her hair into mad spirals.

Max was cooking eggs and bacon when Emily Potter came into the kitchen. Emily was small and noisy and inquisitive, and made Max think of a mosquito. He nodded to her, and continued to read his newspaper while cooking.

Emily peered into the frying pan. 'Bacon – yum,' she said. 'Is there any going spare?'

'No,' said Max repressively. There were only three rashers, and he had thrown up his lunch somewhere in the middle of the afternoon, on a choppy Channel crossing.

'We've been shopping.' Emily wore a low-cut, close-fitting black dress that emphasized her magnificent bosom. 'Tilda and I haven't eaten *all day*.'

Max remembered picking Tilda up from the kitchen floor, when she had fainted. She had been impossibly light, her bones delicate, like a bird's. He said, suddenly worried, 'Tell Tilda she can share this, then.'

Emily leaned against the table, her bosom displayed to its best advantage, looking at him, her dark little eyes bright with her discovery.

'Oh, *Max*. Don't worry, I won't tell.' She tore off a crust of bread, and dipped it in his egg yolk. 'And I'm not heartbroken, either. You and I would never do. I've learned to leave the dark, sultry men to Tilda.'

She swayed seductively out of the kitchen, and Max cursed her under his breath. He had acknowledged several months ago that he had fallen in love with Tilda Greenlees. The realization both irritated and amused him. It had changed nothing, though, and never would. He was old enough and experienced enough to avoid the more risible symptoms of lovesickness, and responsible enough to take the relationship no further than friendship. He would not make love to Tilda, even if she wanted him to. He liked her too much. Anna's summation of the way he separated his emotional and physical needs rang horribly true.

He had just returned from Germany again, having stayed a month with his friends the Hansens. He had realized, whilst witnessing the changes in both Munich and Berlin, that he missed Tilda. He refused to allow himself the pleasure of imagining taking Tilda to a foreign city, though, and made himself concentrate on his work. He had been commissioned to write a series of articles for the *Manchester Guardian*, one of the few daily papers to come anywhere near to understanding the implications of Hitler's rise to power. In Berlin, a fight had broken out in a nightclub. His overriding memory of the evening was of garishly made-up men in evening dresses and cocktail gowns exchanging blows with brown-uniformed *Sturmabteilung*. Breaking his own rules, Max too had joined in, and had been hit over the head with a chair for his trouble. At night, unable to sleep, he had prowled round Gussy Hansen's kitchen, a tea towel filled with ice cubes clutched against his head, thinking of Tilda. He thought of it as an illness that must eventually pass.

Provoked, perhaps, by her difficult birth, Caitlin Canavan continued to disrupt the Hall. At three months old, she was still unable to tell the difference between night and day, and never slept more than a few hours at a time. Jossy had been too ill to breastfeed her, and Nana was too old to cope with endless night feeds, but Daragh insisted on taking over, sleeping in the night nursery on a little put-down bed, warming Caitlin's bottles and spending hours gently coaxing the baby to take an extra half-ounce. Looking out of the window to the grey, frosty lawn, his daughter sleeping against his shoulder, Daragh was happy. He had found love again. He was a passionate man, and he needed love. Though this was a different sort of love from that which he had felt for Tilda, it recalled to him the depth of feeling that they had shared.

Around her fourth month the miracle happened, and Caitlin changed from a little, red-faced, screaming changeling to a bonny, well-grown baby, sometimes capable of contentment. When Daragh put her to bed, she slept through the night. When Jossy or Nana tucked her up in her cot, she'd refuse to settle, or would wake a few hours later, howling. Daragh comforted Caitlin when her first tooth came through; Daragh showed her off to admiring visitors. When the weather grew milder he wheeled Caitlin around the garden in her pram, watching her laugh at the pattern of the windswept leaves, or reach out her tiny hand towards the sun.

Daragh's love for his daughter initially distracted him from a problem that grew more troublesome as the months went on. He and his wife no longer made love: Dr Williams' prohibition had been confirmed by the expensive Mr Browne. At first, when Jossy had been ill and Daragh himself had been tired by the demands of the child, it had not distressed him. But as his natural urges had returned and as Jossy had recovered and begun to shuffle clumsily round the house, Daragh had realized the implications of the situation. Jossy herself asked him back to her bed. He agreed, for a night or two, but found t a torment. She insisted on cuddling and caressing him, yet he was denied the relief of finishing off what she had begun. He was not a eunuch or a priest. It was not that he found Jossy particularly attractive – since Caitlin's birth she had not regained her figure – but he needed a woman, any woman. He even found himself looking at the dimwitted nursery-maid with desire, or wondering whether any of Jossy's horse-faced schoolfriends had grown bored with their husbands. Daragh removed himself to another bedroom. Jossy wept great, globby tears that patched her pale face with scarlet. Daragh, in desperation, went to see the priest.

The priest was sympathetic, but to Daragh's tentative and guilty suggestion that they employ mechanical means of avoiding another child, was adamant. God would give him strength, said the priest, and Daragh walked gloomily out into the early spring sunshine, a lifetime of celibacy stretching greyly in front of him. Choices bleakly offered themselves to him. He could go against the teachings of the Church and use a French letter, and burn in hell. He could take his wife, regardless of the frailty of her body, knowing that to make love to her could kill her. He could continue, guiltily and furtively, to give relief to himself. Or he could take a mistress.

Daragh buried his face in his hands. The conviction, born on his wedding night, that he had, because of Sarah Greenlees' interference and Jossy's infatuation, stepped on the wrong road, grew stronger. He had imagined a lifetime with Tilda. The physical and emotional longing he had felt for her was still vivid and painful. He knew that Tilda was living in London, in a room in the same house as Emily Potter's brother. Daragh clenched his hands and rested his chin on his fists, thinking. Emily's brother had been called – God,

he could almost remember it – Ronald. No. Robert?
Richard?

Roland. Daragh smiled.

Anna dropped the letters into Max's attic before she went
to lunch. 'Bills, darling, always bills.' Max inspected his
post. Three bills and a letter. The letter had a Brighton
postmark.

The single sheet of paper told him that his mother was
engaged to be married to a man called Leslie Bates. *He
is a retired businessman, and was once a captain in the
Guards*, wrote Clara Franklin proudly. Max grabbed his
coat and hat and dashed to Victoria Station to catch the
Brighton train.

He reached his mother's flat by three o'clock. She
was dressed in a new outfit, and the glossy dress
boxes scattered around the apartment told him that
her spending spree had been thorough. He made tea
and tried to coax Leslie Bates's address out of her.
'You're not going to be horrid to him, are you, Max?'
said Mrs Franklin, cautiously. He tried to reassure her,
but was unconvincing and succeeded in reducing her to
tears. He had the address, though.

Leslie Bates wore a houndstooth suit and an Old
Harrovian tie, and lived in a depressing room in a
back-street hotel. He had false teeth and thinning
hair, but maintained the upright stance that Clara
Franklin was so often attracted to, and which was,
presumably, evinced to support the Harrow and Guards
fiction. He offered Max a Scotch and a seat in a
greasy armchair, both of which Max refused. Max
knew that Leslie Bates understood perfectly why he
was there.

Max made clear the reality of his mother's financial

situation, but Mr Bates did not, like some of his predecessors, immediately and embarrassedly withdraw from the engagement. Instead, eyeing Max's old but good shoes and shabby Burberry, he said, 'But there is money in the family, I assume?'

Max groaned inwardly. 'My father's investments lost most of their value in '29. And you must take my word, Mr Bates, that I have no private income. If you marry my mother, then you must expect to be responsible for some fairly substantial bills.'

Bates twiddled his moustache. 'Clara is very attached to me. To break off the engagement would distress her. But an unhappy marriage might, don't you think, cause her greater pain in the end.'

Max wanted to seize the fellow by his horrible dog-tooth lapels and shove him through the window to the pavement below. Instead, he took out his cheque book and said, 'How much, Mr Bates?'

He paid one hundred and fifty pounds so that his mother might continue to live as a single woman and Leslie Bates might leave Brighton. When, an hour later, he explained to Clara Franklin that the wedding was not to take place, she wept and would not be consoled. During the night, Max's fitful sleep on the sofa was interrupted by his mother's prowling footsteps, and the sound of bottles clinking in the kitchen. She took the glass and the gin bottle into her bedroom, where she wept again.

In the morning, when his mother rose at eleven, Max made her tea and gave her aspirins. She looked old and fragile, her dark, lovely eyes swollen by tears. She drank her tea and said shakily, 'I've been very silly, Max. I am so sorry.' He took her hand, and then she dressed and they took the dog for a walk.

He caught the late afternoon train back to London. The compartments were full, so he stood in the corridor, looking out of the window, smoking. He was very short of cash – the cheque to Leslie Bates had cleaned out his savings account – and he was aware of a weight of depression that he did not seem able to shift. He knew that his mother was just looking for love. What love his father had been able to give her she had long ago destroyed. She wanted too much, and was constantly disappointed.

Back at 15 Pargeter Street, he was unpacking his overnight bag when there was a knock at the door. He had forgotten that it was Wednesday, and thus Tilda's German lesson. The sight of her made more raw the pain that he felt. He glanced at the exercise she had prepared, stabbed several red lines through it, and said shortly, 'If you can't cope with the past tense of "to be", then you're going to find German conversation rather limited.' He saw her flush.

They were reading *Emil and the Detectives*, chapter by chapter. Tilda read, Max corrected her pronunciation and helped her translate. As she turned the pages, he prowled restlessly around the room, straightening ashtrays, replacing books on the shelf. Her mispronunciations jarred him, and after he rectified them she immediately made the same mistakes again. He said impatiently, 'For heaven's sake, Tilda – did you leave your brain at Leo Hastings' house?' and he saw her rise from her seat, and begin to pick up her books and pens.

'Where are you going?'

'Back to my room.' She glanced at him. 'You're obviously not in the mood, Max.'

He almost let her go, but realized just in time that if

he did he would hate himself. He stopped her before she reached the door. 'Tilda – please.'

She paused, indecision on her face. 'You're right, Max – I can't concentrate. Let's forget it.'

He had the suspicion that if he let her walk down those stairs, she would not come back. He saw suddenly how empty his life would become. He ran his hands through his hair, and said, 'I'm sorry, Tilda – I've had a bad day. I shouldn't have taken it out on you, though.'

She hugged her books to her chest. Her grey eyes studied him, waiting for an explanation.

'I've been in Brighton, paying a very large sum of money so that some cad would not marry my mother.'

'Oh, Max.' Tilda's expression altered.

'I'll think I'll just shoot the next one,' he said, trying to make a joke of it. 'Borrow a rifle, and shoot the blighter. I'd hang for it, but it would be cheaper.'

She didn't laugh, but dumped the books on an armchair, and put her arms round him. 'Poor Max.' Because he couldn't have borne just to stand there like a dummy, he hugged her back and stroked her hair. In that moment of contact he made the discovery that the touch of someone you love is in itself a comfort. Her touch healed him, it was as simple and as miraculous as that. It was not something he had known before, and because the realization unnerved him, he pulled away from her.

The attic – the bed visible through the adjoining door – seemed just then too small, too full of risk. He said, 'Shall we give up on the German and go out for a drink?' and was relieved when she agreed. They went to a pub at the end of the road, with little patched velvet-covered seats in the saloon bar, and a barrage of noise from the adjoining public room.

He told her about his family. It was as though a gate had opened and all his customary reticence had been drowned by a stronger emotion. 'I was at school when my parents were divorced. It was a very stuffy school – my father was quite well off at that time. The divorce was in some of the papers. Some of the other boys read about it, and they . . . well, you can imagine. I thought of running away, but I knew that they'd just haul me back. I learned to pretend that it didn't matter. I got quite good at that, and after a while, of course, they stopped ragging me. The funny thing is . . .' Max stubbed his cigarette out in the ashtray '. . . the funny thing is that was when I started thinking about journalism as a career. I saw the power of the press, I suppose. Before the newspaper articles, I'd just been boring Max Franklin, who played a reasonable game of cricket for the House and won the odd prize on Founders' Day. Afterwards, I was the Max Franklin whose mother was a drunk and a tart. Much more interesting.'

She put her hand on his. 'Max.'

He smiled. 'Another drink?' He rose, and went to the bar. He thought, savagely, waiting in the crush, how dull, to talk so endlessly about yourself. He pushed forward and ordered two more halves. Back at the table, he gave Tilda her glass of cider.

'Roland told me that your parents are dead, Tilda.'

She nodded. 'I was brought up by my aunt.'

'And she died . . .?'

She shook her head. 'Aunt Sarah's still alive, as far as I know.'

He frowned. 'You don't write home?'

Her eyes were wide and dark. 'We haven't spoken

for a year and a half. I had a letter from home this morning. Not from Aunt Sarah, though. She doesn't know my address.'

He said nothing, just looked at her. After a few moments, she fumbled in her pocket and drew out a folded piece of notepaper. Though he could not read it, Max glimpsed the writing: strong and black and undisciplined.

'It's from Daragh Canavan. I never thought I'd hear from him again.'

The naked pain in her voice seared him. He remembered, a long time ago, Anna saying, *She has a broken heart.*

'You are in love with him.'

She looked up, and shook her head again. 'I *was* in love with Daragh. Not any more. He married someone else. My aunt helped to arrange the marriage.'

The journalist in him was curious to ask more, but he sensed how much pain the subject caused her. 'I suppose the fear that lingers,' he said tentatively, 'is that you'll make just as much of a mess of things as your parents did. Marriage, I mean. Family life . . . all that.'

'I sometimes imagine having a family,' said Tilda. She smiled. 'A real family. Lots and lots of children and a big, rambling house . . . and a garden with little paths and ponds with tadpoles.'

'And bonfires in the autumn. Roasting chestnuts in a log fire.'

She laughed. 'Max. You old romantic. I'd never have guessed.'

He said, 'Perhaps if you know what not to do, then you can make a better job of it.' Another great leap of understanding, he realized. The second in one evening. Max, you old sod, he thought, maybe you're learning at last.

The light that filtered through the frosted window glass gleamed gold on Tilda's shoulder-length hair. Her lids were lowered over her calm grey eyes. He would have liked to be an artist, to draw her. He would have liked to caress with his hands, his mouth, his tongue her translucent skin, dusted with tiny golden freckles.

Yet there was the letter, bunched in her hand. 'What did he want?'

'Oh.' She glanced down. 'To see me. I won't, of course. I won't reply.'

Max was aware of a deep and drowning relief.

Jossy liked to watch Caitlin as she slept in her cot, but her daughter's furious bouts of crying produced in her feelings of panic and inadequacy. She was never sure that she was holding Caitlin the right way, or feeding her the right way, or even talking to her the right way. Caitlin herself reinforced all Jossy's doubts. In the baby's rare moments of contentment, Jossy was aware of a pleasure in her company; too often, though, Jossy found herself howling with her daughter, or simply handing over the red-faced, furious thing to Nana or the nursemaid or Daragh. They all seemed so much better at it. She knew that she was failing again, failing in something a woman was supposed to find easy and natural.

She did not at first mind that she and Daragh could not make love. The process of childbirth had been so much worse than her most nightmarish imaginings that, when she had eventually been capable of coherent thought, she had known that she could not bear to go through it again. The brief conversation she had with Dr Williams produced a mixture of embarrassment and relief. But as she recovered, she began to remember, and to miss, what she and Daragh had shared. Before her marriage, she had regarded her body and its mysterious female workings with shame and distaste. Daragh had changed that: he had coaxed such joy from her.

When she was able to squeeze herself back into her evening dresses, Jossy accepted a few invitations out. She and Daragh went to a theatre in London and a restaurant in Cambridge, and then to a cocktail party hosted by an old schoolfriend of Jossy's. Elsa Gordon was tall and slim and blonde and, although she had two children, her stomach was as flat as a board. Jossy introduced Daragh to Elsa. Elsa, shaking hands with Daragh, registered admiration. Then she turned to look at Jossy, her pale blue eyes inspecting her from top to toe, and she drawled, 'My, what a frock, Joscelin. So original.' Jossy, hooking her arm through Daragh's, felt proud.

Somehow, though, in the course of the evening, her pleasure dissolved. She kept finding Daragh and then losing him. She'd turn aside to accept a cocktail or receive introductions, and when she looked back he'd have gone. Without Daragh at her side, she felt lost, gawky, uninteresting. She saw that Daragh, unlike her, revelled in these occasions. He moved from group to group, always welcomed, never at a loss for words. He never seemed to scrabble around for a topic of conversation as Jossy did; never seemed to find himself, like Jossy, pinned to the wall by a red-faced colonel, and forced to endure a long monologue about hunting.

Eventually, glancing out of the window, she saw a flicker of movement. Daragh and Elsa Gordon were walking through the moonlit garden. Anger gave her strength, and Jossy said a loud 'Excuse me' to the colonel and pushed past him, heading through the crowds to the French doors.

They were standing beside the rose bed. She thought that Elsa's hand was resting on Daragh's arm, but in the poor light she could not be sure.

'I'm tired, Daragh,' said Jossy.

He looked round. 'It's only' – he glanced at his watch – 'half past nine.'

'I want to go home.'

Daragh frowned. Jossy began to march back to the house. When he drew level with her, he hissed in her ear, 'You're making me look a fool!' but she kept on walking.

In the hall, waiting for their coats, she caught sight of their reflections in the looking-glass. Daragh's good looks were only heightened by anger, but she—

She wore a black lace dress that had been part of her trousseau. Yet she seemed to have changed shape since she had bought it: her bust had flattened and her stomach protruded in spite of her corset, so that her figure was pear-shaped. And she must have caught a heel in the hem, because a length of lace trailed, fraying, at the back of the dress. Her hair had frizzed in the heat of the room. *How original*, Elsa had said, and smiled.

Driving home, leaving the town for the flat, raised roads of the Fens, Jossy said, 'You were with that woman for hours.'

'We were talking about the children, that's all. Elsa has a little girl the same age as Caitlin.'

'*Elsa!*' she shrieked. 'You're on first name terms, are you, Daragh?' The car swerved.

He yanked the steering wheel, straightening the car. 'God, you'll have us both killed.'

'She was laughing at me, Daragh. Did you realize that?'

'Then you shouldn't have given her cause to laugh.

Running around after me as though I was a puppy-dog and you were tugging the lead.'

Jossy accelerated down the long straight road that led to Southam. 'I have a right to your company. Elsa Gordon doesn't. I'm your wife!'

'I suppose so,' he muttered. 'Of sorts.'

She gasped. The lights of the Hall grew out of the darkness. Daragh's handsome profile was outlined by moonlight. Jossy swung the car up the drive, and parked in front of the house. Her anger dissolved, and tears stung her eyes. She whispered, 'I know we can't do *that* any more, but we can still kiss and cuddle—'

'Mary mother of God. I grew out of that at sixteen.'

She stared at him. He climbed out of the car and slammed the door. Then he looked back at her. 'Jesus – you didn't think that you were the first, did you?'

Her silence answered him. He laughed as he strode towards the front door. 'I'm twenty-six, Jossy. Did you think that I was saving it for marriage?'

'*I* did.'

'It's different for a woman.' He unlocked the front door and started up the stairs.

She wanted to say, How many? Who? but he had gone ahead of her. She ran to catch up with him, and at the top of the stairs she put her arms around him, and pressed her body against his. 'I love you, Daragh,' she murmured. 'All I want is to be with you.' The warmth of him, the scent of him – a mingling of the slight salty smell of sweat and the cologne that he wore – made her drunk with delight and despair. Sometimes, when he was away, she went to his room and opened his wardrobe, and clutched the lapel of an overcoat, or the sleeve of a cashmere sweater, breathing in his familiar perfume.

When he pulled away, she followed after him, her

high heels clacking on the floorboards, the fallen hem of her dress picking up dust. At the nursery door he turned back to her. 'I'm going to London for a few days.'

'I'll pack some things.'

'No, I'm going on my own, Jossy. Business. It'll only take a day or two. One of us needs to be here for Caitlin.'

In the nursery, she saw the expression on Daragh's face when he looked down at the sleeping child in the cradle. She realized with a sudden stab of pain that he had never looked at her like that. Never.

He came to her, as she had known he would. When she arrived home one day after work, Emily intercepted her and hissed in her ear, '*Daragh*'s in our room! I gave him a cup of tea. I couldn't think what else to do.'

Daragh was now a married man. They would be friends. Tilda pushed open the bedroom door. He was standing at the window. When he turned to her she knew, in one small, crushing moment, that they could never be friends. That his presence allowed her at the most only the pretence of composure.

Yet she went to him, smiling, and kissed his cheek. 'Daragh. How lovely to see you. Are you well?'

'I'm fine. And you look marvellous, Tilda.'

She wondered whether he, too, pretended. Or whether the acquisition of Southam Hall had deadened his capacity for passion. She said smoothly, 'And Jossy and Caitlin? Are they well?'

'They're both grand. Tilda, I'm in London for a while. I thought I'd look up some old friends. Are you free tonight?'

'It's not a good time for me, Daragh.' Her voice shook a little, betraying her.

'Tomorrow, then.'

'I've an engagement, I'm afraid. I'm learning German. It helps me with my work.'

He fell silent. She moved around the room, tidying shelves, straightening the bedspread. 'We've a busy week, haven't we, Em?'

'Just a hectic social whirl.' Emily smiled brightly.

He just stood there, watching her. When Tilda took off her hat and slid her hands from her gloves, she felt as though she was naked. Her skin burned. He said suddenly, 'If you should change your mind . . . I'm staying in the Savoy Hotel.' Then he smiled, and left the room.

She went to the window and watched him walk up the street, his hands in his pockets. She guessed that he was whistling – 'Galway Bay', or 'The Star of the County Down'. Tears stung her eyes, but she blinked them back.

'The Savoy,' said Emily enviously. 'Lucky him. Better than this dump. You won't go, will you?' She glanced at Tilda. 'Tilda, he's *married*, for heaven's sake.'

Daragh was tenacious and he had a streak of self-interest that Sarah Greenlees had taken advantage of. Tilda imagined him sitting in his room in the Savoy, waiting for her day after day. Or she might come home from work and find him on the doorstep of 15 Pargeter Street. She imagined the letters that he might send, the telephone calls that he might make when he discovered where she worked. She wondered how long it would be before her will dissolved, before she let him take what he wanted. There was a way, she thought, of sending him away for ever. Daragh, after all, did not know everything.

'I might go.'

Emily closed the door. 'And what about Max?' she hissed. 'You know that he is in love with you. They are all in love with you, of course – Michael, Fergus, Stefan – which is an absolute bore for me, but Max is different. You know that, Tilda. You shouldn't flirt with someone like Max.'

She said calmly, 'I never flirt.'

'No. You don't have to, do you?' Emily scrabbled in her bag for cigarettes. 'Tilda, stop being so bloody . . . *unreachable*.'

Tilda took her knitting from the drawer and sat on the end of the bed, picking up stitches. The yarn was a fine, silky blue, the colour of the sky.

Emily lit her cigarette. 'Daragh's no good for you, Tilda. I know that he's terribly handsome and that one just wants to die for him, but you mustn't go to him. He wants to make you his mistress.'

Tilda had begun the complicated bit around the neckline. 'I know.'

'Then you won't go?'

She was counting stitches. 'I might, Em.'

'You won't be able to resist him. You think you will, but you won't. Daragh won't ever leave his wife for you, Tilda. He's a Roman Catholic and they don't allow divorce. Then you'll have lost Max, who's worth ten of Daragh.'

When she looked up from her knitting, Tilda saw that Emily was furious. Yet she could not explain: the sense of shame persisted, marking everything she did.

Emily stubbed out her cigarette in a saucer. 'You are so obstinate!' The door slammed as she left the room. Tilda began to knit again, but she had lost count of the stitches.

Two days later she went to the Savoy Hotel. Daragh

had a large room on the second floor, overlooking the Thames. There, he poured two glasses of sherry, handing one to Tilda. Tilda broke the tense silence. 'Tell me about your daughter, Daragh.'

He smiled at last and took an envelope from his pocket and spread out a handful of photographs on the table in front of her. 'This is Caitlin.'

She looked down at the pictures. A dark-haired baby laughed back at her. 'She's beautiful, Daragh. How old is she now?'

'Seven months,' he said proudly. 'She can sit up all by herself.'

There was another silence. Tilda, cradling her sherry glass between her fingers, said suddenly, 'Why did you come here, Daragh? Why didn't you leave me alone?'

'I wanted to explain to you about Jossy.' He rose and went to the window, his hands on the sill, looking out. 'I wanted you to understand how it was.'

'I *know*,' she whispered. 'I *know* how it was.'

'Tilda.' Daragh's voice, and the expression in his eyes, pleaded with her. 'Tilda, please try to understand. I was nothing in Ireland, and nothing still when I came here. I came to England to make something of myself, but I hadn't realized how hard it would be. I didn't propose to Jossy – she proposed to me. I had no idea. I thought she was going to offer me a job . . .' The words trailed away. Then he said, 'Your Aunt Sarah. It was her fault.'

'Sarah pulled the strings,' said Tilda bitterly, 'but you jumped, didn't you, Daragh?'

'Oh, I jumped.' There was self-disgust in his smile. 'Like a marionette. But to own that land, that house – have you any idea what that meant to me? I'd been shut out all my life, not even allowed to *look*. And then, to have all that offered to me –

mine, and not a soul to take it away. How could I refuse?'

She said coldly, 'I was born with nothing, Daragh. I had you, though, for a while, and that meant more to me than all the fine houses. But you threw it away.'

'Yes, God help me.' There was pain in his eyes.

She could not stop herself asking. 'Do you regret it?'

'I regretted it the day I married. I regretted it as I stood at the altar.'

Another long silence, and then Tilda pointed to the photographs. 'And now, Daragh?'

'I'll not lie to you, Tilda. I love my little girl. She is the light of my life.'

She whispered, 'And Jossy?'

'I feel nothing for her. I never have done. I can't breathe, sometimes. She is . . . possessive.'

She thought that he was telling the truth. She felt a flicker of pity for Jossy, who loved Daragh. He sat down beside her again. She heard him say, 'I know I've nothing to offer you. But love is something, isn't it?'

'But you haven't love to offer any more, have you, Daragh? Don't you see?'

He closed his eyes very tightly. 'Tilda, I loved you the moment I set eyes on you, and I've never stopped loving you. I've made a mess of things, I'd be the first to admit. But for God's sake . . . I'm not entirely to blame, am I?'

He seized her hand. His fingers curled round hers, his thumb caressed her palm. She whispered, 'No. You are not entirely to blame.' She had forgotten everything except the proximity of him, the warmth of him. When he drew her to him, she rested her forehead against his shoulder, and her eyes closed as he stroked her hair.

'You haven't asked me why I came here, Daragh.'

He was caressing the small bones at the top of her spine.

'I came here to say goodbye,' she said, and she felt his fingers, stroking the back of her neck, stiffen. 'To say goodbye properly this time.'

Sitting up, she saw the mixture of disbelief and hurt on his face. 'Is there someone else?'

She thought of Max, but she shook her head. 'No. No-one else.'

'I'd leave Jossy if I could, Tilda. You have to believe me.' But she put her fingers against his mouth, silencing him. He drew away from her and they sat side by side on the sofa, no longer touching. Daragh looked down into his glass. 'Love fades, I suppose. Just – dies. I killed it. I was angry and I was greedy and I killed it.'

'No. No.' It would have been better to lie, perhaps, but she would not. 'It's because of what you are, Daragh. *Who* you are. Who Jossy is.'

'Jossy?' He looked bewildered. 'What has Jossy to do with this?'

'Oh, Daragh.' She felt at that moment terribly tired and terribly sad. 'Jossy is my sister.'

A voice called out her name as Tilda ran down the stairs and across the foyer.

'Max . . .' His face was blurred by her tears.

'Emily told me where you were.'

She glanced at him sharply. 'Oh.' She stood still in the middle of the foyer. Guests in evening clothes jostled her.

Max's expression was grim. 'I was concerned about you.'

'A fate worse than death?' Tilda laughed unsteadily. 'You needn't have worried.'

He watched her for a moment. 'Would you like a drink?'

'No. I hate this place.' She shuddered.

'Then shall we go somewhere else?' He offered her his arm.

They walked to the Embankment. The evening sunlight glittered on the waters of the Thames. Barges and pleasure boats jostled on the river, their brightly coloured pennants caught by the breeze.

'Has he gone?' said Max eventually.

'Daragh? I've no idea.'

They had reached the river. They leaned against the railing. 'I would imagine,' said Tilda, 'that he'll get very drunk and then sleep it off and go home tomorrow.'

They were both silent, watching a dinghy row out to one of the larger vessels. Tilda said softly, 'I wish that I was on one of those boats and that I could sail away and never come back.'

'That bad?' asked Max.

She rubbed her eyes, and leaned her head against his shoulder. The sailor in the dinghy threw a rope up to the boat and was lifted aboard.

Max said, 'Do you want to talk about it?'

She thought that perhaps she could tell him. That maybe she owed him something. For bothering about her. For picking her up off the floor, actually and metaphorically, more than once.

'I've no intention of becoming Daragh's mistress, Max.'

'Which is why, presumably, he's getting plastered.'

She shook her head. 'Not quite. I told him that his wife is my half-sister. Which makes Daragh my brother-in-law. It would have been almost incest to sleep with him, wouldn't it?'

He didn't say anything, just looked at her.

'It's true, Max. I found out eighteen months ago. That was why I came to London.'

He gave her his handkerchief and she dabbed her eyes. Then she told him the whole story: Daragh and Aunt Sarah, and the letter that Aunt Sarah had written to Joscelin de Paveley. And, lastly, about her mother, and what had happened to her.

'Are you shocked?' she asked, when she had finished.

He shrugged. 'It's a rotten, pitiless law, the one that put your mother in the asylum. And the rape laws, too – not much better.'

'I sometimes wonder,' said Tilda thoughtfully, 'which one of my parents I take after. The mad one or the wicked one.'

'The beautiful one,' he said.

'Max.' She turned away. The boat set sail along the Thames; Tilda watched it decrease in size until the dinghy, towed in its wake, was no longer visible. 'When I came to London,' she said slowly, 'I tried to pretend that I hadn't a past. I thought that I could start again, remake myself like an old dress – shorten bits, sew on new buttons, make it look different.'

'You've done pretty well.'

'I am ashamed,' she whispered.

'You've nothing to be ashamed of,' he said gently. 'You're neither the mad one nor the wicked one. You are Tilda, and you are beautiful and clever and delightful, and you can make of your life what you wish. You can work – or you can have a family—'

'I think I should like a family.' She needed lots

of people, she thought. Lots of people to fill up the gaps.

'Yet no-one but Daragh will do for you?'

She glanced sharply at him and shook her head. 'I'm through with that sort of love, Max. It's like – oh, riding one of those fast, noisy motorcycles. Exciting, but exhausting.'

He said bluntly, 'You haven't said that you don't love him.'

'No.' She pressed her fisted hand against her heart, as though it hurt. 'I will be able to one day, though. It'll just take a while.'

'Then . . . would you consider marrying me?'

She heard her own quick intake of breath.

'I never thought I'd ask anyone.' He grimaced. 'I'd planned on becoming a revolting old bachelor – you know, a dreadful maroon dressing gown, and not doing the washing-up for a week. But you seem to have distracted me, Tilda. I love you. I can't think of anything nicer than spending the rest of my life with you.'

'Max – dear Max—'

'You are conscious of the honour I do you, but you must regretfully etcetera, etcetera?' There was pain beneath the flippancy.

She walked away from him, sitting down on a bench, trying to think. When he called back to her, 'Tilda, I'm not asking you to say that you're madly in love with me—' Several passers-by turned and stared, and she shook her head again.

'I enjoy your company.' She made a list on her fingers. 'You make me laugh, and you're good to talk to. You're kind—'

'Oh God!' He bent his head in mock despair. 'How crushing—'

'Don't be silly, Max. We like the same sort of things. We think the same way about things. We're both *running*, I think.'

'But . . .?' he said.

'You're rude and arrogant and difficult, of course.' But she stopped teasing him, and said simply, 'Max, I don't want to be madly in love with anyone. Not ever again. If you're prepared to accept that, then – yes, I think that I might marry you.'

She saw him close his eyes for a moment, and then he straightened, and walked over to the bench. She stood up, and he put his arms round her and kissed her. She thought that if it hadn't been for Daragh, then it might never have come to this. They'd have circled each other for months or years, both too bruised by the past to admit a desire for a common future, drifting apart eventually, need and liking killed by hesitancy and lack of trust. He kissed her again, and then held her for a long time, her head cradled against his shoulder.

She heard Max say, 'I'm not asking for all of you. I'm not asking you to give me what you gave to Daragh. If you still love him a little, in your heart, then I can live with that. But I couldn't bear that you should cheat me, Tilda. I couldn't bear that you should betray me. You have to understand that I couldn't live with that.'

She thought that she had made a good bargain. She had exchanged passionate love for something gentler and more reasonable, less liable to give pain, and perhaps more enduring.

She made her promise easily. 'I won't betray you, Max. I'll be a good wife to you. I'll never hurt you.' She kissed him, and felt the tension fall away from him.

CHAPTER SIX

The garage phoned me to tell me that my car was repaired; I took advantage of the journey to Oxfordshire to collect some material from The Red House. Tilda had left hospital, but was staying with Melissa at her house in Surrey.

I went through the contents of the boxes over the next few days. They were a jumble of old diaries and receipts and letters. On first glance, the diaries were disappointingly unrevealing. Their entries were of the 'Pay milkman' type, and the fact that there wasn't a full set showed that Tilda, too, had thought them unimportant, no more than an aide-mémoire. I dutifully read them through, listing only the meetings with the rich or famous people that Tilda had charmed or badgered into supporting her various ventures, and skipping the children's dental appointments and music lessons. My only excuse for my lack of observation is that I still felt edgy and found it hard to concentrate. I had been convinced for a week now that Toby would ring.

When the phone did ring, I jumped with nerves and barked my number down the receiver. Charles's voice said, 'Rebecca? Is that you?'

'Sorry, Charles – I thought you were Toby.'

'*Toby*. Good grief – that hasn't started again, has it?'

I explained about meeting Toby at the party, and found myself agreeing to go to the cinema that night with Charles. It would get me out of the house; it would take me away from the telephone.

I met him inside the cinema. He bought choc ices and huge buckets of popcorn. Watching the adverts, he said, 'I can't believe you are contemplating the loathsome Toby again, Rebecca.' Charles came to dinner with Toby and me once, and they detested each other on sight.

'I'm not,' I said, but he went on as though I hadn't spoken.

'After what he did. I mean, I may not be the most sensitive chap in the world, but even I wouldn't dump a woman just after she'd miscarried my child.'

The film began then, thank goodness. It was something melancholy and French, and it took me a while to get a hold of myself and to make the effort to follow the rather tenuous plot. Afterwards, we went to a café for coffee. Charles asked me about my progress on the biography.

'Tilda's been ill,' I explained. I began to tell him about that exhausting day, from my car breaking down to my horrible, memorable nightmare about Edward de Paveley. He interrupted me when I mentioned Patrick Franklin.

'Patrick?'

'Tilda's grandson.'

'How old?'

'My age. Early thirties.'

'Married?'

'I've no idea. Probably not. He might be more human if he was.'

'Patterned sweaters and a stamp collection?'

I laughed. 'Oh no. Not at all. Rather attractive, in fact.'

He said, 'You sound ... smitten.' He was stirring sugar into his coffee; his head was bent, and I couldn't see his expression.

I shook my head. 'Not my type. Too much like hard work. That's why you're so restful, Charles – I don't feel I have to make an effort with you.' I thought of Patrick. 'And he's a lawyer. Not another lawyer – I couldn't, could I?'

On Monday I looked through the diaries again and noticed at last what I should have seen the previous week.

'See headmistress re Caitlin' was the entry in the mid-September of 1947. And then, in the spring of 1948, 'Melissa, Hanna, Caitlin to dentist.' Daragh and Jossy's daughter had been called Caitlin. It was an unusual name – even more unusual, I guessed, in the England of the 1940s. Could the Caitlin that Tilda had taken to the dentist on 9 February 1948, possibly be Caitlin Canavan? And if so, why?

I'd phoned Joan, Tilda's housekeeper, the previous Friday, and knew that Tilda had left hospital, but had been ordered to rest for a couple of weeks. I sat with my elbows on the desk, chewing my nails, trying to work things out. I went back to the diaries and looked at them more carefully, noticing how the names came and went over the years. Hanna and Erich appeared in mid-1940, but there was no mention of Erich after 1949. Tilda had not yet given me the diaries for the 1950s. Max's name, I realized suddenly, did not appear after mid-1947. Perhaps, I thought, searching frantically for the 1948 diary, Tilda had divorced Max, and married Daragh, her childhood sweetheart and the great love of her life, in 1947.

But there was no mention of Daragh in the 1948 diary. If the Caitlin who was then Tilda's responsibility had been Caitlin Canavan, what had happened to Daragh and to Jossy? I could not imagine that loving, indulgent father allowing anyone else – even Tilda – to care for his daughter.

I considered telephoning Melissa, but I did not know her number, and anyway, I did not want to disturb Tilda. Then I thought of Patrick. I didn't know his number either, but there was a way of finding it out. Lawyers all know each other. I picked up the phone and dialled Toby's chambers. I detected pleasure (or triumph?) in Toby's voice when he came on the line, but an increasing sulkiness as the conversation wore on, but he knew Patrick Franklin, and gave me his phone number.

I telephoned Patrick before I had time for second thoughts. A secretary answered me and told me frostily that she would check whether Mr Franklin was available. I was left on hold, listening to *The Four Seasons*.

'Rebecca?' Patrick's voice, interrupting 'Spring', made me jump. He sounded impatient.

I apologized for disturbing him and said quickly, 'Patrick, there's something I need to find out.' There were no encouraging comments, so I ploughed on. 'When I looked through Tilda's diaries, I saw that there was a Caitlin living with her in 1948. That wasn't Caitlin Canavan, was it?'

There was a longish silence. Then he said, 'Yes, it was.'

'Why? What had happened to her parents?'

'Joscelin Canavan died in 1947. Daragh disappeared after the floods. You know about the floods of 1947, I assume?'

'I've read a little. Daragh disappeared in the floods? You mean he was drowned?'

'No. *After*. He disappeared after the floods.'

The line was crackly and I wasn't sure whether I'd heard him right. I said feebly, 'Disappeared. Where did he go?'

'No idea. Now, if that's all – I am rather busy—'

I thanked him profusely and put the phone down. I added Jossy's death and Daragh's disappearance to the time-line I was making, and tried to continue to work methodically through the letters and diaries. I couldn't concentrate, though, and I felt uneasy. In 1947 Jossy had died and Daragh had disappeared and Caitlin had gone to live with Tilda, and Max . . . I had forgotten to ask Patrick what had happened to Max.

I worked through the afternoon in the reference library, making notes. There were no books about the Fens, but I found a rather dull tome about rivers and inland waterways, with a chapter on the 1947 floods. I remembered the man in the blue jersey at the party, and the lock he had made from celery and pistachio nuts. The thought of food reminded me that there was nothing in the house, so at five o'clock I left the library and walked to the supermarket. I pushed the trolley through the aisles, and then hauled four bulging bags home with me, their thin plastic handles constantly threatening to break. When I reached the end of the street, I saw a blue Renault parked outside my house.

Patrick stepped out of the car as I drew level. He glanced at my carrier bags. 'I was going to ask you whether you'd like supper, but perhaps you've company.'

'No—' As I unlocked the front door, one of the bags split and oranges rolled across the pavement. Patrick fielded them efficiently.

He followed me into the house, taking the oranges and the broken bag through to the kitchen. 'No, you haven't company, or no, you don't want supper?'

I dumped the shopping and books on the table. 'No, I haven't company, and yes, I'd love supper.'

'Good.' His back to me, he was rinsing the oranges under the tap.

I put away the shopping and escaped to the bathroom to slap on some make-up. Patrick's invitation astonished me. I wondered what he wanted.

'Wheeler's, I thought,' he said, as I emerged from the bathroom. He added, with only a flicker of amusement in his blue eyes, 'I know you're keen on shellfish.'

We ate oysters and drank white wine in a room as dark and narrow as one of The Red House's corridors. Polite conversation at first: music and books and the endlessness of the recession. After a glass of wine, I had the nerve to ask him about his father.

'You're Josh Franklin's son, aren't you?'

He prised another oyster out of its shell. 'I told you – some of us are rather peripatetic.'

'You must have had an interesting childhood.'

'At first. I had to go to boarding school eventually, which was rather less interesting.' He topped up my glass. 'And you, Rebecca? Have you family?'

'I've a father and a sister and two nephews. Jack's three, Lawrie is eighteen months.'

'I have a four-year-old daughter,' said Patrick, and I almost choked on my oyster.

'You're married?'

'Separated. Ellie lives with her mother.' His eyes were expressionless.

I remembered the diaries. 'Tilda and Max split up, didn't they?'

He nodded, and dropped his last oyster shell onto the heap of empty ones.

'Because of Daragh?' I persisted, and he shrugged.

'I've really no idea. It's all history, isn't it?'

'And best left alone?'

The waiter took our plates away and Patrick ordered coffee. 'I didn't say that.'

'But it's what you think.'

'Perhaps.'

'Is that why you asked me out? To warn me off again?'

He looked at me. 'Well, no. It wasn't, actually.'

I felt all my nerve endings become hot, and prayed that the restaurant was too dark for him to see me redden.

He said smoothly, 'I thought I might be able to answer a few more of your questions. I'm afraid that I was rather abrupt on the telephone this morning.'

I mumbled something about being sorry to have interrupted his work.

'I was quite glad of the interruption, to tell the truth. You can get swamped in things, so you can't see clearly.'

I knew just what he meant. 'Tell me about Daragh. He can't have just disappeared.'

'But he did.' Patrick frowned, rubbing his forehead. 'I don't know much about him – as I said, it was a long time ago, and Tilda's always played things close to the chest –

but Daragh Canavan does seem to have put everyone's backs up. And he was in a financial mess. Southam Hall was sold in the late Forties.' The waiter arrived with the coffee. 'Have you been there, Rebecca?'

I shook my head. I had been oddly reluctant to visit Southam, afraid, perhaps, that the real place might not come up to my imaginings. 'Have you?'

'Once years ago, with my father. It was all rather depressing. The Hall was being used as a furniture warehouse, and Tilda's old cottage was derelict – it was about to be knocked down. The land had been sold to the council. It was winter, and everything was grey and brown and frozen. Although' – Patrick's eyes narrowed as he remembered – 'I do remember being rather stunned by the flood plain between the Hundred Foot Drain and the Old Bedford river. We'd travelled down from the north by train, my father and I, and I remember how the railway track seemed to skate over the ice. That was all you could see, to either side of the carriage – just a great white plain of ice. Even my father was impressed.' He blinked, coming back to the hot, crowded restaurant. 'Anyway – Daragh. My guess is that he hoofed it. Realized that he was in a mess of insoluble dimensions and ran. It happens, you know. I've defended men who've pocketed the petty cash and taken the first boat to the Continent. Daragh was clever enough not to get caught, that's all. I think he just upped and went.'

Without his daughter? I thought, but did not say. The waiter arrived with the bill. I took out my purse, but Patrick pushed the notes away.

'I dragged you out, remember. You'd probably have preferred a quiet evening in, eating oranges.'

*   *   *

The next weekend, I drove up the M11, past Cambridge and out on the old A45 to Newmarket, turning off and heading north at Quy. The land between the villages became flatter, young green corn piercing the black soil. It had rained heavily overnight, and the fields were blistered with silver streaks of water. Because the drained peat of the fields had dried out and sunk, the shored-up roads were uneasy bridges across a disappearing land, their tarmacked edges crumbling. The scattered houses were of yellowish-grey brick, their front doors several feet above land level, surrounded by rusting farm vehicles.

Southam village was strung along the roadside, a straggle of variously sized cottages, a dozen semi-detached council houses, and a small estate, The Beeches, whose red-brick walls and fiddly white porches made no concession to the vernacular. There was a tiny supermarket and an antique shop, and a shop that sold terracotta pots and wind-chimes. I parked outside the church.

It was easy to find the de Paveley graves. They had pride of place, walled off behind little iron railings, or raised up in pompous tombs of black marble. As though there is distinction even in crumbling bones. The same names – Edward and Christopher for the men, Joscelin and Cecily for the women – recurred for generation after generation. I found my Edward de Paveley under a yew tree, his monument a relatively modest granite slab inscribed with his names and dates. The lichen blooms on the stone were smaller than those of his more distant ancestors. I thought that though Edward de Paveley's crimes had been heinous, he had surely paid for them, over and over again, in Flanders. History comforts and fascinates me, but there are bits of it that I cannot read about without fear and horror.

The Holocaust, of course, is one, but the First World War, with its terrible death knell of battles – Ypres, the Somme, Passchendaele – is another.

I looked then for the grave of Edward de Paveley's elder daughter. I found it after a while, slightly cut off from the rest of her family, an acknowledgement, perhaps, of her conversion to Roman Catholicism. With its marble cross and metal flower container, now empty, it seemed rather isolated and forlorn. Cut off from her history and her family even in death, I thought. I read the inscription. 'Joscelin Alicia Canavan 1911–1947. Beloved of Daragh, her husband.' She had been only thirty-six, poor Jossy. I wondered what had killed her. A broken heart, perhaps? I took photographs of the gravestones, feeling slightly crass, as though my curiosity might disturb the sleep of the dead, and then I walked back to the shop with the terracotta pots and the wind-chimes, and asked the girl who worked there for directions to the Hall. She couldn't think where I meant at first, and I thought for a moment that the de Paveleys' destruction might be complete, that their house might no longer stand. But an older woman put her head round the door, and said, 'She means the Davises' place. Four Winds. Back through the village, love, and then turn up the track to your left. They always meant to do the road, but they never got round to it.'

I saw what she meant as soon as I retraced my path through Southam and took the fork that led up through the fields. The track was unsurfaced, ridges of mud patched with puddles. The poor Fiesta lurched and slid through the deep channels, and I feared for its well-being. After twenty yards or so, I parked and climbed out and walked the rest of the way.

From everywhere except the village, with its fringe

of trees, you must have been able to see the house for miles. It was a great square lump of a building, Georgian-windowed, unornamented. Quite ugly, though it must once have possessed a certain confident dignity. The wall of Leylandii that marked its borders, the huge double garage, complete with Range Rover, and the clutter of terracotta pots and window boxes, a futile attempt at prettiness, destroyed that dignity.

Three For Sale signs from different estate agents flapped forlornly in the wind. Someone's dream had turned to dust. I walked alongside the acid-green ranks of Leylandii, treading the border of the field, aware of my disappointment. Neither Jossy, with her blindfolded love, nor faithless Daragh haunted that house. When I reached the corner of the grounds, I looked around. To one side of me was the house, to the other the village, and before and behind was a vast field of green and black. The dike bisected the land between the village and the house. It seemed to go on for ever, rising above everything else.

I climbed up the bank, slipping on the wet grass. Here, ten foot or so above the level of the fields, the wind was fierce. It belled out my jacket and tangled my hair. Time shifted, and I could have been standing there ten years ago, or fifty, or four hundred, when the land had first been stolen from the water. When I looked around, I saw what Daragh must have seen when he had walked with Jossy: the ripples on the trapped water, the vast grey silence of the sky, the awful emptiness. The way that the horizon presses down, so that one knows instinctively that the land is below sea level. I wondered whether if he'd been born today, Daragh Canavan would have made the same choices. Whether he'd still have married the girl that had the land. I thought that Patrick had probably been right. Swamped by a financial mess of his own making, Daragh had run away. He'd run away before, after all, when he'd left Ireland. He hadn't taken his daughter with him because, for the first time in his life, he'd been unselfish. He had recognized that what he could offer Caitlin was no longer enough.

I began to walk along the dike. I saw the long, squat building at the far boundary of the field and realized, with a thrill of recognition, that it must be Christopher de Paveley's house. There was something repellent and disturbing about the windows that were half smothered with ivy, and the patches on the walls where lumps of pebbledash had fallen, like open sores. It looked as though it had not been lived in for decades.

I saw that the island on which the de Paveleys' house was built was lower than that crested by Southam church. I imagined some ancient, arrogant de Paveley shaking his fist and daring the waters to steal back what he had seized. I imagined how the floodwater must, in the calamitous spring of 1947, have burst through the strong walls of the dike, and drowned the surrounding land. And it began to rain, so I bowed my head and headed back to my car, thinking again of Daragh Canavan, who had walked here, as I had done, and who had just faded away, lost, a ghost.

*

After his journey to London, after he had learned that Tilda would not – would never be – his lover, Daragh had returned to Southam Hall. There, he tried to comfort himself by reminding himself that he still, after all, had Caitlin. And he still had the money and the status.

Yet, somehow, his possessions were not quite the

comfort that they once had been. Jossy and Tilda were half-sisters. The discovery seemed to poison almost everything he did. It rubbed in the fact that he loved the one sister, yet had married the other. It reminded him how Sarah Greenlees had manipulated him, how she had employed his ambition to satisfy her own desire for vengeance. The discovery mocked him, and altered his attitude to Jossy, so that what had once merely irritated him, he began to despise. He compared Jossy's features to Tilda's, noting the coarseness of the one sister's appearance, remembering the beauty of the other's. Sometimes, when he found Jossy's love particularly claustrophobic, he found himself wanting to tell her the truth, just to wipe from her face its expression of patient, beatific adoration.

He did not, though. Instead he drank a lot, and rode a lot, and went out as much as he could, just to be away from Jossy. He also flirted. He confined himself to flirtation at first, and then, at a party in Cambridge, he saw Elsa Gordon again. Daragh danced first with his wife, steering her dutifully around the perimeter of the room, and then with several other ladies, but he did not yet dance with the woman whose eye he had caught as soon as she stepped out of her fancy motor car. He'd make Elsa Gordon wait for him. Every now and then, circling the room, Daragh caught a glimpse of her neat little polished blonde head, her small, sinuous body, the firm calves and ankles encased in smooth seamed silk. Eventually her husband, a dull but wealthy fellow, went off to play cards. Daragh made his move.

First they danced, and then he suggested they escape the heat of the ballroom. In the quiet mustiness of the garden summerhouse, she pressed him against the wall, and laid her body against his, and kissed him. Through her thin dress he could feel rubbing against him her small hard breasts, her jutting hips, her pubic bone. Her small hands undid his shirt buttons and loosened his trousers. Her eyes were glassy, her lips moist. When he pulled up her skirt and pushed himself between her legs, she laughed with delight. He tried to make himself last, gritting his teeth and thinking of dull things like bills and accounts, but his years of abstinence almost let him down. But she came quickly, thank God, and Daragh let himself climax, a shuddering convulsion of pain and pleasure that made her contorted face swim black in front of his eyes.

A few days later, Elsa telephoned. Daragh managed to take the call, and to mention that he'd be driving out to Newmarket the following day, to look at some horses. He saw her car parked at the side of the road, halfway to Newmarket. They drove up a little winding farm track and made love in the back of Elsa's Daimler. The heady perfume of the leather seats was drowned by the scent of sex, and he realized that she liked to be taken like this: rough and crude and with no preliminaries.

Max insisted on a six-month engagement, in case, he said, Tilda changed her mind. He also insisted, because Tilda was still under twenty-one, on getting Sarah Greenlees' permission for the marriage. They took the train from Liverpool Street to Ely one Saturday, and caught the bus to Southam, a tortuous, winding journey through a bleak, grey countryside. Never had Max seen fields so flat, never had he seen a sky so vast, so ominous.

At Southam, they alighted. Max, who had lived in London most of his life, glanced at the clutter of cottages and shops. He kept thinking there must be more just round the corner. But Tilda led him along a track that was pitted with puddles, to a cottage. Sarah Greenlees, opening the front door to them, expressed surprise that Tilda had wasted money on the bus fare and had not walked from Ely, and told them to wipe their feet on the mat. When Tilda introduced Max, Sarah glared at him suspiciously, but shook his hand.

Inside the cottage, he looked around as Sarah and Tilda talked. It occurred to Max forcefully then how different his background was from Tilda's. It wasn't something he had thought about much. Yet this place, with its tiny windows hung with curtains – patched out of old underclothes, he suspected – its earth floors and huge dresser covered with crockery, no two pieces of which matched, shocked him. In his home, cups had been thrown away if they had the smallest chip. Curtains had been made at Harrods or at Liberty. And there had been, of course, a cook-general and a woman to do the heavy work. Max guessed that Sarah Greenlees cleaned her own floors, cut her own wood, strangled her own hens when they no longer laid.

They had sandwiches and cake in the kitchen and Tilda told Sarah about the wedding. 'We'd like you to come,' she said. 'My friend Emily's brother could drive you to London in his motor car.'

'Motor car?' Sarah was affronted. 'You know that I don't believe in motor cars, Tilda. I shall catch the train.' Then she began to clear up the dishes. The corners of Max's mouth twitched.

They married in the early spring of 1935. It was a register office wedding, with a buffet reception afterwards in a small hotel. Tilda wore a cream-coloured costume that she had made herself, and Emily was her bridesmaid. Roland toasted the bride and groom with a glass of champagne from the case that was Anna's wedding present, and took photographs. Mrs Franklin cried, and snow began to fall as they left the hotel for the station.

They were to honeymoon for two nights in Eastbourne. As the train moved out of Victoria Station, Tilda threw her bouquet and Emily caught it, and soon the waving figures on the platform were reduced to tiny black ants. Max let out an enormous sigh of relief, and said, 'Thank God that's over.'

'Wasn't the food awful?'

'Hideous. And Fergus was plastered.'

'And the wedding presents . . . have you seen them, Max?'

'Egg cosies.' In the corridor of the train he kissed her. 'Three equally appalling cruet sets.' He kissed her again.

'No plates or bowls. We shall have to eat out of vases. Oh, Max' – Tilda's hands were around his neck, pulling him to her – 'do you think we should go into a carriage?'

They found an empty carriage and pulled down the blinds. Tilda sat on Max's knee. When the ticket collector saw the carnation in Max's buttonhole, and the 'Just Married' that Michael had painted on their suitcase, he went out again, shutting the door behind him, not bothering to check their tickets.

Tilda always believed that Melissa was conceived in Eastbourne, a place of great gentility that had, surely, imprinted itself on her unborn daughter, marking out her neat, organized character. On the first day of their honeymoon, they got up late and walked along the beach, watching the rain pockmark the grey swell of the waves. On the second day, they did not get out of bed at all. Sometime during the intervening night, Tilda had discovered that making love to Max was, simply, a tremendous pleasure. It was more fun than dining in the smart hotel room, more fun than dancing to the piano trio after dinner, and more fun, even, than sitting at the desk in the Residents' Lounge, pretending to write letters on the thick, crested hotel notepaper. Any lingering doubts that she'd done the right thing in marrying Max Franklin, any suspicion that the sort of love she could offer to Max would not, in the end, be adequate, retreated to a small, neglected corner of her mind.

They went back to the flat they had rented in Fulham. They had chosen the flat for the privacy of its separate entrance way, and for its large, bay-windowed bedroom. There was a little boxroom that Max could use as a study, and a basement kitchen with steps that led up to a small, grimy back yard. The shops, doctor's surgery and Tube station were only a brisk ten-minute walk away.

Tilda cleaned out the cupboards and put away the wedding presents. Sarah had given them sheets and towels, Clara Franklin had given them a pretty Clarice Cliff coffee set, Max's father a crystal decanter. They had two dinner plates and two saucepans and no broom, dustpan, iron or bucket. They had, to begin with, no mangle, so all the washing had to be done in the kitchen sink and wrung out by hand in the back yard, often in the evening, with much giggling. Afterwards, they tended to end up in bed, so that 'Shall we do the washing?' became a code.

The geyser was temperamental and unreliable, but Tilda became expert at it, coaxing it into life in the early morning, refusing to give in to its defeatist shudders and groans. Max went back to Germany in May, and while he was away the doctor confirmed what Tilda had suspected for weeks: that she was pregnant. The baby was due in December, about a week before Christmas. She dreamed of the baby, and of the house in the country that they would buy when they could afford it, with a garden and swings and huge open fires. When Max came home he guessed Tilda's news before she had the chance to tell him. They shared a bottle of beer and went to bed, and made love, carefully, for hours.

She'd timed the pregnancy well. The summer of 1935 was hot and dry, but Tilda's pregnancy did not begin to show until it was over. Until the last four weeks she felt well enough to continue the long journey to Professor Hastings' house. Then she said a tearful farewell, and Professor Hastings gave her a set of encyclopaedias for the baby, and his housekeeper gave her a bale of terry cloth. For the next month she sewed: four dozen nappies, muslin and terry, and a dozen cot sheets, and half a dozen tiny white nightgowns. Clara Franklin discovered Max's old cradle and had it sent up by carrier van. A feathering of white stretch marks appeared overnight on both sides of Tilda's belly, and Max kissed them and rubbed olive oil into them. They discussed what to call the baby and could agree only that they would not use family names. The child would be a new beginning.

The baby was due on 18 December, but the midwife told Tilda that first babies rarely arrive on time. But a week before Christmas she was making mincemeat in the kitchen when she felt a pain in her back. She bent over the table, gasping, her splayed hands among the currants and cherries and suet. Max was upstairs in his study, finishing his article. When she could eventually move, Tilda plodded up the steep basement stairs and stood in the doorway, just looking at him. She saw all the colour drain from his face, and then he helped her into the bedroom and ran for the midwife. She had to call him back from the front door to remind him to put on his coat and hat. It was frosty outside, ice crackling the puddles that lined the gutters.

The baby was born at ten o'clock in the evening. Although it hurt more than she could have imagined, there was a triumph in discovering that her body, of its own, knew what to do, that it repeated rhythms as old as time to create a new life. When her daughter was born, with a slither and a twist and a final, searing pain, Tilda knew that the past no longer controlled her, that she had made a different future.

The midwife cleaned the baby up and wrapped her in a blanket and gave her to Tilda to hold. Through the bedroom curtains, she could see a speckling of stars in a bright black sky. The child was pale and perfect. Tears of exhaustion, pride and delight swelled from Tilda's eyes. When Max came into the room, she said, 'Melissa. She is called Melissa.' The name, which she had not previously considered, had just come into her head and she had recognized it instantly as her daughter's.

They sat for a long time, Max's arm round Tilda's shoulders, the baby sleeping peacefully between them. Max registered his daughter the next day as Melissa Emma, taking her second name from his favourite Jane Austen novel. They celebrated their first Christmas together a week later, a small family: father, mother and daughter.

Tilda's life revolved around Melissa. She was a contented, organized baby, waking at six o'clock for her morning feed, taking her late night feed at eleven, and sleeping the intervening seven hours with predictable reliability.

She was dark-haired and blue-eyed, like Max. At four weeks old she smiled; at five and a half months she'd sit on a blanket in the middle of the kitchen floor, happily playing with rattles and wooden spoons. She rarely caught colds and was tolerant of the attentions of honorary grandmothers and aunties. Max's mother, who had taken to Tilda, dropped in whenever she was in town, showering Melissa with little dresses bought in Harrods and fluffy toys to pin to her pram. Both Tilda and Max knew that Melissa was the most beautiful, clever and adorable baby in the world, but tactfully refrained from mentioning this in the hearing of parents of lesser babies.

Emily was devoted to Melissa. She visited two or three times a week, calling in after work.

'You are so lucky, Tilda,' she said enviously. 'A lovely husband like Max, and a gorgeous baby' – Emily kissed Melissa, who was sitting on her knee, playing with her beads – 'and not having to do beastly shorthand and typing.'

'How's the new job, Em?'

Emily made a face. 'Awful. Simply awful. So dull, and the man I work for is happily married.' She gently prised the string of beads out of Melissa's mouth. 'I have resigned myself to remaining a spinster.'

Tilda shook more salt into the stew. 'You'll stay to supper, won't you, Em? Max is bringing someone home.'

'A man?'

'Harold Sykes works for one of the newspapers that Max writes for.'

'Married?' said Emily.

'Fraid so. Harold has three daughters.'

'Oh dear,' said Emily. 'Perhaps I'll become a nun.'

But Max brought two men home for supper, not one.

Jan van de Criendt was Dutch, tall and blond and quiet, Emily's opposite. Emily's stream of inconsequential chatter faded away beneath the admiring gaze of Jan van de Criendt's blue eyes. Tilda bathed Melissa and put her to bed. When she came back to the kitchen, the three men were drinking beer in the back yard, and Emily was laying the table.

'He's just too beautiful,' hissed Emily.

At dinner, Emily pushed her food around her plate, and knocked over her beer with her elbow. Jan leapt up to find a cloth. Harold and Max argued about Spain. 'Country's a mess anyway.' Harold Sykes was big and greying; his moustache sprouted cheerful curls, and his suits never seemed to fit. 'Could do with a bit of firm government.'

'Dictatorship, you mean, Harold?'

'You sound like a ruddy Commie, Max, old chap.'

'I'm not a Communist. I just don't want Spain going the same way as Germany.'

'More peas, Jan?'

'Thank you, Mrs Franklin. I must apologize for imposing myself on you—'

'Germany's supplying Franco's lot with men and weapons, for heaven's sake, Harold.'

'It's no trouble at all, Jan. I like Max to bring people home.'

'You shouldn't believe everything you read in the papers, Max.' Harold chortled at his own wit.

'Hitler will use Spain as a testing ground for the Luftwaffe. They'll learn how to bomb Spanish towns so that they can destroy us more efficiently in the future.'

'Are you a journalist too, Miss Potter?'

'I work in an awful office, Mr van de Criendt. Tilda, I'm sure I can hear Melissa – it's all right, I'll go—' As

Emily ran from the table, her knife and fork clanged to the floor.

'There could be a staff job coming up soon, Max, old boy,' said Harold. 'I had a word with Freddie. Yours for the asking.'

Max said, 'I'll pass, I think, Harold. You know I'm not much good at keeping to the party line.'

'Steady income,' Harold reminded him, through a mouthful of mashed potato.

Tilda found a babysitter and arranged a trip to the cinema for herself and Max, Jan and Emily. Trapped in the opulent darkness of the cinema, Emily's self-consciousness was conquered by Jan's quiet admiration. As they left the cinema, Emily whispered in Tilda's ear, 'He's asked me out!' and pressed her knuckles against her mouth in an agony of anticipation.

Jan, who owned an import business in Amsterdam, returned to Holland a week later. Emily's mood became dependent on the frequency of his letters. When a couple of days went by without one, she would sulk in Tilda's kitchen-basement, picking over the minutiae of her relationship with Jan, eating cream cakes. When a letter arrived, she would hurl herself down the basement steps, sweep Melissa into her arms and cover her with kisses. When Jan wrote that he was to visit England again, Emily spent a fortune on clothes, lipstick and nail polish, and had her hair permed. The perm was a disaster: Tilda worked for hours trying to dampen down the wild curls. Muttering suicidally, Emily wore a hat to meet Jan at the station. Yet when he alighted from the train and took her in his arms, she knew from the expression in his eyes that he loved her and the frizzy hair ceased to matter.

*　　*　　*

Jossy and Daragh were invited to the christening of Jossy's friend Marjorie's first child. Afterwards, there was a buffet luncheon at Marjorie's house. The day was hot and bright and headachy, and once Jossy had admired the baby and eaten a little lunch she longed to go home.

She wandered around the garden, looking for Daragh. Couples sat under trees or on benches beside the wall, escaping the heat. She thought she saw him beneath the pergola, a tall, dark-haired man, but as she drew closer she realized that it was a stranger. She returned to the house, where the maids were clearing up the remains of the buffet and she could hear, in the distance, Marjorie's baby howling in the nursery. Jossy felt, as she started up the stairs, that she had been searching for Daragh for hours. It occurred to her that it was always this way round – she was always looking for him. She had to fight the wave of oppressive despair that washed over her.

When she heard the noise coming from the bedroom, she thought at first that someone was ill. A peculiar gulping, groaning sort of noise. She stood in the corridor for a moment, undecided whether to look for a maid or for Marjorie, or whether tactfully to offer help herself.

When she pushed open the door an inch or two and saw the couple on the bed, her first thought was, ludicrously, But it's a *christening*! Of all things, that they should do that at a christening. Of all things, that they should do that in Marjorie's house, on Marjorie's bed, at three o'clock in the afternoon!

Of all people, that it should be Elsa Gordon whom he betrayed her with. Jossy stumbled silently back from the doorway. Elsa, whom she had always looked down on; Elsa, who had been nothing until she had married Hamish Gordon; Elsa, whose father had been a house-painter.

With the crabbed, faltering steps of an old woman, Jossy went downstairs. Sitting alone in a corner of the drawing room, she felt physically sick from the shock. Every time she closed her eyes she saw them together, Daragh and Elsa, their clothing awry, writhing on the bed.

A voice said, 'The little darling's fallen asleep at last. He was so tired, poor love,' and Jossy looked up and saw Marjorie.

Some of her pain must have shown on her face, because Marjorie said, 'Are you all right, Jossy?'

'I have a headache.'

'Shall I get you a glass of water? Shall I fetch Daragh?'

'Just the water, thank you, Marjorie.'

Alone again, she stood up, holding the arm of the sofa for support. She was going to tell Hamish what his wife was doing, and she was going to smack Elsa's bland, pretty face. Then, as Marjorie came back into the room, Jossy's anger suddenly evaporated and was replaced by hopelessness. She fell back onto the sofa. What if Daragh had fallen in love with Elsa? She took the glass from Marjorie, and muttered thanks and began to sip the water, but inside she was crumbling. What if Daragh deserted her? If he left her, how could she bear to return to the dull, featureless life that she had known before she met him?

She couldn't sleep that night or the next. Elsa Gordon's face haunted her dreams. She had been aware that Daragh missed sleeping with her, but it hadn't occurred to her that he missed it that much. Jossy thought for a while of ignoring what the stupid doctor had said, and inviting

Daragh back to her bed. But she remembered the ordeal of Caitlin's birth, and shrank from risking that again. Several times she almost confronted Daragh with her knowledge of his infidelity, but she always drew back from the brink. If she forced him to choose between herself and Elsa, what answer might he give?

She had built her life around Daragh; his contentment had been her purpose. Jossy's peace of mind disintegrated, shattered by self-doubt and fear. When Nana, a few days later, told her that Caitlin was unwell, Jossy hardly listened. But then the doctor came and the illness was diagnosed as scarlet fever, and the whole house seemed to shift into a different gear. Voices were hushed and curtains drawn. Daragh sat beside the cot, bathing Caitlin's forehead with a cold flannel. When the telephone rang after lunch, Jossy answered it. The line went dead as soon as she said her name.

Caitlin's fever burned a red-hot rash over her tiny body. A nurse was engaged, but Daragh remained in the nursery, his hair uncombed, dark shadows smudged around his eyes. Caitlin's fever rose and her breathing became short and hurried. Jossy cradled Daragh's head against her, stroking his curls. He said, 'If we should lose her—' and could not go on. Jossy hushed him, comforting him as he wept. As he clutched at her, as if to draw strength from her, her fear and despair disappeared. She knew then that Daragh would never leave her, because he would never leave Caitlin. Jossy, looking down at the child in the cot, willed Caitlin's temperature to fall, and breathed steadily as if to persuade her daughter's struggling lungs to echo her own.

In the early hours of the morning, the fever broke, and Caitlin began to mend. A month later, when the child was out of danger, Jossy gave a dinner party.

She invited Marjorie Tate and her husband, and the Talbots, who farmed to the east of Cambridge, and the Gordons.

'What a treat, Jossy,' said Marjorie, when the roast pheasant, trimmed with splendid tail feathers, were brought in. 'Gorgeous. One always feels coddled here.'

Jossy said, 'It is so important to keep up standards, don't you think, Elsa? After all, there aren't many of us old county families left. So many estates have been sold off and bought by people in trade.'

Elsa gave a little laugh. 'Aren't you being rather old-fashioned, Jossy?'

'Ownership is important. One wants to keep what one is entitled to. I'd hate to think of this' – Jossy's gesture encompassed the house, the estate, and Daragh himself, sitting opposite her – 'used by someone who was not entitled to it.'

There was a silence. Jossy smiled. 'How is your new nanny, Elsa? Hamish told me that you'd had difficulty finding the right woman. Choosing servants is such a bind if you haven't the experience.' It delighted Jossy to realize that Elsa was afraid to answer back.

'Elsa picked the most frightful creature the last time, didn't you, old girl?' Hamish Gordon's broad features were red and happy with claret. 'John hated her. Made her apple pie beds, that sort of thing.'

'John is to start prep school in September,' said Elsa, proudly.

'Did you manage to get his name down at a decent place? I could put in a word for you, if necessary.' Jossy's eyes met Elsa's. Elsa's mouth opened as if to speak, and then she closed it again in a small, thin line. Daragh seized the claret bottle and refilled the men's glasses, and began to talk about shooting. The dinner party staggered on until around eleven o'clock, the bravado display of old money undercut by an exhilarated vengefulness on Jossy's part and humiliated apprehension on Elsa's. Daragh drank heavily. He was a good host, as usual, but his face was white, closed, knowing, and he always had a glass in his hand. The Gordons left first, Hamish dragged away by Elsa, and the other two couples followed soon after.

When they were alone, Daragh muttered, 'Why did you have to be so bloody rude . . .?' and Jossy turned to him.

'Oh, I think you know, Daragh.'

The remaining colour bleached from his face. He went to the sideboard and took a cigar from the box. His back was to her as he clipped the end from his cigar.

'Elsa Gordon is a slut, Daragh.'

There was silence. Then he said, 'Sluts have their uses.'

Jossy said stubbornly, 'You can't *love* a woman like that.'

He looked back at her, his green eyes wide, his features shadowed by candlelight. 'I don't love Elsa.'

'But you sleep with her.'

Daragh smiled. 'If you wish to call it that. To tell the truth, sleeping's about the only thing I haven't done with her.'

His words shattered her frail composure. 'How could you, Daragh? Don't you see how you've hurt me?'

He blinked. 'I didn't intend to. It wasn't something I'd thought about.'

'You thought I wouldn't mind?'

'I thought you wouldn't *know*.' He frowned. 'Though now I think about it, I don't much care whether you mind or not.'

Jossy gasped. Her pain was physical. It took more courage than she had known she possessed to voice her next question. 'Don't you love me any more?'

Daragh poured himself another glass of whisky. She knew from the glitter of his eyes that he was very drunk.

'Any more?' he said. 'I never loved you, Jossy.'

'That's not true! You did! I know that you did! It was love at first sight – think of your letter!'

'Letter?' He frowned. 'Oh, *that* letter. Well, I told you that I didn't write it. Someone else did.'

She cried out, 'Don't talk like that, Daragh, please! You're drunk, aren't you?'

'I am drunk, Jossy, that's so. But I'm telling you the truth. You can believe it or not, as you wish. You don't have to worry about Elsa Gordon, though. I was getting tired of her anyway. I don't love her, I never did, and she's some funny little ways about her. I don't love you either, I've told you the truth about that, but I'll not leave you, and if I find someone to replace Elsa then I'll be discreet because of Caitlin. I lost the only woman I ever loved when I married you, you see.'

His voice was slurred by alcohol, but Jossy could still make out the words. *I lost the only woman I ever loved when I married you.* She stared at him, her heart pounding.

He muttered, 'You don't know her. Though, by God, you ought to.'

As he turned away from her, she seized his sleeve, pulling him back. 'Who? Who do you love, Daragh? Tell me!' She was screaming, and her clenched fists battered his chest. He took a step backwards, but she would not let him go, and her hands clawed at his face and hair. He seized her wrists.

'You want to know, do you? Then I'll tell you. Your half-sister, Jossy. Your father's little by-blow. Got on the wrong side of the blanket, all that.' He scowled, pulling her to him, shaking her to emphasize his words. 'Your father fucked Tilda's mother, don't you see? The old bastard got her pregnant. Tilda's aunt hated him for that. So she – the aunt – wrote that letter. She guessed that you wanted to bed me, and she thought, what a joke, to pass her niece's old lover to the daughter of the man who'd ruined her sister.'

Jossy saw that she had hurt him. A trickle of blood trailed from the corner of his mouth. She began to cry.

'What a joke,' Daragh repeated, 'that Edward de Paveley's fancy daughter should lower herself by marrying a good-for-nothing Irish peasant.'

He let go of her at last, and she sank to the floor, still weeping. As he opened the door, he said, 'You don't look like your sister at all, you know, Jossy. Tilda is ten times more beautiful than you.'

She remembered her father's funeral, and cried out, 'That girl – the one you were with in Southam—'

He paused. 'We were to marry.' The words stabbed her.

Tilda realized that she was pregnant again in the autumn of 1936. The unplanned baby made its presence felt by relieving Tilda of her breakfast each morning, something that she had not experienced with Melissa.

Max returned from Spain in mid-November, grey with exhaustion. Tilda waited until Melissa was settled in her cot, and they had dined, and were alone in the basement, and then she told him about the new baby. She saw his eyes widen and the small vertical line between his eyebrows, which had formed during the course of the year, deepen.

'I'm sorry, Max. I know you wanted to wait.'

He put his arm round her waist, pulling her towards him. 'Don't be silly.'

'Melissa's in the big cot now. The baby can go in the cradle. It'll be all right, Max.'

'Of course it will. It'll be terrific.'

Yet though he kissed her head, his good humour seemed forced.

'Are you worried about money?'

Max shrugged. 'We'll manage.'

'We always said that we wanted lots of children. It'll be good for Melissa to have a brother or sister.'

'Of course it will.' His voice was flat and expressionless.

'Then what is it, Max? Tell me!' She could feel him shutting himself off from her.

He was silent for a moment, and then he said, 'It's what I saw in Spain, Tilda. And it's what I've seen for years now in Germany. I am afraid. Before we had Melissa, I still had a bit of optimism. Not much, but enough. I don't have that now.'

'But that's over there, Max,' she said. 'It's awful, but at least it's not happening here.'

'We will not be untouched,' he said simply. 'There will be another war, and I feel . . . I feel *guilty* for bringing a child into this world. That's the truth, Tilda.' Max fumbled in his pocket for his cigarettes. 'Baldwin and most of those idiots in Parliament think that if they talk nicely to Hitler, then he'll leave us alone. But he won't, Tilda, I know he won't. I spent most of the journey back from Spain writing an article that explains that. And no-one will print it. Today I went from editor to editor, and the only paper to make me an offer was a left-wing rag that no-one reads. Too gloomy, they told me. Doesn't look on the bright side.'

Tilda stroked his hair. 'Poor Max.'

'I even thought of fighting for Spain. Lots of people have joined the International Brigades.'

'Fergus has gone. You won't, will you, Max?' The idea appalled her.

'Of course not. You know that I'm not one for joining things.' He shook his head. 'I used to pride myself on that, but now I find that I rather despise myself.'

She had to ask him. 'Max. Do you mind about the baby?'

'Oh, Tilda.' His eyes were sad. 'How could I? How could I possibly mind?'

Emily married Jan van de Criendt in the spring of 1937, the white wedding followed by a huge reception in Ely. The arrival of letters from Holland each week compensated a little for Emily's departure. Emily pressed Tilda and Max to visit, but they hadn't the money for the ferry passage. Tilda felt as though her circle of friends was inexorably shrinking. Emily was in Amsterdam and Fergus was in Spain, and Michael had been offered a lectureship at Edinburgh University. Roland Potter called in every now and then and, when Tilda could face the Underground train with a baby and carrycot, she went to see Anna at 15 Pargeter Street. Her visits became less and less frequent. Although she had stopped feeling sick, she was always terribly tired. The doctor said she was anaemic and told her to eat liver.

Joshua was born in June, when Melissa was eighteen months old. He was a breech baby and two weeks early, so the head midwife herself attended the delivery. Blurred with pain and gas and air, Tilda had none of the sense of triumph that she had experienced when Melissa was born. She felt only an overwhelming sense of relief that it was over and, when she looked into the dark blue eyes of her newborn son, an instant and intoxicating love.

Joshua was not, like his sister, an easy baby. He caught his first cold at three weeks old, and screamed with misery. Only Tilda could console him. Max went back to Germany, a journey he had put off because of the expected confinement. Tilda's stitches hurt, and her breasts wept milk that the snuffling baby struggled to take. Melissa loathed Joshua and pinched him in his cradle. Clara Franklin came to help, but both the stove and the geyser refused to work for her.

Joshua woke for a feed three times each night. At the age of six weeks, he still needed to be fed seven times in every twenty-four hours. The books said to keep him to a strict schedule, but the sound of his crying was like fingernails drawn across Tilda's heart, and she could not bear to make him wait the regulation four hours between feeds. The nurse at the clinic suggested a piece of rusk last thing at night, but Joshua sicked it up. Tilda began to think of sleep as a luxury, something other people did. She lived in a sort of haze. If she didn't write herself a list, then she forgot most of what she had meant to buy at the shops. It took almost an hour to get ready to go shopping. Both children had to be changed and dressed, and Melissa tended to bury her shoes in her sandpit. The pram had to be hauled up the area steps, no mean feat. Tilda had to find her purse and shopping bag and, if one or other child wasn't howling or wet by then, to run a comb through her hair. The pram was too big to fit into most shops, so she had to do everything with one eye continually glancing back to the doorway.

To begin with Melissa slept in the cot in Max and Tilda's room, and Joshua slept in the cradle. But though he was frailer than his sister, Joshua was also more adventurous. At three months old he hauled himself to the rim of his cradle and pivoted there, laughing. Tilda caught him before he plunged to the stone floor. At the weekend, she and Max made Melissa a little bed in the boxroom and Joshua was promoted to the cot. Melissa loved her tiny room, but Max now had to work in the bedroom or, if Joshua was asleep, in the kitchen. Once, Melissa knocked a cup of cocoa over an article Max had just finished writing, and he had to type the entire piece again. Tilda saw the whitening of Max's face, and knew that they trembled on a precipice, something chaotic and frightening just visible. The moment passed, Max took a howling Melissa onto his knee and cuddled her, and Tilda went back to the ironing, her shoulders aching with tension.

She hadn't realized how much more expensive two children would be than one. Melissa's tiny shoes cost almost as much as Tilda's own sandals, and the medicine for Joshua's earache cost ten shillings a week. Although she was expert at making stews from scrag end of lamb, or eking out a broiling fowl to last four days, that sort of cooking took time. Often she cooked with Joshua tucked under one arm, and a jealous Melissa clinging to her legs. She made all the children's clothes, but material and needles and thread cost money. She and Max were frequently too tired to talk to each other in the evenings.

Max was away from home a great deal. She missed him; his absences distanced him in more ways than the purely physical. When he returned, though she tried to make him talk about what he had seen, he would be tired, depressed, and would have closed off another little part of himself from her. When he was away, when the children had colds, or when she just couldn't face the effort of getting them ready to go to the park, then Tilda felt as though she had returned to the isolation of her childhood. Sometimes an entire week passed when the only adults she spoke to were the grocer and the milkman. When she tried to make friends with the other women at the clinic, conversation was disrupted by Joshua's screams of frustration when Melissa stole his rattle. They rarely had enough money for the cinema or a concert. Max's sweaters had more darns than knitting, and Tilda could not remember when she had last bought a new pair of stockings. She felt trapped by the poverty she'd never thought she would mind.

In October it rained ceaselessly, and Melissa caught a cold. Joshua went down with it a few days later. He had just begun to sleep through the night; now he woke at three in the morning and Tilda could not settle him until five. Melissa, always an early riser, woke for her breakfast at half past six. When Max left the house at half past seven, escaping the howls and the wet nappies and the running noses, Tilda, just for a moment, bitterly envied him his freedom. Her own throat was sore and her head ached. She queued for two hours at the doctor's for Joshua's eardrops. On the way home, she bought buns for the children's dinner, using up the remainder of the money in her purse, feeling guilty, but unable to face cooking. The cold, sharp wind made her cough. After she had hauled the pram down the steps and opened the kitchen door, she guessed from the icy air that the stove had gone out. Melissa discovered that she had left her favourite doll at the doctor's, and began to cry. Joshua joined in for good measure. Tilda got Joshua out of his snowsuit and unbuttoned Melissa's coat, and looked at the stove. The layer of ash was cold and grey and sullen. There were no matches in the drawer. Max had returned and was working upstairs in the bedroom; his coat was hanging in the hall, so Tilda went upstairs to fetch his lighter from his pocket. As she came back down, her damp shoe slipped on the steps and she fell the rest of the way, hitting her head on the banister. Tears of pain burnt her eyes, and she sat on the bottom step, her head in her hands. The children howled louder, their mouths wide Os of fear and indignation. Max emerged to discover the cause of the noise. When he saw the bruise on Tilda's forehead he bundled up the two children in their outdoor clothes again, and took them out of the house. Tilda crawled up to bed and fell asleep.

Max pacified Melissa and Joshua on the Tube by giving them chocolate drops. Joshua coughed his up; Max looked at him unsympathetically. In Fleet Street, he carried the two children, one under each arm, up the three flights of stairs to Harold Sykes's office, pausing every now and then to wipe noses.

Harold looked at the two infants with a measure of distaste. 'Nanny's day off, Max, old son?'

'Tilda's not well.' Max sat Melissa on Harold's desk, and cradled Joshua in the crook of his arm. 'I've come to ask about that staff job, Harold. Is it still on offer?'

Harold raised an eyebrow. 'You know that Freddie's been courting you for months. What's prompted the change of heart?'

'I've been a selfish blighter,' said Max bluntly. 'Cling-ing to my precious bloody principles while Tilda tries to bring up these two in a slum.'

'Bloody,' repeated Melissa carefully. 'Bloody.'

Harold gave a croak of laughter. 'You'd better give them to Lorna and come and see Freddie.' Lorna wrote the agony column. 'She loves brats. I can't bear them till they begin to be civilized.'

They moved out of the Fulham basement in the February of 1938. Max's salary, almost double what he had earned as a freelance journalist, allowed him to pay off their debts, and to put down a deposit on a house in a better district of London. The new house was narrow and four-storied, with a dark and mysterious strip of garden and a white-painted front that looked out onto a small fenced square of lawn and bushes. A girl came in three mornings a week to help with the heavy housework, and Melissa and Joshua each had their own bedroom. The house had electricity and, because of Max's job, they had a telephone installed. Tilda spent the first few months emulsioning walls and making curtains and cushions. When the weather eased, she and Melissa planted bulbs and cuttings in the garden, which was a tiny wilderness of narrow paths and dark, sooty shrubs.

In the summer, they all travelled to Holland to stay with Emily and Jan. Emily was pregnant; the baby was due in November. Jan and his younger brother, Felix, owned a boat, and they spent a week sailing on the Waddenzee, Emily sitting cushioned at the prow, the children tied by lengths of rope to the mast. They celebrated Joshua's first birthday on board the *Marika*, the single candle on his cake guttering in the fidgety wind. The whack of the sails and the frill of white water at the hull delighted Joshua, and he danced with excitement. Jan taught both Tilda and Max the rudiments of sailing. The rush of cold air, the exhilaration as the sails seized the wind and the *Marika* began to scud across the waves – all were intoxicating to Tilda.

They returned to England. Harold Sykes's daughter, Charlotte, who hadn't the least idea what to do after she had finished school, offered to help with the children. For the first time since Melissa's birth Tilda had time to herself. She made herself new clothes and attended constrained little coffee mornings to raise money for this or that. In the afternoons, she took Melissa to tea parties with her small friends or they all went to the park. Sometimes, in the evening, they went to a cocktail party or to dinner at the home of one of Max's colleagues. Tilda told herself that she was happy. She and Max and the children lived in a lovely house in a nice part of London and they wanted for nothing. She joined a sewing circle and a music club, and, sitting in a neighbour's drawing room, listening to a recording of Myra Hess playing Chopin, she found herself thinking, for the first time in years, of Daragh. Wondering what he was doing, how he was. Whether he ever thought of her. She pushed the thought ruthlessly away, but felt unsettled and frightened. She wanted another baby, but she knew that after the Munich Conference and the subsequent dismemberment of Czechoslovakia Max's resolution against having another child had hardened. When it's over, he said, and the *it* was a black, amorphous thing, growing larger, coming nearer.

Max was in Berlin when Herschel Grynzspan, a seventeen-year-old Polish Jew, shot and killed the Third Secretary at the German Embassy in Paris. Max heard the news over a crackly telephone line in a bar at the Hotel Adlon. He had been intending to leave for London the following day, but he stayed on, waiting for the inevitable retribution. *Kristallnacht* – the Night of the Broken Glass – erupted on 9 November. All over Germany, synagogues were burnt to the ground and Jewish shops and homes were invaded, their contents, down to every last teacup, smashed. Thousands of Jewish men were rounded up and sent to concentration camps. Max, standing in the shadows, watching the prayer books belonging to the frail residents of a Jewish old people's home smoulder in pyres on the street, found that his fists were clenched so tightly that his nails had drawn blood from his palms.

Kristallnacht altered him, showing him that there was no limit to the cruelty that human beings were capable of inflicting on their fellow men. When he went home, he wanted to shut himself inside his house with his beautiful wife and his beloved children, and never leave it. Outside, the world he knew was disintegrating, and he could not bear to imagine what that falling apart would bring in its wake. Here there was a gentle sort of order behind the chaos: though the floors might be littered with building bricks and dolls' clothes, there was always food on the table at supper-time, clean shirts hung in his wardrobe, and the children tucked up in bed at seven o'clock at night. He didn't know how Tilda did it, but he knew that he needed it.

He did not speak to Tilda about the things he had seen. To tell her about old men beaten in the street, or babies snatched from their mothers' arms, would sully their home: he would feel that he had brought evil into it. Yet he could not escape the shadows of what was to come. The trenches in Hyde Park, the air-raid shelters built in neighbours' gardens, the gas masks on their pegs in the hall, all were ominous realities. At night, he dreamt of bombs falling on London, destroying his home, burying his family. When he made love to Tilda now, it was with a sort of desperation, a desire to lose himself in the softness and beauty of her body.

Though a mood of greater realism followed the false euphoria of Munich, Max was still constrained in what he could write. Getting ready to return to the Continent, he was aware of frustration, mixed with dread. When he went to the bedroom to pack, Tilda was folding her blouses into a neat pile.

He said, 'Are you going to stay with Sarah?'

She shook her head. 'Aunt Sarah's coming here. I'm coming with you, Max. It's all arranged. Aunt Sarah and Charlotte will look after the children, and we can have a few days together, just the two of us. I'll stay with Emily while you visit Germany – I'm longing to see her baby.' Tilda put the blouses in her case, and turned to him and took him in her arms. 'It'll be better, won't it, Max, if I come?' He drew her to him and kissed her: hot, hungry kisses that made both of them gasp for breath.

They drove to Harwich the following day, taking turns at the wheel. The passage across the North Sea was grey and windswept and they stood on the deck, Max's arm round Tilda's shoulders, until the sky darkened. Docking at the Hook of Holland the following morning, they caught the train to Amsterdam. That night, they dined with Emily and Jan, and admired William, the van de Criendts' son, who was large and blond and placid. In the morning, they caught the train to the border. Max wanted to see the German troop emplacements.

Yet he discovered a different story from the one he had expected to tell. When they alighted at a station near the border, Max saw a dozen women waiting on the platform, trolleys of sandwiches and cakes in front of them. A train whistled, and a thick caterpillar cloud of white smoke formed along the distant railway line, and emerging from it Max could discern an engine, followed by a long snake of carriages. The women on the platform began to pour lemonade into beakers and to remove greaseproof paper wrappings from sandwiches and cakes. The train rushed into the station, brakes screaming. Max could see faces pressed against the windows. As the engine slowed and the smoke cleared, features solidified. All the passengers were children. The boys wore tweed suits, and the girls were dressed in thick winter coats, buttoned to their chins.

Max turned aside to speak to one of the women. She told him that the children on the train were German Jews, from Berlin, on their way to Britain. The children were given food and drink at the station, and a toy. The German authorities had allowed each child to take only one small suitcase and ten marks. Soon they would travel on to the Hook of Holland, and then to Harwich.

Max looked for Tilda, to explain this extraordinary exodus to her, but could not find her. Then he caught sight of her, moving away from him through the crowds, towards the children. He saw her stoop and smile, her hair golden in the winter sunshine, and take a small boy's hands in hers, and speak to him until he too smiled. She was surrounded by children, lost in a sea of children. Max, standing back, watched her move away from him, until he could no longer see her.

Kristallnacht had brought home at last to a self-deceiving British government the urgency of the plight of the German Jews. Entry requirements were eased, permitting the transport of Jewish children into Britain. A few days after she returned from Holland, Tilda started voluntary work with the Refugee Children's Movement, the organization responsible for the *Kindertransporte*. She had intended to spend two mornings a week with the RCM, while Charlotte Sykes looked after Melissa and Joshua, but the need was vast, particularly for someone who could both type and speak German, and somehow the RCM began to swallow up more and more of her time.

At first there were two children's transports each week, from Berlin or Vienna, travelling to Britain via Holland. Though the children for the *Kindertransporte* were selected in Germany, letters flooded into the Bloomsbury offices of the RCM, letters that pleaded desperately for help, that enclosed photographs of smiling, dimpled children. Every child who arrived in Britain had to be found either a bed in a hostel or suitable foster parents. Tilda and Max travelled to Harwich to meet a boatload of child refugees. The port was grey and bleak, and the wind curled breakers from the sea. As they walked through Customs, some of the children, frightened by the uniforms of the officials, began to empty their pockets onto the tables: a pathetic assortment of pencils and string, hair ribbons and sticky boiled sweets.

Few of the refugees spoke any English. Tilda greeted them, trying to put them at their ease. The photographer who had driven up from London with Max and Tilda took a picture of a pretty dark-haired girl, clutching the doll she had been given in Holland. The children were taken by bus to Dovercourt, a few miles along the coast. Dovercourt was in the summer a holiday camp, with pebbledashed chalets and a communal dining hall. Now the wind lashed the fragile little buildings and in the distance the sea had retreated, showing shiny dun mud flats. Tilda helped the other volunteers to serve tea. A group of girls huddled together in a corner of the room, and the boys, determined to put on a brave face, bit their lips to keep the tears from their eyes. Returning to London that night, the photographer fell asleep in the back of the car. Max, driving, was very quiet. Tilda knew that Max, too, was imagining what the parents of those children must have suffered, to send them alone to a foreign country.

The RCM took over Tilda's life. If she wasn't at the office or meeting new arrivals in Harwich, then she was fund-raising or coaxing warm clothes and food from anyone she could think of. When she was elected to the post of secretary of her local committee, it became her responsibility to organize the selection of foster homes and their twice-yearly inspection. The foster parents collected their children from a large, gloomy room near Liverpool Street Station.

As the train slid into Liverpool Street, the refugee children jammed their faces against the carriage windows. Attached to every child was a brown luggage label with a number written on it. Lines of foster parents stood along the platform. Some children shrieked with recognition and pleasure as they alighted from the train; others hung back, exhausted by their long journey, confused by unfamiliar faces and a strange language. Tilda spoke to them reassuringly in German, and shepherded them to the nearby reception centre, where other volunteers sat behind desks, filling in forms. Every child had to be matched to its foster parents. Some parents failed to turn up on the correct day, others arrived to find their adoptive children missing, taken from the train at random by the Gestapo at the border with Holland, and returned to Germany. Some of the smaller children cried, cold and alone and bewildered. The older boys, who would eventually be taken to a hostel, kicked their heels and talked loudly. The crowds thinned out until only the older boys and a girl were left. The girl stared resolutely down at her boots.

Tilda glanced at her watch. It was almost half past three. She beckoned to the solitary girl. '*Wie heisst du, liebchen?*'

'Rosi,' whispered the girl. 'Rosi Liebermann.' She was rather stout, and her mousy hair was swept back into an unbecoming pigtail.

Tilda heard the clack of high heels. A woman was crossing the room towards them. She wore a smart wool coat, a little felt hat with a feather, and was impeccably made up.

'Are you Rosi's befriender, Mrs . . .' Tilda glanced at her list. 'Mrs Stannard?'

'I am Mrs Stannard.' A leather-gloved hand was briefly extended to Tilda. Mrs Stannard glanced at Rosi, and then she moved a yard or two away and whispered to Tilda.

'I thought she'd be prettier! She isn't like her photograph at all.'

Every now and then, a foster child did not live up to its adoptive parent's dreams. Tilda said patiently, 'Rosi is twelve, Mrs Stannard. Children change very quickly at that age. The photograph was probably taken a few months ago.'

Mrs Stannard stared once more at Rosi. 'It won't do,' she said suddenly. 'I'm sorry, but it just won't do. And I really must go, or I shall miss my train.' She marched back across the hall, heels clattering.

Tilda had the impression that although Rosi knew no English, she had understood every word of that conversation. Rosi's nose was suspiciously red, and her lips pressed very tightly together. Tilda ran the possibilities through in her head. There was the hostel, but that was intended for older children. Or she could try to contact one of the foster parents whose child had been detained in Germany, to see whether they would consider taking in this young girl instead. The same thing might happen: Rosi might be rejected again. Years ago, she had failed little Liesl Toller: she must not fail another child.

She took the girl's hand. 'Rosi. Would you like to come home with me?'

By the time all the forms had been filled in and Rosi's few belongings had been assembled, it was already four o'clock. Then the Tube trains were packed, and because of Rosi's suitcase they couldn't squeeze into the first two trains that stopped at the station. Rosi's feet, clad in stout boots, struggled to keep up with Tilda as she almost ran home from the Underground station.

Voices assailed her as she unlocked the front door and walked down the hall.

'Mummy, Daddy dropped the jelly and it went all over the carpet—'

'I have to put a call through to Paris—'

'Mrs Franklin, Joshua rubbed syrup in his hair, so I gave him a bath.'

She put her arm around Rosi and drew her into the dining room. 'Joshua – Melissa – there's someone I want you to meet.' Gently, Tilda drew Rosi forward. 'I want you to meet Rosi Liebermann, who is your extra sister.'

CHAPTER SEVEN

'Rosi was the first of my extra children,' said Tilda, after she had introduced us. It was Tilda's eighty-first birthday party.

I shook hands. I estimated that Rosi Liebermann was now in her late sixties. She was tall and Junoesque, draped in colourful scarves, her long grey pigtail wound in a coronet around her head.

'I was a dumpling,' Rosi said, and laughed. 'I grew four inches in my twelfth year, and acquired a magnificent bosom. No wonder that poor woman ran from me on sight.'

'Rosi is a writer,' said Tilda, but I knew that, of course. In my mid-teens, I had been addicted to Rosi Liebermann's long, escapist, historical epics.

One of the great-grandchildren grabbed at Tilda's knees and in spite of her age, in spite of her frail health, she scooped him up and the crowds closed around them. Her family had spread through The Red House; they shrieked and argued everywhere. Cars were parked along the street, visitors squeezed through the tall, tight ranks of box hedges, and were spat out onto the forecourt of the house. The doorbell rang constantly, and the sound of champagne corks was like a drumbeat. The room heaved and throbbed with Tilda's confident, noisy, successful relatives. Those who did not dress elegantly, dressed originally; those who were not beautiful were stylish or unusual. There wasn't a plain, dumpy, dull person there.

I turned back to Rosi Liebermann. 'So many of Tilda's children and grandchildren seem to be terribly illustrious.'

Her pleasant face creased in a smile. 'Oh, I think that I'm forgotten already. My sort of fiction doesn't last. Joshua is famous, of course. It's a pity he couldn't be here today.'

'I can't see his son,' I couldn't resist saying.

'Patrick?'

Whenever I heard a car draw up outside, I looked out through the open window, but it was never the blue Renault. I felt exasperated with myself for looking; I told myself that Patrick had invited me to Wheeler's to help with the book. That was all.

'Tilda has always been very close to Patrick,' said Rosi. 'He stayed here in the school holidays when he was a child.'

The Red House, with its secret gardens and tall trees, must have been a wonderful place for a child. 'And you, Miss Liebermann?' I asked. 'Did you once live here?'

'I holidayed here, that's all. I was married by the time Tilda bought The Red House.'

'I've been researching the *Kindertransporte*,' I told her. Ten thousand children had been scooped up and saved from Nazi Germany in 1939 – a fraction of the doomed six million, but a significant number nevertheless. 'The train journey ... Holland ... getting ready to leave Germany ... Do you remember it?'

Rosi put aside her glass. 'I can't remember the

weeks before I left Berlin. I suspect that my parents must have tried to make life normal, unmemorable. Although those were not, of course, normal times. I didn't really understand what was happening until we were at the station in Berlin, and it was time to leave. I thought I'd see my parents again in a few weeks' time, you understand. But when the engine started up, I saw how my mother went behind my father and put her hands over her face. She could not bear to see me go. She could not bear to think that it might be the last time.'

I whispered, 'And was it?'

'Oh yes. Both my parents died in Auschwitz.'

I mumbled something inadequate, appalled by such a separation, such loss.

'Tilda and Max became my family. Tilda and Max and Aunt Sarah. I stayed with Aunt Sarah for much of that first year in England. I was unwell – tonsillitis – and the doctor thought I needed country air, so Tilda sent me to the Fens. When Max was sent abroad by his newspaper in 1939, he didn't think it safe to take me to Paris. I hadn't a proper passport or visa, you see, so I went back to Aunt Sarah. The Franklins returned to London in December, and we all spent Christmas together. Then, in the New Year, Max was posted to Amsterdam.' Rosi paused. 'I knew that Tilda found it hard to choose – whether to go abroad with Max, or to stay in England so that all her children could be together – so I told her how much I enjoyed living in Southam. And it was true, I did enjoy it. I was a city girl, so the country was a great adventure to me.'

Someone yelled, 'Rosi! Rosi – come over here and tell Tilda what Professor Hermann said—' and Rosi Liebermann excused herself and disappeared into the throng.

I heard feet crunching on the gravel below, and looked down again. I glimpsed Patrick's fair head first and then, framed by the box hedge, I saw the dark-haired woman who walked beside him, and the little girl who held her hand.

I guessed who they were, of course. The woman must be Patrick's wife, and the child must be his daughter, Ellie. I grabbed a glass of orange juice from a tray and ducked through the crowd, escaping along the corridor, heading for the little room that Tilda had set aside for me. I had fallen into the routine of driving to The Red House on Monday, talking to Tilda and staying overnight, and returning to London on Tuesday afternoon. I spent the rest of the week writing up my notes and doing background research.

The room was cluttered with box-files and notebooks referring to the *Kindertransporte* and the Refugee Children's Movement. Looking around, I acknowledged that I felt miserable because, compared to Tilda's, my own family was pale and anaemic. A father, a sister, two nephews and a brother-in-law. The sum total of my living relations. My father and I invariably irritated or upset each other, my nephews were too young for sensible conversation and, if my brother-in-law wasn't working, he was so tired that he snored in an armchair in front of the television. Though I love my sister, we both seem to want what the other has. I envied Tilda her large, noisy, colourful family. It was what I should have liked for myself, and I did not enjoy the feeling of exclusion that an outsider must inevitably endure at a celebration such as today's.

I tried to distract myself by thinking about the question that had recently preoccupied me: the events of the year of 1947. I had asked Tilda, but she had said, maddeningly, 'We have only reached 1939, Rebecca. I am too old to dart around the years.' Tilda was organized and autocratic and, over the months, I had become very fond of her. She had never lost the energy and impulsiveness of her girlhood; her enthusiasm and love of life made me feel tired and cynical.

I collected some documents, enough to keep me busy through the weekend, and slipped out of the house. I thought that Tilda, surrounded by her relatives, would not notice that I had left without saying goodbye. I had almost reached the gate when I heard footsteps behind me. I looked back.

Patrick was running down the path, a small child clasped in his arms. The documents slipped out of my hands and swooped and fluttered, clinging to the wide topiaried boxes like posters on a billboard.

He said, 'I saw you from the solar.'

I grabbed at the papers. The action filled in the typically awkward silence that followed. 'I have to go.'

'Joan's about to serve the food.'

I shook my head. 'It's a family thing, Patrick.' I made sure I didn't sound too forlorn. 'And I've work to do.'

'I'll walk you to your car.'

I said sharply, 'Won't your wife miss you?' and he looked down at me.

'Jennifer? I don't think so.' He sounded weary rather than bitter. The little girl wriggled in his arms, looked at me briefly, and said, 'Put me down, Daddy. I want to play in the trees.'

Patrick said, 'Ellie, this is Rebecca. Rebecca, this is my daughter, Ellie,' but she had gone, jumping out of his grasp, ducking under the twisting yellow branches of the box.

'She's beautiful,' I said, and she was.

'She's a livewire.' He watched her adoringly. 'She spent the weekend with me. She won't sit still for more than ten seconds at a time, will you, Ellie?' He held out a hand, and she squirmed out from the box tree and ran to him, and he hugged her.

We walked along the road to where I had parked my car. The countryside was at its best: a froth of May blossom on the hawthorns, leaves uncurling on the trees. I unlocked my car door and put the documents on the back seat. Ellie, in blithe disregard of her white party dress, played happily in a puddle at the side of the road. Patrick, like his daughter, looked fidgety.

He said, 'I've been so damned busy, but I meant to phone you.'

'About Daragh?'

'Daragh?' He looked bewildered. 'No. I thought that we—'

'Patrick. Oh, *Ellie*. Patrick, how could you?'

I looked up. Jennifer Franklin, her beautiful face creased with displeasure, marched along the verge and pulled her daughter out of the puddle. 'Patrick, her *dress*. I bought it in *Paris*.'

I thought it time to go. I called a quick farewell, climbed into my car, and drove away.

The doorbell rang just as I tipped the contents of the box onto the floor. When I peeped out of the window I saw Toby. My hand shook as I took the chain off the door.

'I thought I'd call in on my way home,' he said. He stood on the front step, untypically hesitant. 'Bit of a nerve coming here like this, I know, but there are things we should talk about.'

He followed me into the living room. I said, 'I thought everything was said last October.'

'I was a bastard. A complete bastard. I don't blame you for hating me.'

I felt an ill-natured pleasure in his discomfort. 'I don't hate you, Toby,' I said lightly, as I heaved a pile of books from an armchair so that he could sit down. 'I did once, but I don't now.'

'You're indifferent to me. I think that's worse.'

I wanted to say all the harsh, vindictive things I had not been capable of saying when he left me. Then I saw the misery in his eyes, and I felt ashamed of myself, and went into the kitchen to make coffee. The simple, repetitive actions calmed me: measuring the beans, grinding them, pouring on the boiling water, arranging biscuits on a plate. I thought of my mother, scrubbing the kitchen floor after my father had come home from college in one of his more rancorous moods, or Jane, rinsing out baby clothes in the sink, her eyes sapphire chips set in planes of stone.

I carried the coffee in, poured it out. Black, no sugar: it irked me that I had not forgotten. I said, 'Why now, Toby? After so long?' I had built a fence around myself in the months since we had parted; I did not want him to breach it.

'I tried before, but I couldn't. And the longer you leave it, the more difficult it becomes – the more aware you are that you should have done something weeks or months ago. Then I thought I'd write, but that would have seemed cowardly.' He looked up at me. 'When we lost the baby, I just couldn't cope. Nothing like that had ever happened to me, you see, Rebecca. I couldn't accept it, I wanted to pretend that it hadn't happened.'

My first feeling was one of surprise. Then a flicker of relief. I had always assumed that Toby had left because of me, because I was somehow not up to scratch. That the failure of our relationship was my responsibility. Yet Toby's version of events convinced me: it fitted my knowledge of the man I had once loved. Toby Carne was the only child of doting parents. He had been to Westminster and then to Cambridge and he had become a successful barrister. He had probably had everything he wanted until the day his child had begun to bleed from my womb, six and a half months too early.

'I'm not trying to make excuses,' he added. 'I just wanted to explain. I don't think I was particularly rational at the time.'

People react to loss in different ways. After our mother died, my sister Jane fell in love with Steven, got married, and had two children, all in the space of three years. Whereas I put on a stone and a half, and wept whenever I saw a fifty-fivish woman in a blue suit. Quite a lot of fifty-fivish women wear blue suits.

There was a long silence. Of course, Toby's explanation had come too late. Although, if I was honest with myself, a month would have been too late, or a week, or a day, or an hour. *I don't think we should see so much of each other*. Those words had sown a seam of distrust that I was unable to rid myself of. I shrugged. 'It doesn't matter now.'

He smiled, interpreting my muttered words as forgiveness. I realized then that I was free of him. Once his smile would have melted my heart. Now, not a vestige of that sharp, sudden initial attraction lingered, and for that I felt profound thankfulness.

He said suddenly, 'I saw that television programme you made.'

'*Sisters of the Moon*? Rather an appropriate theme, don't you think? Lost babies, I mean.'

The smile faded. A considerable proportion of the

documentary had been devoted to attempting to track down the daughter of Ivy Lunn, the woman who had been raped and incarcerated in a mental institution. I had found Ivy's child – a pensioner herself now – living in a council house in Letchworth and, with the permission of both women, we had filmed their reunion. Tacky, I suppose, but touching all the same.

He asked me what I was doing now, and I explained about Tilda. Toby's eyes narrowed and he said, 'She's some relation to Patrick Franklin. You telephoned me—'

'Tilda is Patrick's grandmother.'

'I've come across him a few times. And I know Jenny, of course.'

'Patrick's wife? What's she like?'

'Beautiful. Quite stunning.' I had seen that for myself. 'She modelled for a while, you know.'

'But . . . difficult?'

Toby looked surprised. 'Not at all. Jenny is perfectly sweet. They split up because of the family, didn't they? Poor old Jen couldn't cope with the in-laws. She said they closed ranks, made her feel an outsider. Wouldn't let her in on the family secrets.'

I was about to say that I hadn't thought that there were any family secrets, when I recalled Tilda's diaries and the eventful year of 1947. Jossy had died, and Max had gone, and Daragh had disappeared somewhere in the middle of a cold, lonely night. I glanced at my watch.

'I'm expecting a pupil in a few minutes.'

'Good Lord, Rebecca – are you teaching again? I thought you hated it.'

My annoyance returned. 'I do. But I need the money, you see, Toby.' I stood up to show him out.

*   *   *

'We were in Paris when war was declared,' said Tilda. 'I remember that Max and I walked along the banks of the Seine that evening, and wondered what it would mean to us. I tried to make him promise that nothing would separate us, but he wouldn't, of course. Max always took his promises seriously.'

It was the end of May, half-term week. Tilda had invited me for lunch. There had been a tableful of us: Melissa's three grandsons, who were now playing cricket noisily on the front lawn, a middle-aged man who had once been one of Tilda's Red House extra children, and Matty, who was supposed to be revising. 'They're just school exams,' she said, cushioning her head on her books, and plugging in her Walkman. 'They don't count.' Now we sat in the garden behind The Red House, in the little clearing with the stone nymph. Matty was lying along the path, bordered by clumps of lavender. Her dress code did not seem to permit her to make any concession to the heat: she wore black from neck to ankle. Bees buzzed at her and she brushed them carelessly away.

We talked about the events of 1939 for a while, and then there was a distant crash: Matty, whose headphones shut her off from the outside world, did not look up, but Tilda started and rose out of her chair.

'Excuse me a moment, won't you, Rebecca?' She walked slowly back to the house.

I put aside my pad and pen. The garden, with its secret paths and festoons of roses, should have cheered me up, but failed to. I was to visit my father for the remainder of the week, a prospect that filled me with gloom. And though I would have liked to have been able to say that I had hardly given Toby a thought during the days that had passed since his visit, it would not have been true.

When I thought about him, I shuttled in a futile fashion between anger and regret. My anger was with myself, for not seeing him clearly long ago. The regret was that he should have come upon me at my worst: a cluttered, dusty flat, hair that needed washing, and a career all too obviously struggling.

Tilda reappeared. 'Roddy hit the ball into the cucumber frame,' she explained. 'The boys have cleared up the broken glass, but he was upset, so I said he could make tea.'

'Treacle sandwiches,' said Matty, who had unplugged herself. 'Roddy always makes treacle sandwiches. *Gross.*'

'Will you stay, Rebecca?' asked Tilda.

I declined, less because of the treacle sandwiches than because I had to get ready for my trip to Yorkshire.

'Melissa has invited Joan and me to spend the rest of the week at the cottage,' added Tilda. The Parkers had a cottage in the West Country. 'There isn't a telephone. If you should need anything . . .' She frowned. 'Have you Patrick's home phone number, Rebecca? No? He has a key, which he could lend you, if necessary.'

My father's house – detached, built of stone – is beside a road that leaps and curls through the North Yorkshire Moors. The stone has darkened over the hundred and twenty years since its building, and when it rains, water from the hillside gathers in pools in the back garden. The house is a mile from the nearest village, eight miles from a doctor's surgery or a supermarket. My father does not drive and, since deregulation, the bus passes his house only twice a day.

I arrived late on Monday afternoon, having become entangled in Bank Holiday traffic. I squeezed my car up the driveway and hauled my bag indoors. We ate Eccles cakes and drank tea in the kitchen, while conversation stuttered like my Fiesta attempting a steep hill. The kitchen combined Spartan neatness with an underlying level of grime that shocked even me. The house was too big for one person – my father's last dream, he and my mother had moved to Yorkshire two years before she died. The stairs were, like the drive, both steep and narrow, the sash windows temperamental and leaky. The bathroom had an overhead cistern and a high-sided cast iron bath that took hours to fill. In winter, clouds would form from your breath when you stuck your head out from beneath the blankets.

I drove my father to the supermarket the following day. Most of what I tried to put in the trolley he took out, tutting at the price. I had seen that his small fridge was almost empty, containing things like half-full tins of meatballs covered with greaseproof paper, or a single sardine nestling menacingly on a saucer. My father boasted that he could with careful management make a loaf of bread last the week. I cooked dinners for him of the traditional British food men of his generation prefer – stews and roasts and pies. No pasta, no garlic or spices. I scrubbed the grease and dust from the quarry-tiles in the kitchen and cleaned out his cupboards with a vigour and energy I rarely apply to my own. I hacked away at the weeds in his garden, found a grocer who promised to deliver supplies and, in the evenings, I read. My father has hundreds of books; he used to teach English Literature. In literature, he delights in the passionate and the exquisite, yet in reality he dismisses passion as false and self-indulgent. His favourite era encompasses the Elizabethan and Jacobean, all those jewelled little sonnets, those perfect miniatures of verse. My mother, who was a calligrapher, illuminated some of his favourites. One was framed in the room in which I slept. *I long to talk with some old lover's ghost, Who died before the god of love was born . . .*

On the morning on which I was to leave, my father cycled to the village to buy me ham for my sandwiches. I could have explained to him that I didn't need sandwiches, that I could stop at a motorway service station. Or that I don't even much like ham. But I didn't say anything because I knew that he wanted to do it for me. I watched him put on his flat cap and fit cycle clips round his turn-ups and set off on his old sit-up-and-beg bicycle for the village, slow and wobbling as he climbed the hill. And I had to turn away and blow my nose, and go quickly back into the house.

The drive back to London was slow and tedious. All three lanes of traffic stuttered to a halt outside Northampton. The car radio informed me that a Deranged Person had found his way onto the motorway, and that there had consequently been an accident. Pewter-grey clouds blanked out the blue sky, and the air was still and heavy, appropriate weather for lunacy. When I arrived home, two hours later than I had anticipated, Jason Darke, my most aggravating pupil, was waiting on my doorstep, smoking a quick ciggie. Jason – nineteen, good-looking and incorrigibly lazy – had failed his History A level the previous year, and looked likely to do so again. When he did not complete the homework I set him, which was most weeks, he employed a clumsy charm that was irritating rather than endearing. He had a good brain, but preferred to avoid using it. Most annoying of all, his blithe confidence in his future was probably justified; his father was Something in the City, and Jason expected him to use his influence successfully.

He was more irksome than usual, flirting with me in a condescendingly half-hearted way, not bothering to disguise his yawns. After we had struggled one-sidedly with the decline of the Liberal Party for an hour and he had left the house, the realization that I would have to take on more pupils next year simply to maintain my mediocre standard of living was infinitely depressing. *Good Lord, Rebecca – are you teaching again?* I dragged the latest box from Tilda's house out from beneath the desk, but could not interest myself in its contents. On top of the pile were some yellowing photographs cut from a newspaper: a fishing boat; a portrait of a younger Tilda, her hair long and loose, with a serious expression on her face. I went to the fridge and poured myself a large glass of wine, but the alcohol failed to raise my spirits. I was pursued – albeit in a rather desultory fashion – by old lovers and callow youths. My financial situation was precarious: my advance would barely cover my living expenses over the eighteen months or so it would take me to complete Tilda's biography. I was in my early thirties, without a partner or a child or a steady income. The wine blurred things, staving off the possibility that I might just sit in the middle of the carpet and howl. I realized that I hadn't eaten since the sandwiches on the motorway, and wondered if I'd enough money for a pizza. I scrabbled in my bag for my purse, opened it, and took out the scrap of paper on which Tilda had written Patrick's home telephone number.

If I hadn't been a little drunk, I'd never have dialled. I rose unsteadily to my feet, picked up the receiver, and stabbed the buttons. When Patrick answered, I had no idea what to say.

'Hello? Hello?' Patrick's tone altered as he repeated the word, growing more impatient. 'Who's calling?'

'It's Rebecca,' I managed.

'Rebecca?' he said. 'I was going to phone you.'

I blinked, and stared at the receiver. 'Why?'

'I'm going to look at a house tomorrow. I wondered whether you'd like to come with me.'

'House?' I said blankly.

'I'm thinking of buying a place in Cumbria. The estate agent has sent me particulars.'

'I saw you as more of a Docklands sort of person, Patrick. A weekend place?'

'Something like that. Well?'

I imagined he was like that in court, barking short, incriminating questions at hesitant witnesses. 'All right,' I said.

He picked me up from my flat at seven o'clock the following morning. Friday's gloomy skies had cleared, and the haze of cloud thinned as we drove out of London. I realized as we left the city behind that I felt happy. I had almost forgotten what it was like, to feel happy.

As we headed north, I said, 'I'm travelling to the Netherlands at the beginning of June to look at the places where Tilda lived. I've got some names out of her address book – people to look up.'

He focused on the road ahead. 'Who have you spoken to?'

'Jan van de Criendt, and a woman who was Tilda's neighbour in 1940. And Hanna Schmidt's daughter. She lives in Scheveningen.'

I talked a bit more about Holland, and then I let the subject drop. I still sensed Patrick's hostility to Tilda's decision to make public the story of her life, and I didn't want to spoil the mood of the day. Telemann and Vivaldi sang from the tape-player and we stopped every now and then for coffee. Somewhere north of Nottingham, the countryside rucked and rose, shedding the green and brown dullness of middle England. Sunlight glittered on silvery lakes trapped by hills, and trees rose from slopes hazed azure with bluebells.

We stopped briefly for lunch, and then drove on. The trees became sparser, the grass replaced by heather, boulders showing through the earth like bones. Patrick consulted the map. 'There should be a side road and then a track to the left.'

The side road proved to be the width of the Renault, circling up through the fells. We almost missed the track, two parallel ruts in the heather, climbing up the hillside at an unreasonable angle.

'We'll have to walk a bit. Have you suitable shoes?'

I was wearing sandals. I thought of adders, and then put them firmly out of my mind and climbed out of the car. When I looked back, the road was just a grey ribbon and the pub where we had eaten our lunch was less than a matchbox.

The fellside soared above us, rising up towards the sky like a great grey and purple tidal wave. Patrick said, 'There it is.'

I could see nothing but a few tumbledown farm buildings, high up on the fell. Then I glimpsed, incongruously, the estate agent's board, pinned to a fence, flapping frantically in the wind.

'*That?*'

Patrick walked ahead, flattening a path through the heather. Though in the valley it had been windless, up here the breeze was both capricious and cold. Eggs of snow curled in the shaded hollows around the peaks. As we neared it, I saw that the farm consisted of three buildings – a farmhouse and two outbuildings. Sunlight glimmered on the thick roof-slates; in winter the fellside would shelter the house from the snow and winds of the north.

I was out of breath by the time we reached the house. Too much sitting at a desk and not enough exercise, I told myself sternly. I would sign up for an aerobics class in the autumn. Meanwhile Patrick had taken a key from his pocket, and was flicking through the estate agent's flysheet.

'We might as well start with the farmhouse. We can look at the byre and outhouse afterwards.'

He fitted the key to the lock. It creaked resentfully, and when he pushed it open I smelt cobwebs and damp, evidence of a building too long deserted. I heard tiny scurrying feet, and my eyes struggled to adjust themselves to the lack of light.

'I should have brought a torch,' said Patrick. 'You don't mind spiders, do you?'

Not in moderation, I wanted to say. I could not see how he could possibly consider buying such a heap, even as a weekend retreat. Then he pushed open a door and, all of a sudden, I did see. Light streamed through the big stone window, larger even than the window in Tilda's solar, and painted long white bands on the stone-flagged floor.

'Heavens,' I whispered.

'Exactly.' He was smiling.

I've never been good at judging distances, so I could not say whether from that window you could see for five miles or for ten or for fifty. All I know was that it was as though you could see the whole world, in all its splendour, like a tapestry spread out before you. The chain stitch of the roads and dry stone walls; the herringbone of the rivers and streams; French knots of boulders and barns, and lakes and tarns of cloth of silver.

I dragged my gaze from the view and looked around the room. It was vast, its height reaching the vaulted roof, the fireplace immense and baronial. I imagined it with curtains and rugs and burning logs and candles in sconces. When we went through to the next room, the kitchen, I saw that it too was huge.

'At least there's an Aga.'

'Circa 1925,' said Patrick, inspecting it. 'Coal-fired.'

It would take about three hours, I thought, to warm up an M & S Chicken Kiev for one. We toured the rest of the house, in which a bathroom was conspicuously absent, and then went to look at the outbuildings. Heavy clouds had gathered on the peaks while we had been inside. They blackened the fellside.

'The ... um ... facilities,' said Patrick, glancing dubiously at the brochure and then opening a door.

There was a sort of bench, set with a wooden plank in which three holes of diminishing circumference were cut. Father, Mother and Baby Bear. I shut the door quickly.

Patrick strode to the next building. 'The byre,' he said, opening the door to a huge barn. 'To protect the sheep in winter.'

While we were inside inspecting the dark cavern, the rain began. It drove down in silvery stair-rods, flattening the heather, bouncing on boulders buried in the gorse. We were both wearing jeans and T-shirts. I stood in the doorway, watching the rain, and Patrick came to stand beside me. Where his body touched mine – shoulder, elbow, hip – my skin tingled.

'What do you think?' he said.

I stared at him blankly. His eyes were blue in the

centre of the iris, a ring of charcoal grey around the outside.

'The house,' he added patiently.

'*Oh* . . . well, it's wonderful, of course.'

'Stunning, isn't it? In London one feels so hemmed in. Here – well, you can breathe, can't you?'

'But it would be an impossible place to live, Patrick. Difficult . . . and inaccessible.'

'I've always liked the difficult and the inaccessible.' His eyes still held mine. 'So much more of a challenge.'

I said quickly, 'You'd go mad after an hour or two. So isolated. You'd miss the pubs and clubs and restaurants.'

'I wouldn't. Not in the least. Nor would I miss the traffic jams and the Tube at rush hour and the poor sods you see begging on the Embankment. Some of the company I'd miss, though.'

He leaned forward and his lips touched my forehead. The rain had thickened.

'Me?' I whispered.

'Mmm. If I abandon the law and become a gentleman farmer, would you miss me, Rebecca Bennett?'

I didn't say another word. Instead, I touched his lips with mine, small, delicate kisses that made me close my eyes, drunk with the nearness of him. His hands rested lightly on my waist and then travelled up my spine beneath my T-shirt, his palms gliding over my bare skin.

The rain drummed against the stone roof of the byre. I had forgotten that it was possible to want someone so much that you don't care where, or how. I had forgotten how much more powerful are the desires of the body than the warnings of the mind. I made love to him, lying in the straw, with the barn door open and the rain beating down, breaking the silence of the hills.

*

Caitlin Canavan started at her new school in the January of 1939, when she was five. Daragh had put the day off as long as possible, and had suggested a governess, but Jossy had been insistent. With Caitlin at school, she would have Daragh to herself again.

For her first day, Caitlin wore a navy gymslip and white blouse, a grey tweed coat and a grey felt hat trimmed with a blue band, pulled over her black curls. Daragh took a photograph of her standing on the front steps of the Hall, her tiny leather satchel clutched in her hand. 'Don't you look the little princess, Kate,' he said, and hugged her before they climbed in the car. Then they drove to Ely, and escorted Caitlin through the exclusive gates of Burwood School. A teacher took Caitlin from them, and they were left empty-handed as their daughter joined a long crocodile of little girls heading into the building.

Daragh watched Caitlin until she could no longer be seen, and then he turned on his heel and walked briskly back to the car. He tossed the keys to Jossy. 'You drive back, Joss. I've business here. I'll walk home. I could do with a walk.'

Jossy sat in the car, the keys in the ignition, but did not yet start up the engine. She felt, as she always did on such occasions, a terrible disappointment and grief. Her grief was not for her daughter, who had begun a new stage of her life, but for her husband. She knew that Daragh would spend the morning with a woman. She knew that she, as always, had hoped for too much.

As she drove back to Southam, Jossy repeated to herself all the things she always said on such occasions. That Daragh was hers, and that none of his affairs lasted for more than a few months. That she, and only she, slept under the same roof as him at night, and dined at the same table. That his wedding ring was on her left hand, and that she had given birth to his daughter. That he would eventually grow out of his need for those other women. They might hurt her, but she need not fear them.

She feared only Tilda, whom she had never seen. Tilda, her sister. She often thought about Tilda; it was like scratching away at an unhealed sore. She believed Tilda to be the twin of those imaginary sisters of her childhood, lighthearted and beautiful and charming. All that she herself was not. She guessed that Tilda was the sort of person for whom everything was easy. Jossy hated her.

The winter, which was ice-cold and wind-ridden, claimed the life of Christopher de Paveley that February. At the funeral, great draughts shrieked through the gaps around windows and doors, and seared the stained glass with ice. The mourners – ancient old schoolfriends of Christopher's, decrepit comrades-in-arms of his service in the Great War, and red-faced shooting companions – wore their furs and overcoats. They brayed the hymns and joined in loudly in the responses. Though Jossy's uncle had been dead only a few days, Daragh found that it was an effort to remember what he had looked like. Stooping, thin, whey-faced, like his son. Daragh's gaze alighted on Kit de Paveley. The fellow had bronchitis or something, and wheezed like an old bellows as he struggled to bear his father's coffin.

The service was brief and pallid, like all Anglican services. The burial that followed was an ordeal of wind and cold. Tiny spots of snow polka-dotted a leaden sky. When it was over, Daragh and Jossy and Kit stood at the lych gate, shaking hands with the mourners. Sympathy was muttered, condolences expressed. Daragh was bored, utterly bored, until the woman cut him.

Elizabeth Layton was an acquaintance of Jossy's, and on every do-gooding committee in Cambridgeshire. She shook hands with Kit and then with Jossy, and then just walked past Daragh. He felt a jolt of anger, but told himself that it had been a mistake, not a deliberate insult. Yet the small incident rankled, and when, a few moments later, the last of the mourners left the churchyard, Daragh looked out into the road and saw her again, and walked to her side.

When she turned to him, he saw that she had dark, intelligent eyes.

'I'm afraid that I haven't had the opportunity to thank you for coming today. I just wanted you to know how much we appreciate your being here.' Daragh smiled his best smile, the one that always won them over, and held out his hand. She looked down at it, but did not take it, so he added, floundering, 'You must accept my apologies if you were overlooked—'

'You did not overlook me, Mr Canavan. I did not choose to shake hands with you.'

She turned to go, but he grabbed her elbow. 'I demand that you explain yourself!'

'You have no right to demand anything of me. I had hoped to avoid speaking of such a subject on this occasion. But since you insist, Mr Canavan, I do not approve of the company that you keep. Of course many men stray once in a while, but when they do so it should be with one of their own class, who knows the rules. It should not be with a feather-headed little servant.'

He couldn't think what she was talking about at first, and then he remembered Cora Dyce. Cora was nursemaid to a family in Cambridge; Daragh had met her through one of Caitlin's friends.

The snow was falling thicker now. The woman said, 'Cora Dyce is expecting your child, Mr Canavan. Did you know that?'

Her words struck him like a blow. 'But I only saw her once or twice . . .' he said feebly.

Mrs Layton's smile was unamused. 'Once or twice is enough, isn't it?'

He muttered, 'I had no idea . . .'

'Although Cora is silly, she is not vicious. I don't think the same can be said for you, Mr Canavan. Cora's mother works for me. She came to me when she discovered her daughter's condition. And you need not worry, she will ask nothing of you. The matter will be dealt with discreetly. Not to protect you, Mr Canavan, but because I like and respect Mrs Dyce.'

Elizabeth Layton walked away, leaving Daragh standing alone at the roadside. Motor cars had begun to drive back to the Hall, making twin herringbone tracks in the soft covering of snow. There was an odd, empty feeling in the pit of Daragh's stomach. He crossed the road to Jossy.

'I'll walk back, if you don't mind, Joss. I've a bit of a headache.' He gave her a peck on the cheek, and headed for the path through the fields.

Little blots of snow danced in the air, but the black bones of the ploughed fields showed through the incomplete covering of white. The land spread out to either side of him, as flat as a board, with only the dike to interrupt the eye before it found the horizon. There were no people, and even the birds, Daragh thought, huddled together in the reeds, out of sight. The cold, sharp air stung his lungs.

He climbed to the top of the dike, and saw how the long narrow length of water, trapped by the clay walls, had begun to turn to ice. He sat down on the bank, his head in his hands, not caring that the snow gathered on his shoulders and head, as it gathered on the land around him. His self-loathing was absolute. When he looked back over the last few years, he saw that he had lost sight of what he had meant to do with his life, and that he had acquired the careless dissolution of the English upper classes whom he had always scorned. Worst of all, he had let down Caitlin. He was not a father she could be proud of.

He saw how his longing for Tilda and his resentment of Sarah Greenlees' interference had eaten away at him through the years of his marriage. With Tilda, he had been a better person. His fingers slid slowly down from his eyes, and when he looked round he noticed that even in the brief period of his sitting, the bands of ice that clung to the banks of the dike had begun to widen, spreading their dull grey grip across the water. Soon, if nothing halted it, the floes would meet in the middle, and the water would be stilled. His own life had begun to harden, something cold and poisonous seizing it, so that he had become, without intending it, worthy of contempt.

He stood up slowly; the chill had already entered his bones. He wanted to tear off his clothes and plunge into the dike so that the icy water could purify him, so that he could start again, but he knew that the cold embrace would kill him. He wanted to run as far as he could from this devilish place, but he would stay, he knew, for Kate, whom he loved.

He looked across the fields again. Part of the trouble was that he, who had always been able to turn his hand to anything, was now idle. Idleness did not suit him; it had let his mind drift to occupations that diminished him. Daragh walked back to the Hall, the fast tread of his shoes leaving hollows in the snow.

Daragh called at the steward's house the following morning. By then the snow had settled, so that the roof of the house was brighter than the whitewashed walls. When he rapped on the front door, the housekeeper showed him in.

Glancing through doorways, Daragh saw that all the rooms were much the same, that there was no differentiation between dining room and drawing room and study. They were all full of books and old-fashioned furniture and rows of stones and dirty bits of pot, with hardly a fire lit. The place needed a woman's touch, but Daragh could not imagine the woman who would choose to marry Kit de Paveley.

Kit was in a square, ill-lit room at the back of the building. He nodded to Daragh; Daragh muttered condolences, and clapped him on the shoulder. He could feel the younger man's bones through his clothing.

Daragh said, 'I thought, now that your father's gone, we should talk about the estate.'

Pale eyes, fringed with white lashes, glanced warily up. 'The estate?'

'The farm. You're working now, aren't you, Kit?'

Jossy had told Daragh that Kit was teaching at a

boys' school in Cambridge. Daragh thought that it wasn't much of a job for a man.

'I'm teaching classics,' said Kit.

'That's great,' Daragh said breezily, and glanced at Kit's thin, hunched frame. 'And I suppose you wouldn't be up to farming, anyway?'

Kit's pale eyes narrowed. 'You're planning to take over the farm.' It was a statement, not a question.

'It didn't seem right to barge in while the old fellow was alive, but it's what I've always wanted. My family owned a farm in Ireland, of course.'

The corners of Kit's mouth twisted. 'The Fens aren't like Ireland, you know. They've a geography and a history all of their own. You have to understand the land. I can lend you a book or two—'

Daragh brushed the offer aside. 'It's your father's record books I've come for.' He glanced at his watch, longing suddenly to escape the cold, airless house. 'Bring them up to the Hall this afternoon, won't you? Oh—' Daragh, as he turned to go, recalled Kit's peculiar hobby. 'Jossy said to tell you that it's all right about your digging. As long as you don't get in my way, it won't bother me at all.'

In 1939, Max thought, you could hear the nails being hammered into the coffin. Spain had fallen to Fascism in January, and Hitler had seized the weakened remains of Czechoslovakia in March. Mussolini, ever the opportunist, bombed Albania in April. The newspapers printed cheery headlines: HITLER GETS THE JITTERS, NO WAR THIS YEAR.

Clara Franklin had a fall and broke her hip. Tilda, who was fond of Max's mother, had wanted to drive down with Max to the nursing home, but could not, in the end, get away. 'Slippery lino,' explained a white-faced Mrs Franklin from her hospital bed, but Max, checking his mother's flat that evening, saw the gin bottles in the dustbin.

Brighton always induced in him a measure of gloom and anger. He celebrated his return to London by quarrelling with both Harold and Freddie. He did not get home until half past eleven at night. Tilda was in bed, asleep, and his dinner was congealing in the oven. As he scraped food from the plate into the bin and found cheese and biscuits, he calculated that he and Tilda had not spoken to each other for three days. He had been in Brighton, or working, or she had been involved with the RCM. He sat down at the kitchen table, his head in his hands. He longed for a drink, but resisted the temptation. He must be out of the house early the following morning to interview some tedious politician, to write yet another mendacious, morale-boosting article.

He dreaded that his and Tilda's future would become one of increasing separation. He saw how people gathered themselves to her, and feared that there might one day be no room for him. He knew how easily events could come between people, levering them apart, dissolving the glue of common experience. His father had worked long hours, and Max could remember his mother's slow descent from bewildered loneliness to a frantic gaiety that had led her to seek company elsewhere. In the aftermath of a depressing couple of days, it crossed Max's mind to wonder whether Tilda would be quite so otherwise engaged if she had married Daragh Canavan. Max imagined Daragh as a sort of Irish Rhett Butler. Good-looking, in an obvious way, and utterly unprincipled.

He realized that he was becoming self-pitying – a

revolting failing – so he carried his plate and glass into the sitting room in search of the newspaper to read. The room was littered with children's toys, and the square foot of space for his plate on the table was obtained at the expense of a heap of Joshua's paintings. Josh's idea of art was to cover an entire sheet of paper with red paint (always red), applied with the thick brushes that Tilda made for him out of rolled-up newspaper. Melissa's paintings were of an altogether different character. Max had hopes of Melissa: at three and a half she drew figures with limbs and features that were even, sometimes, recognizable.

He finished his supper and glanced at his daughter's painting. Melissa had drawn Max wearing his Burberry and hat, and Tilda in the blue dress that he had bought for her birthday. Joshua, as in all of Melissa's paintings, was disproportionally small, as though to diminish his importance. Max put the painting aside. Then he went upstairs and for a while watched Tilda sleeping, hardly able to bear to acknowledge to himself how much he loved her, and how much he sometimes feared that she did not love him in quite the same measure.

Through the year of 1939, the ages of the children on the *Kindertransporte* dropped dramatically. Babies and toddlers began to arrive in Harwich, having been looked after throughout the long journey by their older brothers and sisters or, sometimes, just pushed through the carriage window by a desperate mother into the lap of an unknown elder child. They broke Tilda's heart, those babies, who had wept through Germany and Holland and across the North Sea in the arms of unfamiliar thirteen- or fourteen-year-old minders.

The boat-train now arrived in Harwich almost every

day. The offices of the RCM were chaotic, understaffed and lacking professional help, chronically short of both money and suitable foster parents. All funding for the children had to be raised privately; the government refused to help beyond easing entry restrictions. Every now and then a foster placement that had appeared to be eminently suitable was shown to be anything but: a twelve-year-old refugee girl would be found slaving as a maid-of-all-work, or a boy, already disturbed by his experiences in Germany, would be beaten for wetting the bed. Throughout the summer, Tilda felt as though she was frantically applying sticking plaster to a wound that constantly threatened to re-open. At night she dreamt of those children: the girl who had escaped persecution in Germany to find a different, subtler sort of torment in England; the baby who had travelled to Harwich in the arms of a stranger, a ten-mark note and a letter explaining his circumstances enclosed by his mother in the uppermost of the six nappies she had pinned to him to keep him dry through the long journey.

Late home one evening, Tilda found Max in the kitchen. She kissed him on the cheek. 'Sorry, darling – there was a last minute problem.'

He said, 'I gave the tickets to Charlotte.' His back was to her.

Her hand flew to her mouth. They had arranged to go to a concert. 'Oh, Max—'

He was flinging the dishes so forcefully into the hot, soapy water that she feared they would break. 'Max, I'm so sorry—'

'You could have telephoned.' His voice was taut. 'At least you could have telephoned.'

She muttered miserably, 'I forgot.' Somewhere in the long, frantically complicated day, the treat that she had been looking forward to for a week had slipped from her mind.

'Didn't you bother to write it in your diary? Along with all the other appointments – among the committee meetings and the fund-raising activities – wasn't there a "meet husband"?'

His sarcasm wounded her. She tried to explain. 'I did write it down, but I forgot to look in my diary. I didn't have time. Max – you'll break that jug—'

He slammed the jug onto the draining board. 'What shall I do, Tilda? Shall I make another appointment to spend an evening with you?'

In the silence that followed, a voice echoed distantly. Daragh's, saying, *Where do I fit into your scheme of things, Tilda?* She whispered, 'Max – I'm doing something useful at last – not much, just sticking fingers in a dam – but oh, Max – if you could see those children!'

He dried his hands and lit a cigarette. 'And your own children – Melissa and Josh and Rosi – which are more important to you?'

'That's not fair, Max,' she said slowly. Tears stung at her eyes. 'Our children are the most important thing in the world to me.'

'But they are not enough.'

She stared at him, suddenly appalled. She loved her family more than she could have believed possible; she would have given her life for any one of them. And yet—

'We are not enough,' repeated Max. He sounded tired. 'Are we, Tilda?'

She looked away from him. At home, she had felt confined and bored. When her work with the *Kindertransporte* had begun, it had been as though she had fitted the final piece into a jigsaw. There was something lacking in her, she thought miserably, her unsettled, itinerant childhood had left her unfit for normal family life.

'I've been offered a new post,' said Max abruptly. 'I'd intended to turn it down because it would mean going abroad, leaving you, but . . .' He shrugged.

As we hardly ever see each other anyway . . . The remainder of his sentence hung in the air, unsaid. She sat down at the kitchen table, her face turned away from him, her knuckles pressed against her teeth. Her whole life, she thought, had been a series of desertions. The father who had never acknowledged her, the mother who had died, the lover who had betrayed her. And now Max.

'You want to go away . . . because of me?'

He flung out his hands in a gesture of despair. 'I want to go away because I can't bear to write any more duplicitous little pieces about how Hitler's going to back down because Britain and France have made a pact with Poland. And I want to go away because if I write anything that might show the loyal British public just how close we really are to war, D-notices are clamped on it almost before the ink is dried. And because—' He broke off, and shook his head. Then he added, 'So I made a fuss, and they've offered me a foreign correspondent post at last. It would give me more freedom, but it would mean living abroad.' He lit another cigarette, and stood at the window, his back to her, smoking. It was midsummer, and through the open window Tilda could smell in the darkening air the thick, oily scent of lavender. She asked Max the question she had never previously dared to voice.

He swung back to her. 'War? Oh – a week. Perhaps two or three. No more, Tilda.'

War. She felt an almost physical fear as she saw how war diminished everything else. How it would rob them all of the right to decide their futures. And how, just now, it clarified everything for her.

'You must take the post, Max,' she said. 'I know how much you want to.' She rose from her seat and began to dry plates and cups and put them away, as though by impressing order upon her home she could control a shapeless, frightening future.

'And you?'

'Perhaps we shall come with you.'

He stared at her. 'Tilda, I said that there will be a war—'

'And when there is, we shall go home.' All the china was stacked neatly in the dresser; she shut the double doors. 'You'll know, Max, when we must go.'

'And the children? Rosi? It wouldn't be safe to take Rosi abroad – she hasn't a full passport.' The dying sun shadowed the lines and planes of Max's face, casting hollows around his dark blue eyes, carving runnels from nose to mouth. He said, 'And the *Kindertransporte*?'

'The transports will cease as soon as war breaks out. You know that too, Max. They will be trapped.' And she saw in her mind's eye the faces of the children pressed against the windows of the carriages, the shadows of tree and lamp cast across the glass like bars.

After the declaration of war at the beginning of September, Daragh tried to join up, but was told that his was a reserved occupation. He felt a mixture of disappointment and relief. He would have liked the activity and perhaps the danger of war, though not the squalor or the tedium. It would have been a relief to escape Jossy for a while, but he would have missed

Caitlin dreadfully. He would have been glad to get away from the muddle in which Christopher de Paveley had left the estate, but he remained confident that he could sort things out.

Although Jossy watched him like a hawk, he had not strayed since the débâcle with Cora Dyce. The reverberations of that episode still echoed. Shunned by certain people, struck off invitation lists, Daragh knew that Elizabeth Layton had talked. At first, for Caitlin's sake, he cared, but as the coldness continued he gave up trying to seek the county set's approval. 'They're just strutting peacocks,' he said to Caitlin, as he gave her a riding lesson. 'We don't need them, do we, Kate? We're better than the lot of them.'

Caitlin trotted her pony round the paddock. 'We're better than the lot of them,' she sang. 'We're better than the lot of them.'

Daragh had his hands full with the farm. Somehow he had expected that the place would more or less run itself, as his granda's farm seemed to have done. It did not, though, and he lurched from one crisis to the next. The fencing collapsed and the sheep escaped into the new wheat; a ditch became clogged with reeds and flooded a field. In spring, when the snow melted, the water lay on the land, refusing to drain away, sullenly reflecting the sky like a black mirror, rotting the crop of potatoes that he had sown. When he looked back through the records, Daragh discovered that the farm had made little profit since the war. Edward de Paveley had lived off his capital, and that and the death duties had eaten away at the estate. What had, upon his marriage, seemed unlimited wealth, was in reality a dwindling source of income. He tried to economize, but it was difficult. They were already short of servants – only a cook, maid and nanny for that great barn of a house. The gardener had died and his boy had been called up, so Jossy attempted to keep the garden tidy. Caitlin's smart school cost a mint of money, but what was the point of anything if she didn't have the best? She had a wardrobe fit for a princess – a black velvet coat with a fur collar, a silk tussore party dress, a tiny little riding jacket and jodhpurs, and a pony of her own. He gave her everything she asked for.

That autumn, two evacuees were billeted at the Hall. Jossy tried to wriggle out of it, but Daragh, recalling the photographs of whey-faced slum children in the newspapers, drove to the reception centre and picked out a pair of brothers. Norman and Arthur Green came from the Isle of Dogs. Their knees were black with dirty scabs and their mouths permanently open, wet with saliva as they breathed adenoidally. Daragh handed them over to Nana to give them a bath, and the screams echoed through the house. At supper, they stuffed egg sandwiches whole into their mouths and refused to drink their milk without a dash of tea in it. Caitlin looked on, hardly eating, her dark eyes filled with disgust.

Norman and Arthur attended the village school. Most days, they would return to the Hall with their knees and knuckles even bloodier than before, because the village boys, sensing them to be different, had set on them on the way home. Daragh suspected that Norman and Arthur could look after themselves. Jossy largely ignored them, and Caitlin continued to regard them with repelled curiosity, as though they were a new sort of animal that she had not hitherto encountered in one of her picture books. And they ran rings round Nana.

After Norman and Arthur had been at the Hall a few weeks, Daragh thought that Caitlin seemed under the weather. She hadn't her usual enthusiasm for her daily ride, and she kept scratching her head. The following day, he noticed that Arthur and Norman, too, were always scratching. With a feeling of horror, he went through Caitlin's curls with a fine comb. They were seething with lice. When he seized Norman and Arthur and dragged them into the bathroom and inspected their heads, Daragh hated them, though he knew his hatred to be unreasonable.

'They'll have to go,' said Jossy, when he told her that evening.

He knew that she meant the boys, not the lice. This time, he did not argue. Norman and Arthur were found another billet the following day, in a cramped little cottage in Southam. Daragh spent hours combing through Kate's hair, until it was clean again.

CHAPTER EIGHT

Because I wanted to see as far as possible what Tilda had seen, and experience what Tilda had experienced, I drove to Harwich and sailed to the Hook of Holland. I'd had my car expensively serviced at a garage a few days before, to be sure that it lasted out the journey. The boat docked at half past five in the morning and, as I travelled north to Amsterdam, I thought what a neat, bright little country it was, the fields and dikes and rows of flowers everything they should be.

Amsterdam was messy, though, curls of litter on the cobbles beside the canals and graffiti on the walls. It was hot and the traffic was awful, and by the time I found my hotel my silk shirt was stuck to my back with sweat. I lugged my suitcase up to my room, showered, and collapsed on the bed, the towel wound round me. I wanted to sleep but could not: my mind would not wind down. It leapt with disconcerting facility from Tilda to Daragh to Patrick; it muddled up the chill bleak waterways of East Anglia with the tidy canals I had glimpsed that morning. It conjured with an aching desire the illusion that Patrick was beside me, that his naked skin touched mine, that the warmth of the sunlight from the unshuttered window was the warmth of his body. I longed for him: with every obsessive thought, with every fast pulse of my heart. It was only when I sat up straight, heart pounding, eyes wide open, having heard the aeroplanes dive-bombing the glittering roofs of Amsterdam, that I knew I had slept and, if only for a moment or two, had returned to the summer of 1940.

I dressed and, armed with a map, went out to find coffee. I had visited the city twice before, with Toby. I remembered the Rembrandts in the Rijksmuseum, and the water-buses on the canals at night, their reflections shimmering in the moonlight. I had only two days in Amsterdam; on Thursday I would drive to Scheveningen to interview Leila Gilbert, Hanna Schmidt's daughter, so I could not afford to waste time. I caught the water-bus and sat with the students and the tourists, looking down at the olive-green waters of the canal and across to the old houses of the wealthy merchants. Tilda and Max had moved to Amsterdam at the beginning of 1940. Before that, they had spent a few months in Paris. Holland had maintained a neutral status after the outbreak of war, though Max, of course, saw the fragility of Holland's position. Rosi Liebermann, as she herself had told me, had remained in England with Sarah Greenlees. Max had been convinced that to take Rosi abroad would be to risk her life. Not for the first time, nor for the last, Tilda had had to make an agonizing choice between people that she loved. But Tilda had enjoyed Amsterdam: Jan had joined the Dutch army, leaving Emily to run the business while Tilda worked as a volunteer in the refugee hostels. Their friendship flourished once more.

Alighting from the water-bus, I began to walk to the van de Criendts' house. Jan van de Criendt had sold furniture and fine rugs. He had imported the rugs from the East, and the furniture from all over Europe, including

England. He had retired to the coast years ago, and now the van de Criendts' former house was a bar, and tourists gathered at the little tables on the forecourt. I sat down at a vacant table and ordered a sandwich and a beer. I peered into the darkened interior of the house, but failed to imagine Tilda and Emily laughing together amongst Persian rugs and chests and old clocks. While I waited for my lunch, I took my notebook out of my bag and leafed through it. In April 1940 the German army had invaded Norway, and Max had almost sent Tilda and the children home. But Joshua had measles and was too ill to travel, and by the time he had begun to recover the British navy had reached Norway with the intention of securing its liberty. Max's pessimism had bowed, nor for the first time, to Tilda's optimism and joie de vivre. She had been unable, she had explained to me, to believe that the worst could happen. Tilda had looked at the canal-boats laden with red and yellow cheeses and gorgeously coloured tulips, at the housewives scrubbing their front steps, and had been unable to believe that such tranquillity could be brutally and deliberately destroyed.

I drank my beer and ate my sandwich. Then I wandered slowly back to my hotel, enjoying the early evening sun on my bare arms and legs. The city seemed populated only by lovers: they lounged at the bridges, adoring their reflections in the water; they kissed at street corners, limbs entwined, their mutual passion excluding the rest of the world. I thought of Patrick, of the afternoon at the farmhouse and of the night we had spent at the small hotel in Penrith, and I closed my eyes and shut away the noises of the city, and longed for him. And I wondered whether Tilda's fear of separation from Max – an uncharacteristic fear for so independent and spirited a woman – had not been connected in some way with Daragh. Whether under-occupied and alone, her thoughts – her desires – returned to her first love. I thought of Tilda here, in Amsterdam, in 1940, waiting for the storm to break.

*

She never slept well when Max was away. In the early hours of the morning, she heard his key turn in the lock. Tilda switched on the lamp.

'*Max.*'

'Ssh.' He put his finger to his lips, and came to sit on the bed beside her. He had been away for a fortnight; he still wore his raincoat, and Tilda saw that his shoes were caked with mud. There were deep shadows of weariness around his eyes, and his face looked thinner.

'Are you hungry?' She seized his hand. 'Shall I make you something to eat?'

He shook his head. 'I'm sorry, darling – didn't mean to wake you. Go back to sleep.' He peeled off his raincoat and jacket, and unknotted his tie. She did not sleep, but watched him.

'Was it awful?'

'Pretty bad.' He never said more than that. Max had two compartments to his mind: the work one and the family one. He took great care to keep the two divided.

'Are you coming to bed?'

'Not yet.' In the dim light, his eyes seemed not blue, but black. 'Tilda, I've booked a passage back to England for you and the children and Charlotte.'

'When?'

'Tomorrow. I meant to get back sooner but I was held up. You must leave, Tilda.'

'And you?' she whispered.

'I'll be staying on for a while. Martin Willet will pick you up at lunch-time and drive you to the Hook of Holland.' Martin was a stringer for one of the Amsterdam newspapers. 'I have to leave before midday.'

She felt cold inside. 'Max, you must come with us.'

'I can't.' His expression was grim. 'I have to stay until the end, don't you see?'

She thought that 'the end' had such an ominous ring. She was leaving Max alone in a crumbling, dangerous Europe. She hugged him, pressing her face against the folds of his shirt so that the tears that stung the corners of her eyes were blotted, invisible.

In the morning, the task of packing, of deciding what to take and what to abandon, did not detract from the anxiety of seeing Max leave. Tilda took the lucky coin that she wore around her neck, that she had found all those years ago in Southam, and put it over Max's head. Then she held him very tightly. When he had gone, she stood for a moment at the window, her back to the children, her eyes closed. Then she became very busy again, running round the house, making sure that they had left nothing vital behind. She found a rag doll under Melissa's bed, and a snowsuit belonging to William van de Criendt stuffed down the back of a chair. When Martin Willet arrived, she helped him assemble the children and Charlotte Sykes and put the luggage in his car. Then she locked the front door, put the key through the letterbox, and did not look back.

Now that the decision had been made, the journey through the network of narrow, cobbled streets and humpbacked bridges seemed frustratingly slow. She wanted to be away, she wanted to be settled again. Martin stopped the motor car outside Emily's shop, and Tilda grabbed William's snowsuit, and ran in. The shop was deserted, the dark, polished tables, the painted chests and carved mirrors gathering dust. Tilda called out, and climbed the steep, narrow stairs.

Emily was in the kitchen; William was sitting in his high chair. Emily looked pale and drawn.

'I think William's going down with a cold. He was up all last night.' Emily looked at Tilda. 'What is it, Tilda? Tell me.'

'We're going home. We're to take the midday ferry.'

'Oh.' The single sound was a small, painful gasp.

'Come with us, Emily, please. If Max says we're to go, then it's because he thinks that Germany's about to invade.' Tilda saw the tremor of shock in Emily's eyes. 'He's usually right about things like that. You can't stay here, you might not be safe. Come back to England with us.'

'I can't leave Jan.' The sunlight cast dark hollows onto Emily's face. She tried to smile. 'I'll be all right. I've loads of tins of sardines and things stored up in the cellar, just in case. And it won't last long, Jan says. The Germans can't defeat Holland and Belgium and France, can they?'

Tilda's throat ached. She remembered Ely and Miss Clare's Academy, and how both Emily and she had fallen in love with Daragh Canavan. She said gently, 'You don't look well, Em.'

'It's just the curse, I think.' Emily's skin had no colour, and her eyes seemed to have sunk back into her skull.

'I'll have to dash.' Tilda's voice faltered.

'Good luck, old thing.' Emily turned aside, but not quite quickly enough.

'Emily?' The expression on Emily's face frightened Tilda. 'Emily, what is it?'

Emily gasped. 'Nothing. Nothing.'

'*Emily.*' Tilda covered Emily's clenched fist with her hand. 'You're ill, aren't you?'

Emily didn't speak at first, and then the words tumbled out. 'I have the most awful pain in my side. I've had it for two days now and it's getting worse and worse. I'm afraid, Tilda—' She broke off and closed her eyes, and when she spoke again it was with a trace of the old, confident, bouncy Emily.

'It's all right, it's nothing. You must go, Tilda – you'll miss the boat. Go. Please.' She turned her face away.

Tilda hesitated, and then hugged Emily, and ran back out to the car. Throughout the drive from Amsterdam to the Hook of Holland, the children asked her questions and demanded drinks and entertainment, and she answered them mechanically. Holland's green, flat countryside unreeled behind her, but she did not see it. She saw only Emily's face, sick and frightened and alone.

At the Hook of Holland, Martin unloaded their luggage from the car, Charlotte took Melissa's hand and Tilda carried Joshua. They pushed through the crowds of soldiers and sailors. Joshua almost swooped out of Tilda's arms, eyes wide, when he heard the hooting of a ship's funnel. Gulls shrieked, and the air was thick with fish and salt and diesel.

The queue at the ferryport snaked across the foyer. Tilda turned to Martin. 'You go back to Amsterdam, Martin. We're fine now.'

'Max said—'

'Honestly, we'll be fine.' She stood on tiptoe and kissed his cheek. 'You get back to the office.'

Martin raised his hat, and disappeared into the crowds. The queue shifted slowly forward. Melissa grew bored, so Tilda played I Spy with her. Joshua wriggled out of Tilda's arms and shuffled around the hall on his bottom making hooting noises. Tilda hauled him back every now and then and thought about Emily. Jan was away, Emily did not know where. William had a bad cold. Jan's only relative was Felix, his younger brother, miles away in north Holland. Most of Emily's neighbours were single men or old couples: she knew no-one well in Amsterdam, and her Dutch was still uncertain. Tilda bit her nails and wiped Joshua's nose and escorted Melissa to the lavatory and remembered the way Emily had said, *I have the most awful pain in my side.*

They had reached the counter where their tickets were checked. 'Four passengers?' asked the steward.

'Three,' said Tilda suddenly, and handed Joshua to Charlotte. 'I have to go back to Emily. She's ill.' The decision, now that she had taken it, was unavoidable. Charlotte gaped at her. She looked frightened.

'You'll be fine, Lottie.' Tilda scrabbled in her purse and extracted all the English money that Max had given her. 'Get a train from Harwich and a taxi from Liverpool Street. Here are the house keys. I'll be back in a day or two – I have to make sure that Emily's all right.' She moved a step forward; she could hear grumbles from the queue behind her.

'Mr Franklin—' said Charlotte nervously.

'Max will understand. And besides, I shall be back before him.'

From over Tilda's shoulder, an upper-class English voice said loudly, 'I say, do put a step on there—'

'Remember Joshua's chest-rub and make sure you watch Melissa when she brushes her teeth at night, or she'll eat the toothpaste.'

'*Frightfully* inconsiderate—'

A steward had taken their luggage; Charlotte stepped onto the gangway, Joshua in her arms, Melissa holding her hand.

'And they must both take their malt extract. Josh likes his spread on a rusk.'

Melissa, her eyes and mouth wide with alarm, stared at her retreating mother. Josh waved a grubby hand. Melissa's face screwed up and she tried to pull away from Charlotte. An elbow jabbed Tilda in the small of her back. Charlotte looked back once, smiled a watery smile, and disappeared with the two children and the steward into the ferry. Melissa's wail was a thin, high-pitched lament at her abandonment.

There was a pain beneath Tilda's ribs. She thought it was her heart. She stood aside, aware of an awful loneliness, and a conviction that she had done something irretrievable. A group of travellers, the men in striped blazers and straw boaters, the women in silk dresses, pushed past her. Tilda took a deep breath and elbowed her way back through the ticket office, towards the railway station.

All her doubts disappeared when, back in Amsterdam, she ran up the stairs behind the van de Criendts' shop, and found Emily curled up on the couch, a hot-water bottle on her stomach. William was playing on the floor. Emily's eyes widened when Tilda opened the door, and she tried to get up. Emily protested; Tilda promised to catch the night ferry if the doctor said that Emily was well enough to be left alone. But the doctor, hauled by Tilda out of his surgery, diagnosed appendicitis and operated that evening. Tilda remained in Emily's apartment, looking after William. It was 5 May. On the evening of 9 May, Emily discharged herself from the nursing home and took a taxi back to her home.

On the morning of 10 May, the German army invaded Holland.

Tilda was giving William his breakfast when the first of the aeroplanes swooped over Amsterdam. To begin with, she cursed it because she was afraid that the noise might wake Emily, who had had a bad night, and then, when that plane was followed by a second, and a third, she was seized by a terrible fear. When William had finished his bottle, she put him back in his cot and ran outside in her dressing gown. The street was full of people, looking up. The aeroplanes drew circles in the sky, and on the tail of each one was a swastika.

With Emily propped on the sofa, wrapped in blankets, Tilda watched the soldiers dart around the roads and the high, narrow buildings, as though they were playing a game of hide and seek. Throughout the day, rumours reached them – that the Dutch had capitulated, that the Germans had been overwhelmed and had withdrawn, that Nazi paratroopers had landed in the polders of north Holland and were blowing up the dikes that protected the land from the sea. On 11 May the order went out for all German refugees in Holland to remain inside their houses. On 13 May, Emily's neighbour, tears streaming down her face, told Tilda that Queen Wilhelmina had taken ship for England. Emily refused to believe her. The bakers' shops were still open, the housewives still cleaned their steps; everything seemed so normal. The following day, the man who sold flowers in the streets told them that the Nazis had bombed the port of Rotterdam and that thirty thousand people had been killed. The dull pounding and the distant plumes of black smoke lent credence to the rumours.

Tilda packed her bag and stayed up through the night

washing and cooking, so that when she left Emily would be able to manage on her own. Emily had dragged herself out of bed, shuffling around the flat, the persistent pain of the stitches making her stooped and old. The wireless was on constantly, Emily retuning the dial as the signal was lost in crackles and screeches. The news from the BBC was optimistic. They could only understand parts of the Dutch broadcasts. When, every now and then, she found a German station, Emily cursed and flipped over the dial, her small round face creased with fury.

On the evening of 15 May, there was a hammering at the door of the shop. Tilda ran down the stairs to open it. An elderly woman stood on the doorstep, two children beside her. She spoke in Dutch, too fast for Tilda to follow her, but her gestures and expression were distressed.

'She says that there's a boat sailing from Ijmuiden to England tonight.'

Tilda turned to see Emily, crouched on the stairs in her dressing gown.

'This lady's husband sometimes works for Jan,' Emily explained. She asked the woman something in halting Dutch. Another torrent, incomprehensible to Tilda, followed.

'I think she's saying that the children – Hanna and Erich – are German refugees, of Jewish extraction, but Christians, and that she must get them to Ijmuiden so that they can board the ship to England. But she can't drive and hasn't a car. She wonders if I can help.'

The woman fell silent, exhausted. The children, a teenage girl and a boy of about nine or ten, looked white and frightened. Emily said, 'You must take them, Tilda. You must take Jan's car and drive to Ijmuiden.'

She smiled. 'William and I can manage. I'm better now. You must go home, Tilda.'

Within half an hour, she was driving out of Amsterdam. The roads were clogged with people: cars and bicycles and coaches and small, hurrying groups of pedestrians. The children, Hanna and Erich, sat beside Tilda on the wide front seat. The car, which Jan used for transporting furniture, was big and heavy. Her arms ached as she swung the lumbering vehicle round corners, overtaking vans and bicycles, driving as fast as she dared through the crowded streets.

On the road to Ijmuiden, their pace slowed. Cars jostled with army trucks and jeeps. A soldier flagged them down, and peered through the window. The little boy, Erich, seemed to shrink into himself, to become stiller than Tilda had thought it was possible for a child to be. Tilda tried to explain where they were going, and the soldier waved them on. A long queue of cars trailed slowly along the other side of the road, heading back to Amsterdam. Fear squeezed her stomach again. A second soldier stepped in front of the car, forcing Tilda to brake suddenly. Again, Erich froze. Hanna put her arm round him. The soldier barked questions at them, and they were waved on once more.

She had to be in time. She had to be.

The flat fields, with their grazing cattle and their narrow dikes, so familiar to Tilda from her childhood in the Fens, crawled slowly by. There was not room enough to overtake the traffic, and the steady stream of motor cars and bicycles back to the city was ominous. Tilda's jaw ached with tension. At last, they were in sight of the port. She could see the silhouettes of the ships in the dock. She parked the car at the side of the road, gave

Hanna and Erich their suitcases, slung her own bag over her shoulder, and ran, a child's hand clutched in each of hers. Voices – British voices – echoed around her. British soldiers had landed at Ijmuiden. Her heart lifted. Clouds of smoke clogged the horizon, and the sparks and flashes that intermittently brightened the darkening sky were like fireworks. Aeroplanes swooped overhead. Cars and coaches clustered around the dockside. Tilda could see the ship, a battered steam freighter. She could read the name written along its bows: the SS *Bodegraven*. She was within a hundred yards of it when it upped anchor and began, very slowly, to sail out of the port.

She stood there for a moment, gasping for breath, staring at the ship. The horror of her situation almost overwhelmed her. She was stranded in a Europe about to be engulfed by war, the immense distance of the North Sea between herself and her family. She might be separated from Max and the children for weeks, months, years. Dutch and British voices shouted to everyone to clear the port. Aeroplanes screamed as they dive-bombed the SS *Bodegraven*. She was not afraid for herself, she was afraid only of the acres of time and space that separated her from those whom she loved most in the world. Then she saw that beside her the boy Erich had sunk to the ground and curled up in a small, stiff ball. Tilda knelt down and stroked his curved spine. He rocked to and fro, humming softly to himself. Hanna was staring at her, her eyes wide and anxious. Tilda picked Erich up in her arms and carried him back to the car.

When the British blew up the pier and the Royal Dutch oil tanks, the flames reached into an ultramarine sky, tarnishing it, casting a black shadow across the sea. The roads had cleared as Tilda drove back to

Amsterdam. When she reached the city and saw the lights that burned in every window, she knew that Holland had surrendered.

Emily fed the children, and Tilda sat on the sofa, eyes wide, staring at the wall. She couldn't think what to do, her mind no longer seemed to be working properly. Emily pressed a cup of tea into her hands, but Tilda could not yet drink it. The striped wallpaper, with its framed pictures of Emily in her wedding dress, and Jan and Felix sailing the *Marika*, blurred whenever she thought of Melissa and Josh.

She blinked and her sight cleared as she stared at the photograph of the boat. She remembered happier days: herself and Max on board the *Marika*. The tea slopped in her saucer, and she whispered, '*Felix*.' Then she stood up, and began clumsily to put her coat back on.

'Tilda?' Emily moved away from the children, who were seated at the table. 'Tilda, where are you going?'

She told her. Emily stood quite still for a moment, eyes wide. Then she disappeared into the bedroom, and Tilda heard her open a drawer. When she came back, she was carrying something wrapped in a length of cloth. She sat on the sofa beside Tilda.

'It was Jan's father's,' Emily whispered. 'Jan made me keep it when he went away. Just in case.' Emily unfolded the cloth to reveal the old army revolver. 'It's loaded,' she said softly. 'You must take it, Tilda.'

Tilda wrapped up the gun in the cloth again and slid it into the deep pocket of her coat. Just in case.

The roads were empty now. There was an eerie, uneasy silence, as though the city itself could hardly believe its defeat. For the second time that day, Tilda steered the heavy motor car out of Amsterdam.

She had to switch on the headlights because it was dark and she did not know the road well, yet their conspicuousness in the quiet countryside alarmed her. Hanna and Erich sat beside her, as before, Erich's small hand clasped in Hanna's. The map was spread out on Hanna's lap. Emily had given Tilda detailed instructions of how to find Felix van de Criendt's house in Den Helder. She and Max had visited Felix several times, but she did not trust herself to find the way in the dark.

As they drove north, the road became less even and the car rattled and lurched in the potholes. The sky was clear, inky black, pocked with stars. The aeroplanes had gone. Tilda went through it all again in her head, just to make sure. The route took her through north Holland, via Alkmaar, past the dikes and dunes that held back the North Sea.

She smiled at the children, beside her. 'Not far to go now.' Hanna smiled. The boy worried Tilda. He did not speak at all. Hanna had told her that Erich was ten years old, but the expression in his eyes seemed much older. The road was unfamiliar and narrow; afraid of overturning into a ditch, Tilda slowed down. Thoughts of Max, of the children, of the precarious future darted into her head, and were pushed ruthlessly away. She focused her mind on the task in hand: reading the map, looking for roadsigns, reaching the coast before daybreak. The countryside was flat, crisscrossed by dikes, the only trees tall, spindly willows. It occurred to Tilda that such a countryside offered nowhere to hide. A sudden movement to the side of the road made her jump, but it was only a fat red cow, strayed out of her field. She broke off bits of chocolate and fed them to the children;

Erich stored his furtively in the pocket of his shorts. It was late; she estimated that they had only thirty miles or so to travel. She had been awake since half past five that morning; her eyelids were growing heavy. Let Felix be at home, Tilda prayed, let him be at home. *Grant that no hobgoblins fright me, no hungry devils rise up and bite me.* Something moved at the side of the road. 'It's only another—' Tilda began, and then she gasped, a sudden sharp intake of breath, and stamped her foot on the brake. The car shuddered to a halt in the middle of the road.

*

I reached Scheveningen, on the Dutch coast, in the early evening. The town glittered in the sunshine. I booked into a small hotel, and quickly showered and unpacked. I had arranged to visit Leila Gilbert at half past seven. Mrs Gilbert's apartment was only a ten-minute walk from my hotel. She greeted me warmly, and showed me into her living-room. Through the front window I saw that the North Sea was now Prussian blue, flecked with silver, instead of the sullen grey that had accompanied my voyage from Harwich. A few children lingered on the beach, piling sand into plastic buckets.

I heard Leila Gilbert say, 'It is beautiful, no?' and I turned round as she placed a tray of coffee and biscuits on the table.

'Beautiful,' I echoed.

'My sons think that Scheveningen in the dullest place on earth. But I like to be by the sea.'

Leila Gilbert, who was Hanna Schmidt's only child, had two teenage boys. The apartment was littered with evidence of them: Doc Martens in the hallway, a rack of

T-shirts dripping in the bathroom and loud music from one of the bedrooms.

I indicated a photograph on the sideboard. 'Your mother?'

Leila nodded. 'She died three years ago, as I told you. I still miss her dreadfully.' She handed me the photograph and I looked down at it. There was a marked similarity between mother and daughter: both had high, broad, bony foreheads, long, thin noses, and bushy, light brown curls. Hanna had become a surgeon, Leila taught at a girls' school in The Hague.

Leila poured coffee, and called to her son to turn down the music, and I flicked back through my notebook. 'Your mother lived with Tilda after she left Holland, didn't she?'

Leila handed me a cup and saucer. 'At the end of the war, she went back to Europe, to see whether any of her family had survived. They hadn't, I'm afraid. So she returned to England and took up a scholarship at Cambridge, to study medicine. Rosi Liebermann went up at the same time to read English. They both stayed with Tilda in the vacations. Later, Hanna studied in Paris for a while, and later still she worked in Israel. We travelled a great deal. I was born in Paris, but I went to school in Belgium, and I married an Englishman. And now I live in the Netherlands.'

'I'm interested in how your mother came to leave Holland in 1940. I've spoken to Tilda already, but I wondered whether Hanna ever described the journey to you.'

'She told me about it a few weeks before she died. She was so ill that I think she had begun to live more in the past than the present. I knew some of it already, of course.'

I sat, pen in hand, scribbling notes as she spoke. Much of what Leila Gilbert told me I had already learned from Tilda. Hanna Schmidt had left Austria in 1938 and had been adopted by an elderly Dutch couple living in Amsterdam. Although Hanna was a Christian, she was of Jewish origin, and thus persecuted by the Nazis. In 1939 the Dutch couple had adopted a second child, a boy, Erich Wirmer. Hanna had felt safe in Amsterdam, and had believed that her parents and elder brothers would eventually join her there. That illusion crumbled in May 1940, when Germany invaded. Because Hanna and Erich were not of the Jewish faith, they were in touch with few other refugees in Amsterdam, and failed to receive the vital message telling them of the coaches that would take them to Ijmuiden. When they heard that a ship had been chartered to ferry the Jews to England, Hanna's adoptive parents, who had no car, asked Mrs van de Criendt if she could drive the children to Ijmuiden. Mrs van de Criendt was unwell, but an English lady staying with her offered to help.

'Tilda,' said Leila. 'The English lady was Tilda. My mother always remembered seeing her for the first time in Mrs van de Criendt's shop. She said that she was like an illustration of a princess in a Hans Andersen book,' Leila smiled.

Tilda had driven the two children to Ijmuiden. Leila mentioned, as Tilda had done, the many interruptions to their journey. The Dutch army had not been forewarned about the SS *Bodegraven*.

'The ship was half empty – many more refugees could have been taken to safety had they been able to reach the port in time. Tilda and Hanna and Erich were too late – the boat had already sailed. After the first shock was over, my mother wasn't frightened. She was always a level-headed person, and besides, as soon as she met Tilda she was convinced that she would be safe. But poor Erich . . .' Leila shook her head. 'He had seen such terrible things. He was only ten years old.'

They had driven back to Amsterdam, to Emily van de Criendt's house. Leila told me that Hanna had remembered that Emily had given them special little chocolate biscuits to eat. Then, before she had time to finish her tea, she had to put on her coat again, and they had driven out of Amsterdam once more.

Leila left the room to tell her son to turn down the volume of his CD-player. I looked out of the window again. The little groups of children had left the beach. I knew the next part of Leila's story. Tilda had driven from Amsterdam through north Holland, to the town where Felix van de Criendt lived. She had woken him up, and—

Leila took up her story again. 'It was late, and Hanna was very tired. She kept drifting off to sleep. She read the map for Tilda and held Erich's hand because she knew that he was frightened. Hanna wasn't frightened at all until the soldier stopped them.'

I looked up. 'Soldier?' Tilda hadn't mentioned a soldier.

'A German soldier. A stray paratrooper, I suspect, who had become separated from the rest of his battalion. He was wounded – my mother noticed that he was limping. Anyway, he flagged down the car.'

I had stopped writing. Nirvana pounded from a nearby room, but I hardly heard it. 'Was he armed?'

Leila nodded. 'My mother said that she began to be afraid when he spoke to them in German. He told them to get out of the car. He was pointing a gun at them.' She paused. 'So they got out of the car. My mother's legs were shaking so much that she was afraid she would not be able to walk. The soldier told them to stand at the side of the road. Then Erich began to scream about his things, and he ran back to the car.'

I asked, 'What things?'

Leila looked sad. 'Apparently, he'd a few items belonging to his family in his suitcase. Nothing of value, but they were all that he had.'

I repeated, 'Erich ran back to the car . . .'

'The German soldier raised his pistol. And Tilda shot him and pushed his body into the dike.'

I stared at Leila, unable to speak.

*

She started up the car again. There were scarlet flecks all over her clothes. Hanna was crying. Erich clutched his suitcase to his chest. A sour smell filled the car. Tilda saw that Erich had wet himself.

She couldn't steer properly at first; they veered from one side of the road to the other, as though she was drunk. But she managed to get hold of herself, and to straighten up, and to tell Hanna to pick up the map from the floor. She thought that she ought to speak to the children about what had happened, but she couldn't. She didn't think that she'd ever be able to speak about it to anyone. She did what Max did, and put it in a little compartment in her mind and shut the door.

Hanna had unfolded the map again. The tears had dried on the cheeks, and she had begun to follow the line of the road with her finger. The air that issued through the open window smelt salty. They were near the sea, thought Tilda, and her heart lifted slightly. In the aftermath of what had happened, she felt terribly tired and all her muscles ached. Hanna read out directions and she followed them like an automaton. When, after another hour's driving, they reached Den Helder, she braked and sat for a moment, unable to move.

The girl, Hanna, stepped out of the car and opened the driver's door. 'Here,' she said timidly, and handed Tilda a handkerchief. When Tilda glanced in the wing mirror, she saw that her face was spotted with red. She spat on the handkerchief and scrubbed her face hard, and then, leaning out to the verge, she was very sick.

Afterwards, she felt better. She stripped off her coat and flung it into the back seat of the car, and helped Erich change into dry clothes. His skin was pale and waxy and his eyes glassy, and he still hummed the tuneless little song. Then she gathered suitcases and bags and children together. Though it was still dark, she found Felix's house easily. When she hammered on the door the sound, breaking the ancient silence of the port, was as shocking as a gunshot.

After a few minutes, Felix opened the door. '*Tilda!*' His hair was tousled, but he was fully dressed. 'I've been listening to the wireless,' he said, as he ushered them into the house.

She explained quickly about Emily's illness, and Hanna and Erich and the SS *Bodegraven*. Felix, seventeen years old, looked excited rather than concerned. She did not tell him about the German soldier. When she had finished, she added, 'Felix, I have to get back to England. Hanna and Erich will not be safe in Holland. I wondered—'

'The boat,' he said. His eyes, the same grey-blue as Jan's, were big and round and delighted. 'You want me to sail you back to England.'

'Yes.' Voiced, the idea seemed ridiculous. Mad

and dangerous and irresponsible. 'Jan—' she began uncertainly.

'Jan wouldn't let me join up. But this'll be much better fun. I was planning a fishing trip next weekend, so she's all fitted out. And there's tins and things in the larder.'

He turned to go, but she grabbed at his sleeve. 'Felix, it'll be dangerous. I don't want you to get hurt.' Though he was six foot tall and rangy, Felix seemed suddenly so young. 'Maybe we shouldn't—'

'It'll be splendid,' he said. Smiling broadly, he snaked his hand and made shooting noises. 'Don't worry, Tilda, she can get up quite a good speed with the wind behind her. Almost four knots.'

Two days after leaving Holland, they dropped anchor near Aldeburgh on the Suffolk coast. There was barbed wire on the beach and a great fuss of oldish men in assorted uniforms, one of whom brandished an ancient rifle until Tilda wearily explained who they were, and why they were there. Now, wrapped in borrowed blankets, they sat in the firelit parlour of a pub. The man with the rifle still watched them, though his suspicion was gradually being replaced by disappointment.

The English coastline had been swathed in fog. Once, orange sparks and an intermittent crackling noise had told them that someone was firing at them. Felix had sworn under his breath and cursed the difficult sandbanks and tides of the eastern coast. The wind, which had filled the sails and blown them across the North Sea, had died. Felix had started up the little outboard motor; its chugga-chug-chug had broken the silence and taken them towards a pebbled beach. The floor still moved beneath Tilda's feet.

'They've got that number for you, lovey.' The inn-keeper's wife gestured to the telephone. The children were curled up together in front of the fire; even Felix had fallen silent.

The effort of crossing the room to the telephone was almost too much for Tilda. Her legs shook, and she leaned against the bar as she took the receiver.

'Harold? Harold, it's Tilda – Tilda Franklin.'

Harold Sykes's voice boomed at the other end of the line. 'Tilda! Lottie told me you'd stayed behind in Holland.'

'I'm in England now, Harold.' The line was bad, and she had to shout. 'I'm in a pub in Aldeburgh. On the Suffolk coast. Max is still in Europe and I've no English money, and I didn't like to disturb Lottie so late, and I thought perhaps you . . .' Her voice wobbled; she was horribly near to tears. She felt none of the delight she had anticipated on reaching England, only an almost unbearable desire to be in her own bed, in her own house, with her family around her.

'Suffolk?' Harold seized on the salient point. 'How on earth did you get to Suffolk, Tilda?'

'By boat,' she said. 'Emily's brother-in-law – you remember Emily, don't you, Harold – has a boat.'

There was a pause. Tilda wondered if she had been cut off. But then Harold said, 'Tell me the name of the pub, darling Tilda, and just wait there. I'll drive up to fetch you.'

*

I took the overnight ferry back to Harwich. A wind had got up, and in the restaurant my plate slid drunkenly from one side of the table to the other. The restaurant was almost empty, the weather putting people off their food. In the bar, a woman sang and played keyboards. I listened to her for a while and then wandered up to the deck. Grey-faced passengers, like a Ford Madox Ford painting of emigrants, huddled on benches. I folded my arms on the barrier rail and looked out. The waves were iron-grey, crested with foam, the clouds that massed in the sky a similar shade. I imagined crossing this sea in a little Dutch fishing boat, as Tilda had done. The wooden hull lurching with every wave, spray crashing over the bows and soaking the deck. And it had been wartime: every dark shadow in the sky could have been an enemy plane; every distant vessel must have given Tilda and Felix reason to fear.

The newspaper articles about Tilda's voyage had been written by Harold Sykes. Harold, that seasoned journalist, had given Tilda – against her will, I suspected – her first taste of fame. Her triumphant story ('ANGEL OF AMSTERDAM'S HEROIC VOYAGE') would have been a useful antidote to the dark days after the fall of France. The rescue of the two refugee children from Holland had brought Tilda to public notice for the first time. From that small beginning her celebrity had grown. A practical woman, she had used her fame to further the causes dearest to her heart, to open doors hitherto closed to her, to help the unhappy children she loved.

But I thought that I understood now the cause of Tilda's reticence. For her, the escape from Holland would always be tarnished by an incident that she had hidden. If what Leila Gilbert had told me was true, then there was an aspect of Tilda that she preferred to keep from the rest of the world. However justified the killing of the Nazi paratrooper had been, to have taken another human life must have haunted her. What bothered me –

what hurt me, I suppose – was that she had not confided in me. I had thought I knew her well; now I began to wonder whether I knew her at all.

I left the deck, aware of an urgent need to be back in England. I needed to look again at Tilda's story, to see it in a slightly different light. I wondered what Patrick was doing, where he was. I slept little that night. The ferry rose and plunged with the waves, and its engines, which sounded as though they were in the next door cabin, roared alarmingly. When we docked at Harwich the following morning, I was relieved to drive out of the ship's hold into the sheeny drizzle of an English June.

I spent the weekend with Patrick in his flat in Richmond, a tasteful little mews with ivy-leaved geraniums and an entryphone. Inside, the rooms had polished beech floors, cream-coloured blinds, and furniture that was matching, elegant and expensive. When I complimented him, he said, 'Jen chose it,' and silenced any further conversation by kissing me.

We did not leave the flat; we scarcely talked. The language of the body: skin against skin, the echo of another's heartbeat behind layers of muscle and bone, and air expelled fast from the lungs. We parted on the Monday morning, Patrick for his chambers, me for my flat. I sang as I flung back curtains to let in the sunlight, and when I opened the windows even London air seemed sweet to breathe. I made myself coffee and idly leafed through yesterday's Sunday papers as I drank it. Government scandals, Northern Ireland, the drought.

I could so easily have missed it, but I did not, it seemed to sear my eyes, that small, unimportant paragraph tucked in at the foot of a back page.

Human remains have been discovered in a Cambridge-shire dike. The grim discovery was made by workmen during routine repair work to the bank of a dike near the village of Southam. The waterway was rebuilt following the floods of 1947, and Cambridgeshire police, investigating, believe that the body may have been concealed at that time.

Daragh, I thought. I can't explain why I was so certain. Daragh.

PART TWO

CHAPTER NINE

She dreamt of 1940, sailing across the North Sea with Felix and Hanna and Erich. The tiny craft exposed on the great expanse of water. The fog that surrounded the English coast had magnified the sound of the sea lapping against the bows, and the shouting of the men on the beach.

Tilda awoke. Lying in the darkness, she remembered how Harold Sykes's newspaper article about the crossing had changed her life. 'Tilda Franklin? Didn't you . . .?' people had said when she had introduced herself, adding some ludicrously inaccurate version of her flight from Holland. At first she had tried to explain that she had just needed to get home to her children, but that too had been misinterpreted. ANGEL OF AMSTERDAM SAYS, I DID IT FOR MY BABIES! She had resented the intrusion into an episode that she would have preferred to forget, just as now, sometimes, she had to swallow her resentment of Rebecca's questioning. There had been fear behind her anger at the assumption that her life had become public property, fear of the pointing fingers, the invasive questions, the crass curiosity about her origins. That fear lingered. She had never shaken off the shame she felt at her procreation, her birth, her earliest years. And the uncritical admiration of strangers had driven further the wedge between herself and Max. Max had seen her flight from Holland rather differently: an unnecessary risk, the breaking of a promise. Promises had been important to Max.

Though it was June, she felt cold. Younger, she would have walked for miles to chase away her demons, or surrounded herself with her family. Old age reduced you to essentials, and to memory. A frail body and a tormenting memory. She hoped that when she had told Rebecca everything she needed to know, she herself would be free.

Now, though, she was still enchained. The war years lingered, in all their danger and drama and tedium. When she closed her eyes, trying to shut out the darkness, she saw the faces of those whom the war had taken. Clara Franklin. Felix van de Criendt. In 1941, Clara Franklin had been dancing in a nightclub when a bomb had struck a direct hit. Tilda remembered scouring a battered London for a bunch of the scarlet lilies that Clara had loved. Max, working abroad as a war correspondent, had been unable to attend his mother's funeral. Another brick built into the wall with which he had surrounded himself. Max had been able to grieve properly neither for the mother who had died, nor for the mother he might have wished to have had. The snatched, unsatisfactory days that she and Max had been able to spend with each other during the war years had been marked by physical and emotional exhaustion. He had been reluctant to talk, she too busy to coax him. She had feared that they would never regain their old intimacy, or worse, that it had been hollow, built on sand.

Irony had haunted her throughout the war: the irony of saving Hanna and Erich from almost certain death, while losing their saviour. Felix van de Criendt had joined the RAF as soon as he had turned eighteen. He had been killed in 1942, when a German plane had shadowed his bomber as he had flown back to England. Felix had been gunned down within sight of his airfield, almost home, a pitiless death, a mockery of bravery and youth. Tilda had wept for Felix and had felt a complicity in his death, because she had brought him to England.

And the irony of surviving the Blitz, only to have her home destroyed by a V-2 rocket in the last year of the war. She had felt safe, she had told Max, when he had remonstrated with her for remaining in London in the autumn of 1940. She had sent the children to Sarah, in Southam, but she herself had returned to London, because she had work to do. When the worst of the Blitz was over, the children had come home. Then, years later, in the January of 1945, returning from the shops, Tilda had seen the plume of smoke rising from the street where she lived. The bomb had struck the row of terraced houses, destroying her home and those to either side of it. The little square of trees and grass had been littered with splintered branches and fallen leaves, and a pram had lain on its side on the pavement, its wheels buckled. At the corner of the square had been a motor car, the dust a grey shroud for its motionless occupants. Someone had made her a cup of tea, taking her silence for shock or despair at all she had lost, but she had felt only a sense of relief so intense that she had almost fainted. The children were safe: the loss of the home that she and Max had built up over ten years had seemed unimportant compared to that. When they returned from school, Josh had run among the rubble and dust, delighted by the strange new landscape, and

Melissa had wept. Such a mess she had said, all my things are in such a mess. Hanna and Rosi had been sensible and comforting, as usual, and Erich had stared at the ruins and coughed his habitual little cough, and chewed at the tags of skin around his fingernails. Then they had taken what could be salvaged, and had gone to live with Sarah, in Southam.

Tilda's eyelids had grown heavy . . . She did not want to think of Southam. She had not wanted to return to Southam then, and she did not wish to do so now. Yet the images persisted. May 1945. VE Day. Putting up bunting in the village hall. Feeling not joy, but relief and weariness and a persistent sorrow. Escaping the chatter of the women and children, and running along the path by the church to the dike. Sitting on top of the bank, and looking out across the fields to where puffy blue clouds nestled on the horizon. Closing her eyes, breathing in the scent of the flowers . . .

Meadowsweet and mayweed. She could smell them still.

I remember . . .

Brushing blades of grass from her dress, Tilda stood up, looking for Josh. 'That *boy*,' she said, exasperated, out loud. Josh was a wanderer.

The fields were deserted except for a solitary man, walking the perimeter. Tilda hailed Kit de Paveley as she ran down the bank.

'Mr de Paveley!'

His face was shadowed by the brim of his straw hat. Tilda had seen Kit de Paveley half a dozen times since she had returned to Southam, alighting from the bus on the way back from the school in which he taught, or queueing for stamps in the post office. She never thought of Kit de Paveley as her cousin, any more than she thought of Joscelin de Paveley as her sister. She tried not to think of their relationship at all.

'I'm sorry to bother you, but I wonder whether you've seen a little boy ... eight years old ... wearing ...' Tilda struggled to recall what Josh had dressed himself in that morning '... shorts and a striped jersey.'

Kit shook his head. Then he said, 'Where did you get that?' He was staring at her lucky coin, reclaimed from Max, strung again round her neck.

'This?' Tilda glanced back at the dike. 'At the foot of the bank. I can't remember exactly. I found it years ago.'

'May I see it?'

She pulled it over her head and gave it to him. 'Is it very old?'

'It's Roman. Silver. Quite rare. I've found plenty of pottery shards but very few coins, and those only bronze.' Kit's pale eyes were shining. 'The Romans were the first people to drain the Fens. I believe that there was a settlement here – I've found tesserae in the vicarage garden, and there are signs of earthworks all over the estate. Of course, there's some disagreement over whether they settled in any numbers this far east, but I intend to prove—'

He broke off suddenly. 'I do beg your pardon, Mrs Franklin. Your son—'

'Josh will turn up. He always does. Would you like to keep the coin, Mr de Paveley?'

A flush stained Kit's pale skin. 'I couldn't possibly—'

'Please.' She smiled at him. 'I'd like you to have it. When you are famous, and you have an exhibition in the British Museum, then you can write on the label

"Donated by Mrs Tilda Franklin", and I shall feel very erudite and honoured.'

Something woke her: a bird's cry, or the rumble of traffic from the road. Tilda sat up in bed, her heart beating too fast, staring at the darkness. If she pulled aside the curtain, would she see The Red House's tangled, beautiful garden, or the flat fields and narrow waterways of Southam?

Her aching body, as she leaned across and switched on the bedside lamp, reminded her that she was old now, and in Oxfordshire, and alone. The lamplight illuminated her bedroom, but she longed still for dawn. In the early hours of the morning, all her fears gathered, and she was aware of her close proximity to death. Her mind, plagued by the past, raced along avenues of self-reproach. *If . . . if . . .* The awful relentlessness of the past. The immutability of it.

Rebecca's visits, so necessary to her intention, tormented her. They stirred memories that had long lain hidden, memories that fluttered to the surface, colourful and jarring, sweet and painful. She thought of Kit again, holding her coin in the palm of his hand, his eyes, as he looked down at it, bright with a sort of longing. It occurred to her that Rebecca and Kit plied a similar trade: they both delved in the darkness for nuggets of silver, fragments of truth.

*

Badgering Patrick's protective secretary, I managed to get through to him at his chambers. I read him the newspaper report. *Human remains have been discovered in a Cambridgeshire dike . . .* 'In *Southam*, Patrick.'

'Hell,' he said.

'Patrick, it could be Daragh.'

'It could be anyone.'

'But if it is—'

'I'll make some enquiries. Leave it with me.' A pause. 'Don't say anything to Tilda yet, Rebecca. No point in upsetting her unnecessarily.'

I agreed readily. We talked a little, but he seemed rushed, so I said goodbye and put the phone down, aware of my unease.

Hell, he had said. He should have sounded surprised, or shocked. But he had not. He had been angry.

Patrick phoned a few days later and asked me to come to his flat that evening. There, he poured me a glass of wine. 'I managed to talk to someone in the Cambridgeshire police. Informally, of course – he owed me a favour.'

I glanced up at him. 'And? Was it murder?'

'The hands and feet had been bound. They found the remains of the strips of leather.' He smiled grimly. 'Yes, they think it was murder. There's not much forensic evidence, but the fact that it was hidden in such a manner . . .' He did not finish his sentence.

'Have the police identified the body?'

He shrugged. 'There were no convenient watches or rings. The skeleton was male, somewhat above average height, youngish. That's all.'

Daragh, at the time of his disappearance, had been in his mid-thirties. And he had been tall. I had pinned a copy of his photograph to the board above my desk: I thought of it now, that innocent, vulpine face.

'Can they tell when he died?'

'The dike was breached in the floods of March 1947 and repaired over the following weeks. They've only just begun to look into it, but there doesn't seem to have been much work carried out since on that part of the earthworks until this summer, when the body was found.'

Which meant that the body had been concealed in April 1947. Daragh Canavan had disappeared in the April of 1947. I looked across the room at Patrick.

'Come here,' he said.

I went to him. He took my glass out of my hands and put it on the table. Then he began to unbutton my shirt. 'They can't rule out the possibility,' he said, as he bent and kissed my breasts, 'that the victim was buried alive.'

I shivered. 'Are you cold?' he said.

I shook my head. My shirt slithered to the floor. 'Such a horrible way to die. I can't imagine anything worse.' He straightened, and I kissed him, drawing him towards me, exploring his mouth with my tongue, as if by immersing myself in his warm, breathing body I could shut out the images that crowded into my head.

We made love on one of the bleached cream rugs, our need for each other too urgent to walk the few yards to the bedroom. Patrick's skin tasted of salt and when his hands touched my body my nerve-ends burned. Just for a moment, when he was inside me, and I could feel the weight of his body on mine, I thought of Daragh, alive in the darkness of the dike, spadefuls of earth weighting down his chest, his lungs, his heart. But then the aching pleasure gathered force and could not be resisted, and I heard my cry of delight echo against the walls and window panes.

We spent the night together, rising early the next morning; Patrick had to fly to Edinburgh on business.

I took a taxi back to my flat and showered and drank coffee and tried to concentrate on my work. I had spent the last few days studying the war years. Though the V-2 rocket that had landed on Tilda's house in January 1945 had destroyed some records and diaries, she had become a minor public figure, so I was able to get information from newspapers and magazines. Tilda had continued to work with the *Kindertransporte* children throughout the war, and in 1944 had become involved with arrangements for evacuating children from London during the terror of the V-1 doodlebug bombs. I imagined her darting around Britain in crowded trains, or cycling through unlit, unsignposted country roads to check on the suitability of her charges' billets.

Charlotte Sykes had joined up at the end of 1940; Tilda had afterwards relied on Sarah Greenlees to help her with the children. Max had stayed on in Germany after 1945 to cover the Nuremberg trials; by that time Tilda's work had largely fizzled out. Yet the war had changed her. It had allowed her, as it had allowed so many women, the opportunity to use all her gifts. Ancient minutes of committee meetings showed me her organizational skills; letters to uncaring or ignorant officialdom proved her passion. She had possessed a valuable and unusual mix of talents, the greatest of which was her ability to attract love. Not only the love of men, but of women and, of course, children. She had a warmth, an ability which made everyone feel that they, and only they, were the person she most wanted to be with. I too had sensed that; I too felt drawn to her.

Today, though, I could not concentrate. My body recalled Patrick's, and my mind persisted in drifting to a lonely earthworks, and a man bound hand and foot and buried alive. My desire, my horror, made me shudder. I pushed aside the laptop, and doodled aimlessly on my notepad. I was certain that those workmen, repairing the dike, had found Daragh Canavan's body. Though, again, I had agreed with Patrick that we should say nothing yet to Tilda, I myself had no doubts. The skeleton had been that of a tall young man. It had been buried at the right time, in the right place. I looked at the snapshot on my pinboard, and thought, what did you do, Daragh Canavan, to merit such vengeance?

I began idly to scribble on my pad. Daragh had had money troubles; Daragh had been a womanizer. Cambridgeshire in the late 1940s must have been littered both with his creditors and with cuckolded husbands, any one of whom might have felt angry enough to kill him. I sat back in my chair, chewing my pencil as it occurred to me that there were other names I could add to the list I was making. Jossy's name, for instance. Daragh had humiliated Jossy for years – might the worm have turned at last? Might Jossy's obsessive love have been turned to hatred by one last, appalling betrayal?

My heart began to beat a little faster. What could have hurt Jossy more than if Daragh had seduced the half-sister she had never acknowledged? What if Daragh and Tilda had, at last, consummated their love? In 1947, Daragh had vanished and Tilda and Max had parted. I recalled the promise that Tilda had made to Max when she had married him. Though she had admitted that she still loved Daragh, she had sworn not to betray Max. Had she, in the difficult postwar years, broken that promise?

I added Max's name to my list. Perhaps Tilda had made love to Daragh, and Max, maddened by jealousy, had killed him. Perhaps Max had struck Daragh on the head and tied him hand and foot, and buried him in the half-repaired dike. Perhaps Tilda had guessed what

Max had done, and that was why she had resisted having her biography written for so long. In her old age, she could have assumed her secrets safe. But the past had re-emerged, bones forcing their way up through the soil, relating a different story to the one she had intended to tell.

I drove to Oxfordshire the following morning. It was a fine, bright day, and Tilda was sitting on the terrace at the back of the house. I asked her about the postwar years.

'Did you stay in Southam after the end of the war?'

She poured me a cup of coffee. 'I wanted to go back to London, but it was impossible. There was a housing shortage, you see. And Sarah was unwell. She had a heart condition. She wouldn't go to hospital to have it investigated – to Sarah, the hospital was the old workhouse.'

I remembered the photograph of Long Cottage. 'It must have been rather cramped – seven of you in that little cottage.'

'Eight, when Max came home in 1946. But the garden was marvellous – almost an acre of land, which meant that we could grow our own fruit and vegetables.' She explained to me, 'Less queueing, Rebecca. Food was still rationed. Erich helped me look after the garden. He never settled at school, I'm afraid – the other children used to tease him, because he was different, so as soon as he passed his fifteenth birthday he left.'

'He was Austrian, wasn't he?'

'Erich was born in Vienna. I never knew much about his childhood – he wouldn't speak about it – but I found out a little through the Refugee Children's Movement. His mother died when he was a small boy, and after his father was killed by the Nazis Erich lived by himself on the streets of Vienna until someone found him a place on the *Kindertransporte*. He was nine years old, Rebecca – can you imagine, a child of nine, scavenging for food, living with such memories?'

She looked across at me. Her eyes were bright – with anger or with sorrow, I could not tell. I thought of Tilda's other two adopted children.

'And Rosi? She lost all her family, didn't she? What about Hanna?'

'None of Hanna's family survived. She had four sisters – they all died in Dachau. Rosi accepted her loss, but Hanna could not. Max found out for her what information he could through the Red Cross, but Hanna went back to Germany when she was eighteen, to look for herself.'

I drank my coffee, wrote my notes, and was aware, as I had been when I had spoken to Rosi Liebermann at Tilda's party, of the slightness, the triviality of my own experience.

'Of all my children, Josh was happiest in Southam.' Tilda smiled. 'He loved it. The rivers . . . the open spaces. He was always in trouble, though – he'd leave school at midday, pretend he was going home for lunch, and just roam about. Once he thumbed a lift to Denver Sluice. He didn't come home until late at night, and by that time Max had called the police. Max was furious, and took him out of the village school and insisted he weekly board. Max thought he was running wild, you see. I knew that he was just Josh.'

The famous Josh Franklin was, as far as I knew, still roaming about. There had been a postcard on Patrick's mantelpiece from some remote part of China.

Tilda had fallen silent. I wondered, looking at her,

what it had been like to go back to Southam after all those years. I said tentatively, 'Did the children know about your connection with the de Paveleys?'

She shook her head. 'I never spoke about it to them. Max thought that I should, but I didn't. I couldn't. I saw later that I should have done. Secrets are so destructive. At the time, I felt that I was protecting my children from an unpleasant truth. I remembered how it had hurt me when Sarah had told me about my father, and I didn't want to inflict that pain on them. Though it was . . . *unsettling* when Melissa and Caitlin struck up a friendship.'

She looked away from me. I sensed many things unsaid, and I thought both of the German paratrooper she had shot, and the body unearthed from the dike. I said, 'And Daragh? Did you see much of him?'

Tilda's profile was set against the background of blue sky like a cameo.

'Not at first,' she said slowly. 'But then . . . when Josh went missing, Daragh organized the men to search for him. And when Melissa broke her collarbone, he drove us to the hospital. It was always Daragh who would bring Caitlin to our house to play with Melissa. Never Jossy.'

I imagined Daragh, that practised seducer, that consummate opportunist, watching, waiting. How he must have wanted Tilda, who had been beautiful, and who should, but for Sarah Greenlees' interference, have been his.

'Daragh kept away, of course, when Max was at home,' Tilda added.

'Was Max away a lot?'

'He stayed in London part of the week, and the rest of the time he worked at home. Freddie, his editor, wanted him to go back to Germany, but Max refused. The war changed him, Rebecca – he couldn't settle. He became more and more restless. He was deeply unhappy, in fact. And as always he tried to keep his unhappiness to himself. He shut himself off from me . . .'

*

Harold Sykes persuaded Max to accompany him to the pub to celebrate Lorna Clarke's engagement. 'Chap's been sniffing after her for years,' confided Harold, over Scotches. 'Never thought he'd come up to scratch.'

The pub was crowded, men jostling for space at the bar. They pulled chairs round a small table: Harold and Max and Lorna and two new boys, Reggie Gates and Basil Dayton. Basil, who had drunk too much, was talking loudly, gesturing with his cigarette. 'So old-fashioned. Dismal little photographs, long-winded articles forever harping on about the war. People don't want to read about the war any more, do they?'

Max knocked back his whisky rather quickly. Harold said amiably, 'Rather a big thing to ignore, old boy.'

'People are looking to the future, and so should we.'

'You mean,' said Lorna, 'draw a line under it, forget it?'

Basil Dayton was fair-haired, pink-cheeked, and he looked, Max thought, as though he should still be in sixth form.

'People don't want to plough through endless depressing paragraphs about ancient old Nazis in prison in Germany. They want something short – snappy – bright.'

Max drawled, 'An interesting journalistic challenge. Write a cheerful piece on the Nuremberg trials, using words of no more than two syllables.'

Lorna sniggered. Basil flushed. 'I just meant that we should look ahead . . . be less hidebound . . .'

Reggie Gates lit himself a cigarette, and glanced across the table at Max. 'After all,' he said, inhaling, 'does anyone *read* those impenetrable essays you write, Max?'

Scenting danger, Harold offered to buy another round of drinks. Max, who had months ago classed Reggie as bright but obnoxious, said lazily, 'One or two plough through them to the end, I suppose.'

'I mean,' and a smoke ring circled to the ceiling of the pub, 'what was your last sermon about? Something to do with the Jews and Palestine? People would rather read about football, or some nice scandalous film star. They're not interested in *Palestine* – most of them don't even know where the place is. As long as there's some cheap little kike to make their suits—'

Max's fist struck Reggie Gates's chin. Reggie's chair fell back and there was the sound of breaking glass. Harold said, 'Max, for God's sake—' and Lorna's hand gripped Max's sleeve, halting him. Reggie climbed unsteadily to his feet. 'You shit, Franklin,' he said, as he dabbed at his bloody nose with his handkerchief. Max left the pub.

Harold caught up with him when he was halfway down Fleet Street. Rather portly, Harold struggled for breath. 'Max – what the hell—'

Max shrugged and kept on walking.

'Slow down, damn you. And what in God's name did you do that for? Reggie Gates is a ghastly little twerp, but for heaven's sake, Max, you have to work with him—'

Max stopped at last, his hands dug into his pockets. It was bitterly cold, and he noticed for the first time the flakes of snow that spun in the air. 'No, I don't, Harold. I'm giving in my notice.'

Harold gaped, open-mouthed. 'Don't be an idiot, Max.'

Max shook his head. 'It'll be the most sensible move I've made in months. I've had enough, Harold. I'm chucking it in.' Because Harold was an old friend, he tried to explain. 'Harold, it has all seemed so utterly futile since I came back from Germany. And I feel so *old*. Those kids – Basil and Reggie and their like – they are the future. Smart, brash little grammar-school boys. They can't spell, and they can hardly construct a sentence, but who cares about that nowadays? You and I are leftovers, Harold. Our clothes – our manners – our backgrounds – we don't fit in any more. Things have moved on, and I don't care to run along, trying to keep up.'

He walked away then, and Harold made no move to follow him. The snow thickened as Max left Fleet Street, and when he looked up he saw the flakes darting against the topaz light of the streetlamps, a frantic, jiggling polka-dot pattern. Max thought how loathsome England had become: a shabby, worn-out little country, the streets still cratered by bomb damage, the population shambling and grumbling, lacking imagination, drained of energy. He no longer felt part of it. None of the postwar visions – neither the idealistic socialism of Attlee's government, nor the material goods that the people longed for – were his. He could only stand aside and watch it all with a distaste that was both futile and impotent.

Nana had died early in the war, and Cook had left service to earn better wages in a munitions factory. A woman from the village came up several times a week to scrub floors and do the washing, but that was all. The Hall, with its large, numerous rooms and formal gardens, had consequently lost much of its former austere grandeur. Jossy, who rarely noticed her surroundings, didn't mind. She tended the kitchen garden so that they had fresh fruit and vegetables and, with the aid of Mrs Beeton, taught herself to cook. Because Daragh liked to fish and shoot wildfowl, and because he had many useful contacts in the seedier London pubs and clubs (Jossy tried to avoid thinking of it as the Black Market), their rations were not too restricted.

The Hall, like everywhere else, had the dreary, slightly disreputable look of a building that has not seen a lick of paint in seven years. But it was still the Hall, Jossy's childhood home, the home of her ancestors for centuries. That her hands were blistered with digging, or that she, queueing for meat at the butcher's in Ely, was indistinguishable from all the other tired women, did not trouble her, because she knew that her breeding was in her speech, her blood, her name, her ancestry.

She minded only one of the changes that the war years had brought. Since Tilda Franklin had come back to Southam, Jossy had watched Daragh constantly. *Tilda is ten times more beautiful than you*, Daragh had said, long ago, and Jossy, seeing Tilda, had acknowledged that he had spoken the truth. When he had first told her of Tilda's existence, Jossy had made discreet enquiries. Cook, who had worked at the Hall only since the mid-Twenties, had been unable to help, but Nana, her memory carefully prompted, had recalled Deborah Greenlees. Nana's version of Deborah Greenlees' disgrace had been different from Daragh's. Nana, like everyone else in Southam at the time, had believed Deborah Greenlees to be flighty, promiscuous, the author of her own troubles.

It was only later, thinking of her father, that Jossy began to doubt the truth of Nana's version. Jossy remembered her father's uneven step on the stairs, and how the sound had always produced in her an instant and inescapable fear. A child, she had seen herself through her father's contemptuous eyes: plain, stupid, worthless. Her childhood had been governed by her fear of him; though he had rarely struck her, she had always sensed his capacity for violence. Her fear of him was still too vivid to be dismissed. Though she tried to reassure herself of her father's innocence, she was haunted by doubt.

During the latter years of the war, she had realized that Daragh had begun to see other women again. An obliging widow from the village; a shop assistant in Ely. No-one who threatened her. Though his affairs hurt her, Jossy hid her pain. Though she loved Daragh with an undiminished passion, she knew him to be weak. Daragh's good looks had not lessened in the fourteen years of their marriage, but the quality of Jossy's love for him had altered. Not the quantity of it: that was unchanged. But she understood him now, and his capriciousness enchanted her as much as it tormented her. She knew herself to be a plodding, mundane person, her nature so different and so inferior to Daragh's mercurial brightness. She knew that Tilda, and only Tilda, was a threat to her.

At first Jossy had tried to ignore Tilda Franklin's existence. But weeks and months had passed and Caitlin, riding through the village one day, had struck up a friendship with Melissa Franklin. Because Melissa was, superficially at least, the only other girl in Southam sufficiently well-bred to be a companion for Caitlin, and because Jossy had kept secret from everyone Tilda's supposed relationship to her own family, she had been able to make no real objection to the friendship. And besides, Caitlin was useful. Caitlin could keep an eye on Daragh.

Today, Caitlin had spent the afternoon with Melissa, and Daragh had collected her from Long Cottage and brought back to the Hall in time for tea. After tea, Jossy went upstairs with Caitlin to help her comb out her plaits before her bath. Caitlin, who loathed having her hair done, liked to sit at her mother's dressing table, distracting herself with the scrapings of cosmetics left in the gilt glass pots.

Jossy unknotted Caitlin's ribbon. 'Was he talking to her?'

Caitlin dabbed her nose with the swansdown powder puff. 'Only a bit. I said I was hungry.'

'What were they talking about?'

Caitlin shrugged. 'This and that.'

'*Kate.*'

'The weather. Some boring thing in the newspaper. That exam Melissa's taking.'

Jossy was relieved. She began to draw the hair-brush through Caitlin's thick, dark curls. Caitlin painted her lips. She said, 'And then that woman thanked him and said that she thought he was a marvel.'

Jossy stiffened. 'Ow,' said Caitlin. 'You're pulling my hair, Mummy.'

'That woman said that Daddy was a marvel?'

'Miss Greenlees' barn door won't shut properly and all the sacks of potatoes were getting wet, so Daddy carried them into the scullery.'

'Surely,' said Jossy coldly, 'Mr Franklin could have done that?'

'He's away.' Caitlin squinted. 'He's always away.'

Jossy's eyes narrowed, and her hand gripped the hairbrush hard. 'Away? What do you mean, Caitlin?'

'He's in London. Melissa's really fed up about it.' Caitlin, dabbing at her eyelashes, sounded bored. But Jossy, all her anxieties suddenly doubled, stared at her daughter's reflection in the mirror.

Caitlin's dark eyes emerged from a white skin, and her lips were carefully drawn in scarlet. She is only thirteen years old, thought Jossy with a pang, and she is already beautiful.

After they had dined, they sat in the kitchen, the wireless tuned to a Bach recital. Max closed his eyes, but Tilda knew that he was not sleeping. Eventually she said hesitantly, 'Max. Do you think that we might have another baby?'

His eyes opened. 'Tilda—'

'You said, after the war . . .'

'We have five children. Isn't that enough?'

'Babies are' – and she struggled to put her feelings into words – 'babies make everything all right. A new baby would be a new start. We need a new start.'

He stared at her. 'We have Hanna, who weeps every night for her family. We have Rosi, who is in love with that frightful curate. We have Josh, who is quite impossible, and Erich who cannot cope in normal society—'

She knew all these things. 'A baby might distract Hanna from her grief and Rosi from the curate. And Erich is so good with kittens and day-old chicks and things like that, that I thought he might be able to love a baby.'

'Where would you put it?' said Max. 'In the coal hole?'

She flushed. 'Max, I'm thirty-two. Josh is nine. I've always wanted another child. We both wanted a big family, didn't we? If we leave it much longer, it'll be too late.'

He looked at her. 'No,' he said. 'No, Tilda. No more children.'

For a moment she did not speak. Then she whispered, 'Never?'

He closed his eyes again, shutting himself away from her. Tilda stared out of the window. All through the years of the war, she had looked forward to a third baby. She had imagined another daughter, to name after Sarah. Since her work with the children of the *Kindertransporte* had tailed off, she had quelled her returning restlessness with the prospect of another baby. She wondered for the first time whether Max had met someone else. She imagined a glamorous woman, platinum blonde, red-lipped. Not the sort who wore second-hand cotton dresses or shabby corduroy trousers. Whether that woman existed or not, she knew that she was losing Max, that he drifted further and further away from her. He had always been reserved, emotionally cautious, a man typical of both his class and his nationality, but it seemed to Tilda now that reserve had hardened to coldness, and that caution had become indifference.

In January, Max started work in Whitehall. An officer he had known on Field Marshal Montgomery's staff found him the job. Though he never admitted it, Tilda knew that he hated the work; she knew also that he was deeply unhappy. She had thought that the end of the war would reunite them, but it had not. Max, who had always tended to cynicism, had nevertheless lost something during the war – some sort of fundamental faith in humanity. Increasingly Tilda feared that some of his unhappiness was centred around her. He rarely spoke to her about anything other than the superficial. Worse, it had been weeks since he had turned to her in bed. Because of the weather, Max stayed in London more and more frequently. Her marriage was crumbling, and her efforts to shore it up felt increasingly desperate.

Towards the end of the month, on Max's birthday, Tilda took the train to London. She met Max outside his offices and they went to a restaurant in Knightsbridge. The food was dull and badly cooked, and Max talked too little and smoked too much. After they had exhausted the topics of the children and the weather there didn't seem to be much to say. They had become, Tilda thought miserably, like the other married couples one saw in pubs and restaurants, their gazes flicking around the room for diversion.

They walked back to the hotel where Max had booked in for the night. It began to snow again, new flakes settling on the dirty mounds of the old. Inside their room, ice greyed the inside of the windows. Tilda took from her pocket a small package.

'Happy birthday, darling.' She watched Max unfold the brown paper. 'I found it in a second-hand bookshop in Ely. Is it all right?'

It was an early edition of Hakluyt's *Voyages and Discoveries*. She quoted, '"There is no land unhabitable, nor sea innavigable",' and smiled. 'I like that.'

'Such optimists, the Elizabethans,' said Max. Tilda nestled up to him, her arms around him, beneath his overcoat. Kissing him, she thought for a moment that it was going to be all right. They had drifted apart but they would come together again.

She said, 'I thought perhaps you could begin to look for somewhere in London, Max.'

He drew away from her, hanging his coat on the peg on the back of the door. 'I've done so already, Tilda.' He lit another cigarette. 'Can't afford a place like this too often, and Harold's sofa is damned lumpy. I've found a couple of rooms in Bloomsbury.'

She frowned. 'A couple of rooms? That's not big enough, darling. I'll have to bring Sarah – I can't leave her on her own. And the girls must have a room to themselves in the vacations.' Rosi and Hanna had started at Cambridge the previous October.

'I meant,' said Max, 'a couple of rooms for myself.'

It was as though he had hit her. She sat down on the edge of the bed, winded, cold. She heard him say: 'The expense – the arrangement we have at present is quite impractical.'

She said, 'Is there someone else?'

'Don't be ridiculous, Tilda.' He sounded angry.

She caught a glimpse of herself in the mirror over the basin: the shadows beneath her eyes, the beginnings of two lines to the sides of her mouth. She had never bothered much about her looks; just for a moment she regretted that. She wondered whether he was lying to her.

'Why, then, Max?' she whispered.

'I told you. Because it is impossible for me to keep travelling between London and the Fens. Impossible, expensive and exhausting.'

'Then we shall all move back to London.' Tilda reiterated the decision she had come to several days ago. 'Melissa would love to live in London again, and I'd be able to find a local school for Josh so that he wouldn't have to board, and—'

'No,' said Max.

She stared mutely at him, silently pleading with him for something, for some small sign that he still loved her. He moved restlessly about the room, and she looked down at her hands, threading her fingers together, then drawing them apart. The gold wedding band blurred, but she forced back the tears and made herself speak. 'You've been unhappy since you came home, Max. It's because of what you saw in Germany, isn't it? Why don't you tell me about it? It might make it better, and at least . . .' The words trailed off.

'No,' said Max again. His voice was taut, brittle.

'Max.' She knew that she was fighting for her marriage, for her family, for all that was most important to her in the world. 'How can I understand what you're feeling if you keep it from me? If you don't give me some idea of what it is that haunts you?'

'For God's sake, Tilda—'

'Is it to do with the concentration camps?' She saw him flinch. 'Talk to me, please, Max.'

He spun round. 'So that you can place sticking plaster over the wound? So that you can make things better like you do with the children?'

'I didn't mean that. You know I didn't.'

He did not seem to hear her. 'Has it occurred to you, Tilda, that not everything can be repaired? Do you really think that you have made everything all right for Rosi – for Hanna – for Erich?'

She gasped. 'I tried . . . that's all. I tried. Do you think I shouldn't have?'

'I doesn't matter what I think, does it?' His face was white, and there were bluish hollows beneath his eyes. 'You've never paid too much attention to what *I* think, have you, Tilda?'

She stared at him. 'What do you mean?'

He flung out his hands. 'Crossing the North Sea in a cockleshell. Staying in Holland after I begged you to go home. Gathering up all those waifs and strays—'

'They just happened, Max! I was there, and I had to do something. I couldn't have left Rosi alone at Liverpool Street, and I couldn't have abandoned Hanna and Erich in Holland.'

'But don't you see, Tilda,' he said softly, 'that Erich was destroyed long ago, and that Hanna will probably spend the rest of her life searching for sisters who were put to death in some hell-hole?'

She said miserably, 'At least they are *alive*,' and he turned away, and stood at the window, smoking. She sat on the edge of the bed, staring at the discoloured basin, the tarnished mirror, seeing through his eyes her role of the last nine years: bumbling and amateurish and naive.

'You're fooling yourself, Tilda. You can't really make any difference. No-one can.'

She rose slowly to her feet, and pulled her coat back on. Max's words, condemning her, echoed around the room. He said, 'Where are you going?' and she said, 'To the station,' and walked out, shutting the door behind her. He did not come after her. She thought he might, but he didn't.

She walked to Liverpool Street. She was just in time for the last train. Snowflakes dissolved in the steam from the funnels. She climbed in the carriage as the engine started up. When she sat down tears flowed silently from her eyes, though she pushed at the bones of her face with her fingertips to stem them.

*   *   *

Daragh had regretted the ending of the war. He'd enjoyed the Home Guard – his social standing and his comparative youth and energy had meant that he had run the show. His men had been a mixture of the very young and the very old, and those with reserved occupations and a few crocks unfit for military service. He'd enjoyed knocking them into shape, making soldiers of them. He hadn't put up with any slackness, and he thought they'd respected him for that. The end of the war had left a hollow in his life; the constant possibility of drama replaced by the certainty of tedium.

Now, in the first bitter months of 1947, the snowflakes floated through the leaden air like puffy white feathers, and the blizzard howled and shrieked like a banshee. All the things that Daragh was supposed to do – sowing crops, clearing ditches and dikes – the snow made impossible. He built snowmen with Caitlin, and he cut and stored wood and tried to keep the old Bentley running. Because of the weather, the trains and ships could not get through to the power stations, which threatened to run out of coal. Power cuts dimmed the towns and cities. Though the Hall had its own generator, there wasn't enough petrol to keep it running, and there was no coal to be bought. Daragh hacked down a couple of trees, but the vast fireplaces consumed them within a week. Jossy took to wearing her fur coat indoors. Daragh didn't mind the cold, but on the day he found Caitlin sitting in a window seat, pinched and blue, he took an axe to one of the garden sheds. It burned gloriously, kindled by the letters and bills he had discovered in his desk.

When the weather trapped them indoors, Daragh had too much time to think. In spite of the cold, he sometimes woke in a sweat in the early hours of the morning, knowing that he was in a worse mess than he had ever been in his entire life. All his borrowings had been the answer to an immediate crisis; each loan had, he had thought, been the last. He had borrowed from credit companies in order to repay the bank; he had borrowed from moneylenders to repay the credit companies. Yet the chain of loan and debt that he had so carefully put together was breaking apart. Letters and telephone calls pursued him to the Hall. He burned the letters without reading them, and slammed down the receiver without speaking. He avoided certain parts of London: they would not have been safe for him.

His worst fear was that his troubles would affect Caitlin. The school was already making a fuss about overdue bills. Daragh did what he always did when he had problems: he tried to distract himself. He couldn't run away this time because of Caitlin, but he could spend the odd evening at the Pheasant in Southam, and once or twice he battled out to the neighbouring farms to see a cockfight. The brutality of it – the bloodied, featherless birds – disturbed him, but took his mind off things.

And there was Tilda, of course. Before Tilda had come back to Southam, he had accepted his lot – Caitlin, the Hall, Jossy. He had begun, almost, to feel happy. Then, one morning, he had ridden into the village with Caitlin, and he had looked up and seen Tilda. He had had no warning of her return, and the shock had struck him with an almost physical blow. He had wanted to shout for joy, or to weep, but he had done neither, because of Caitlin. He had known then that what he had taken for happiness had been only an illusion; that he had slept and, seeing Tilda, had woken.

His joy soon dissipated, replaced by frustrated desire and bitterness. Her physical presence tormented him, and at night he dreamed of touching her, of undressing her, of losing himself in her slender body. To subdue the pain of his longing, he struck up an acquaintance with the obliging wife of a labourer, and called, now and then, at a certain house in the back streets of Ely. But these were only palliatives, not remedies.

Daragh began to hope when he perceived the obvious disarray of Tilda's marriage. He saw a chance for himself: Tilda was lonely and isolated from her London friends; Max was rarely at home. Daragh visited Long Cottage more frequently, helping with the heavy work that the boy Erich was not fit enough for, and offering the occasional lift to Ely.

Driving home from a cockfight one afternoon, the car, Jossy's father's ancient Bentley, spluttered to a halt three miles from Southam. Daragh, wrapped up against the cold in coat, scarf and hat, fiddled about under the bonnet. Then he saw Tilda.

She had a knapsack on her back, and was walking across the fields. She was wearing a longish flowered skirt under a short blue coat, and wellington boots. She looked, he thought, about seventeen. He waved his arms and hailed her, and she waved back and tramped through the snow towards him.

She'd been to Ely, she explained, to get medicine for Erich's bronchitis. Her eyes were bright, her long dark gold hair escaping from her velvet beret. He thought what a great girl she was, walking twelve miles to get medicine for a kid who wasn't even her own. To Daragh's question, she explained that Max was still in London, and that he'd started a new job, but she didn't meet Daragh's eyes while she said that.

Tilda looked at the bonnet of the Bentley. 'What's wrong with it?'

'Fan belt's gone,' he said. 'I need' – he glanced

at Tilda – 'a stocking or something to get me home.'

Because her cheeks were pink with the cold, he could not tell whether she reddened or not. She said, 'Then you'll have to look the other way.'

He sneaked a look. He heard her kick off her gumboot, and then he peeked and saw her, her skirt above her knees, peeling off her stocking. Her legs were long and slim and brown. The sight stabbed at him, producing an immediate physical response that he had not anticipated. He almost wished he hadn't looked, he wanted her so much. It was weeks since he'd slept with a woman, and that with some raddled old whore. He insisted on giving Tilda his overcoat to make up for the stocking. He fixed the fan belt, and then he drove Tilda back to Southam, but he hardly spoke, he ached so with desire.

Always, she expected Max to come home. Through the commonplace disasters and excitements of family life – through placating Josh's headmaster after her son's most recent absence without leave, through Rosi's unrequited passion for the curate, who had boils on his neck, through Hanna's nightmares and Erich's silences – she expected him to come home. To Tilda, her family was the hub at the centre of a turning wheel: she had believed it to be the same for Max. That it was obviously not so, that he could deliberately cut himself off from those he claimed to love most, eroded the foundations of her world.

So the snow, which had floated from a leaden sky for weeks, was a welcome distraction. The difficulties it created she welcomed too. The bus did not come, the wheels of her cycle would not turn, supplies could not get through to the village shop. All these things meant that her days were filled with hard work, so that she had less time to brood. Drifts blew as high as the hedgerows and curtained the lower windows of cottages. Thick grey ice stilled the water in ditches and dikes, and froze up the diesel pumps. The drains that should have taken the water from the land were frozen solid, blocked by snow.

When Erich was ill, Daragh cut the wood. Tilda watched him through the open door of the barn, splitting log after log. When he flung off his jacket, the dance of his shadow as he swung the axe was just as it had been years ago, when they had been young. She had to turn aside, go back into the house, make pastry, scrub the floor. Anything to distract her from the awareness that Max did not love her, and from the sudden, painful memory of an older love.

In March, the thaw set in. It began to rain, a steel-grey curtain that saturated the reeds that roofed the cottage. The wind got up, toppling chimney stacks, felling trees. Walking along the summit of the dike, Tilda saw that the water almost reached the top of the bank. On Sunday, rising early, she found Sarah, dressed in mackintosh and gumboots, standing in the parlour, staring out through the window at the flat, waterlogged, wind-lashed fields.

'She's going to blow,' said Sarah. 'I've been out and looked at her.'

'The dike?'

Sarah nodded. 'We must take the furniture upstairs.' She began to drag an armchair across the room. Her lips were violet-blue.

'Erich and I shall do it.' Tilda placed her hand on Sarah's sleeve, halting her. 'I'm desperate for a cup of tea. You'll make one, won't you, Aunt Sarah?' Their eyes met, and Tilda saw the outraged pride in Sarah's eyes, but Sarah did not shake off her hand.

Tilda woke the children. She set Melissa the task of carrying crockery and china up to the bedrooms, and sent Joshua into the barn to fetch logs. With Erich's help, Tilda carried upstairs whatever furniture would fit up the narrow staircase. In Sarah's bedroom they stacked bottles of pickles and preserves and sacks of flour and potatoes. They caught the hens, who squawked in their wicker cages on the landing, and packed into orange boxes all the little, worthless treasures that Sarah had amassed over the years: the chipped china cups, the mottled old books, the photographs and letters and keepsakes.

At midday Tilda went out to check on their nearest neighbour, an old widow who lived alone. On her way back, the wind was almost too fierce for her to stand. Men were running in the direction of the dike, their progress impeded by the gale. Tilda wrapped her coat round her and ran after them. Her gumboots splashed through deep puddles; but beneath the water, the earth was still iron-hard with frost. Scattered like spillikins by the wind, branches of elder and willow littered the path that led down the slope from church to field. Rain beat down on Tilda's head, plastering her wet hair to her face. As she approached the dike, someone shouted, 'Go back, lass! Go home!'

She stood for a moment, watching with horror the men's frantic labour as they hurled sandbags on the summit of the dike. She saw where water, black and menacing, had begun to seep from the foot of the bank. The waters that the earthworks held back, maddened by wind and thaw and rain, cast up waves that lashed against those struggling to preserve the defences. She feared that this was a war already lost. This invader could not be turned back. Tilda retreated, running home to her children.

When one of his labourers pounded on the door in the morning, telling him of the imminent disaster, Daragh hurried his wife and child into the car and drove them to Ely. Returning from Ely, thankful that Caitlin was safe with the Tates, Daragh's progress was blocked by the branches that the wind had thrown across the drove, and by the deep puddles that had begun to spread from the overflowing ditches. Carefully negotiating these obstacles, he had time to think. A stark choice confronted him. He could save his home, or he could do his duty and help the men – the villagers, many of whom were his labourers and had been under his command in the Home Guard – to defend Southam. He could almost hear the whispering of sand in the hourglass: his luck trickling away, used, spent.

Daragh left the car, its wheels made immobile by thick black mud, its petrol tank almost empty, in the village. Then he ran down the slope to the field. Through the shimmering rain, he could see the men working on the dike. Some straddled the top of the bank, grey figures silhouetted against a malevolent sky, others grovelled in the earth at the edge of the field. Daragh moved among them, joking with one, encouraging another. He, like them, dragged wet, heavy sandbags to the top of the bank; he, like them, dug clay, barrowing it to the shifting, leaking foundations. It lifted his heart to know that his presence cheered them: that his magic – his looks, his charm, his luck – still counted for something. It almost compensated for his suspicion that this task was hopeless, that they could not possibly resist this black monster. 'Haddenham pump went this morning,' someone yelled at him through the terrible wind and, later, 'Bank's blown at Over!' Daragh's hands were raw and bleeding, every thread of his clothing soaked.

The water seeped through another section of the bank. Half a dozen men ran to it, shovelling clay against the leak. 'Here too!' shouted a boy, and they dashed a hundred yards or so to where a thin spray of water spat through the undergrowth. The rain was relentless. On the summit of the bank, where waves pounded the weakening structure, a lad slipped and fell into the water, and had to be hauled out with a rope. Daragh, looking up, every muscle straining with exhaustion, could see that the sandbags made the structure top-heavy. They could not win: either the flood would overtop the bank, or the force of the water would eat away at foundations already weakened by the severe frost. Yet he still worked among the men, encouraging them, helping the half-drowned lad back to the safety of the church, offering exhausted men a mouthful from his hip flask.

A jet of water rushed out through the matting of docks and nettles that covered the slope. As soon as they stopped up one leak, another sprang. The narrow spray gushed, the earth bulging, clods of grass torn from their roots, unstoppable now. A voice shouted, 'She's going! Every man to high land!' and they threw down the shovels and the sandbags and ran for the safety of the church.

Daragh, shambling along the track on legs that almost refused to bear him, heard the bank blow. It was the noise of a thunderclap. The blast shocked him, so that he reached out for something – anything – to cling on to. Someone supported him and a voice said gently, 'She've gone, sir. Can't do no more,' and he allowed himself to be helped into the church, knowing that in the great roar and rush of water lay the wreckage of his hopes.

CHAPTER TEN

'And Daragh disappeared . . .?' I asked.

'A few weeks after that.'

There was a silence. Tilda and I were sitting in the garden room at The Red House. Clouds of blue plumbago were set against whitewashed walls and, because it was evening, the flowers of the hoya put forth their honey-scented dew. For a long time afterwards I associated that perfume with duplicity.

During the floods of 1947, the combination of rain, frozen earth and thawing snow had inundated thirty-seven thousand acres in the South Level. The army and fire service had been called in to help deal with the devastation. The Dutch government, experienced in similar disasters, had lent a pontoon crane.

'Southam village was flooded,' explained Tilda, 'and the Hall was under six feet of water. Daragh lost so much – furniture, paintings, rugs – all destroyed. And his land . . . crops that he had sown swept away, fields covered with black mud. He believed himself ruined.' She pressed her hand against her eyes, and I disliked myself for making her recount a past that was so obviously painful to her.

She told me that she was tired, so I left her and went to work in the little boxroom. I was looking through a photograph album when the telephone rang. Joan had gone for the evening to Oxford; I dashed along the corridor to answer it.

A woman's voice said, 'I wish to speak to Tilda Franklin.'

'She's just dropped off, I'm afraid. Can I take a message and ask her to call you back?'

A pause. Then, 'Are you the housekeeper?'

I explained who I was, and what I was doing at The Red House. There was another silence, and then, disturbingly, a peal of laughter. 'You are writing that woman's biography? How extraordinary!'

I felt affronted. 'Who is this, please?'

She didn't answer. Instead she said, 'Another sycophantic little piece about the Angel of Amsterdam, I suppose.' A second peal of laughter, and then the tone of voice altered. 'Shall I tell you the truth? Shall I tell you how that saint – that *angel* – threw a penniless, friendless fifteen-year-old into the street? I think I reminded her of *him*. I reminded her of what she couldn't have. I reminded her of what she had destroyed.'

I said again, more urgently, 'Who is this? Who are you?'

'She killed him.' Some of the anger faded from the taunting voice, and was replaced by pain. 'She killed my father. I always wondered, and now I know.'

My heart was pounding painfully in my chest. I knew, suddenly, to whom I was speaking. 'Caitlin?' I whispered, but she had already rung off.

I dialled 1471, to find out where she had been calling from. By the time I put the receiver down a few moments later, I knew that Caitlin Canavan was, in the flamboyant manner of her father, staying at the Savoy Hotel.

* * *

My intention to stay the night evaporated; I had to be alone. When Tilda woke, I made her tea and chatted to her, and did not meet her eyes. Throughout the drive home, that angry, taunting voice echoed in my head. *She killed my father.* I had assumed that Caitlin Canavan was either dead or long out of touch with the Franklins. Caitlin had been a bit player, Jossy and Daragh's spoilt only child. Now, she had forced herself into centre stage.

Back in London, I phoned Patrick and left a message on his answerphone. Puzzles constantly rearranged themselves in my mind. Tilda and Daragh had had an affair, and Max had discovered them and killed Daragh and buried his body in the dike ... Or Jossy, maddened by jealousy of her more beautiful half-sister, had murdered her faithless husband ... And now a new and terrible possibility, one I had not previously considered: Tilda herself, who had always loved Daragh, had realized that he would never leave his daughter for her, and—

So when the following evening, halfway through dinner, Charles, after talking endlessly about himself, looked up from his Thai green curry and said, 'How's Tilda? Found any skeletons in the cupboard yet?' my face must have given me away. He put down his fork and said, 'Oh, *Rebecca*, do tell.'

I shook my head. 'It's probably nothing. I'm just letting my imagination run away with me.'

He poured me another glass of wine. 'You may not believe it, but I can be discreet.'

So I found myself telling him about the body in the dike and about Caitlin Canavan's telephone call. 'I thought that Max, Tilda's husband, might have had something to do with it, but it never occurred to me that Tilda herself . . .' The words trailed off; I was unable to voice my worst fears.

Charles took a mouthful of coconut ice cream, and waved his spoon at me. 'A gift for you, though.'

'What do you mean?'

'Don't be dense, Rebecca. I'm sure that little brain of yours has been ticking away. Dame Tilda Franklin a murderer. They'll be fighting for it in the bookshops. It's like discovering that Mother Teresa was a child prostitute.'

I looked down at my coffee. I knew that he was right. Sinners are so much more newsworthy than saints.

'Dynamite, don't you think, darling?' He had put down his spoon, and his pale green eyes had narrowed, and there was an expression in them that, just for a moment, I interpreted as anger. How silly. Why should Charles be angry? Charles was detached, elegant, amusing, unthreatening. That was why I liked him.

'Could cause you a tiny *crise de conscience*, I suppose,' he said smoothly, adding, 'I heard on the grapevine that you're seeing a bit – or rather a lot, in fact – of the grandson. The handsome, brooding Patrick. I have to say, I didn't believe it. But . . .'

It wasn't any of his business, but I said, 'I've been out with Patrick a couple of times.'

'Such an unsuitable expression, *going out*. It usually means quite the opposite.' He looked up. 'It's true, then?'

'Yes. You sound surprised, Charles.'

'I thought you were still pining for the oleaginous Toby.'

'I'm not, and he wasn't oleaginous. Over-ambitious. Pompous. Pretentious, perhaps.'

Finding suitable adjectives to describe my ex-lover

was the sort of game I would have expected Charles to join in, but tonight he did not. Instead he said, 'Are you in love with him?'

'Patrick? I don't know. I thought I was in love with Toby. I'm never too sure what it means, *in love*.'

'It means thinking about someone all the time. It means that when you're with the object of your love, you don't want to be anywhere else. You don't want to be with anyone else. You don't want to *be* anyone else.'

In all the years I've known him, I can't remember Charles seeing a woman for more than a few weeks at a time, and that only occasionally. His mannerisms, his lack of close involvement with women – even our friendship – have all made me wonder whether he might be gay, yet for some reason have remained in the closet. 'Charles, you surprise me,' I said, but my mind had drifted once again to Tilda and Daragh. *She killed him*, echoed Caitlin Canavan's angry voice.

'You know I've adored you for decades, Rebecca darling,' said Charles, and I patted his hand, and fished in my purse for my share of the bill.

Charles walked me home. As we turned the corner of the street, I saw the blue Renault parked beneath a streetlamp. Patrick was sitting in the driver's seat, drumming his fingers on the steering wheel.

'I'll go, then,' Charles said tactfully. We said goodnight, and I tapped on the Renault's window. Patrick followed me into the flat. He looked exhausted: bluish shadows around his eyes, fine white crow's feet beneath his tan.

He refused my offers of coffee and an armchair. 'I've been driving all day. You left a message on my answerphone, Rebecca.'

I took a deep breath, and began to tell him about

Caitlin Canavan's phone call. He interrupted my first sentence. 'Oh God. I was hoping she wouldn't hear.'

'Patrick – it could be her father . . .' I broke off as the implications of his words sunk in. 'You *know* her?'

'Of course. The wretched woman's been a thorn in the family flesh for years.' He twitched angrily. His restlessness made the room seem too small, too claustrophobic.

'I thought . . . I assumed that you'd lost touch with her ages ago.'

'Unfortunately, no. What did she say?'

My mouth was dry. I searched for a tactful way of framing Caitlin's accusations.

'Come on, Rebecca. What did she want?'

'She's heard about the discovery of the skeleton. She assumes it's her father.'

I heard him swear softly. He looked across at me. 'There's more, isn't there?'

There was no tactful way. 'She accused Tilda of killing him.'

The restless prowling stopped momentarily. 'Good God.' Patrick went to the window and placed his palms on the sill, looking out, his back to me. 'Damn,' he said softly. 'Damn, damn, damn.'

Yet again, it unsettlingly occurred to me that his response was one of anger, instead of shock. But I went to him, and put my hand over his, and he turned to me and said, 'I expect she was drunk. It'll have been the alcohol talking. Thank God Tilda didn't answer the phone.'

I said bluntly, 'She might do the next time.'

He stared at me. 'Yes. She could phone again, of course.'

'How well do you know Caitlin Canavan, Patrick?'

He shook his head. 'Hardly at all. I just oversee the financial arrangements when my father's abroad.'

'Financial arrangements?'

'We help her out a bit. Caitlin's been married three times, but none of the marriages lasted. She's always had expensive habits and consequently a heap of debts.'

'So you send her money?'

'Have done on and off since the Sixties.' His eyes narrowed as he saw my expression. 'There's nothing sinister in it, I assure you. Caitlin is family. She is also untrustworthy and hysterical. You can't believe a word she says. When she moved to Dublin she asked Tilda for a loan so that she could find a house. Tilda stumped up – she never saw the money again, of course – but a few years later Caitlin was back, asking for more. My father – Josh – could see how Caitlin upset Tilda, so he took over the wretched woman so that Tilda wouldn't be bothered. Dad's away a lot, so he eventually asked me to deal with things. I just pay her rent, for God's sake.'

Yet it didn't make sense to me. Caitlin Canavan's blood relationship to Tilda Franklin was through Edward de Paveley – Tilda's father and Caitlin's grandfather. Hardly a connection for which Tilda should feel any responsibility. Even if Tilda had looked after Caitlin in the years after her parents died, the financial obligations that Patrick had described seemed disproportionate.

I had to turn away, afraid that my face might betray my disquiet. I heard Patrick say, 'I'd better speak to Tilda, I suppose. Only I'm in the middle of a case, and there's things to sort out with Jen, so God knows how I'm going to find the time—'

I recalled my brief glimpse of Jennifer Franklin: her sleek dark hair, her magnolia-pale skin. I went to Patrick and put my arms round him. 'I could break the news to

Tilda, if you like. Tell her about the discovery of the body, I mean.'

'There's no need to say anything else.' His arms enfolded me, and his mouth caressed the top of my head. 'After all, Caitlin's miles away. Maybe she'll simmer down a bit after she's had time to think things over.'

I realized I had not told him that Caitlin Canavan was in London. I opened my mouth to speak, and then shut it again. Perhaps Patrick was right. Perhaps Caitlin had been drunk. Perhaps she was mad. There was, it had occurred to me, only one way to find out. I must go and see her myself.

Meanwhile, there was Patrick. As his hands slid from my back to my buttocks, and his palms caressed me, I forgot about Caitlin, about Tilda, about Daragh. 'Stay the night,' I whispered.

'Sorry,' he said, and kissed me. 'Can't. I have to work.' He drew back.

He left soon afterwards. I opened my desk drawers and began to search through the diaries. Caitlin's name appeared frequently from the summer of 1947 to mid-1949. After the May of 1949, she was not mentioned in Tilda's diary. She had been – I scribbled on a scrap of paper – fifteen and a half in May, 1949. *That saint, that angel, threw a penniless fifteen-year-old into the street.* I looked back through the 1947 diary. Max's name, I had noticed before, appeared only rarely after April. Tilda had implied to me that her marriage to Max had disintegrated largely because his experiences as a war correspondent had exaggerated in him a natural tendency to avoid close human contact. Max had been with the British army when Belsen had been liberated, an experience which had permanently scarred him.

Now I questioned whether Tilda had told me the

whole story. Had she edited the truth, as with the episode of the German paratrooper in Holland? In the April of 1947, Max had left Tilda, and Daragh had disappeared. Or Daragh had been murdered. Too many coincidences, Rebecca, I said to myself grimly. Far too many coincidences.

I sat on the bed, wrapped up in the duvet, looking through the diaries. Carefully, this time, reading each entry. The repetitive action, the small, dull words began to hypnotize me into a sort of languor. I was drifting, fully dressed, into sleep when I heard the footsteps on the path at the side of the house. Crunch, crunch, crunch on the gravel. A small noise, but sufficient to make my heart hammer against my ribcage and the diary slide out of my hand. I couldn't remember whether the back door was locked.

There's never a blunt instrument to hand when you want one. I picked up a fat library book about the Fens, and tiptoed into the kitchen. The door was locked, and the light on. The yard and the path were deserted. I told myself that it must have been a cat, out hunting, but I slept badly that night.

On Monday, I told Tilda about the unidentified body in the dike, and Caitlin Canavan's telephone call.

I did not tell her, of course, about Caitlin's accusations. Just that Caitlin Canavan assumed the body to be that of her father. Tilda heard me out, her face unrevealing, and then she rose and went to the window. Rain silvered the tangle of rose and honeysuckle in the garden. Damp weather always exaggerated her rheumatism; she moved stiffly.

'I never believed that Daragh ran away,' she said. 'He would not have left his daughter.'

I only realized that I had been holding my breath when I heard the slow exhalation of air. 'Tell me what happened, Tilda,' I said. 'Tell me the truth.'

She turned to me, her features imperious, her brows raised. 'Isn't that your task, Rebecca? To distinguish the truth?' She sat down. Her eyes were half shut, her voice low. 'People had to start again. Spring crops had to be resown so that the harvest was not lost. Houses washed clean of mud, flood damage put right. But there are some things that cannot be put right . . .'

*

The full moon was doubled in the floodwater that still patched the fields. Stars sparked the inky sky, their reflections shifting with the fitful breeze. A rank perfume issued from the debris caught in fence and ditch: a drowned rabbit, yellowed spring cabbages, a grey rag doll. Daragh, walking around the perimeter of the field, pulled the collar of his coat up to his ears. Nights like this, he hated the Fens. Nights like this, he remembered green hills and seawater lapping a rocky shore, and air so cold and tart and salt it made you drunk to breathe it. He took the hip flask from his pocket, his numb fingers faltering with the screw-top, and swallowed deeply. Nights like this, with his boots clogged with mud, and ruin behind him and before him, he wanted to run, to hide, to start again.

The huge, monstrous army of the engineers' earth-moving equipment stood not far away, the bulk of the machinery menacing, the angular metal arms reaching out for him. Daragh thought at first that the footsteps that he heard were the rhythmic pounding of his own heart. Then he glanced back, and saw his pursuers like a black cameo against that pale, wavering moon. He hadn't thought they would come for him here. They were creatures of the city: small and dark and verminous, feeding off black alleyways and city sewers. He began to run. The earth, laughing, grabbed at him, clogging his boots, tripping him, so that he stumbled and slid with a clumsiness unnatural to him. The tower of the church, outlined with silver, and the bright windows of the public house were only half a mile away. Safety. Daragh's ribs squeezed his thorax, and his lungs gasped for the thin, watery air. The wet furrows slowed his pace, as though he were running in a nightmare. His luck whistled through the hourglass, and he cursed this unforgiving land.

Daragh slipped in the mud and landed hard on his knees. Their footsteps sounded in his ears like thunder. Hands seized the shoulders of his coat, pulling him to his feet. The first blow struck his stomach, the second his chin, and after that he lost count.

At eleven o'clock, Sarah and the children were asleep, and only Tilda lay awake, curled in a double bed that was too big, too empty, trying to read herself to sleep. The tapping at the door wasn't much of a noise at first. Owls' claws on the gutter, mice in the skirting board, and then she thought: *Max.*

She flung a shawl over her nightdress and ran downstairs and drew back the bolt. He was leaning against the porch, black shadows flooding his features, his body bent. She heard herself exclaim. 'Sorry, Tilda,' said Daragh. Then he fell forward into her arms.

Most of all, as she helped him into the kitchen, she felt angry. Angry with Daragh for not being Max, angry with herself for believing that Max had come back to her, angry with Max for making her endure this.

In the brighter light of the kitchen, she looked properly at Daragh, and whispered, 'Dear God,' and grabbed her coat from the back of the door. 'I'll phone the doctor . . . the police . . .'

He stopped her. 'There's no need for that, Tilda.'

'Daragh, someone did this to you.'

'The bastards almost beat me to a pulp. But we had . . . an arrangement.' He gave a croak of laughter. 'Not the sort of arrangement I would care to discuss with the police.'

She stared at him, realizing that he was deeply in trouble. Part of her wanted to tell Daragh to leave, the part that wanted these days to draw away from other people's pain, because it reminded her too much of her own. But he was shivering convulsively, so she poured him a measure of whisky and folded his cold hand around the glass. 'There's a shirt and trousers of Max's in the wardrobe. I'll go and get them.'

'Is Max away?'

'He's in London.' Tiptoeing upstairs, she took Max's old summer clothes from the wardrobe. When she went back to the kitchen, Daragh had stripped off his shirt and was standing at the sink, sluicing the mud from his torso. His tanned skin was patched with red bruises, and smeared with dirt. She did not want to be needed, yet now Daragh, for the first time in years, needed her. She took a clean flannel and began mechanically to help wash his shoulders. 'What sort of trouble are you in, Daragh?'

'Money trouble,' he said. He grimaced. 'It makes a change, Tilda. It was always women with me.'

She did not smile. 'How bad?' She wrung out the flannel, and thought. 'I could lend you twenty pounds or so.'

'It's a sweet thought, darlin',' he said. 'But it's a mite worse than that.'

She didn't really want to know. She had troubles enough of her own, and had no wish to share Daragh's. He had let her down years and years ago: she owed him nothing. Yet a small voice in the back of her head reminded her that since she had returned to Southam, Daragh Canavan had been a good friend. He had organized the search party when Josh had gone missing, he had cut logs for her, and had checked that she was safe during the flood. He had asked for nothing in return.

'How much worse, Daragh?'

The expression in his eyes disturbed her. He said slowly, 'I thought I was a rich man when I married Jossy. That house . . . the land . . . But it's not as easy to be rich as I thought it was. The farm hasn't made money since the Great War. On a good year it breaks even, on a bad year there's a loss. There's been a lot of bad years – wet springs that wash away the seedlings, poor harvests. I tried to sell a field or two, but no-one was buying, so I mortgaged the house. We have such expenses – Kate's school and the servants and labourers and the horses—'

He took Max's shirt from the back of the chair, and pulled it on. 'Mortgaging the Hall got me straight for a while. When I couldn't pay the mortgage, I sold a few paintings and bits of furniture. Jossy didn't mind: I didn't sell anything that made much difference to the way we live. I told her that I was selling my motor car because there wasn't any point having two with petrol rationed, but the truth was that a fellow was threatening to take me to court.' He took a deep breath. 'Then I tried raising money in other ways. The horses, mostly. I was lucky at first.'

Now, Tilda thought, after the years of separation, they had something in common. Now they had both watched their dreams crumble. The family that had meant so much to her was dispersing; the wealth and status for which Daragh had abandoned her was turning to dust.

'I had to raise another loan. Not the banks, of course – they shut the door in my face. Different sorts of fellows.' Daragh smiled. 'I met up with them just now, back in the Fen.'

He was shivering again, so she stroked his shoulders, trying to rub warmth into them. 'Hush now. Does Jossy know?'

He shook his head violently. Then he looked up and said, 'Tilda, I shall lose the house,' and she saw in his familiar green eyes an utter despair.

'You'll have to tell Jossy.'

Daragh pressed his knuckles against his chattering teeth. 'She worships me,' he muttered. 'God knows why – I don't deserve it, that's for sure. How can I tell her the truth? How can I tell her that she's been wrong, all these years? God knows, I haven't been much of a husband to her – I never loved her, I didn't even much *like* her – but she doesn't deserve that. I've got used to her – we rattle along – it's not much of a marriage, but—'

His voice broke. She took his hands between hers, trying to warm him. His body, more muscled with the years, had become unfamiliar, but when she laid his clenched fist against her face she remembered the warmth of his skin.

'Such a tangle,' he said, and took a shuddering breath. 'Anyway, I'd the money from the early harvest earmarked to pay them off, and there was a little scribble in the dining room that someone told me was worth a thousand or so. Only the flood has washed away the crops and turned the picture to a pulp, and oh, Tilda, I don't know what to do!'

She put her arms around him and let him rest his forehead on her shoulder. His entire body shook. He whispered, 'I was always lucky . . . but it's gone, Tilda. I can feel it running out—'

She stroked his hair and he pulled her tightly to him. She patted his back and muttered soothing words, but could feel the tears in her own eyes, taste them salt as they trailed down her face. She heard him whisper, 'Tilda, what is it? I'm so sorry . . .' and then felt him kiss her tears, small, soft pressings of his lips against her face. 'Darlin' girl,' he said, 'you mustn't cry for me, I'm not worth it, never was—' and she knew that she should turn away, make some light-hearted remark, boil the kettle for tea.

Yet she did not. It was as though they were finishing at last what had been begun years before. His kisses changed in quality, lingering on her skin, coaxing from her a longing she had believed dead. Daragh wanted her; Daragh did not believe her old, undesirable, useless. With Daragh she was the young, optimistic, energetic Tilda that she once had been; with Daragh she could slough away war and loneliness. His touch brought her back from a sort of death, kindling a flame that seemed to set fire to her. When his hand slipped beneath the thin covering of her nightgown and he touched her breast, she wanted to cry at the exquisite, terrible pleasure of it. She had forgotten that she was capable of such pleasure. Daragh's mouth traced the path from her neck to her cheekbone, and when their lips touched, she was lost.

*   *   *

Jossy, watching from the landing window, heard first the crunch of Daragh's boots on the gravel, then the song that he whistled. It was half past midnight.

As he fumbled with his key in the lock, she ran from the landing to her bedroom. She crouched under the covers as he ran up the stairs and slammed the bathroom door. After a while, when there was silence, Jossy crept along the corridor to the bathroom. There, she touched Daragh's shaving brush, still damp, and his towel, trying to stifle the misery of her suspicions with this second-hand proximity of him. She lifted the lid of the laundry basket and took out his shirt, holding it to her face, breathing in his scent. Then, opening her eyes, she caught sight of the unfamiliar laundry mark. And the name tag. *Franklin*, it read.

Jossy sank to her knees, moaning softly to herself.

Max had wanted to explain to Tilda that he needed time to think, time to recover the equilibrium that he had so resoundingly lost. He should have told her that it was he and not she who had changed, but her wounded eyes had reproached him, and he had shied away from emotional involvement. If she touched him, or if he had allowed himself to touch her, then he might have broken into a thousand little pieces. He had stood on the edge of that precipice once, and he would do anything to avoid doing so again. He had, in the end, said all the wrong things, things that he suspected she had misinterpreted, but he knew that his clumsiness had been symptomatic of his state of mind.

In his rooms in London, it was easier. There was an armchair and a table and a basin and a wireless set that he hardly ever switched on. It was damned cold in this appallingly cold winter, and because of the fuel crisis the heating was off for most of the day, but both boarding school and the months he had spent with the Allied army in the winter of '44–45 had taught him to tolerate cold. Here no-one hurled themselves at him shouting 'Daddy' in a way that made him, ridiculously, jump. Here no-one expected affection or intimacy, things he no longer felt able to give. He ate in the dingy little dining room, and his rooms were cleaned once a week by a preoccupied, silent woman who grieved for the son she had lost at El Alamein. The chap whom he now worked for tentatively suggested a trick cyclist, but Max waved away the suggestion, and nothing more was said. He knew that he was not shell-shocked, as so many of those who had survived the first war had been. It was just that he had seen things that no man ought to have seen, and they had left him with such a deep pessimism that, just now, he saw no point in anything. Max knew that men killed women as lovely as Tilda and tortured children as dear as Melissa and Josh, and that they took pleasure in doing so. The faces of his own children had constantly reminded him of that. He knew that he was not being fair to Tilda, that his absence wounded her, but he had no alternative.

He found solace in the dull routine of his life. Now, he rarely saw a newspaper, and all the magazines had had to close down because of the fuel shortage. He read only the most meaningless books, and listened only to the lightest music. He had photographs of Tilda and the children, but he kept them in a drawer. He used the excuse of blocked roads and icy railway lines to avoid returning to Southam at the weekends. It was not that he did not love them, only that he had nothing left to give. Sitting in his rooms, Max watched the snow fall, and was thankful for the white blanket of silence that muted the city.

Yet the snow thawed, and spring came at last, and he found himself thinking of his family more and more. He took out the photographs, arranging them on a chest of drawers. He went to a concert, and did not weep. After work one day, he met his father in the Savoy. They talked about rugby, and about the government's plans for nationalizing the iron and steel industries, and then Max told his father about his new job.

Mr Franklin blinked. 'Didn't think you liked that sort of thing, old boy.'

'I don't,' said Max bluntly. 'I detest it. But I didn't want to write any more.'

'What does Tilda think?'

Max evaded his father's eyes. 'Tilda and I have been living apart since January. I was working in London, and with the snow it became impossible to travel home, and . . .' He shrugged.

Mr Franklin coughed. 'I know that it's damned difficult to find decent housing these days, but if one has money . . . You know that I have a bit put by, Max.'

Automatically, Max shook his head. His father substituted money for love. Affection was not his currency; only the cheques that Max always refused.

The waiter arrived. Mr Franklin poured water into his whisky and coughed again. 'I let Clara down. Didn't give her what she needed. Didn't realize until it was too late.'

Max could not recall his father ever before talking about his marriage. He was almost stunned into silence, but he made an effort, guessing what those few fractured sentences had cost the older man.

'Tilda's not to blame. It's all my fault. I saw some frightful things in the war, Dad, and I couldn't get them out of my head. Still can't. You must know what I mean – you fought in the first show.'

This time the silence persisted. At last, rising from his seat, his father said, 'When I first met your Tilda, I thought what a lovely girl she was. What a diamond.' Mr Franklin gathered up his hat and umbrella, and his hand briefly rested on his son's shoulder. 'Don't throw it away, Max. That's what I did.'

Often she remembered Daragh's leaving of her. He had turned away from her (they lay sprawled on the kitchen floor, their clothes scattered, gasping for breath) and he glanced at the clock and said, 'Mother of God, Jossy will have sent out a search party.' Then he sprang to his feet and, as he dressed, he whistled to himself. *No maid I've seen like the fair colleen that I met in the County Down* . . . Turning to go, he had seen his muddy clothes and scooped them up. Then, stooping, he had kissed her, and then he had gone, shutting the door behind him.

She had gone up to her bedroom, and had poured cold water from the jug to the basin, and had washed herself all over. Then she had sat, wrapped in a towel, on the edge of the bed. The dim light of the oil lamp had picked out shadowed reminders of the man she loved. His old dressing-gown, on the peg on the back of the door, his typewriter, on top of the chest of drawers, a packet of cigarettes on the mantelpiece. And their wedding photograph, silver-framed, on the bedside cabinet. *Oh, Max*, Tilda had whispered. *Oh, Max – what have I done?*

At last, she wrote to him. *Dear Max*, she scribbled, *Sarah is very ill. In fact, I think she is dying. Everything is wrong since you went away. Please come home, Max, I need you so much.*

She signed the letter and blotted it. Then she stood up and moved to the window, pulling the curtain a few inches aside. She felt exhausted with guilt and dread and fear of the future, but she knew that she would not sleep. She longed to turn back the clock. Just then, she saw justice as Sarah did, a primitive weighing of good and bad. A reckoning. The heart suspended on a balance and found wanting. She had betrayed Max, and for that a price must be paid.

Jossy drove to Cambridge. Water still blistered the fields, but the main roads were passable and the work of repairing the banks and dikes was well under way. In Cambridge, she made her way to a department store. There, in the beauty salon, she had her hair cut and tinted to hide the strands of grey. Then she spent a further half-hour while a disdainful girl in a white overall painted her face and lectured her on her failure to take care of her complexion. When Jossy opened her eyes and looked in the mirror, a new face stared back at her: the small lines around her mouth and nose disguised by powder and foundation, her dark eyes, always her best feature, given depth and size by liner and mascara.

After the beauty salon, she went shopping. She had bought nothing new for ages, so although clothing was still rationed she had plenty of coupons. With the help of an assistant, Jossy eventually selected a cream-coloured blouse and a knee-length black skirt. She would have preferred something calf-length – the 'New Look' that had been in all the magazines – but clothes were skimpily cut to save cloth. 'Very smart, madam,' said the girl as Jossy looked at her reflection in the changing-room mirror. *Smart*, thought Jossy savagely, as she began to take off the new clothes. Never beautiful. *Tilda is ten times more beautiful than you.* Her hands shook as she undid the buttons.

Back at the Hall, some of the bravado induced by the shopping spree faded. To begin with, the devastation of her home hadn't upset her, because Daragh was safe. When she'd heard that the dike had blown, she had been seized by a certainty that she had lost him, convinced that though against the odds she had kept him from the greedy desire of other women, the floodwater had stolen him. Learning of his safety, she had not wept at what the waters had done to her home. Instead, when the waters had retreated, she had helped Daragh and the men drag sodden rugs and furniture from the lower level of the house, and then she had set to work, mopping out the residue of black silt.

Now, the paper that hung from the walls in tarnished shreds, and the bare, blackened floorboards, seemed to echo her sense of loss. At a time when she desperately needed to hold on to what she had, everything was disintegrating.

She served dinner at eight o'clock. Daragh's eyes widened when he saw her. 'You look very splendid, Joss.'

Very splendid. Ships and cars and houses were splendid. She saw herself as lumbering, broad-hipped, lacking all Tilda's delicacy and elegance. But she smiled and said, 'I've made us a special dinner, Daragh.'

His horse had thrown him the other day; he rubbed

at the bruise on his chin. 'Have I forgotten a birthday?' he asked lightly. 'Are we celebrating?'

'I've some wonderful news, Daragh. I'll tell you after we've finished.'

She had made three courses: soup, fish and dessert. The vegetables and fruit were from the garden, the fish plump trout that Daragh had caught the previous day. The bareness of the room was alleviated by the flames of the log fire and the candlelight. She brought the wireless from the kitchen and tuned it to the Third Programme, and music played softly as they ate. Daragh was as sparkling as he had been when he had begun the affair with Elsa Gordon.

After coffee and brandy, Jossy went to him as he stood by the fire, and nestled her head against his shoulder. She told him that she had visited the doctor that morning, and had learned that there was now no possibility that she would have another child. 'It's the change of life, Daragh. It comes earlier with some women than others, Dr Williams said.'

He hugged her, rather absently. 'That's rough. Poor old Joss.'

'Daragh,' she said. 'You don't understand. Don't you see what this means? It means that we can be man and wife again. It means that you can share my bed again.' There were tears in her eyes. She stood on tiptoe, her mouth seeking his. Her small kisses touched very gently his cut lip, and the bruise on his jaw. She drew him to her, adoring the feel of him, the scent of him. Though a flicker of fear persisted, she knew that she had made the right decision.

She seduced him, this second honeymoon. She undressed him, she caressed him, she made him want her. When she felt him shudder inside her, she knew that she would win. Daragh would choose, as he had always done, the easiest path.

The following day, Jossy went to Southam post office to buy stamps. Walking back through the village to the Hall, she recognized the man alighting from the bus. Purposefully, she marched forward.

She had to tap Max's shoulder to gain his attention. Then she said, 'Good afternoon, Mr Franklin. I'm glad to see you back in Southam. Perhaps, in future, you would take care to keep your wife away from my husband. That would be better for both of us, don't you agree?' Then she spun on her heel and walked back down the street.

He almost ran after her, seized her, shook her, forced her to withdraw her filthy accusations. Then he thought, *what if . . .* and stood in the middle of the road, staring at Joscelin Canavan's retreating back. A tractor, loaded with gault to repair the dike, lumbered up the road towards him, but he did not see it until the driver leaned forward and yelled at him.

Max picked up his suitcase and began to walk to the cottage. He felt surprisingly calm. He thought back, remembering. Tilda, climbing up the stairs of the Savoy Hotel to Daragh Canavan's room. Afterwards, walking with her along the Embankment, when her eyes had been bruised with grief. *You haven't said that you don't love him. I will be able to one day. It'll just take a while.*

Later, Tilda, restless in domesticity, wanting something more than he had been able to give her. Their children, the *Kindertransporte*, the busy days and nights of her work with evacuees – had it all been an attempt to fill her days, to substitute for *this*, for the true love that she had found and lost?

He reached Long Cottage. She was in the garden; he saw her, hoe in hand, bending over a furrow in the soil. She possessed a freedom of spirit that he envied and had wanted to take for his own. What had been extinguished in him by a middle-class childhood, school, work, still burned in her. He guessed that it burned also in Daragh Canavan, though it seemed to Max that in Daragh independence had been perverted to carelessness, and passion indulged until it became depravity. Max watched her for a while, stooped over the earth, her dark gold hair escaping out of its ribbon, her profile severe and perfect, and then he turned to go.

He must have made some sort of sound, because he heard her call out his name. He kept on walking, heading back along the drove to the road that led to Ely. He heard her footsteps drawing near to him, rubber boots splashing in the puddles. When she touched his shoulder, trying to pull him round, he almost hit away her hand.

'Max . . .' She was gasping for breath.

He said, 'I just spoke to Mrs Canavan. Or, rather, she spoke to me,' and he watched Tilda's face change, saw the fear, and knew that she had betrayed him.

'I'd hoped she was lying,' he said. Her hand slipped from his arm. 'Or mistaken. But really, it doesn't seem very likely. After all, you've been in love with him for years, haven't you?'

'Max . . . please . . .' They were standing outside the post office. A lace curtain twitched; a woman paused in the street, pretending to check her purse.

'We have to talk.' Her eyes pleaded with him.

'What is there to talk about? Mrs Canavan implied to me that you were having an affair with her husband. I almost told her not to be so cheap, so tawdry. But then

344

I thought that perhaps it was true.' He looked down at her, and he wanted to shake her until she told him the truth. 'Is it, Tilda? Is it true?'

He heard her whisper, 'I don't love Daragh, Max, I love you. I loved Daragh once, but then I learned to love you, and I shall go on loving you for the rest of my life.'

But he no longer believed her. He had lost the capacity to believe in miracles. He said, 'But you made love to him,' and when she shut her eyes, unable to meet his, he spun round on his heel, yelling at the woman with the shopping bag, the watchers in the cottages, 'Leave us alone, *damn* you!' Then he picked up his bag, and began the long walk back to Ely. He felt exhausted, all his anger dissipated in a terrible awareness that he was not enough for her, had never been enough for her, had deluded himself into thinking himself the sort of man that someone like Tilda could love.

Again, her footsteps followed him. Her voice was a howl of despair.

'It was just *once*!'

Tears were streaming down her face. Max's anger returned in full force. 'You promised me,' he said softly. 'You promised me.'

Jossy had expected to be triumphant, but was instead exhausted. She went to her bedroom soon after supper, leaving Caitlin making sandwiches in the kitchen, expecting to doze for ten minutes or so.

When she woke, she knew by the intense blackness of the sky that she had slept for hours. She was still fully dressed. She felt a moment of intense disorientation. She glanced at the clock. It was half past two in the morning. She had slept for more than eight hours. Shivering with

345

cold, Jossy pulled her dressing gown over her skirt and jersey and then padded down the corridor to Daragh's room, intending to slip into bed beside him, to draw warmth from his body. She pushed open the door.

He was not there. She stood for a moment, not quite believing the smoothness of the bedspread. She switched on the light, looked around the room. Then she began to search the house, opening one door after another. The picnic things were piled on the kitchen table and Daragh's empty whisky glass stood on the draining board. Daragh's tweed jacket and his galoshes were missing. Which meant that he had walked over the fields to Southam.

Jossy told herself that Daragh had gone to the Pheasant, and from there to a cockfight or poker school. Yet she was unable to sleep again that night, lying awake, watching the sky slowly lighten, listening for his footsteps. At dawn, she rose and made breakfast for Caitlin. Caitlin came downstairs dressed in her jodhpurs and riding jacket, but her mood was touchy and irritable. Jossy started to explain that Daddy wasn't home yet, but Caitlin, sprinkling sugar on her porridge, said stiffly that he'd be back soon, because he'd promised. Caitlin ate two spoonfuls of porridge, and then ran out to the stables to make ready the horses. Jossy scoured saucepans, scrubbed cutlery. The day, which had started fine, clouded over, and soon thick rods of rain pounded the gravel, forming wide yellow puddles. Caitlin retreated to the house at last, but remained at the window, looking out through the shimmering curtain of rain. Jossy, watching her, realized suddenly the depth of her daughter's misery. She placed an awkward arm round Caitlin's shoulders, but though the child did not shake her off, neither did she turn to her. It occurred to

Jossy that Caitlin hardly noticed that she was there, and that they both waited with painful, fearful love for the same man. Their twin sufferings should have allowed them to comfort each other, but did not.

Daragh did not come home that day, or the next. On Monday morning, after she had taken Caitlin to school, Jossy drove to Southam village. It had occurred to her, horribly, that in telling Max Franklin of his wife's infidelity she might have achieved the very opposite of what she had intended. Mr Franklin might have left his wife, and Daragh, who had always loved Tilda, might have seized his opportunity.

Undisturbed by the curious glances her enquiries received, Jossy learned that Max Franklin had indeed left Tilda. Mrs Butler in the post office had seen Mrs Franklin running down the street after her husband, crying. Mrs Franklin, added Mrs Butler, her large, pale eyes fixed meaningfully on Jossy, was no better than she should be. Jossy drove down the spur of road that led to Long Cottage. Children ran in and out of the house; the refugee boy cycled from the village, his bicycle panniers full of spring cabbage, but there was no sign of Daragh. When Tilda left the cottage, a shopping basket on her arm, Jossy looked at her carefully. Tilda's face was pale and blotchy, her long hair straggled anyhow around her shoulders. She did not, Jossy thought, look beautiful any more. In fact, she was as plain as her sister.

Daragh had been gone five days when it occurred to Jossy that he might never come back. The thought came to her when she was bent over the stove, testing potatoes with a knife. She still cooked every meal for three people. The knife slid into the potato and Jossy straightened, pushing her fringe out of her eyes, trying to shake the thought away. Daragh had gone away before. But never for so long. Never without writing.

The next morning she walked across the field to Southam. The breach in the dike had been repaired, and only a few sullen, muddy puddles, choked with rusty tin cans and clogged scraps of sacking, licked the lowest levels of the field. Sometimes Jossy stared at the ground as she walked, looking for minute clues that he might have left – a discarded cigarette packet, or a button from his jacket – and sometimes she scanned the horizon, as though she might glimpse him, six days after his disappearance, his hands dug in his pockets, whistling as he walked back to her.

The next day she went to the police station in Ely. She could tell by their bored expressions that they weren't interested, that Daragh was just another errant husband, so she thumped on the counter with her clenched fist, and said, 'You do realize that my father was Edward de Paveley, don't you, and that he was a magistrate?' Though they scribbled a few details, they still looked bored, and she walked away, thinking how things had changed since the war.

At home, she noticed Daragh's letters, piled on the table in the Hall. Sitting on the morning-room sofa, she slit each envelope with the paperknife, glancing frantically at the sheets of paper. She did not find out where Daragh had gone, but she did learn other things. She learned that they owed Caitlin's school fees, and that there were large outstanding bills to the tradesmen. She learned that the Hall, her home, was mortgaged, and that the mortgage had not been paid for six months. She sat for a while, fragments of paper scattered around her like fallen leaves, stunned by the realization that it was possible to lose the things that you had believed inalienable. Your position in society, your childhood home.

She went to the bank the following day. The bank manager told her that she might lose the Hall. Jossy stared at him stonily and snapped, 'I'm sure it won't come to *that*, Mr Mortimer,' and stalked out of his office. But her legs were shaking. That night, standing at the window, looking for him, she thought that everything familiar was falling apart. If the night sky had lightened, or if the peaty earth had opened up to reveal chasms littered with the bones of dinosaurs, she would not have been amazed.

A month later she engaged a private detective. By then, she had visited London several times, haunting Daragh's favourite places – the Savoy, the Café Royal, his club – leaving Caitlin at home in case he came back while she was out. She went to Newmarket and to Ascot, weaving among the crowds, doggedly scanning every face. She revisited the seaside resorts they had explored when Caitlin was a small child: Cromer and Great Yarmouth and Southwold. Her heart leapt whenever she saw a tall, dark man with a spring in his step.

Mr Oddie, the private detective, was stooped, greying, and his clothes smelt of tobacco. Sitting in the morning room on the yellow silk sofa, he asked a series of impertinent questions. She endured them for Daragh's sake. She endured them because she knew by now that she was pregnant with Daragh's child. She felt for the baby only indifference. All her energy was concentrated on one undertaking. She knew that Daragh was out there, *somewhere*, and that it was just a question of looking in the right place. She refused even to consider the other possibility.

Mr Oddie shuffled around Southam, smoking his

roll-up cigarettes, asking questions. Village gossip said that Daragh had gone back to Ireland, or that he had fled to America, as so many of his forefathers had. Village gossip also suggested, woundingly, that Daragh had run away with another woman. Mr Oddie had investigated this possibility, but Daragh had been in love with Tilda Franklin at the time of his disappearance, and Tilda Franklin still lived alone in Southam. Jossy did not tell Mr Oddie of Tilda Franklin's supposed connection with her own family.

Mr Oddie wrote a report which concluded that Daragh Canavan had fled the country because of his debts, though no trace of his name had been found on the boarding lists of planes and ships. Jossy thanked Mr Oddie and paid him by selling a necklace of her mother's.

Kit called at the Hall. 'The fields aren't sown yet, Joss. Shall I organize the men?'

Jossy shook her head. 'Daragh will sort everything out, Kit, when he comes home.' Kit shuffled from one foot to the other and began to say something, but she silenced him. So long as no-one voiced her worst fears she could shut them away, put up with the physical discomfort that had become part of her day-to-day routine, keep going.

Yet sometimes she found herself thinking, *What if he never comes back?* What if Daragh, who had been the only joy of her life, had gone for ever? The pain of his leaving made her, sometimes, want to die. At night she wept and tore at the sheets, wanting to scream at the absence of him.

Sarah died in June. Tilda found her in the orchard one afternoon, sitting in the old deckchair, her eyes closed, an open book on her lap. She thought at first that Sarah was asleep, and then, touching her chill hand to wake her, knew that she was not. The sky was aquamarine, perfumed with the roses and pinks from Erich's garden.

Tilda helped the nurse lay out Sarah's body. Later, after the funeral, she sorted through Sarah's room. Packing ancient stays and lavender-scented knitted stockings into cardboard boxes, she felt as though she was putting away the past, clearing out her childhood. Waking in the early hours of the morning, she remembered the broken floor brick where Sarah hid her savings, and padded downstairs in her nightgown. Beneath the brick, she found an old stocking, filled with coins. The coins were sovereigns, a dozen of them, old and coated with a thin layer of black silt. She sat at the table, the money piled in front of her, a cup of tea growing cold in her hands as the room slowly lightened.

The future stretched out before her, as bleak and featureless as the fields that surrounded Southam. Sarah had died and Max had left her, and she would never have the third baby that she had longed for. The children who had once needed her – the academic and *Kindertransporte* refugees – now had their own lives. Josh and Melissa were growing older, and her own life seemed to have lost momentum. She thought of Max, and she thought of Sarah and, as she pressed her hands against her forehead, tears trickled through her latticed fingers.

Tilda knocked on the door of Kit de Paveley's house. She heard Kit's wheezing before he slipped the bolt. She began to apologize for her unexpected arrival, but Kit beckoned her inside.

The house shocked her. The floors and walls were blackened, and mould flowered in gaps between the wainscoting. The smell of damp and decay was overpowering. 'The housekeeper won't come any more,' explained Kit as Tilda followed him down a corridor. 'Since the flood. The water took weeks to drop below floor level – I was sloshing about in my gumboots for ages.' He smiled, trying to make a joke of it, but he looked ill. He opened a door. 'I've had a go at this room, though,' he said. 'Will it do?'

He looked at her with such obvious, such unexpected anxiety that she smiled and said, 'It's splendid, Kit. Quite splendid.' The room was better than the others. Bare boards, a few pieces of furniture, old cretonne curtains flapping at the window.

'The dig I'd begun . . .' said Kit suddenly. 'Where you found your coin, Mrs Franklin.'

She remembered giving Kit the coin that she'd worn around her neck. For luck. Her luck, like Daragh's, had run out.

'It was promising. I'd tried a few other sites beside the bank, but I found nothing. Then I discovered some tesserae and potshards. And a lovely little piece of glass. You must understand, you don't often find Roman glass. They reused it, you see.'

Tilda wondered whether he remembered to shop for himself, or to cook, or to launder his clothes. She resolved to ask him to tea.

'But I couldn't dig in the snow, and then the flood . . . Everything swept away . . . destroyed . . .' Kit blinked, and turned aside.

'But you'll try again, won't you, Kit?'

'I don't know. I don't know.' His hands dug into his pockets, he stared out of the window to the dike.

Tilda unfolded the handkerchief in which she had wrapped Sarah's sovereigns. 'I wondered if you would look at these? My aunt left them to me and I thought that I might sell them.'

The coins slid into Kit's outstretched hands. His head bent, he examined them carefully. Through the window, Tilda could see the dike, the thinly grassed slope now the only evidence of the spring's disaster.

The pains in her back persisted at irregular intervals throughout the night. Jossy fell asleep eventually, convinced that when she woke in the morning they would have stopped. They hadn't, but they had eased enough for her to drive Caitlin to school. Sitting in the school car park, crouched over the steering wheel, she wondered whether to go and see Dr Williams. But it seemed too much trouble: all that fuss, all the complicated arrangements she would have to make if Dr Williams were to admit her to hospital. Whereas if she went home, it might go away.

She drove home and sat for a while in the kitchen, sipping a cup of tea. The pain retreated until it was a slight ache, almost unnoticeable. Outside, it was a warm, bright day. The sort of day when Daragh might come home. She always associated Daragh with summer: whenever she pictured him in her mind's eye, he was striding along the top of the bank, his hands in the pockets of his old corduroy jacket, the breeze feathering his short black curls. Jossy rose from the chair and tried an experimental walk to the front door. She felt fine. It was too sunny for a cardigan, so she covered her head with her old straw hat and went outside.

She walked through the gardens, remembering the first time she had walked here with Daragh. She had known then that she loved him, and would always love him. He had been everything she could not be: vivid and bright and beautiful. When she looked back over the years, she seemed always to have been running, trying to keep up with him as he darted just out of her reach, intangible, impossibly luminescent. She did not mind that: she was just then grateful for the experience of having loved.

She passed the tangled raspberry canes and mildewed gooseberries in the kitchen garden and looked out across the field, patched red with poppies and corncockles. Jossy walked to the dike and began slowly to scramble up the slope. The covering of grass and weeds was not yet complete, and her sandals slipped in the clay. When she reached the summit her heart was hammering painfully, so she sank to her knees beside the still black water. She closed her eyes, feeling close to him. She could almost hear his footstep and catch his whispering words, blown on the breeze. His hand might touch her shoulder, and he might sit beside her and look out with her across his lands. She sat for a long time, at peace with herself, and then she became aware of a wetness between her legs. She was afraid to look, and when she stood up and saw the bloodstains on the back of her cotton dress she began to whimper with fear. She half climbed, half slid down the bank, tumbling uncontrollably down the last few feet. Pain stabbed at her back. She wanted to lie down and weep, but she knew that she must not. She had to be strong. She had had to be strong throughout her marriage: through the ordeal of giving birth to Caitlin, through the empty years when she and Daragh had not shared a bed, through his infidelities. Slowly, Jossy hobbled back to the Hall.

When, cautiously, she visited the lavatory, she knew

that she had to get help quickly. There was no-one else in the house. Something terrible was happening, and she could not for a moment think what to do. Crouched in the cloakroom, she tried to think clearly. She had to drive to Ely, yet the pain was so crippling she could hardly move. But she had to live, because if she did not, she would never see Daragh again.

Jossy shuffled out to the old Bentley, parked on the forecourt. Every action – turning the starter handle, opening the driver's door, climbing in – was a torment. But she managed it, her teeth clenched, her breathing laboured. The car rumbled down the driveway and the pain gathered and flowered, making her groan out loud. When she looked down, the towel with which she had covered the seat was crimson.

Ely was too far; she would drive to the village instead. Someone – one of the women who'd safely given birth to a dozen children – would be able to help her. Jossy steered the Bentley out through the gates onto the track. Daragh had always meant to asphalt the track, but had never got round to it. The ruts, dried by the sun, jolted the car. She reminded herself, as agony uncoiled in her spine, that it was only a couple of miles to the village. Her hands slipped from the steering wheel and she rested her forehead against the cool leather, gasping. The Bentley slewed diagonally across the road and came to a halt. When the contraction faded, Jossy tried to steer the car out of the ditch. The engine ticked away, but the wheels spun impotently, sending up dust. After a while, she stopped trying, and gave herself up to the pain. The sun beat down on her head and she closed her eyes. She knew that she was going to die, but because it hurt so much she did not particularly mind. What she minded was that she would never see him again. The word *never* was awful and terrifying. Jossy lay across the front seats, her knees curled up to her chest, and closed her eyes.

Yet in the black heart of the pain, everything else, even Daragh, became insignificant. When it subsided, a battle that each time she almost lost, so great was the relief of the absence of pain that it was almost a pleasure. Every now and then she seemed to lose a bit of time, a little chunk cut out of her ebbing life, expelled like her half-formed baby. As the contractions intensified, she sank into unconsciousness. In the fleeting return of awareness, she remembered that he had always come back to her. She had only to look in the right place, and she would see him.

She was in her bedroom at the Hall, and the baby, a boy, slept in his cradle. She pushed open a door and looked down the long dark corridor. At the end of the corridor stood a man. *Daragh*, said Jossy, and smiled, and ran to him.

Tilda stared at the heap of peel and bean shells. The knife slid into the dirty water, and her reflection gazed back at her: pale and anxious and tired. A loud knocking at the door made her snap back to reality and hastily dry her hands on her apron.

Kit de Paveley was standing on the doorstep. He was wheezing, his fist held against his chest, his face contorted with the effort of squeezing out speech. 'Jossy,' he said. 'In the car . . . She's dead, Mrs Franklin. Jossy's dead.' Kit's lungs struggled audibly. Then he said, 'That bastard – he killed her!'

She half dragged him into the house. Sitting in the parlour, he repeated, 'In the car. On her *own*.'

And that was the most awful part of it. When she had

the rest of the story, and had fetched the priest and had called the doctor (for Kit – she had seen, looking into the Bentley, that it was too late for Jossy), and had driven to Ely to break the news to poor Caitlin and had taken her to Kit, she had thought, how dreadful, to die alone like that. How dreadful, too, to be Caitlin Canavan, who had lost both her parents within four short months. Caitlin hadn't screamed or cried when Tilda had broken the news to her that her mother was dead; she had just folded her arms around her chest and seemed to close in on herself, her eyes coal-black in a small, white face. She had not spoken until Tilda had taken her across the fields to Kit de Paveley's house, where she had stopped suddenly, staring at the battered, dirty building, and had wailed, 'But what about the *horses*?'

Kit de Paveley called again the following morning. His skin was almost transparent, his eyes blue-shadowed. 'Caitlin's gone,' he said. His long, lank, fair hair flopped forward over his face. 'I can't do it, Mrs Franklin. Can't look after her. Hopeless. Even the cooking . . . haven't a clue.'

Tilda touched his shoulder. 'Hush now. There must be someone—'

'There's no-one. No aunts or cousins. A couple of mad great-uncles who can hardly look after themselves. We are not a . . . *prolific* . . . family.'

Tilda cycled to the Hall. The huge iron gates creaked as she opened them. She looked up at the house and tried to imagine her mother working here more than thirty years ago, but the closed doors and dusty panes looked back at her, telling her nothing, their secrets secure. She was a trespasser here, shut out by the history and wealth of the place, and she found herself tiptoeing through the gardens, afraid that her footsteps might disturb angry ghosts.

Grant that no hobgoblins fright me, no hungry devils rise up and bite me . . . She found Caitlin in the stables, as she had expected. The light was dim, the child wrapped in Daragh's old corduroy jacket, her face pressed against the gleaming black neck of her pony. Just for an instant Tilda mistook the daughter for the father; for the flicker of an eyelid Caitlin Canavan adopted the fleeting image of the man who had pulled her life out of shape. But at Tilda's small, stifled gasp, Caitlin turned, and the man's face became the child's once more.

Chapter Eleven

Tilda's recounting to me of the events of 1947 had erased some of the shock of Caitlin Canavan's telephone call. Tilda had admitted to having committed adultery with Daragh Canavan, her childhood sweetheart, but had told me that she had regretted it almost immediately. In describing Daragh's encounter with his creditors, Tilda had reinforced Patrick's conclusion that Daragh's precarious financial situation had led to his disappearance.

I had almost managed to rationalize Caitlin Canavan's accusations. I had misheard them, or misinterpreted them. Or she had been drunk, as Patrick had suggested. Yesterday I had phoned Caitlin and arranged to meet her for lunch in a restaurant in Covent Garden. Before I left the house, I glanced at the photograph of Caitlin and Daragh: the little girl in her velvet-collared coat, button boots and beret, her hand in her father's. They were strikingly similar, strikingly good-looking. Even in that stilted black and white photograph I could sense their greedy hunger for life.

The Covent Garden restaurant was long and dark, tunnelling back into the building. When I looked around, I recognized Caitlin Canavan instantly, sitting at a table in a wrought iron booth, a cigarette in one hand, a glass in the other. She must have been over sixty, yet the child's face lingered, the eyes wideset and watchful, the mouth sensuous, red-lipped. I wormed past the waitresses.

'Miss Canavan?'

'Miss Bennett?' She shook my hand.

'Rebecca, please. May I sit down?'

She laughed throatily. 'I hope you don't mind sitting in the pariah's enclosure.' She gestured to her cigarette, and called the waitress. 'Another G and T, darling, and one for my friend. And could we see the menu?'

I watched Caitlin covertly as she studied the menu. Once more, I experienced that peculiar and exhilarating sense of the boundaries of past and present merging, becoming indistinguishable.

'Pasta . . . frittata . . .' muttered Caitlin dismissively, 'one cannot buy decent food in London these days . . .' She stubbed her cigarette out in her empty glass. 'At least in Dublin one can get a good steak.'

Her accent was an uneasy mixture of upper-middle-class English and southern Irish. 'Do you still live in Dublin, Miss Canavan?'

'I've a lovely little Georgian house on the south side.' The waitress returned to take our order. 'I'll have the prawns, please, darling. And a bottle of that gorgeous Chablis.'

I ordered an omelette and took another mouthful of gin while my first question formed in my head. But she beat me to it, leaning across the table towards me, her eyes dark and intense.

'I want to tell you about my father. I want you to understand what he was like. He was a wonderful man, Rebecca, the best father a girl could have. He taught me to ride, and he taught me to fish and to shoot. And to dance. When my father danced, all the women in the room would turn and look at him and wish that they were his partner. And he was so kind. I remember, at the beginning of the war, he insisted that we took in evacuees – most of the county families managed to get out of it, you understand. Frightful little toads they were too – they didn't stay long, thank God, they were unsuitable for some reason, but at least he tried. All the servants and labourers loved him. And he was so good with the dogs and the horses ... I can still remember how he wept when he had to shoot his old gun dog.' She paused, and lit another cigarette.

I said, 'And your mother?'

'Mummy adored him. She simply adored him. She never looked at another man. It was love at first sight, did you know that? Terribly romantic.'

Jossy remained for me a shadowy figure, her passion for her handsome, fickle husband all that was visible of her.

'I had such a happy childhood.' Caitlin's lips curled into a smile. 'Horses and parties and trips to the theatre. Daddy always made time for me. When I couldn't get to sleep he'd tell me stories of his own childhood in Ireland.'

The waitress arrived with the wine. When she had gone, Caitlin raised her glass in a toast. 'To retribution.'

I struggled to suppress a shiver. Her face had altered, the fleeting impression of youth vanished, her vivacity replaced by cold bitterness. She muttered, 'Cook's daughter wrote to me. She still lives in Southam. She always remembers my birthday and Christmas. After I read her letter, I knew that I had to come back. I went to the police a couple of days ago. I want my father to be buried properly, next to my mother.'

I remembered Jossy Canavan's grave, with its empty flower vase. I said hesitantly, 'You can't be sure—'

'I *know* that they have found my father. I told the police that.' She drained her glass. 'Though they were very offhand.' She sniffed.

Something occurred to me. 'You could find out for certain,' I said. 'DNA.'

She looked blank. I explained, 'They could extract DNA from the remains that were found and compare it with yours. They'd have to take a sample of your blood. Nothing much. Then you'd know.'

'What a marvellous idea,' she said. 'What a simply marvellous idea. I shall take the train to Cambridge tomorrow and *insist*.'

The food was served. I didn't much feel like eating my omelette. Caitlin's long fingers twisted the shells from prawns, scattering them haphazardly over the tablecloth. Then she said, 'They told me that he may have been *alive*,' and her face crumpled and she wept into her greasy hands.

I searched in my pocket and managed to find her a reasonably clean tissue. She dabbed at her eyes and blew her nose. 'I waited for hours,' she said, 'and he did not come home.' The child's grief at the parent's desertion echoed in her voice.

I refilled her glass and topped up mine. She gulped the Chablis. 'He was having an affair with that woman.' She sniffed and dropped the wet tissue among the prawn shells. 'I didn't understand – I was only thirteen, after all. He'd gone to *her*.'

'To Tilda?' My heart began to beat fast.

'Mmm. Dame Tilda Franklin.' Caitlin's voice was

heavily laced with irony. 'My aunt, if you believe her stories.'

'You don't?'

'She could have been anybody's, couldn't she? The girl – her mother – was unstable, of course. Everyone knew that.'

'When did you find out?'

'That we were supposedly related? Josh told me, years later.' She made a dismissive gesture. 'Such nonsense.'

She returned to the prawns, attacking them with efficient savagery. 'Anyway – that night. We were to ride to Devil's Dike the next day, Daddy and I. We hadn't been out riding for ages because of the flood, and Devil's Dike was one of my favourite places. I made the picnic myself. Daddy watched me make it. All his favourite things – Gentleman's Relish and water biscuits and a little flask of tea for if we felt cold.' She glanced up at me. 'You see, don't you, that he would not have willingly broken his promise to me? That he would not have stood in the kitchen and watched me slice bread and wash apples if he had not intended to go with me?'

I nodded. Tilda herself had said that Daragh would not have left his daughter. When I looked at Caitlin Canavan, I saw that her eyes were slightly glazed, and I guessed that she looked not at the crowded restaurant, but backwards, into a different time.

'I remember that he was wearing his best clothes. His Egyptian cotton shirt, his tweed jacket, his silk foulard. He looked so handsome. He was wearing cologne – I noticed it when I kissed him. He'd been drinking that day – he let me pour out his whisky and fill up his little water jug – so I suppose he wore the cologne to mask the whisky. We all do it, don't we, darling?' She laughed. 'It was quite late when I finished packing the picnic basket. I saw him leave the house, and I ran out after him to kiss him goodnight. I asked him where he was going. I remember that he laughed and said, "I'm going to net a little bird." I thought he meant that he was going shooting, though he hadn't taken a gun. He walked out through the kitchen garden and across the fields to Southam. He couldn't walk along the top of the bank as he usually did, because they hadn't finished repairing the breach.' Caitlin's hands were fisted on the table, and her voice had become low and urgent.

I said, 'Did you see him reach Southam?'

'It became too dark. And even by that route, the short cut, it's almost a mile.' When Caitlin looked up at me, I saw that her eyes were burning. 'But he can only have been going to Southam, can't he? If he'd meant to go further, then he would have taken the car. He wouldn't have driven to Southam, you see, because petrol was still rationed.'

I remembered Southam village and its isolation, and I guessed that she was right. An idea occurred to me. 'Perhaps your father was going to the pub. You said that he'd been drinking. Perhaps he wanted to drink in company—'

She shook her head vigorously. 'Dressed in his best clothes? Certainly not! He'd have worn his old corduroys to visit the Pheasant. That's why the men liked him, Rebecca – because he could become one of them.'

Daragh the chameleon, I thought. Daragh who could make himself into whatever it was the other person most desired: one of the boys, or the affectionate father, or the seductive lover.

'And besides,' Caitlin added, 'I *know* that he didn't go to the Pheasant. After my father vanished, my mother engaged a private detective to look for him. I found the report after my mother died. It was in her things.'

I stared at her, my mouth dry. 'Do you still have it?'

'Of course.' She glanced at me. 'Shall I send you a copy of it, Rebecca? Nobody will believe me – they might believe you. Will you tell the truth for me?'

I nodded, unable to speak. She whispered, 'I remember that he was whistling "Galway Bay". He only whistled "Galway Bay" when he was happy,' and I knew that she had returned to the past again, and that she was a child, watching her handsome father walk away from her for the very last time.

'When he was seeing another woman?' I prompted gently.

'Some people might have thought him immoral, but I think that if you are good-looking and charming and kind and funny, then why not make a lot of people happy? That's what my daddy was good at, Rebecca. Making people happy.' She lit another cigarette. 'My mother was not enough for him. Some men are like that. And my parents never shared a bedroom, of course. Mummy nearly died giving birth to me, and the doctor told her that another baby would kill her.' She exhaled a cloud of blue smoke. 'And they were right, and I was left with no-one except Kit, who was hopeless.' Her face creased again, but this time she did not cry. 'So I had to go and live with *her*.'

Caitlin wiped her hands on the napkin, and beckoned to the waitress. 'Finished, darling. Is there a dessert menu?' She smiled brilliantly, and the girl cleared away the plates. 'The unhappiest years of my life,' she went on, leaning across the table towards me, her voice penetrating. 'I'd lost my father and my mother and my home. That woman – Tilda Franklin – took me out of my lovely school and sent me to a council school. She wouldn't even let me keep my dear little pony. We went to live in that awful house with that peculiar man.'

'Colonel Renshaw?' I knew that at the end of 1947, Tilda had moved to Oxfordshire, to become housekeeper to a retired colonel.

Caitlin nodded, and glanced at the dessert menu. 'Profiteroles . . . caramel . . . so dull. Ah, treacle tart. Custard *and* cream, of course.'

I chose fruit. When the waitress had gone, I prompted Caitlin. 'So you lived with Tilda . . .?'

'Until I was fifteen and a half. Then she threw me out.' Caitlin poured more wine into her glass; the bottle was almost empty. 'You do know, don't you, Rebecca, that her own daughter chose not to stay with her?'

'Melissa?'

'She went to live with her father. She couldn't stand it either. And Josh was at boarding school.' Caitlin laughed, too loudly. 'So she may have been an angel with her adopted children, you see, but with her own she was lousy.'

The pudding arrived. I picked at the nice arrangement of cherries and pineapple, but did not yet eat. I was searching for the right words to frame the necessary question, when Caitlin hissed: 'I want you to tell the truth. I want you to tell the world that she killed my father. She killed him because he would not leave me.' As she leaned towards me I saw the grey roots of her tinted black hair and the way her lipstick had leached into the fine lines around her mouth. Beneath the expensive cosmetics and the old-fashioned clubbiness, she was an ageing, unhappy woman.

'He went to see her that night, and he never came back.

I waited for him, but he did not return to me because she had killed him and hidden his body in the dike.'

When I parted from Caitlin and left the restaurant, I did not immediately go home. Instead, I sat outside on a bench, watching the fire-eaters and jugglers and street traders, thinking. It was very warm: I slipped off my jacket, and pushed my damp hair back from my aching forehead. Yet when I looked back at the conversation I had just had with Caitlin Canavan, when I recalled her certainty, I shivered.

Though Caitlin had drunk steadily throughout our lunch, I could not dismiss what she had told me as the fanciful ravings of an alcoholic. Her memories had been too precise, too vivid, to be anything other than the truth. They fitted neatly with what Tilda herself had told me. The flood, the love affair, Daragh's disappearance. Tilda might not have lied, but she could have left things out. *She had killed him and hidden his body in the dike*. Was it possible? She was capable of killing, after all, and capable of evasion – Leila Gilbert's story of Tilda's flight from Holland in 1940 had taught me that. Had Tilda erased Daragh's death from her story, just as she had erased the death of the German soldier?

A street seller waved a copy of the *Big Issue* in my face, and I fumbled in my pocket for a pound coin. I thought of going to see Tilda, to confront her with Caitlin's accusations, but dismissed the idea almost immediately. I had to speak to someone, though. I grabbed my bag, ducked around a clown building an invisible wall, and headed for Patrick's chambers.

London was hot and crowded and bad-tempered. It was half past four by the time I reached Gray's Inn and confronted Patrick's superior secretary. 'Mr Franklin is in a meeting,' she said repressively. I was hot and sticky and my mouth was dry; glancing out of the window, I saw a wine bar on the opposite side of the road. I scribbled a note, and asked Patrick's secretary to give it to him as soon as he was available.

I went to the wine bar, ordered mineral water, and sat down at a small table in the corner of the room. In spite of the water, my headache grew worse, not better. The air in the small, windowless room was still and clammy. I tried to think logically through Caitlin's version of the events of April 1947, to pick out the flaws, but my thoughts congealed, thick and ugly and oppressive.

It was after five o'clock when Patrick appeared, threading through the office workers who had begun to spill into the bar from the City.

'Rebecca.' He kissed my cheek. 'Are you all right? Or is Tilda—'

'I'm fine, Patrick,' I said quickly. 'And so's Tilda, as far as I know. I haven't seen her since Tuesday.'

'Then what is it? Your note said that it was urgent.'

His concern had altered to irritation, and I began to regret my impulse in coming here. But I could not turn back.

'I've just had lunch with Caitlin Canavan,' I said. 'She's staying at the Savoy, Patrick.'

His eyes narrowed. 'I know.'

'Did she telephone Tilda again?'

'She wrote a letter. On headed notepaper, for God's sake.' He glanced at his watch. 'I could do with a drink.' He went to the bar, and returned after a few moments with a bottle of Sancerre and two glasses. He sat down next to me, and poured out the wine.

'Tilda showed me the letter. Caitlin said in it that she'd been to the police.' Patrick slung his jacket on the back of the chair, and loosened his tie. 'I had a word with them. Apparently she was half cut when she went to the police station, so it wasn't difficult to persuade them not to take her too seriously.' He paused for a moment, drinking his wine. 'You had lunch with her? Why, Rebecca? I explained to you the other day that that would be a waste of time.'

My head pounded, and I was angered that he should see fit to tell me how to do my job. I tried to keep my voice level. 'I need to see all sides, Patrick.'

'Don't you trust Tilda?'

'It's not a question of trust.' Tilda herself had told me that it was my task to distinguish the truth.

'Isn't it?'

'No. Not so black and white. Life isn't black or white,' I added, blundering into cliché. 'Two people can remember the same event quite differently, can't they?'

The wine bar was filling up; Eighties leftovers with striped shirts and red braces were braying their orders. The heat gathered, making our corner of the room a stifling little cage. Patrick looked withdrawn and impatient, and the silence was punctuated by the sound of breaking glass and loud laughter from the bar.

'I ran into a friend of yours the other day,' he said suddenly. 'Toby Carne.'

'Toby's not a friend.'

'No?'

'He was a friend.' I sounded touchy. 'But he isn't now.'

'You mean, he was a lover, but he isn't now.'

I said angrily, 'Toby was my lover, but I've barely seen him since we broke up last year.' Though I remembered, too well, that fleeting, unnerving visit a couple of months ago. And I had learned, through Tilda, that though love might transmute to jealousy or hatred, it lingers, a persistent catalyst.

We sat in silence, evading each other's eyes. I thought of Jennifer: beautiful, elegant Jennifer Franklin. Six inches taller than me, and probably, damn it, a stone lighter. My headache was augmented by a feeling of utter misery.

Patrick said stiffly, 'I realize that you need to talk to as many people as possible. But Caitlin is, I think, a special case. She's always been a troublemaker. She drinks a lot, and then she talks a lot, and most of it is rubbish but, you know, mud sticks.'

'You prefer her to stay in Dublin, out of the way.' The words snapped out before I could hold them back.

His head jerked up, his blue eyes wide and angry. 'Christ, Rebecca – you make it sound so sinister.'

He refilled his glass; I refused more wine. I felt slightly sick. 'I can't just ignore what Caitlin says, Patrick,' I hissed. 'I can't just dismiss it – pretend it hasn't been said.'

He blinked. His fingers drummed against the edge of the table. 'So you believe her?'

'No. I don't know. Patrick—'

'Not an unreasonable question, Rebecca. If you didn't believe Caitlin then why did you go and see her?'

'For heaven's sake, Patrick—' I had spoken too loud; some of the boys at the bar turned round and stared. 'Stop trying to catch me out. Stop trying to make *me* feel guilty.'

My heart pounded painfully in my chest. Whereas formerly I had read desire, or even love, in his eyes, I now saw something else. His expression chilled me.

He said slowly, 'I always knew this bloody biography was a mistake.'

'What did you want of me, Patrick? Some anodyne little book showing only one side of Tilda? No-one is perfect, you know.'

'I'd almost become resigned to the idea. Almost begun to welcome it. I thought I could trust you to do a decent job.' His voice was bitter. 'But you're going to write some sensationalist rubbish, aren't you?'

'How dare you—' I stood up clumsily, knocking over my wine glass so that it shattered on the tiled floor. There was a ragged chorus of cheers from the red-braced mob at the bar.

'There are plenty of skeletons in our family closet, Rebecca, but they're just not the ones you're looking at. Ask Melissa what Caitlin did. Ask her.' Patrick's angry voice followed me as I ran out of the bar.

It was rush hour. My Tube ticket refused to go through the barrier; as I stood there stupidly staring at it, the man behind me pushed his ticket into the slot and shoved me through before him. I squeezed onto the Underground train, nauseated by the hot, sweating bodies that surrounded me. When the train stopped in a tunnel and for a few moments the lights went out, I thought of Daragh, in the dike: the darkness, the suffocating weight of the soil.

I discovered, when I finally reached my flat, that I had come out without my key, and I had to fiddle with the little kitchen window beside the gravel path. The telephone began to ring just as I shook the latch free and wormed through the open window onto the sink. I made a mental note to get it fixed and, convinced that

Patrick must be telephoning to make up our quarrel, dashed to answer the phone.

When Charles answered, I began to cry. Because I was hot and tired and miserable, I suppose. Charles was perfectly sweet. 'I shall jump in a taxi *immediately*, Rebecca.' I couldn't put him off because I could hardly speak.

He was at my door in ten minutes, with a huge bunch of flowers, a bottle of wine and a video of *Casablanca*. He found a jug for the flowers, and a couple of glasses for the wine, and looked at my red eyes, and said, 'You're not weeping for the gorgeous Patrick Franklin, are you?' and, though I thought I had got myself under control, I began to howl again.

He hugged me and patted my back, while I tried incoherently to explain.

'Patrick – quarrelled. In a wine bar—'

'Ghastly places, darling.'

'Only trying to do my *job*—'

'There, there.'

''S not my fault if his grandmother's a murdere—'

'Absolutely, darling.'

'*He's* the bloody lawyer—'

'Poor old Patrick's got his reputation to think of, hasn't he?'

At that, I stopped howling, and looked up. 'What do you mean, Charles?'

He offered me his handkerchief. 'Well, as you said, he is a lawyer. Rather a well-known lawyer, in fact. Probably intends to be a QC or a judge or something. Wouldn't do his career much good if people knew his grandma had a habit of socking her lovers over the head and burying them alive in dikes.'

I stared at him. I felt cold inside. 'You mean, you think that he *knows* . . .?'

'I've no idea, darling. Never met the man.'

I thought of Patrick, who had responded to the news of the discovery of Daragh's body with anger, not shock. Patrick, whose family had paid Caitlin Canavan off for years. Patrick, who had persuaded his friend in the Cambridgeshire police force that Caitlin was just a mad old drunk.

'A drink?' asked Charles, gesturing to the wine bottle, but I shook my head. 'I'd rather have tea.' I had drunk enough today. 'Would you, Charles?'

He went into the kitchen. I sat in the armchair, trying to think, but reduced to a sort of mental paralysis by fear and misery. Of course Patrick's reputation – and the reputation of the Franklin family – was important to him. His well-loved grandmother, his illustrious father. At Tilda's party I had met musicians, writers, doctors and scientists. Tilda's family – Patrick's family – were not ordinary. They were not filing clerks or bus drivers or shop assistants. Even Matty, with her nose-ring, intended to read physics at Cambridge.

If Tilda had been involved in the death of her old lover, and if that involvement was to become known – through me – how might that affect the Franklin family? As a dark stain, perhaps, tarnishing generations, blackening both the glamour of their past and their glittering present-day lives.

Charles placed the tray on my desk, and poured the tea. We didn't talk about Patrick or Tilda; instead, he put on the video and we watched it, curled up on my bed, Charles's comforting arm round my shoulders. Afterwards, he offered to stay the night in case I wanted company, but I refused. I needed to be alone. I needed to think. I needed to understand how deeply I had been betrayed.

*   *   *

I was curled up in a foetal postition, my wrists and ankles latched together. I struggled feebly as they shovelled the earth upon me. A clod of wet clay on my feet, another on my chest. It squeezed my lungs, stealing my breath, and its scent invaded my nostrils, heavy and grassy and cloying. Sticky morsels of earth struck my face, rolling into my eye sockets and mouth. I tried to move, but the soil weighed me down. It cut off the light, making me dumb, its weight increasing with each impacting spadeful, pinning me to the darkness, compressing the spongy air sacs of my lungs and the chambers of my heart. The heat, the weight and the blackness intensified, so that I could not move at all . . .

I sat up. I think I screamed aloud. My hand, searching for the light switch, shook so much that I knocked the lamp from the chest of drawers and it fell to the floor, shattering the bulb. It was not yet dawn; the room was inky black, opaque. My heart pounded in my chest. Thud, thud, thud . . . I put a foot out of bed to stumble to the light switch, to escape this awful oppressive darkness, and then I realized that the sound I heard was not in rhythm with the beating of my heart. Thud, thud, thud . . . crunch, crunch, crunch. Footsteps on gravel. I had to clench my fists, to press them against my teeth to stop myself screaming. Fumbling in the darkness, I found the book about the Fens. I climbed out of bed, and knew from the pain in my heel that I had stepped on a fragment of broken glass. Blood pulsed in my ears, and I struggled to get hold of myself. I felt sick, my forehead glazed with sweat. I told myself that I was imagining the footsteps. That they lingered from my dream, the footprints of Daragh's murderer, walking away from that unquiet grave.

I opened the bedroom door cautiously, the book clutched in my hand. The small corridor was unlit: the bulb had gone weeks ago and the socket was high and inaccessible. I tiptoed to the kitchen. As I pushed open the door, I heard the noise again, and then a yowl and the clang of a dustbin lid. A cat. I switched on the light and slid down the wall to sit on the floor, half laughing at myself, half furious. The book slipped out of my hands and fell open. I saw by the date stamp that it was already a fortnight overdue. For some reason this upset me disproportionately: my life seemed to be sliding out of control again. I sat there for a while, hot and trembling with reaction, but as cold as clay inside. The waves of nausea intensified; my stomach lurched and I ran to the bathroom and was extremely sick.

Afterwards, I went back to bed with a glass of water and a plaster for my foot. The nightmare lingered, oppressive and claustrophobic. How ridiculous, I told myself, to have been reduced to nausea by an image of something that might have happened almost fifty years ago. And then it occurred to me, with sudden horrible intuition, that it wasn't only the library book that was overdue. That my sickness might have nothing to do with my dream. I limped into the living room and found my diary and leafed back through the pages. After ten minutes of increasingly frantic checking, I came to the conclusion that I had not had a period since two weeks before I went to Cumbria. Eight weeks ago.

I hadn't gone back on the pill since my miscarriage. Since Toby, I'd gloomily anticipated celibacy, and when Patrick and I had become lovers he had volunteered to take care of that side of things. I had been relieved: I had often felt sick and bloated when taking the pill. But that first time . . . I remembered the straw scratching my back, the echo of the rain, and how Patrick's body had fitted into mine. Neither of us had considered the consequences. There hadn't been time.

I counted the weeks again, certain that I must have made a mistake. The numbers were unchanged: eight weeks. I sat up in bed, my head clutched in my hands. Dawn had begun to seep through the window, showing me what I already knew: that my home, with its three small rooms and a concrete yard instead of a garden, was utterly unsuitable for children. I imagined a baby buggy, Moses basket, changing mat and all the other clutter that babies necessitate added to my own mess. I had glimpsed through my sister the unending effort that looking after a small child entails; I remembered Jane, white-faced and straggle-haired, telling me that she would sell her soul for eight hours' uninterrupted sleep. I pictured myself changing a baby with one hand while typing with the other. I imagined the sniggering glances of the Jason Darkes of this world as I breastfed a baby while discussing the causes of the First World War.

And I began, sitting there in the cold early morning light, to question whether I could continue with Tilda Franklin's biography. Tilda's image seemed to be splitting in two, the private face at variance with the public one. My faith in Tilda had eroded like the dike that had been battered by floodwater, the dike which had once concealed Daragh Canavan's body. I could not dismiss Caitlin Canavan's accusations as the jealous ravings of a lonely, abandoned woman. Tilda herself had admitted that she and Daragh had been lovers, and Caitlin's conviction that Daragh had been going to meet Tilda on the night of his disappearance had the ring of truth. *I'm going to net a little bird.*

Leila Gilbert's voice echoed, too. *Tilda shot him and*

pushed his body into the dike. When I tried to picture the polders of north Holland, I saw instead the long bleak line of Southam dike. The splash and suck of bubbles as the soldier's body tumbled into the water; the earth that had entombed Daragh Canavan as he still breathed.

Had Tilda lied to me about her motive for having her biography written? Had she contacted me not out of a desire to make her mother's story public – a motive which convinced me less and less – but with a less reputable intention? Tilda was old and frail, she must know that she had not long to live. Had she chosen me as her instrument? Was I to see only the fairer face – was I to fix her image for posterity in white marble, indisputable, indissoluble? Was I to enable her to make her last gift to the family who had always been of paramount importance to her – the gift of an untarnished reputation?

And as I followed that thought to its logical conclusion, I remembered my first conversation with Patrick in the garden of The Red House. Myself, sarcastically asking him whether he thought me illustrious enough to write his grandmother's biography. And his reply. *I should think you're as good as anyone. Better than most, perhaps.* It occurred to me, with cold and threatening plausibility, that Patrick had approved my choice *because* of my inexperience, and not in spite of it. Patrick, the lawyer, guessing – or knowing – that Tilda had something to hide, had believed me too amateurish – and too stupid – to recognize the contradictions in his grandmother's story.

The edifice that I had built up was failing, weakened from its foundations. We don't believe in bad blood any more, but we do believe in genes. Little thumbprints, computer dots on a double helix. Is there a gene for evil, that Edward de Paveley passed on to one daughter and not to the other? For poor Jossy had been foolish, not evil. And Tilda – what was Tilda? Had she inherited her father's ruthlessness, his imperiousness? Had she, when she had understood that Daragh had destroyed her marriage, yet would cling on to his own, meted out her own sort of justice to her deceitful, fickle lover? *I do believe in justice*, Tilda had said to me, a long time ago – yet in what justice did she believe? An older sort of justice, I feared, Sarah Greenlees' sort of justice. An eye for an eye, a tooth for a tooth . . .

You cannot write unless you believe in what you are writing, and my belief was crumbling. My belief in Tilda, whom I had learned to love, was ebbing away. I could not be used as Tilda's instrument. Yet without the income from the book about Tilda, I could not support myself, let alone a baby. I went back to bed, but I remembered the spider-webs that had festooned the box trees in the garden of The Red House, and how they had clung to me, a sticky gossamer that I could not brush away. And I wept again, knowing that I had lost Patrick, whom I had let myself love, a little.

When I awoke again at ten o'clock the following morning, the horrors of the previous day and night had receded. I told myself that my nausea was likely to have been the consequence of fear, rather than pregnancy. I had not been regular since my miscarriage and, after all, Patrick and I had only been careless once – since Cumbria we had practised safe sex like responsible adults. As for my work, I told myself that I must make no rash decisions. I decided to have a day off – I had become too embroiled in this book, and had lost the capacity for objectivity that had always been so useful to me. So I cleaned my flat, and borrowed a stepladder from my next door neighbour to replace the light bulb in the hall, and left a message on the answerphone of a joiner to replace the window latch. Then I went to the supermarket and lastly to the library, where I paid the fine and ordered half a dozen more obscure histories of the Fens, gleaned from my overdue book's bibliography.

At home, the little red eye of the answerphone announced that there were two messages waiting for me. *Patrick*, I thought, and when first Charles's and then Toby's voice filled the room I was almost overwhelmed by a raw grief. I could have phoned him, I suppose, but I no longer trusted him. He had accused me of being callous and over-ambitious – such hurt cut deeply. I missed all of Toby's message and had to rewind it. He had tickets for the ballet tonight, he said. Did I want to come?

I was about to phone him and refuse, when something occurred to me. I contacted Toby at his chambers and arranged to meet him outside the Royal Opera House. The ballet was *Giselle*, and the tale of betrayal and madness and doomed love wormed its way into my heart, gnawing at the precarious equilibrium of the day. In the interval, I questioned Toby about Patrick, picking away at the thin scab until it hurt. I didn't care in the least that Patrick Franklin was plainly the last person that Toby wanted to talk about, so I deserved, I suppose, to find out what I did. That Jennifer and Ellie lived in Cumbria, that the farmhouse where Patrick and I had first made love was only a few miles from the town where Patrick's wife now lived.

* * *

In the course of another long, sleepless night, I concluded that Patrick had never loved me, and that, from the beginning of our relationship, he had been using me. Keeping an eye on me, distracting me, trying to ensure that I saw only the admirable side of Tilda's character. Reputation, as Charles had pointed out, mattered to Patrick. The sort of glittering career that Toby coveted, Patrick was seizing for himself. If Tilda had played a part in Daragh Canavan's death, and if I made public her involvement, the scandal would inevitably affect Patrick. Patrick had never wanted Tilda's biography written but, unable to stop her, he had taken the next best route and had attempted to influence the biographer. Rich, handsome Patrick Franklin had found it easy enough to bewitch short, plump, struggling Rebecca Bennett. I had never felt more humiliated.

At mid-morning the next day, the phone rang. It was Joan, Tilda's housekeeper.

'Tilda's in hospital, I'm afraid, Rebecca. I thought I should let you know.'

'Angina?' I asked.

'It's more serious than that. She had a heart attack last night. The police came to talk to her yesterday. And that wretched woman phoned—' I heard Joan's quick angry outward breath. 'I was at the shops, and Tilda answered it—'

'Caitlin telephoned?'

Joan's voice was grim. 'Yes. Anyway, Tilda's not too good. Only immediate family are allowed to visit, but I'll be here as usual on Monday, of course.'

I asked a few more questions, muttered hollow good wishes, and put the phone down. I spent a wretched weekend wondering whether to write to Nancy to tell her that I was going to have to break my contract –

and then wondering how on earth I could repay the advance. And knowing that I should buy a pregnancy testing kit, but being unable to face doing so.

In the end, I drove to Oxfordshire as usual on Monday morning, postponing all decisions a few more days. I had expected to spend a quiet day sifting through old letters, but when I rang the doorbell Joan greeted me and told me that Tilda had asked me to visit her in hospital.

Reluctantly, I drove to the Radcliffe Infirmary. Tilda was in a small side room. 'We told her only family, but she insisted on seeing you,' said the nurse disapprovingly, as she led me along the corridor. Tilda, propped up on pillows, looked small and frail and white. I touched her papery forehead with my lips: a Judas-kiss.

'Just five minutes,' said the nurse.

I began to ask Tilda how she felt, but she grabbed my hand, halting me. Her breath was shallow and quick. 'I had to see you, Rebecca,' she whispered. 'Caitlin said that she had talked to you about Daragh.'

I looked away from her great, wounded eyes. Tilda's hold on life seemed so fragile that I was afraid I had only to say a word, or to frame the wrong question, for the thread to be snapped. So I said nothing.

'I have to tell you about Daragh.' Her words echoed Caitlin's, only a few days before. *I want to tell you about my father.* 'He was a destroyer. It took me a very long time to realize it, and he didn't intend to be, but he was. Daragh destroyed almost everyone who came in contact with him. Jossy ... Max ... Caitlin ... and me, of course.' She closed her eyes for a moment, as though even the act of seeing exhausted her. 'Daragh destroyed that silly girl he got pregnant ... and he destroyed his daughter's inheritance. Caitlin lost everything – the house, the land, everything . . . What Daragh did touched, in the end, my children too.'

Tilda opened her eyes and looked at me. 'I am not saying that I was not also to blame.' Her voice had become stronger. 'And I am not saying that I did not love him once, because that would not be true. I am telling you only that I saw him clearly in the end. Which Caitlin, of course, can never do.'

'Caitlin came with you to Oxfordshire, didn't she?'

'Yes, God help me.' Her words weren't much more than a sigh. 'We had to leave Southam. The cottage was so cramped, and I had begun to detest the place. There was gossip . . . rumour. In so small a village, one has few secrets. I was desperate to leave, but I had little money and there was still a housing shortage.' Tilda smiled weakly. 'Kit de Paveley found me a job. I had offered to look after Caitlin, you see, so he wanted to help me in return. The poor girl had no-one else, and it was obvious that Kit could not bring her up.'

She paused, and seemed to gather her strength. 'Kit found me the post of housekeeper to an old friend of his, Colonel Renshaw, who lived in Oxfordshire. It was perfect – a big house, with only the old gentleman living there, so there was plenty of room for all of us. I had to lie a little, of course,' she added, and her gaze held mine, challenging me. 'You must remember that morality was different then. Stricter, less accommodating. I told the colonel that my husband had been taken ill during the war and was living in the south of France for the sake of his health. I let him believe that my parents had been married, and that they had died when I was an infant. I was desperate, you see, Rebecca. I had to start again. I had to put the past behind me.'

I heard the clack of stout black shoes on the polished

corridor behind me. The nurse said, 'Time for our rest now, Dame Tilda.'

There was a flicker of the familiar impatience in Tilda's eyes. Then she whispered, echoing Patrick, 'You should talk to Melissa, dear,' and turned away from me.

CHAPTER TWELVE

Max had quit his job and sailed for France. Paris in the heat was every bit as awful as London in the heat, and even the decent hotels served only ersatz coffee, so he took the train to Angers, in the Loire valley, and sat in cafés drinking red wine, looking up at the château. France was as shabby as England, paint peeling from the doors and window frames, but somehow, in the sunlight, it didn't seem to matter so much. From Angers, he travelled to Chinon, where he wandered through the ruins of the castle on its rocky crop and looked down at the bridge across the river, decked with flags because it was a fête day. Then Saumur, then Tours. His pace slowed as he went south, almost as though the sun and the heat had entered his veins, subduing the restlessness and nervous energy that had always been part of him.

He stayed a few days in each place, sleeping in cheap pensions, dining in cramped little cafés. The food was better in the countryside, where fields of sunflowers raised their yellow faces to the sky, and the village markets were crammed with stalls selling wild duck and pots of homemade jam. As he travelled south, the sun grew more intense, and Max, like the French, and like the lizards that darted in the shade, began to take a siesta after lunch. Ten minutes at first, then half an hour, then an hour. One day he slept until four o'clock in the afternoon, and then got up and ambled round, looking at the people. His capacity for sleep amazed him. It was as though he was making up for all those years of nervous interrupted dozes in foxholes and jeeps.

Eventually, he went an entire day without wanting to curl up into a little, shaking ball when he remembered Belsen. He still thought of them, those grey shadowy people, and he still wept for them, and that was right, surely. But they had retreated just a little, making the business of living more tolerable. When that pain lessened, though, the other intensified. He had managed to avoid thinking of Tilda: now, every light-haired woman made him turn his head, and every low, melodic peal of laughter became hers. He would have liked to have killed Daragh Canavan, who had succeeded in proving to him what he had always feared: that Tilda had never really loved him. He had been second-best when they had married, and he had remained second-best until the end. He thought of her with bitterness and with anger, and a sense of betrayal. He had arranged with the bank to send money for Josh's schooling and the children's clothes and food, and he wrote to his children frequently – light, descriptive little notes about the places he had seen, the people he had spoken to. He had no contact with Tilda. When he thought of her, he saw her golden body entwined with Daragh Canavan's, and he despised himself for having loved her.

When he reached the village a few miles to the south of Saintes, Max stopped and did not travel any further. It wasn't much of a village: there was a church and a *mairie* and a butcher's and a baker's and a tobacconist's and a ramshackle garage with a *Fermé* sign pasted outside it.

The village was surrounded by bleached dusty fields and by vineyards. Max enquired for a room and was shown to a little stone-built hotel in the square. At night, the sky was a square of blue velvet, spangled with stars, set to the music of cicadas.

A few weeks later he bought the garage with the *Fermé* sign. He had learned a lot about cars during the war. There was a house attached to the garage, of a pale stone that kept the sun out during the hottest part of the day. Part of the roof had fallen in, so Max cut wood to repair the broken rafters and replaced slates. There was no electricity or running water, so he used oil lamps in the evenings, and drew water from the well. He repaired the rusty old petrol pump and acquired second-hand tools from market places and house sales. The woman in the *boulangerie* where he bought his morning baguette began, around the new year, to greet him by name. He dined each midday in the little café, and drank red wine or a marc in the bar at the corner of the square. He abandoned his Players and taught himself to enjoy Gauloises. He was pleasant and friendly, passing the time of day with the black-shawled women who sat out in the sun, or the farm labourers in the bar. But he kept himself to himself, having relearned the dangers of becoming too involved. He liked to sit out on fine evenings, watching the sun go down, a bottle of the sharp local red wine on the table, playing chess against himself. When the curé ambled past one night and professed a passion for chess, Max was obliged to invite him to sit down. The curé called quite frequently after that. He was a good chess player, and didn't talk too much.

He knew that he'd been a rotten father to Melissa and Josh, and that they'd be better off without him. He'd spent much of their infancy working abroad, and then, during the war, they had been separated again. His concerns for them had led him to be severe and distant, like his own father. He suspected that his children feared him as much as they loved him, and that they would react to his absence with relief, not grief.

He often felt lonely and angry, but the hard manual work exhausted him, leaving him blessedly unable to think. The southern sun entered his bones, unknotting muscles, rubbing away the lines of worry on his forehead.

Colonel Renshaw's house was called Poona, and it clung to one side of the Oxfordshire village of Woodcott St Martin. The house was huge, turn-of-the-century, incomparably ugly, a red-brick and stucco façade punctuated by immense bay windows, dormers and balconies. There were three floors: Tilda and her family occupied the top floor, the colonel and his collections the lower two. The garden was vast, and put entirely to the purpose of growing food and supplying fuel for the huge and temperamental stove that wheezed and coughed in the kitchen. Colonel Renshaw, who had been wounded in the Great War, had devoted the remainder of his life to becoming self-sufficient.

'Poisonous,' he said, poking a cabbage with his walking stick as he showed Tilda round the garden. 'Buy this sort of thing in a shop, and they'll have packed 'em full of poisons. Grow 'em yourself, and you know what you're eating.'

The colonel also kept pigs and goats and a great many hens and ducks. He would, Tilda suspected, have kept sheep and woven his own cloth if his hands had not been too arthritic. His arthritis, and the lung complaints which were the consequence of inhaling mustard gas at the battle of the Somme, had forced him, at the age of sixty-seven, to engage a housekeeper.

Tilda mentioned their mutual acquaintance, Kit de Paveley.

'Met the boy when he was at Oxford,' said the colonel, thwacking nettles aside as they walked the perimeter of the garden. 'Archaeology – mutual interest. Clever chap. Went on a dig or two together.'

Tilda's duties were officially to cook, clean and launder the colonel's clothes and linen. In reality, on days when the colonel's arthritis was at its worst, her tasks ranged from writing the many letters of complaint with which he plagued the parish council to shooting the pigeons which were the bane of his existence. The work was arduous, but she welcomed that because it stopped her having to think. Rising at six, feeding the stove with wood and the dried turf that the colonel insisted would make excellent fuel, made her concentrate harder on avoiding frostbite than regretting, yet again, the last disastrous months of her marriage. Struggling in midwinter to give variety to another meal of parsnips, potatoes and cabbage distracted her at least temporarily from worrying about the children. Polishing floors with a beeswax that the colonel extracted from his own hives left her too exhausted to think about what had happened to Daragh.

Their living quarters on the top floor of the house were spacious enough to take all their own furniture as well as that which the colonel had provided. There were four bedrooms: Melissa and Caitlin shared the largest, Josh and Erich had the room with the dormer, Rosi and Hanna, in the vacations, occupied the back bedroom, and Tilda herself slept in the small room with the bay. There was a bathroom, with basin, bath and lavatory of such clanking, rusting size that they seemed to have been made for giants, a small kitchen, and a larger sitting room. Compared to the cramped rooms and low ceilings of Long Cottage, Poona was a palace.

Woodcott St Martin had once been a village as small as Southam, but the introduction of a sprawling council estate and a row of red-brick bungalows had tripled its size. The wall that divided the council houses from the bungalows was typical, Tilda often thought, of the divisions within the village. Those from the council estate frequented the working men's club; those from the bungalows and the big old houses that clustered around the green joined the tennis club or the Dramatic Society. There was a bus to Oxford every half-hour, which Caitlin and Melissa took to the girls' grammar school. Josh would continue to weekly board until he took his Common Entrance.

The cheque that Max sent each month towards the children's keep was unaccompanied by any letter or expression of goodwill, an omission that reopened the thin scab which barely covered the pain of his leaving. Sometimes, when she was scrubbing potatoes or ironing the colonel's vast long johns, some of Tilda's grief turned to anger. Anger that Max should desert his children. Anger that he should be so harsh, so judgemental. Anger that he had believed her to be less flawed than she was.

Caitlin loathed living in Colonel Renshaw's house. In Southam, before they had moved, she had walked each day to the Hall, afraid that her father would return and find her gone. But a For Sale board went up outside the house, and one day some awful people moved in. Dreadful scarlet pelargoniums, which Mummy would have certainly thought common, now grew in the greenhouse, so Caitlin, after making sure that no-one was looking, chucked a stone through the roof. The chime of breaking glass was satisfying.

At first Caitlin had been cold to Tilda, who hugged her, which was awful. Then she was rude to her, but Tilda's patient firmness was if anything more aggravating than the hugging. Then she amused herself with small acts of revenge – a tablespoon of salt in the stew, or a well-aimed kick at the pole that held up the washing line, so that the sheets and pillowcases trailed in the mud – but she caught Tilda looking at her quizzically once or twice, and was more careful after that.

Then they moved to Oxfordshire. The move somehow made permanent all the most dreadful things about Caitlin's new life. Before, she had believed that Daddy would come back, and that they would live at the Hall again, and that everything would be all right. The move eroded that conviction. She was expected to share a bedroom with Melissa, though at the Hall she had had a larger room all to herself, as well as a little dressing room. It was ridiculous and unfair that she had not her own room. Melissa herself regarded Caitlin with an uncritical admiration that was one of the few consolations of her new life, though when Melissa showed her the letters and sketches that Max had sent to her, Caitlin glanced at them, fury welling in her at the meanness of silly little Melissa's knowing where her father was when she did not.

The colonel himself was mad, so Caitlin avoided him as much as possible. The food was horrible and boring, and she never had any new clothes. She started at the grammar school in January. There were thirty girls in each class, and some of them wore down-at-heel shoes and baggy stockings and spoke with country accents. Worse, no-one seemed to notice her. At Burwood School, everyone had known her. She had been Caitlin Canavan, who lived in a big house and had been driven to school by her handsome father, and who took ballet and elocution. At her new school, some of the teachers didn't even know her name and, though at Burwood she'd always been easily top of the class, at the grammar school she was unable to rise above the middle. When she talked about her ponies or about the parties that Daddy had given for her, or about her holidays in Deauville, no-one believed her. Your mother works for that potty old man, they said, and Caitlin felt doubly ashamed. That they should believe Tilda to be her mother, and that Tilda was herself a servant, humiliated her.

No-one seemed to realize that she was special. No-one seemed to notice that she was prettier, cleverer, altogether more interesting than other girls of her age. No-one seemed to admire her, and yet Caitlin knew, looking in the mirror, that she was indeed special. Her father had said so.

They were living in the colonel's house when she found the private detective's report. Her mother's papers had been stored in cardboard boxes when the Hall had been put up for sale, and had remained packed away in the cottage in Southam. After they moved, Tilda offered to go through the boxes with Caitlin. Caitlin refused, unpacking them by herself because they seemed a last, precious link with her former life. Most of what she found meant nothing to her. A very dull diary kept when Jossy had been a child, letters, bills, grocers' receipts. Anything connected with her father Caitlin kept. Then she found Mr Oddie's report. When she realized what it was she flicked quickly through it, bubbling with excitement, certain that she would now know where he had gone. Curling up on her bed, Caitlin began to read the report in detail. As she read, her excitement changed to shock, and then to nausea. She was sick in the creaky bathroom, and when she came back Melissa had come into the room. Melissa looked at Caitlin and asked her whether she felt well, and Caitlin, seeing that Melissa was only a yard or so away from that awful thing, said coldly, 'Did you know that there is the most frightful spot on your chin?' which made Melissa gasp and run to the looking-glass.

Caitlin gathered up the papers and made for the outside loo, the only place where one could be certain of privacy. In the dark, spidery little room she read the rest of what Mr Oddie had written. There were things that confused her (what was 'intercourse'? What was 'a physical relationship'?), but she did understand that Mr Oddie was saying that her father had had lots of women friends. Mr Oddie had made a list: someone called Elsa Gordon was at the head of it, and Tilda Franklin's name was at the bottom.

Erich worked each day on Colonel Renshaw's garden. There was over an acre of land, plus the animals and wildfowl and the copse. Although the colonel, who commonly referred to him as 'that Hun', at first terrified him, Erich grew used to the old man. He realized that Colonel Renshaw couldn't recall any of their names – he always addressed Melissa as 'Lizzy', confusing her with a long-dead sister – and he suspected eventually that 'that Hun' wasn't meant as an insult. Erich's stuttering explanations that he was Austrian and of Jewish origin were ignored, drowned by a lengthy description of a game of football the colonel's men had played with the Kaiser's troops between the trenches in the Christmas of 1914. Erich understood that, compared to his ability to dig thoroughly and collect chicken manure conscientiously, his race and religion were unimportant to the colonel.

The village frightened him. Every now and then he would have to visit the blacksmith to get the shears sharpened, or sell their surplus eggs to the bad-tempered grocer. These outings were an ordeal. His stammer invariably became insurmountable and, though his English was quite fluent, he forgot the commonest words. He could feel people staring at him. Their censorious eyes followed him from behind netted windows and privet hedges. A sheen of sweat would escape from his skin and, though he'd been fine when he left Poona, he'd realize that he needed the lavatory.

Tilda encouraged him to go to church; Erich went once, and then managed to discover something urgent to do in the garden each Sunday morning. To be enclosed with staring strangers was unbearable. To his relief, after a few weeks Tilda told him he didn't have to go if he didn't want to. She insisted, though, that he join in the family game after tea each evening. He didn't mind that, because sometimes Caitlin too joined in, and just to look at Caitlin gave Erich an odd, searing sort of happiness.

Christmas at Poona was sufficiently peculiar to distract Tilda, much of the time, from memories of other Christmases. The generator broke down in the early hours of Christmas morning, and though Josh, who was good at that sort of thing, tinkered with it for hours, they had to light the house with oil lamps and candles. The colonel insisted they all dine together, and poured everyone, including Josh, a measure of very old, very pale sherry. Dressed in their best clothes, they ate the turkey that Tilda had cooked. Afterwards, Hanna and Rosi played mah-jong with the colonel, Josh and Erich went back to the generator, and Melissa and Caitlin helped Tilda with the washing-up.

It was only much later, when the younger children were in bed, that Tilda was overwhelmed by the sheer loneliness of it all. There had been Christmases without Max before, but they had been in wartime, and his absence had been unavoidable. And there had always been *something*: a letter, a card, and once, sent from North Africa, a beautiful silk scarf that he had bought for her in a bazaar. This Christmas, Max had sent presents for the children, but nothing to her. Not a letter, not a card, not even the smallest indication that he cared whether she lived or died. Curled up on the sofa, smothered with rugs and shawls to keep out the wind that whistled through the gaps around the windows, Tilda imagined a lifetime of such absence, such anger.

Hanna placed the tea tray on the hearth. Rosi sat down on the rug. 'I think that Christmas is better without electric lights. More romantic.'

Hanna poured out the tea. 'It was fun, wasn't it? Though the colonel beat us at mah-jong. Twice.'

'He cheats.' Rosi was unthreading her long plait.

'*Rosi*,' said Tilda.

'It's true. He does. Almost as much as Caitlin does.'

'*Rosi*.'

'Come on, Tilda – you must have noticed that Caitlin cheats. And at snakes and ladders, of all things.'

'Of course I've noticed, but I thought it best not to say too much.'

'Because she's lost her mother and father, blah blah blah—'

This time it was Hanna who said, '*Rosi.*'

Rosi looked up. 'Well, so have Hanna and Erich and I lost our parents, and we don't cheat. Or read other people's letters and diaries, or steal their lipsticks.'

Rosi had embarked on a stormy relationship with Richard Vaughan, a junior doctor at Addenbrooke's Hospital in Cambridge. When Rosi had discovered Caitlin reading Richard's letters, she had thumped her soundly.

Tilda said slowly, 'I am afraid Caitlin believes that her father is still alive. She can't mourn him, you see, because she is waiting for him to come back to her.'

Hanna looked up. 'You don't think he will?'

'Oh no.' Tilda remembered Daragh, spreading out photographs of his baby daughter on a table in his room in the Savoy Hotel; Daragh, saying, *She is the light of my life* . . . 'He adored her. I cannot imagine that anything less than death would have kept Daragh from Caitlin.'

Hanna said sensibly, 'Then it's not surprising that she's taking a while to settle.'

Tilda tried to smile. 'And of course, this sort of life is such a change for poor Caitlin. She was an only child, and she's suddenly found herself part of a large family, and she's had to move house and change school. She led such a privileged life, in some ways. And I have tried to talk to her about her father.'

Yet the conversation had been unsatisfactory. Caitlin had affected disinterest, but Tilda had seen through the pretence both hostility and fear. She had in the end balked at killing Caitlin's hope that Daragh would return to her: she had not felt that she had the right. The intensity of Caitlin's anger disturbed her, and Tilda had wondered fleetingly whether Caitlin knew that she herself had been

Daragh Canavan's lover. She had pushed the idea aside. How could Caitlin know? Neither Jossy nor Daragh would have confided such a thing in their daughter. Yet the unease lingered, reborn every time she glimpsed her image in those dark, accusing eyes.

Often she questioned whether she had done the right thing in taking in Caitlin Canavan. Her own motives, she knew, had been a muddle of pity and guilt and an acknowledgement of a blood relationship of which Caitlin knew nothing.

At first, the girl just waved at Max when she cycled past the garage each morning, and then, after a few weeks, she called out a cheerful '*Bonjour!*' She rode out at a quarter past eight, and back at seven o'clock in the evening, Monday to Saturday. She was young, her fair hair caught back in a chignon, and she dressed, even to ride her bicycle, in elegant silk or crisp cottons, her skirts blown back by the wind to show her brown legs. In spring, she called out as she glided past, '*Ça va*, Monsieur Franklin?' and he looked up, surprised that she knew his name. He began to look out for her each day. One evening she was late coming home, and Max glanced at his watch several times as he tidied up the forecourt and set to work on an old Citroën that a farmer had brought in. Just before eight o'clock he heard the clack of her sandals as she walked up the hill, and saw the uneven lope of the bicycle wheel.

'I have a puncture,' she said, flicking a strand of blonde hair out of her eyes, the corners of her mouth bending down. 'Such a nuisance. Could you look at it for me, monsieur?'

Max upended the bicycle and removed the tyre. A long rose thorn stabbed the inner tube. He found her a chair to sit down on and a glass of water to drink while he patched the tear. The heat had lingered into the evening, melting little black pools on the tarmac road.

'You should buy a new tyre – this one's almost worn through,' Max said, when he had finished.

'How much do I owe you, monsieur?'

Max shook his head. 'A rubber patch and a piece of chalk? Nothing.' He wiped his hands on a rag and held the bicycle while she climbed onto it. He found that he was watching her as she cycled away.

Although the next day was Sunday, Max decided to strip down the Citroën's engine. He was unclogging the carburettor when he heard the whirr of the bicycle. She was wearing a smart black dress, and he guessed that she had come from Mass. She unhooked the bicycle basket.

'Where is your kitchen?'

When he gaped at her, she smiled patiently and repeated her question. 'Where is your kitchen, Monsieur Franklin? I have come to cook for you.' She walked into the house, peering into the rooms. 'Ah – my *grandmère* has a stove like that. It will do very well.'

She cooked roast lamb and vegetables followed by an apple tart. Max opened a bottle of red wine. She told him that her name was Cécile Ferry, and that she worked in a dress shop in Saintes. Her parents were dead, and she lived with her grandmother. She had been engaged, but her fiancé had been killed when France had been invaded in 1940. She did not ask Max any questions in return. After they had eaten, she washed up, and cycled away again. Then they went back to waving and calling greetings in the mornings and evenings.

In Saintes, Max bought a bicycle tyre, and slung it over the petrol pump so that she would see it as she rode past. 'For me?' Cécile called, smiling, and braked. He replaced the worn tyre, and on Sunday she turned up with her basket again. He had hoped that she would. *Coq au vin*, this time, followed by cherries.

After they had dined, they sat in the scruffy garden with the overgrown fig and the steps that led down to the *cave* where Max stored wine. Max put out an old blanket on the grass. Cécile told him about the small vineyard she had inherited from her father. And about the woman who owned the dress shop in Saintes, and about her cousin who was to be married in July. And the schoolteacher's fondness for wine, the tobacconist's affair with the wife of the *pâtissier*, and the long-standing feud of the owners of two adjacent vineyards.

'Lord,' said Max, eyeing her. 'I had no idea there was so much going on.'

She smiled, but did not comment. Then she said, 'And you?'

'Me?' Max looked away. 'I run this decrepit garage, that's all.'

'You are English?'

He nodded. 'Born and bred.'

'Your French is very good for an Englishman, Monsieur Franklin.'

'I lived in Paris for several months.' A sudden snapshot of himself and Tilda walking along the banks of the Seine, wondering what the outbreak of war would mean to them.

'But you haven't always repaired motor cars and bicycle tyres, have you, Monsieur Franklin?'

'How can you tell?'

She shrugged. 'You are a gentleman. An English gentleman.'

A crushing judgement, he thought. He said, 'I used

to work for a London newspaper. That's why I was in Paris – as a foreign correspondent.'

'Ah,' she said. 'But . . .?'

'But I stopped enjoying it,' he said flatly.

'You prefer your oily engines . . . your petrol pump . . .'

'Much.'

She stood up. 'I shall wash up now.'

'Not at all. I'll do it later.'

She looked down at him. 'Only if you let me cook lunch for you next Sunday,' she said.

She was wearing a straw hat, and she had brought a picnic. Max had fixed up a battered Peugeot for himself, and they drove down to the mouth of the Gironde, with its marshes and mud flats and oyster sheds on delicate stilts, suspended over the water. Cécile laid out cold chicken and salad and bread and raspberries on the rug, and Max cooled a bottle of white wine in the river. While they ate, Cécile told him the names of the birds that haunted the silvery fringes of the Gironde.

When there was only one raspberry left in the bowl, Cécile picked it up and put it in Max's mouth. Then she kissed him. Her lips tasted of raspberries and wine, her skin smelt of almonds, and her hands, resting on his shoulders, were cool and soft. He drew away from her. She looked at him enquiringly.

'Just friends, Cécile,' he said. 'Please?'

'Max.' She smiled. 'So English.'

Tilda knew that she must take stock, accept that she had lost Max, start again. She had thought that by moving away from Southam she would be able to forget the past. She had done so before, fleeing to London after Sarah had told her that she was Edward de Paveley's daughter.

This time, though, she kept remembering. Remembering herself and Daragh, making love. Remembering Max's face as he had said to her, *You promised me.* Remembering Jossy in the old Bentley, her unborn baby trapped inside her lifeless body. Domestic work did not blot out the memories. Scrubbing floors, she remembered; hoeing the garden, she remembered. She told herself that she needed something to occupy her mind, and attended a Women's Institute meeting, but the other women, enquiring about her husband, looked at her curiously. Dreading questions about the past, she used the excuse of her work to turn down friendly invitations to tea. And besides, the domestic minutiae, the competitions for new ways with eggless cakes, were not enough. Her mind wandered, cluttered with guilt and shopping lists and concerns about the children.

She saw an advertisement for Workers' Educational Association lectures in Oxford, and signed up for a series about the United Nations. One of the lectures was about the work of UNICEF, the international children's emergency fund set up at the end of 1946 to help mothers and children in need after the war. Afterwards, during the discussion that followed, Tilda mentioned the work of the *Kindertransporte*. Then she glanced at her watch and, seeing that it was already half past nine, grabbed her bag and ran for her bus.

She was running along the pavement when she heard footsteps behind her. A voice called out, 'I say! I say – do slow down a little—' She paused, and glanced back.

Gasping for breath, the young man held out his hand. 'Archie Raphael. I was at the lecture. A few rows back.'

Tilda shook his hand. 'I'm delighted to meet you, Mr Raphael, but I have to dash, or I'll miss my bus.'

'I've a motor car. I'll give you a lift.' He scurried along beside her. 'I just wanted to say – you're that woman who rowed across the North Sea, aren't you?'

Tilda stopped suddenly. A man cannoned into her and apologized, raising his hat. She started walking again, very fast, and said, 'It wasn't a rowing boat, it was a sailing boat. And Felix did most of the work, not me.'

He didn't listen. They never did. 'I remember your face from the newspaper. I never forget a face. And you were talking about the *Kindertransporte* just now. And I know Harold Sykes – well, his daughter, Lottie, actually. Sees herself as Ginger Rogers, but obviously *not*, I'm afraid.'

Archie Raphael was about Tilda's height, tow-haired, and, she guessed, about twenty-five. 'I really do have to go, Mr Raphael.' Looking up, she saw her bus approaching, so she ran to the roadside, signalling for it to stop. It lumbered on unheeding, standing passengers spilling out on the platform.

'Oh, *blow*.'

'I say, I am most terribly sorry. My fault for holding you up. But you'll let me drive you home, won't you?' Archie added, 'I am frightfully trustworthy, in case you're concerned. Never drive above thirty miles an hour, and I'm the soul of honour—'

She didn't seem to have much choice. 'You are very kind, Mr Raphael. I hope you don't regret your kindness when I tell you where I live.'

He grinned. 'Edinburgh?'

'Woodcott St Martin.'

'Almost as bad. Come on. My car's parked at the college. I'll drive you home in no time, Maud . . . no, that's not it.' He screwed up his face. 'Don't tell me, I've almost remembered. Mary . . . Millicent . . .'

'Matilda,' she said, putting him out of his misery. 'Matilda Franklin. But everyone calls me Tilda.'

Driving home, he tried to talk to her about 1940. She watched the countryside ebb past, the headlamps of the car picking out the heavily leaved trees and drenching them with gold, and said, 'It was a silly thing to do, and it was a very long time ago. I don't want to talk about it, Mr Raphael. I've never talked about it.'

'But Mr Sykes—'

'Harold made most of it up. You know what journalists are like.'

Yet when they arrived home, Rosi was sitting on the verge outside the house. Tilda opened the car door.

'Rosi . . .?'

'I had to see you, Tilda! I had to come home! I hate Richard! I never want to speak to him again!' Rosi, howling, launched into a torrent of German.

Archie Raphael looked interested. Tilda climbed out of the car and, turning back to him, said firmly, 'Rosi is a *Kindertransporte* child, Mr Raphael. Ferry to Harwich, train to Liverpool Street. Nothing heroic. Thank you so much for the lift.' She shut the car door.

Waiting at the bus stop after school, a boy from the neighbouring grammar school asked Caitlin out.

She shrugged. 'If you like.' It was the first time a boy had asked her out; she felt a rush of triumph, and turned to Melissa. 'Tell Tilda I've tennis practice or something.' Caitlin heard Melissa's wail of protest as she walked away down the pavement. Neither she nor the boy, whose name was Charlton, spoke for a while, and the pleasurable feeling began to fade. She glanced at him, all her old dissatisfaction and boredom returning at the sight of his greyish shirt collar and scruffy blazer.

Then he said, 'You look stunning, Kate. Did anyone ever tell you you look like Vivien Leigh?' and she felt better. When they walked past some girls from her class, Caitlin noticed their envious glances. Charlton was, after all, a fifth former, and she was only in the third.

'What's your name?' she said suddenly. 'I can't call you Charlton. It sounds silly.'

'Leonard,' he said. 'My friends call me Lenny.'

He took her to the new milk bar that had opened in the town centre. The strawberry milk shake was pink and frothy and delicious, and Caitlin drank it slowly, enjoying the fact that she was certainly the youngest girl there, and that Lenny was one of the best-looking boys.

'You don't live in Oxford, do you?' said Lenny.

'I'm staying with some people in Woodcott St Martin. My father's working abroad. When he comes home, we'll go back to my old house.'

When, later, he suggested a walk in the park, Caitlin almost refused. She wasn't sure that she could bear any more long silences. But he coaxed her. 'Come on, Kate. I'll make sure you don't miss your bus,' so they walked through the park, past the mothers pushing prams, past the old people sitting on benches, to where sycamores shaded the lawn. The grass was like straw-coloured raffia. There, he bent and kissed her, his mouth wet and soft, his nose colliding with hers.

It wasn't like in the films. But she let him do it because she did not want him to guess that this was the first time she had kissed a boy, and because it was good to know that someone wanted her again.

Erich, walking to the dairy to buy milk for Tilda, discovered The Red House. The old, gabled building lay to the far side of the village, beyond the shop and the post office and the green and the duck pond and all the smart houses with big cars in their drives. The men who washed and polished their big cars each Sunday afternoon sometimes stared suspiciously as Erich clumped past in his shabby clothes and muddy gumboots, but there were no eyes to watch him from The Red House. It was deserted, unoccupied; he watched it for ages before he was sure of that, before he screwed up the courage to push open the creaky wrought iron gate and step inside.

The first time, he walked along the path, with its huge dark box trees that seemed to push in on him, to the front of the house, and then he darted back to the road, frightened. After a couple more visits, he realized that the trees were there not to keep him out, but to guard the house for him. The watchers could not follow him here. At The Red House, he was free. Glancing through dusty window panes, Erich saw huge empty rooms carpeted by the dried leaves blown through gaps around windows and doors. He concluded from the empty packets of Lucky Strikes and discarded gas masks that the house had been used by servicemen in the war.

It was not the house, though, that fascinated him: it was the garden. The garden was glorious, magical, entrancing. In an old shed he found a fork and spade, and dug and pruned and weeded whenever he had the chance. He intended to reclaim The Red House's garden. To find out what it was meant to be. To bring it back to life. At first, the area behind the terrace seemed a senseless muddle of bramble and old man's beard, but then, as he pulled away the strangling creepers and clumps of weed, Erich realized that it had once been carefully laid out, an intricate weaving of path and plants. The old brick walkways were greened by velvety moss, and shattered by frosts. He made a map, sketching in fragments of path, trying to work out how they had once joined up. Hacking at bramble shoots, Erich discovered evidence of flowerbeds: yellowed, wizened flowers, starved of light by the overgrown shrubs, old-fashioned tulips and primulas and auriculas. In spring, the small dark ponds were alive with tiny, half-formed frogs and newts. Erich watched them for hours.

When he found the marble statue, covered with dead leaves, beneath the willow tree, he thought at first that it was a fallen log. Then, kicking aside a clump of sticky fungi, he saw the small, graceful white hand, the delicate fingers curved as if beckoning him. Erich knelt in the leaf-mould and lifted the statue upright. He knew by its weight and coldness that it was made of marble. He brushed the soil and cobwebs from the face with his fingertips, and the girl looked back at him, cold and beautiful and perfect.

Late August was hot and dusty, the dog-end of the school summer holidays. Tilda made pastry as Rosi played the parlour piano and Colonel Renshaw tested his rifle, which he had recently cleaned, in the garden. Wasps buzzed around the high ceiling.

'That awful noise,' said Hanna, coming into the kitchen, slamming the door. 'Bang, bang, bang from the garden, and crash, crash, crash from the parlour.' Hanna's mousy hair was escaping out of its plait, and her forehead was creased with irritation. 'Stop it, Rosi!' she yelled. 'It is horrible!'

The music stopped. There was another explosion from the garden, and Erich, sitting at the table, flinched. Tilda put the colander of blackberries in front of him.

'Pick out the leaves, Erich, please. Hanna, you'll help, won't you?'

'My *essay*,' began Hanna, fractiously, but Tilda said gently, 'Hanna,' and Hanna sighed, but sat down next to Erich.

Caitlin and Melissa were in the adjoining scullery, supposedly sorting out the washing. Caitlin's voice drifted into the kitchen, to Tilda, sprinkling flour on a marble slab.

'. . . used to spend summers in Deauville. Such super beaches, Liss – you'd adore it . . .'

Then Melissa, glumly. 'I never go anywhere.'

'Daddy always took me to a restaurant for lunch. The waiters would pat me on the head and give me *bonbons*.'

A particularly loud explosion from the garden. The blackberries upended over the table. Hanna scrabbled to pick them up. Erich's face was greenish-white. When Tilda rested her hand on his shoulder, his body went rigid.

She went outside. The sun was a bright, hard white disc above the trees. Her hands were covered with flour and her forehead, from the heat of stove and sun, was damp with sweat. She heard the thunderclap of another shot, and saw that Josh was holding the rifle, aiming it at the tin can the colonel used as a target.

'Josh, put that down.' The sight of Josh with the rifle induced in her a rush of fear and anger.

'Mum—'

'I said, put it down.'

'I've used a rifle at school.'

'*Now*, Josh. And give these scraps to the pig. Colonel, lunch will be about half an hour.'

She went back into the kitchen. Rosi had progressed from the 'Coronation Anthem' to 'Zadok the Priest'. Tilda glanced at the table.

'Where's Erich?'

Hanna looked up. 'He went upstairs. He was upset.'

Erich, Tilda knew, would be crouched in a corner of the room that he shared with Josh, his forehead pressed against his knees, humming the same tuneless little song that she had first heard years ago, in Ijmuiden.

The pastry was greying in the heat. Hanna, book in one hand, was eating the blackberries. Melissa's paints were scattered over the window seat. Caitlin's voice, from the scullery, penetrated through the rifle shots and music.

'I don't see why we should do this. After all, *she's* the servant, not us.'

Tilda paused, rolling pin in hand. Her eyes met Hanna's. 'Finish the pie, please, Hanna.'

Tilda went into the scullery. The washing was still an unsorted heap in the basket. Melissa, glancing up, looked guilty, but in Caitlin's dark eyes there was only antagonism.

'Melissa, go and clear up your painting things.'

'Josh was using them too.'

'Josh is busy. Go on, Melissa.' Melissa walked out of the room, heels dragging.

Which left Caitlin, sitting on an old wicker chair missing most of its canes, legs swinging, looking anywhere but at Tilda. Tilda said softly, 'Kate, in our family, everyone shares the errands.'

Caitlin drawled, 'You and I don't have *quite* the same backgrounds, Tilda. You really should remember that.'

Yet she rose from the chair, and began, very slowly, to pair socks.

She could, Tilda thought, explain to Caitlin that Daragh had come from a poor rural family not dissimilar to her own. She could point out that, in the end, house, land and horses, the paraphernalia of a privileged way of life, had had to be sold to meet debts worth double their value. She could even tell Caitlin what she should perhaps have told her long ago: that they were of the same family. Yet she knew that she would do none of these things. For a proud, troubled child like Caitlin to understand the folly of her beloved father's last years would, perhaps, destroy her. And she herself had never been anything but shamed by her relationship with the de Paveleys. But it was not only those reasons, Tilda acknowledged, that stopped her confronting Caitlin. She sensed that they walked a tightrope; they both feared yet only half recognized what lay beneath them, in the abyss.

Back in the kitchen, Melissa was crouched on the floor beside the window seat.

'My *picture*—' There were two torn scraps of paper in her hand.

Tilda knelt on the floor. She took the two halves from her daughter's hands and fitted them together. From the floor, her family, carefully painted by Melissa, stared up at her. Max, Hanna, Rosi, Erich, Caitlin, Josh and Tilda herself. She and Max were now on separate halves of paper.

'We can mend it, darling.'

'It's spoiled!' Melissa buried her head in her hands, and sobbed.

As she ran upstairs to look for paste and tape, Tilda knew what she would do. She would attempt yet again to persuade Erich to talk to the nice doctor she had found in Oxford. She would make sure Hanna took no books other than the silliest romances with her when she went camping in Scotland with Rosi. And she would find a quiet half-hour alone with Caitlin, and try once more to talk to her about Daragh.

And she would write to Max. She would remind him that he had a daughter, who missed him. For whom letters and postcards and sketches were not enough. She herself might deserve to be punished, thought Tilda as she knocked on Erich's door, but Melissa did not.

The whole village, Cécile explained, helped with the *vendange*. So Max, after a tentative protest, covered up the petrol pump and swapped his oily overalls for ancient corduroys and a shirt his mother had bought him before the war, and picked grapes. The work almost took his mind off the letter he had received that morning. Tilda's anger had been obvious in every sentence of her note; Max had read it with an indignation that matched hers. But as he worked, flanked on one side by the postmistress, on the other by a surly fellow who bought petrol for his tractor at the garage, he was aware of another emotion. Guilt. He had assumed, too easily perhaps, that his children would be glad to see the back of him. Tilda's letter had told him that was not so.

Every now and then, when he straightened, he'd see Cécile, wearing shorts and a knitted top, her hair tied back with a red-spotted silk scarf. By the end of the day Max's back ached and his hands were blistered. Long shadows, the same purple as the grapes, painted the rows of vines. The first spots of rain fell as they wheeled their final loads back to the barn. Cécile hooked her arm through Max's, and led them all back to her grandmother's house. Two long trestle tables were set up in the kitchen. The smell of the beef casserole made Max realize how hungry he was. The wine was rough and sour and delicious and he drank glass after glass to satiate his thirst. Rain drummed on the roof, and when Max glanced back through the open door he saw steam rising from flagstones still hot from the sun.

It was almost midnight when the party broke up. Max thanked the grandmother and kissed her hand, and looked round to take his leave of Cécile. She was standing at the door, a cardigan draped over her slender shoulders. 'I'll walk with you,' she said. 'It's stopped raining, and I need some air.'

They walked in silence through the quiet village. The perfume of rain-washed grass rose from the earth. Crickets chirped in the verges, and an owl, its white ghostly wings outspread, took flight from a derelict barn. When they reached the garage, she followed him inside, as he had known she would. He moved to light the oil lamp, but she halted him and her slim fingers rested on his shoulders as she kissed him. Her full, pointed breasts pressed against his chest, and he could taste the wine on her lips. He pulled her towards him, covering her face with kisses, the darkness intensifying his desire because it concentrated his senses. After a while, she said, 'Max, don't you think we should go to bed?' and he let her go, torn between alarm and desire.

'Max, what is it?'

He lit the oil lamp. 'Cécile – I'm married.'

She said seriously, 'I guessed that, of course.'

He looked at her. She was so different from Tilda: smaller and plumper and her face altogether rounder. 'I mean, I'm still married. Not divorced or anything.'

'But you have lived here alone for over a year, Max, so you are not *that* married.' She approached him. 'Or are you telling me that though your wife does not love you, you still love her?'

'Yes . . . no . . . damn it, Cécile, *no*, the marriage is over. But I have children . . . ties. I'm trying to tell you that I am not free.' Exasperated, he stared at her, golden in the light of the oil lamp. 'And that I'm years older than you, and that you really would do better with one of those nice boys who helped with the harvest.'

'But I don't want any of the boys,' she said softly, coming to stand in front of him. 'I want *you*, Max.'

In the bedroom, a new fear possessed him. It had been a long time since he had made love to a woman. He remembered those nights with Tilda, bending to caress her, and seeing instead of her naked body those ragged, broken women of Belsen. He did not think he could bear the shame of failing to make love to Cécile.

But France had changed him; he had left that doubting, tormented part of himself behind, and moved on. Coupling with Cécile, the release of orgasm left him with such a relief of tension that his sleep was unbroken for the first time in years.

The following morning, after they had made love again and Cécile had left for work, Max wrote to Melissa, asking her to come and stay with him at half-term.

Two days before Hanna went back to Cambridge, she was swinging on the long, low branch of the beech tree, agonizing over the lymphatic system, when she saw Erich scuttling towards the back gate, two terracotta pots under his arm. She leapt off the branch and ran after him.

'Erich, what on earth are you doing?'

He jumped, so she put out a hand to calm him. 'It's only me, silly.'

'Shall I ... would you like to see my s-s-secret, Hanna?'

She almost said no, thinking of exams, and all the work she had to do. But she had always, even as a child in Holland, sensed Erich's fragility.

'Of course I would.'

'Then come with me.' He darted out of the gate and Hanna followed him.

He led her through the village, past the houses and the shops, stopping in front of a big house set back from the road. 'In here,' he said. There was a plaque on the gate: 'The Red House'.

'Erich—'

'It's all right. No-one lives here. Come on, Hanna. Once you're inside, no-one can see you.'

Clouds of raindrops sprinkled from the trees, scattering Hanna's dress as she walked. The avenue of high, bulky, overhanging bushes led to the front of the house.

'Are you sure it's empty?' Hanna realized that she was whispering.

'There's only ghosts,' said Erich.

Hanna guessed The Red House to be several hundred years old. When Erich took her to the terrace that lay behind the house, she looked down at the garden and said, 'Oh, *Erich*.'

He smiled. He smiled so rarely that Hanna's eyes prickled with tears. She saw what he could have been: a tall, dark, good-looking boy. Most people saw only the hunched shoulders, the furtive eyes, the missing front tooth. Most people heard only the stutter and the placatory nervousness. Blinking, Hanna looked back at the garden.

The paths, made of an old weathered brick, twisted together in a complicated knot. Honeysuckles and ramblers drooped over the threads of the knot, and the late flowers of the rose were decorated with raindrops, like diamonds. The garden was studded with tiny ponds and shrubs and trellises. The parterres and paths were free of weeds.

'Oh, Erich,' she said again. 'You did this, didn't you?'

He nodded. 'You're not to tell anyone, Hanna. Not even Tilda. I'm not showing her until it's finished. It'll be a surprise for her, won't it?'

As she walked, fronds of clematis brushed Hanna's face, and the leaves of the wild geranium and lady's mantle that edged the path soaked her feet. In the middle of a clearing paved with bricks stood a marble statue of a girl carrying a horn of plenty. Flora, thought Hanna, trying to remember her classics. Or Pomona—

'Caitlin,' said Erich, as if reading her thoughts. He touched the statue's cold white head. The look on his face made Hanna shiver.

In the autumn term, Melissa fell in love. Martin Devereux was new to the sixth form of the neighbouring boys' grammar. All the girls were in love with him, and Susan Morgan was an object of envy because she possessed a cough-sweet tin containing a sticking plaster that Martin had once worn on his finger. Melissa first saw him from the hockey field, where the girl whom she was supposed to be marking pointed him out to her. She had read about love at first sight, but it had never before happened to her. Later she wrote his name on her pencil case in her best handwriting, with lots of curly bits on the M and the t and the n. A day was good if she saw Martin, dismal if she did not. The day that he brushed against her on the crowded pavement was glorious. The only time she remembered feeling so happy before was the day that her father had come home after the war.

She spent hours doing her hair and dabbing stuff on her spots and looking into the mirror and despairing. She put her straight, fine dark hair in curlers overnight, and howled when she took the curlers out in the morning and it spiralled in chaotic corkscrews. She let down the hem of her pleated skirt to make it more fashionable and nagged her mother for stockings instead of socks. She knew that Martin Devereux wouldn't look at a girl who wore socks. She lay for hours on her bed, thinking about him. She imagined slipping and spraining her ankle in front of him, so that he'd have to pick her up and carry her in his arms. Or dropping something out of her satchel: he'd run after her and strike up a conversation. Her imaginings never got much further than that.

Eventually she told Caitlin how she felt about Martin Devereux, half expecting Caitlin to laugh, or to say something scornful. But Caitlin was understanding, and offered to help set Melissa's hair. They were halfway through, and the room smelt of setting lotion, when Caitlin said, 'Would you like his autograph?'

'Martin's?'

'Of course, dummy. I'll get it for you, if you like.'

'Kate . . .'

Caitlin shrugged. 'If you don't want it . . .'

'Oh, I do!'

The sixth form boys had games after school on Wednesdays, Caitlin explained. She'd slip through the hole in the fence, and ask Martin Devereux for his autograph. Simple.

'You won't tell him it's for me?' She would die,

Melissa thought, if Martin were to find out how much she loved him.

'Course not.' Melissa, watching Caitlin's reflection in the mirror, saw her smile as she twisted the last curler into place.

After school, Caitlin wriggled through the fence that divided the girls' school from the boys', and walked across the football pitch. Standing at the foot of the sports pavilion steps she asked in a bored voice, 'Is there someone called Martin Devereux here?' A tall, lanky boy said, 'It's your lucky day, Devereux,' as Martin Devereux detached himself from the group and walked down the steps to her.

'A friend of mine wants your autograph,' Caitlin said, fishing a scrap of paper out of her pocket.

'A friend?' He smiled knowingly.

'Not me. Too dreary – girlish pashes for sixth-formers. Still – better than the captain of hockey, I suppose. Just write, To M, best wishes from Martin whatever-your-name-was. Something like that.' She yawned.

He scribbled on the piece of paper. Caitlin smiled. 'Actually, she's called Melissa Franklin, and she has the most frightful crush on you.'

'How amusing,' he said, handing her the autograph, but she could tell that he was flattered.

'Too sweet of you. Bye-ee.' Caitlin began to walk briskly back to the perimeter of the playing field.

He caught up with her as she reached the hole in the fence. 'I say – I wonder – would you like to go to the pictures one evening? Um . . . I'm so sorry, but I don't know your name.'

'Caitlin,' she said. 'Caitlin Canavan. Most people call me Kate.' She considered. 'Not the pictures. I'll meet you at the milk bar in Cornmarket Street after school tomorrow.'

Melissa gazed at Martin Devereux's autograph, her heart beating very rapidly. 'To M, best wishes from Martin.' He had such lovely black, curly handwriting.

Caitlin was pulling the navy ribbon from her hair. 'I said we'd meet him after school tomorrow.'

Melissa was speechless at first. Then she said, '*Both* of us?'

Caitlin nodded. 'I'll help you do your hair tonight, Liss, so that you look really nice.'

After school, Melissa and Caitlin walked into town. Melissa was convinced that Martin would not come. He would have changed his mind, or Caitlin would have made some sort of mistake.

But she saw him through the window of the milk bar. 'Caitlin—' she whispered, suddenly wanting to run away, but Caitlin had already opened the door. Melissa scuttled in after her.

'Hello, Martin,' said Caitlin. 'This is Melissa.'

Martin glanced briefly at Melissa. 'Hi there.' He was just as good-looking close to as he was from a distance. His mouth drooped with a sulky little twist at the corners that Melissa was unable to capture with her pencil.

Martin bought two more milk shakes and sat down next to Caitlin. Melissa sat opposite him.

'Oxford is such a dump,' said Caitlin, looking around, raising her slender shoulders.

'My people have just moved down from London. I can't wait to get back there. One feels buried alive.'

'I used to live in the Fens, miles from anywhere.'

'Dear God,' said Martin. 'What on earth did you *do*?'

'I rode a lot. And my father and I weekended in London quite often, actually.'

'I *liked* the Fens,' said Melissa suddenly. They both stared at her: it was as though, she thought, the *table* had spoken. 'I liked Long Cottage and I miss Aunt Sarah and my swing and our den. You liked it too, Kate. And the bower we made – you remember, in the garden, with the bindweed and the old man's beard—' She stopped suddenly, her face hot, realizing that neither was listening to her.

Martin put his hand in his pocket and drew out a handful of change. 'I'll just get some matches. I'm desperate for a cigarette.'

Caitlin said, 'Melissa will get them, won't you, Melissa?' and smiled. The smile was patronizing and conspiratorial, and it was echoed by Martin. It sparked a suspicion in Melissa that she could hardly bear to contemplate. She took the money and stood up and went to the counter, and heard the ripple of laughter as she asked for the matches. She wondered whether they were laughing at her. She was aware suddenly of her pigtails, her flat chest. The assistant placed the matches on the counter, and Melissa, as Martin spoke, stepped backwards a couple of paces, straining to hear.

'*Too* tedious . . . little kids in gymslips running after one . . .'

Then Caitlin. 'She adores you. Aren't you flattered?' And a giggle.

The coins slipped out of Melissa's hand and rolled around the counter. He knew. Caitlin had told Martin that she, Melissa, loved him. The shock of Caitlin's betrayal was almost as painful as the humiliation of Martin's knowing. Melissa stood quite still for a moment, completely at a loss, her mind blank. She wondered whether she should run out of the café, but she still had his change, his matches. She walked back to the table and sat down.

Martin was saying to Caitlin, 'Only one more year's school, thank God. I'll go to Oxbridge, of course, but at least my weekends will be my own.'

'I shall leave school as soon as possible.' Caitlin shook back her dark curls. 'I was going to be presented, but that sort of thing is rather passé, isn't it? So I shall be an actress, or a model or something.'

Caitlin was flirting with Martin Devereux, tossing back her hair, smiling at him, raising and lowering her mascaraed eyelashes. And Martin's gaze rested on her, unable to look away.

'You'd make a terrific model, Caitlin. And I can imagine you on stage.'

Caitlin simpered. Martin Devereux glanced at his watch. 'There's a funfair on the common. Could be amusing. Shall we go?'

'If you like.'

'Perhaps your friend would take your satchel home. Things tend to fall out when one is upside down on the Big Wheel. Would you do that for me, sweetheart?' Martin turned to Melissa and smiled. His smile, that only half an hour ago she would have died for, was now worthless.

Melissa took Caitlin's bag and her own, and walked back to the bus stop. She got lost in the narrow, winding streets, and had to wait twenty minutes for the next bus. But she did not allow herself to cry until she was sitting on the back seat, her face pressed against the window, her tears painful and silent.

* * *

'You hardly said a word,' Caitlin said later as she peeled off her stockings. 'So he thought you didn't like him.'

Melissa knew that Caitlin was lying. They were in their bedroom; Caitlin had come home at six o'clock, and told Tilda that she'd had a netball match.

All Melissa wanted was to curl up and sleep and preferably never wake up again. Her head ached so badly that she thought she might be ill. She hoped she was ill, something serious and long-term so that she wouldn't have to go to school again for a very long time, because if she did go back to school then she might see Martin Devereux, and that would be just too awful. And she could hardly bear to be in the same room as Caitlin. She had never been sure that Caitlin liked her – she had always, she now acknowledged, courted Caitlin's approval in a rather craven way – but to realize that Caitlin cared not one bit for her was profoundly shocking. She saw suddenly that Caitlin was a poisonous interloper, and that after this afternoon she would never again be able to count on the pleasant, dull safety of family life. Melissa pulled the eiderdown over her head and closed her eyes, but saw Martin Devereux's patronizing smile, heard Caitlin's ripple of mocking laughter.

'Cheer up,' said Caitlin carelessly, 'you're going to France soon, aren't you?'

She had forgotten France. Her washed and ironed clothes were in a neat pile on the chair, ready to be packed.

'You'll love it.' Caitlin was sitting at the dressing table, brushing her hair. 'So warm and sunny, not like miserable old England. I had such wonderful holidays here, I used not to want to come home.'

Melissa had lived in France as a child, in Paris, but she hardly remembered it. But the vague memory of feeling happy and safe made tears spring to her eyes again.

'Just think,' said Caitlin, 'you could *live* there if you wanted, with your father. Lucky, lucky you.'

CHAPTER THIRTEEN

'In retrospect,' said Melissa, 'it seems so trivial, doesn't it? But I can still remember how I felt at the time. I saw that I counted for nothing with Caitlin. To see yourself so clearly through another person's eyes is an unsettling experience.'

We were sitting in the chintzy drawing room of Melissa Parker's large, modern Surrey house. Photographs of Melissa's three daughters and her grandchildren crowded the sideboard and mantelpiece. Outside, her husband was mowing the lawn into immaculate stripes; from the kitchen I could hear loud music as Matty crashed about, making herself a snack.

Melissa offered me a cake to go with my cup of tea. Just the sight of the shiny icing and glacé cherries made me feel ill. I declined politely.

'So you stayed in France with your father?' I asked.

'Yes. Now that I have children of my own, of course, I can see how much that must have hurt my mother. At the time, even though I missed her dreadfully, it seemed the only thing to do.'

'Did you tell Tilda or Max what had happened?'

She shook her head. 'Not until much later. I couldn't bear even to think about it. It's odd, isn't it, when you consider all the humiliations one has later to endure – childbirth or losing one's job or reversing one's car into a petrol pump – yet nothing ever seems quite so dreadful as the mortifications of being almost thirteen.' She glanced at her watch. 'I'm afraid I have to go out soon, dear. I've a meeting.'

Melissa's life consisted of meetings, committees, driving her daughter great distances, and hurtling about the country to visit her many relatives. She was shortly to go and stay for ten days with her elder daughter, Annabel, who had just had a baby. I stood up and thanked her for giving me her time, and arranged to come and see her in a fortnight.

I travelled home by train – the Fiesta's clutch needed to be replaced, so I had had to book it into a garage. Before I went to the station, I forced myself to do what I had been putting off all week, and in a chemist in Weybridge I bought a pregnancy testing kit. Travelling back to London, I thought I understood why Melissa had chosen to live in France with Max. Nothing has quite the same ability to wound as an unhappy first love. And Melissa, like Tilda, had an immense capacity for loving. For that to be so deliberately and unkindly rejected must have been painful indeed.

At home, I let myself into my flat and picked up the mail from the doormat. Bills and a royalty statement and a postcard from Lucy Lightman of a Bahamian beach. And a large manila envelope: I did not recognize the wild, black handwriting that scrawled my address. I slit open the envelope, and took out several sheets of photocopy and a covering note. The note was signed by Caitlin Canavan. As she had promised, she had sent me a copy of the report made by the private detective Joscelin Canavan had engaged to search for her missing husband.

The report was dated 30 May 1947. As I began to read it, I forgot everything else – Patrick, and whatever ghost it was that haunted me, and even the pregnancy testing kit, still in my bag.

The detective's name had been Norman J. Oddie; his signature adorned the final page of the report. Like me, Norman J. Oddie had suspected Max Franklin. Mr Oddie had been a conscientious man and had checked thoroughly Max's movements on the night of 10 April. After the bitter parting from Tilda, Max had walked back to Ely and then caught the train from Ely to Liverpool Street. One of the teachers from Josh's old school had been travelling to stay with her sister in London, and had recognized Max on the train. Miss Parsons had told Mr Oddie that Max Franklin had been polite but uncommunicative. He had spent most of the journey smoking and looking at a book without turning the pages. When the train had reached London, Max had lifted Miss Parsons' suitcase down from the luggage rack and opened the door for her, and then had disappeared into the crowds. The landlady of the boarding house in which Max lived had confirmed that he had arrived home just before seven o'clock. He had dined (Mr Oddie even included the menu), and then he had gone to his room. He had been up at seven for breakfast the following morning.

Mr Oddie concluded, as I had, that Max could not possibly have killed Daragh Canavan. Over the weeks I had become convinced that the manner of Daragh's death excluded Max. I could imagine Max killing Daragh in a fair fight, losing his temper and hitting him just too hard, but I could not picture him binding Daragh hand and foot and burying him alive in a dike. What Max had seen in Germany had made him incapable of such deliberate, vengeful cruelty.

I read on. Mr Oddie listed some of Daragh's debts: the reputable ones, to the bank and Harrods and Tattersalls, and the less reputable ones, to a succession of seedy little men in pubs and clubs and racecourses. I thought of gangland killings, bodies encased in concrete bridges over motorways, or weighted down with chains in the murky depths of reservoirs. Not so dissimilar, surely, from a burial in the wall of a dike. I felt hopeful until I flicked a page of the report and read that Mr Oddie had traced a certain Thomas Kenny to a pub in Hackney. Thomas Kenny had been one of the two men who had beaten Daragh up on that fateful night after the flood. 'Why should I kill him?' Kenny had said. 'Haven't a hope of getting my cash back now, have I?'

The private detective confirmed that Daragh Canavan had not been seen in Southam on the evening of 10 April. He had not visited the pub, he had not called on any of his labourers. Mr Oddie, lacking the evidence of a body, concluded that Daragh, burdened by debts he could not possibly pay, had fled the country.

My conclusions were necessarily different. I knew that he had never left Southam. Where else would Daragh, dressed in his best, evidence of his drinking disguised by cologne, have been going if not to meet Tilda, his lover?

The report seemed to bear out everything Caitlin had told me. I put it aside, and went to the bathroom. When the little blue line in the test tube told me that I was expecting Patrick Franklin's child, my legs shook so much I had to sit down on the loo seat, my head in my hands. I was overcome by such a mixture of emotions that I could not, for a while, think. The uneasy calm of the past week was utterly shattered. Yet through horror at the predicament I had so carelessly got myself into, I recognized, to my surprise, a small kernel of joy. My body was giving itself a second chance. I hugged my knees up to my chin, and clasped my bent legs.

I'm not sure how long I sat there. By the time I unfolded my stiff limbs I knew that I had to try, at least, to repair the breach with Patrick. The child was his, too. Whatever Tilda had done, whatever Patrick had tried to conceal, the past should not be permitted to hurt our child. I changed out of my travel-crumpled clothes, and then, cursing the garage for not yet having fixed my car, caught a bus to Richmond.

As I alighted from the bus, the grey roofs of the shops and houses gleamed pink and gold in the rays of the setting sun. Every so often, thick clouds blocked out the rays and cast dark patches on the pavement. As I walked, I planned what I would say to Patrick. I would tell him about my pregnancy, and I would explain to him that I had no wish to exploit Tilda's unhappy past. I would point out to him that my previous book had been scholarly, not sensational, and that I intended this one to be no different. Lastly, I would remind him that Tilda herself had told me that it was my task to distinguish the truth. That was all. The truth.

I turned the corner that led into the mews where Patrick lived. I saw the gleaming red sports car parked outside his house, and I saw the front door open as Patrick stepped from the house to greet the tall, dark-haired woman who was climbing out of the car. And when I saw them embrace, I turned on my heel and ran away.

I just missed a bus, of course. I began to walk home, thinking I'd pick up another bus from a further stop.

I could not bear to wait there, knowing that just a few hundred yards away Patrick Franklin was kissing his beautiful wife. I could almost taste my jealousy in my mouth: bitter and acid, it sparked anger, not tears. I dug my nails into my palms and half ran, half walked through the maze of streets between Richmond Road and Twickenham Road.

More quickly than I had anticipated, it became dark. The first raindrops struck the dry road, blackening it with drops the size of pennies. Light from the headlamps of the cars gleamed on the wet tarmac. I was wearing only a short dress and a linen jacket, and both were soon soaked, and my wet hair clung in rat's tails to my head. I glanced up and down the road, but could see neither a bus nor a taxi. I headed up a narrow alleyway, intending to cut a few yards from my journey. My speed made me breathless, and exorcized my anger. Then I heard the footsteps.

Running, this time. The alleyway was deserted and unlit. The drumroll of rain and the distant rumble of traffic echoed in my ears. I saw how foolish I had been, walking alone through dark city streets. I remembered the child in my womb – tiny as yet, a little curled-up question mark, but I owed it better care than this. The pursuing footsteps grew louder and faster, and I, too, began to run, clutching the bag that contained my purse and credit cards. My feet stumbled in the potholed asphalt. I glanced back over my shoulder and thought I saw a flicker of movement in the darkness, a fleeting glimpse of a face, ghostly-white. My muscles were leaden and my breath sobbed in my throat. The tall buildings seemed to close in on me, unknown and menacing. Every window was blank, every door shut. I turned a corner and crossed a road, searching for a familiar landmark. I recognized nothing: I was lost in the London I thought I knew well. Black shadows pooled in corners, and the rain cast a strange, glittering sheen over the roads and houses, gathering and swelling down the gutters, dragging with it a detritus of old cigarette ends and chewing-gum wrappers. I dashed down another alleyway, crossed another road. At last I had to stop, leaning against a wall, gasping for breath, looking back into the darkness. I could no longer hear the traffic; I was surrounded by a silence that was filled only by the rain and by the frantic beating of my heart. Though I looked back, certain that I would see a face, a shape, emerging out of the darkness, there was nothing. My skin crawled: the silence, the unfamiliarity of the city streets was unnatural. I waited, unable to move, expecting to see walking towards me the shade of Daragh Canavan, his insubstantial footsteps making no mark on the ground.

Fear propelled me along the alleyway, and pushed me through the narrow gap between two buildings, out into the main road. When I looked around, I wanted to laugh and then to cry. What had seemed strange was not so; I had just been seeing it from an unfamiliar angle. I realized that I was in Isleworth; I had walked along this road every day during the months that I had worked with Charles. In the distance I could see the building which housed Charles's offices. I began to run towards it, hurling myself across the busy road, regardless of the hoots and howls of rage from the drivers. Then, praying that Charles was working late, I pressed the bell for Lighthouse Productions.

Charles's voice, strangely disembodied, answered me. 'Charles Lightman—'

'Charles – it's me, Rebecca,' I said, between gasps for breath. 'Can I come up?'

The entryphone buzzed, and I opened the door. I looked behind me but could see no-one. Each stair was an effort for my weary legs.

I hadn't been to Charles's offices since we'd made *Sisters of the Moon*. Now, when I pushed open the door, I was shocked at what I saw. Charles has never been a particularly organized person, but the level of chaos astonished me. Heaps of files, papers and video cartridges littered the small room. The waste basket was overflowing, and the desks were piled with letters and faxes. The window sills were crowded with plastic coffee cups and discarded sandwich wrappings.

'Drink?' Charles said, waving a whisky bottle at me. He was wearing dark trousers and a rather grubby white shirt, and his hair, which needed cutting, kept flopping over his eyes.

I shook my head. My lungs still hurt.

'Bit of a mess. Clear yourself a seat, Rebecca.' He glanced at me. 'You all right?'

'Fine,' I said unconvincingly, as I hauled files and papers off a chair and sat down. 'It's raining,' I added. I was beginning to feel rather foolish. 'And I hadn't an umbrella.'

'Only you seem a little *distraite*.'

'I thought someone was following me.' I didn't mention ghosts; he would have thought I was mad. 'I thought I heard footsteps. So silly. My imagination's out of control these days. I'm hearing all sorts of bumps in the night ...' I laughed, and changed the subject. 'How about you, Charles? You look ... busy.'

'Everything's going really well. I've simply masses of new ideas on the go. I've stayed up the last few nights, trying to organize all my proposals, get things down. It's funny, isn't it, how sometimes you don't have a decent idea for months and then you have one after the other.' Charles was talking very fast, and he moved restlessly from desk to chair, chair to window sill. He reminded me of those clockwork toys one sometimes sees, dashing frenetically and aimlessly to and fro. As he began rapidly to describe the television programmes he intended to make, I wondered fleetingly whether he was drunk, or was keeping himself awake with amphetamines. But, masking my sudden concern for Charles, I saw, as if imprinted on my inner eyelid, Patrick and Jennifer embracing, and I wanted to howl my grief aloud. Patrick and Jennifer were still in love; that much was obvious to me. I had been nothing to Patrick – or, worse, I was a threat. And yet I carried his child.

'What on earth are you doing in this neck of the woods, Rebecca?'

Charles's voice broke through my thoughts, catching me off guard. 'Visiting Patrick,' I said. 'But he wasn't in,' I lied.

His back was to me as he picked an armful of files from the floor. 'I was going to call you. I wanted to talk through an idea with you. But if you've still got a thing going with Patrick Franklin—'

'I haven't,' I said bleakly. 'I thought I might have for a while, but I haven't.'

When he turned to me, I saw that his gooseberry-green eyes gleamed. 'You're sure?'

'Positive.'

'In that case . . . D'you remember the last time I saw you, you said that you thought Tilda Franklin might have been involved in the death of her old lover?'

I nodded warily. 'Something like that. Charles—'

'Bear with me. The series I was telling you about just now—'

I looked blank. I hadn't been listening.

'*Through a Glass Darkly*,' he said impatiently. 'Showing that Christopher Marlowe wasn't quite the Elizabethan James Bond we'd all like to think he was, and that Florence Nightingale was a pain in the neck. Debunking popular history, in other words.'

'The skull beneath the skin.' I thought of Daragh.

'Exactly.' Charles smiled widely, and began inaccurately to stuff files into a drawer that was already overflowing. 'And I thought, how simply marvellous, to do someone more contemporary.'

I could hardly bear to watch him. Papers were floating to the floor like falling snow. I crossed the room and took them out of his hands. 'Let me.' I suddenly understood what he was suggesting to me. 'You don't mean to expose *Tilda*, do you, Charles?'

'Transmission could coincide with the publication of your book. Terrific publicity for you – imagine the sales. It'd be stunning, wouldn't it? That is, if you're of the same mind that you were last time. If you still think that Tilda Franklin isn't exactly the angel she's supposed to be.'

I shook my head vehemently. 'No, Charles. Forget it. It's a horrible idea.'

When I gathered up the ragged jottings that had fallen to the floor, it took me a while to realize that they were ideas for programmes. Some were just a single word – 'Madness', or 'Jealousy'. Others were long, rambling sentences without punctuation or capital letters. Glancing at them, my earlier concern for Charles resurfaced.

He went on as though I hadn't spoken, 'Just think. Footage of misty waterways. Gloomy skyscapes. The dike where they found the body – we could film in winter, when it's snowing, perhaps. Interviews with the man who found the body – and the police. It could work, I know it could. And I'd need a researcher, of course.'

I shoved all the scraps of paper into a large envelope. 'I told you, Charles – forget it.'

'We work well together, don't we, Becca?' He looked across at me. 'Or are you afraid of the consequences?'

He was smiling now. I shut the filing cabinet drawer firmly. 'What on earth do you mean, Charles?'

'Well.' He poured himself another slug of whisky. 'Patrick Franklin's got a lot to lose, hasn't he? How far would he go to hold on to his reputation?'

'Libel laws, you mean?'

'One can only libel the living.'

I glanced up at him sharply. Tilda was eighty-one years old, and just now in hospital following a heart attack. I understood what he was saying: that Tilda might die before the programme went on air.

'Actually' – and with a single sweep of his hand, he cleared his desk of a heap of papers – 'actually, I wondered whether you felt physically threatened. I mean . . . footsteps . . . noises in the night . . .'

'By Patrick?' I glared at him. 'Don't be silly, Charles,' I said, but his insinuations lingered, and could not quite be brushed aside.

*　　*　　*

When I finally went home that night, there was a message on my answerphone. When I began to replay it, and Patrick's voice filled my living room, I switched off the tape, and wiped it clean. Anger and adrenalin pumped through my veins; I saw everything with bitter clarity. I could abandon the biography, somehow repay the advance, look for other work. The after-effects of the recession remained – I might be unemployed for months, and neither my sister nor my father had money to lend me. Who would choose to employ a pregnant, out-of-work biographer? If I abandoned my publisher's commission, then I must also abandon my child. Everything in me rebelled against that route.

Or I could accept Charles's offer, and work for him. I'd earn more money and Tilda's book would have every chance of success. I'd be able to keep my baby, move to a bigger flat, find more work, have a decent life. But in doing so I should betray both Tilda and Patrick. Whatever they had done – whatever betrayals they still practised – they were both blood relatives to my child. Tilda's story was teaching me the importance, the intransigency of that bond. Even before its birth, the infant would be the inheritor of treason. If I worked for Charles, all Patrick's most wounding accusations would be borne out.

Though my feelings for Patrick had become closer to hatred than to love, I began to see what I must do. Daragh Canavan had been murdered on a clear spring night, tied hand and foot and buried alive in the earthworks of the half-built dike. The crime had remained undiscovered for forty-eight years. I must find out who had killed him. I must unpick the skeins of history and reveal the truth, because my fate – and my child's – had become entangled in the secrets of the past.

I took out the list that I had begun weeks ago, of people with the motive and means to kill Daragh Canavan. I had already crossed off Max's name, and I now seriously doubted whether Daragh's creditors would have found it profitable to murder him. I glanced at the next name on my list. Jossy had had every reason to kill Daragh. I felt a flicker of hope when I thought of her: Mr Oddie, of course, had not felt able to question Jossy's movements. Tilda had told me that Daragh was a destroyer – had Jossy, too, finally recognized that? Had she seen the hopelessness of her love and annihilated its object?

Though I wanted to, I could not quite convince myself. Four months after Daragh's disappearance, Jossy had died of an unattended miscarriage. Could she have killed the father of her second child? Both Tilda and Caitlin had described to me Jossy's search for her missing husband. Nothing I had discovered about Jossy Canavan led me to think that she was devious enough to go through such a charade, all the while knowing that her husband was buried less than a mile away in the dike. And she had loved Daragh: even her tombstone, inscribed with his name, proclaimed her love. I did not think Jossy responsible for Daragh's death.

So I headed my list with another name. Tilda's. Tilda Franklin had had both the means and the motive to kill Daragh Canavan. Tilda had reason to hate Daragh. He had destroyed her marriage, and he had betrayed her twice. I, who had also been twice betrayed, understood the bitterness and anger that she must have felt. Had Tilda the physical strength to kill a strong young man like Daragh Canavan? For much of her life Tilda had worked on the land: first, with Sarah Greenlees; then, during the war, growing food to feed her family; later, looking after

433

Colonel Renshaw's household. Tilda hadn't bought her roasting chickens plastic-wrapped in Sainsbury's: she had strangled and gutted the hens she herself had reared. She had shot pigeons in the colonel's garden, she had slit the throat, perhaps, of the pig that had been fattened for bacon. Though she was now old and frail, the ghost-image of her earlier robustness lingered in her straight spine, her square shoulders. Compared to Tilda, I felt feeble, pampered, over-dependent on the dubious machinery of the late twentieth century.

With Tilda, Daragh would have been been off his guard. If he had intended, dressed in his best, to go to her, he would have intended also to seduce her. He would have been complacent: he had had her once – why not a second time? With everything else falling about his ears, Daragh, the charmer, must have remained confident only of his sexual prowess. I imagined him lying on the grass, eyes closed, expecting kisses. I imagined Tilda looking down at him and realizing what he had done to her, realizing too that he would never understand, and would never care. I imagined how she might have hated him then. How she might have struck him with a stone, or with a shovel abandoned by the workmen who were rebuilding the dike. If she had hit him hard enough, then she would have been able to truss him like an old hen for the pot and immure him beneath the clay. I imagined her dragging the body to the earthworks, just as she had hauled the German soldier's body across the grassy polder.

Of course, the person to whom I most wanted to speak was wretchedly out of reach. I would, I thought, have given a great deal to talk to Daragh Canavan, that wrecker of dreams, that destroyer of hopes. I glanced at his photograph again, and said his name, but he just laughed back at me, careless and secretive, intriguing even in death.

I long to talk with some old lover's ghost,
Who died before the god of love was born . . .

CHAPTER FOURTEEN

'What's "intercourse"?' she said. She needed to know.

He looked shocked. Martin Devereux, whose self-professed ambition was to drink dry the cup of life, actually looked shocked. 'Bloody hell, Caitlin – what a thing to ask.'

'Don't you know?'

'Of course I do.'

'Tell me, then.'

His eyes were lidded. Only a sliver of pale blue iris was visible. 'I'd rather show you.'

'OK.' She shrugged, and looked round. 'Where?'

'Not here,' he said, reddening. They were in a pub. 'I haven't the cash for a room. It'll have to be the car.'

He drove until they came to some woodland and then he swung the motor car into the trees. The ruts in the track were clogged with dead, coppery leaves and, as they jolted along the uneven ground, the last of the leaves, like fragments of burnt paper, were torn from the trees by the wind. It was raining: dark, swollen drops that slid along the naked branches of the trees and plopped onto the windscreen of the car. Martin pulled on the handbrake.

'We'd better get into the back.'

In the back of Martin's father's car, Caitlin unbuttoned her blouse and Martin took her nipple into his mouth, kissing her breasts, squeezing them with the palms of his hands. She felt slightly bored: they'd done much the same on previous dates. But then he reached under her skirt and began to fumble with her knickers. She pushed him away: he was breathing very fast and loudly, and his eyes had an intent, determined expression that alarmed her. He muttered, 'I thought you wanted me to show you,' and she had to swallow her embarrassment and her fear, and tell him to go on. She felt stupid, exposed, squashed up on the back seat of the car without her knickers on. When he pulled down his own trousers and underpants, and she saw the awful thing that lay beneath them, she cried out, but he did not seem to hear her.

She was glad that it didn't last very long. He pushed it into her before she realized what he was doing. It hurt, and she shouted at him, and then he shuddered and yelled and collapsed on top of her, and lay very still. For one peculiar, disorienting moment, she thought that he was dead. She imagined lying there for ever, Martin stuck inside her, both of them buried eventually by the falling leaves. The rain still thudded onto the windscreen, and at last Martin muttered, 'God, that was terrific.'

Caitlin sat up, shoving him off her, and pulled her knickers back on. There was an unpleasant dampness between her legs, which frightened her. She thought, *That was what my father and Tilda did*, and then she pushed the thought away, and climbed into the front passenger seat. She decided that she would not go out with Martin again. She enjoyed the chase, not the kill.

It was as though, Tilda often thought, she had been standing on a pier jutting out over the water, and someone had kicked away the stanchions. She was flailing in choppy water, unable to find much to hold on to. She had deserved to lose Max; but she could not understand why Melissa had chosen to leave her.

She continued to look after the children and the colonel, but now only rarely attended her lectures in Oxford. She disregarded offers of friendship, rejecting invitations from even her oldest friends: Anna and Professor Hastings and Emily van de Criendt. Her father had abandoned her, and so had Max, but neither desertion had inflicted so terrible a wound as the loss of her child. From her remaining children she tried to hide the depth of her misery, knowing that she must not inflict her pain on them.

Now, Hanna and Rosi were making Christmas cards on the kitchen table, and Josh and Erich were collecting fallen branches from the copse to use as fuel for the stove. Tilda glanced at her watch. Caitlin was visiting a friend. She had promised to be home by six o'clock, and it was now almost seven. Tilda's unease increased as she washed up. At half past seven, she put on her mackintosh and walked out to meet the bus. The cold fine rain stung against her face. The bus slowed as it emerged out of the half-dark, its wheels curling waves from the puddles. Three women and a boy climbed out.

At the telephone box at the corner of the road, Tilda asked the operator to put her through to Mrs James, the mother of Caitlin's friend.

'It's Mrs Franklin,' said Tilda. 'Caitlin's guardian. She isn't home yet – has she stayed for tea?'

There was a silence. Then Mrs James said, 'Caitlin isn't here, Mrs Franklin. Sylvia's been at Guide camp all weekend.'

Tilda muttered something about having made a

mistake, put the receiver down, and walked back to the house. The streetlamps illuminated the road with a yellowish glaze, but the sky and trees and fields were intensely black. Caitlin claimed to have spent the last three Saturdays with Sylvia. Tilda went home, but there was a cold feeling in her stomach, a certainty of disaster. She muttered, 'I should phone the police, perhaps,' but Rosi, sticking loops of red paper ribbon to cards, said, 'She'll have gone to the cinema and forgotten to tell you. You know what she's like.'

'But it's almost—' began Tilda, and then saw the flicker of movement between the hedges that flanked the front path. She ran to the back door, breathless with relief and anger.

'Kate. Where were you?'

'The bus was late.'

'You didn't come home by bus. I went to the stop. You didn't go to the Jameses either. When you were late, I telephoned.'

'Oh,' said Caitlin, and shrugged.

Tilda, looking closely at Caitlin, saw that she was wearing make-up and nylons. The nylons were snagged, her blouse done up on the wrong buttons.

'Kate. Were you with a boy?'

Caitlin shook her head. There was a dead look about her eyes that alarmed Tilda just as much as the snagged nylons and smeared lipstick. Fifteen, she thought. She had been only two years older when she had met Daragh. She remembered the intense sweetness and pain of first love, its terrible compulsion.

'You are very young to have a boyfriend, Kate,' she said, forcing herself to speak more gently. 'I know that you're grown-up for your age, but you are still only fifteen.'

Caitlin stood on the rug, rainwater dripping from the arms of her gabardine mackintosh. Daragh's child, thought Tilda. She could see him now in Caitlin's stubborn pride.

'If you are fond of someone, then why not bring him home for tea? Then we can all meet him.'

Caitlin spoke at last. 'What? To this place? So that Erich can offer him the bowl of c-c-cabbage? So that he can find out that my guardian is a servant?' The emptiness in her eyes was replaced by anger and contempt. 'Anyway, I haven't a boyfriend. Not any more.'

She turned on her heel and left the room. Tilda looked down at herself. Her dress was covered by a dirty apron and her hands were red and raw, her fingernails black with mud. Her heart was beating so fast that it sickened her. She sat down on the bottom stair, her head in her hands.

'It's *burnt*,' said Melissa.

It's steak, Max wanted to say. It's steak, and what with the war and rationing, you probably can't remember what steak looks like. But he took Melissa's plate from her and replaced it with his own.

'Have mine, then.'

She looked down at it and sighed with a martyred air. 'You know I don't like onions, Daddy.'

The trouble was that he didn't. He had forgotten – or had never known – that his daughter didn't like onions, cabbage, or skin on her hot milk. And he had forgotten that she never remembered to polish her shoes unless he reminded her, and that she spent hours in the bathroom in the morning, so that for the first few days of her stay he had had to attend to his early customers unshaven. He had forgotten that she would insist on going for long cycle rides alone each weekend, yet each evening would demand a night light. Her inconsistency confused him.

Max finished his glass of wine. 'I talked to the head teacher at the school this afternoon, Melissa. She says that you can start after Christmas.'

Melissa stared at him.

'Just mornings to begin with,' he added coaxingly. 'Until you get used to it.'

'*Daddy*—' Tears were welling up in Melissa's eyes.

'You have to go to school, sweetheart – it's the law. They'll make allowances for your French.'

Tears dripped down Melissa's nose. Her knife and fork dropped with a clang on the plate, and she pushed back her chair and ran from the table. He heard her bedroom door slam, followed by loud sobbing. Max sighed, and pushed away his dinner, his appetite gone.

He cleared up the half-eaten food and, standing in the kitchen doorway, lit a cigarette. He remembered the call that he had made six weeks ago to a telephone box in Oxfordshire, at a prearranged time. Somehow the sound of Tilda's voice, carried all those hundreds of miles, had not induced in him the anger he had anticipated. Over the crackly line he had sensed her deep hurt and bewilderment and, after he had replaced the receiver, he had tried once again to persuade Melissa to return to England. But she had said (her face crumpling up, as it had a habit of doing), 'Don't you want me, Daddy?' so he had hugged her, and said, 'Of course I want you, darling. You know that I want you.'

Outside the frost had begun to outline each blade of grass. Melissa had swept back into his life, Max thought, and had forced him to look again at an existence which he had previously found satisfactory. Nothing seemed right for her. The house (a tin bath, Daddy!), his work (you looked nicer in your suit, Daddy), and, of course, his cooking (bread and cheese *again*) – all came in for criticism. He had been made to see his life as she saw it – Spartan, rather bleak, perhaps even (the thought horrified him) slipping into the pathetic, faded mustiness of bachelordom.

He had not yet introduced Melissa to Cécile. Cécile had remained tactfully absent for the week of Melissa's holiday and, when Melissa had made her unexpected decision, Max had written a hasty note, explaining the situation. He knew that he had been evading the issue. It was ridiculous that he should allow his social life to be constrained by a twelve-year-old girl. He decided to ask Cécile to dinner.

Max scrubbed the cigarette butt into the flagstone with his heel, and went back into the house. He could still hear the sobbing. Just for a moment, he looked back with longing to the easier days of infancy, and then, praying for superhuman tact and patience, he tapped on Melissa's door.

Max made a great effort with the dinner. He bought a duck from the wizened old woman at the market, and carefully wrote down her instructions for cooking it. He chose a *tarte aux prunes* from the *pâtisserie* and discovered that one could not buy custard powder in France. He filled the basket with logs and lit the fire in the living room, and bought matching plates from a shop in Saintes, and candles for the table.

Cécile, elegant in black, arrived promptly at eight o'clock. Max looked round for Melissa.

'She's probably still in the bathroom. It seems to take her an hour to do her hair.'

Cécile smiled.

'Glass of wine?'

'That would be lovely, *chéri*.'

Cécile was halfway through the glass of wine when Melissa appeared. She was wearing her oldest clothes: a jersey that needed darning, and a skirt so short it revealed her bony knees. Max decided to say nothing.

'Melissa – this is Cécile. You remember that I told you that she was a friend of mine. Cécile, this is my daughter, Melissa.'

Melissa, looking at the floor, mumbled a greeting. Max felt a flicker of irritation, but decided to serve the duck.

He knew before they had finished eating the first course that the evening had been a mistake. To all Cécile's attempts at conversation, to his own coaxing efforts, Melissa remained monosyllabic. Her mouth twisted down at the corners, and her fringe, which needed cutting, flopped over her eyes. If his cooking did not come in for the usual searing criticism, then that was only because she remained sulkily uncommunicative.

Afterwards, Melissa stomped upstairs to bed, and Max poured himself and Cécile a brandy.

'Sorry.'

'What for, *chéri*?'

'She was terribly rude.'

Cécile smiled. 'She is thirteen, Max.'

He sat down next to Cécile, and put his arm around her. 'Is that an excuse?'

'She sees me as a rival. An enemy.'

Max said, exasperated, 'I explained to her that you were a friend. Nothing more.'

Cécile's face was turned away as she picked up her brandy glass. 'Nevertheless, Max, Melissa loves both you and her mother. She is bound to see any other woman as an interloper.'

He said self-pityingly, 'I can't do a bloody thing right, Cécile. She finds fault with everything. I keep thinking she'll say that she's had enough, and wants to go home.'

'Is that what you want?'

He was silent for a moment. Then he said, 'No. No, of course not. She drives me to distraction, but . . .' He had not realized that his daughter loved him so much. Through a muddle of other emotions, he had recognized that he felt honoured and touched that she had chosen to stay with him.

Cécile touched his hand. 'Do you want to tell me about it?'

'About what?'

'*Max.*' When she looked at him like that it was as though she were fifteen years older than he, and not the other way round. She explained patiently, 'Melissa loves you, or she would not be here, and she loves her mother, or she would not have behaved as she did. The simple solution to the problem of Melissa would be for you and – Mathilde, is it? – to live together again.'

Max shook his head. 'That's not possible.'

'Why not?'

He had never voiced it before. It was an effort to get out the ugly words. 'Tilda was unfaithful to me.'

'During the war?'

'Afterwards. Though she'd been in love with the fellow for years.'

Cécile was silent for a few moments. Then she said, 'And your wife is still with this other man?'

'Oh no.' Max, rising, chucked another log on the fire. 'It was just the once that they . . . Apparently he went away soon after. Left his wife and child and disappeared into the undergrowth . . .' And how typical of Daragh Canavan, Max thought, to desert a pregnant, dying wife – and how typical of Tilda, too, to take in the wretched man's child. And then suddenly to up and leave Southam, and become housekeeper to a complete stranger. The thought of Tilda's job, and the peculiar ménage that Melissa had described, made Max feel uneasy. It all sounded horribly hard work. He told himself that Tilda had, as usual, done exactly what she wanted to do, but all the same, he found himself feeling vaguely guilty.

'*Once* . . .?' repeated Cécile.

He glanced back at her. 'Once . . . twice . . . fifty times . . . It doesn't matter, does it? It's still a betrayal.'

She was looking at him in a way that was not entirely sympathetic. He had expected her to understand. He said, justifying himself, 'Faithfulness in marriage is so important, isn't it? My mother played fast and loose with half my father's business colleagues. I saw what it did to him. I couldn't have endured *that*.'

'So you left your wife,' said Cécile slowly, 'because you discovered that she was like your mother?'

He flushed. Put like that, it sounded ridiculous. 'No, of course not. Tilda isn't in the least like my mother. It was just – damn it, Cécile, I had the right to expect constancy, didn't I?'

'Of course, Max,' she said gently.

He fetched the brandy bottle, and refilled their glasses. He would have liked to have drunk until the uncomfortable thoughts that echoed in his head began to recede, until he was no longer made to look back and question his own behaviour, that he had until recently believed unimpeachable.

Cécile leaned over and kissed him. 'I think that I must not stay the night, Max. We would have to be very quiet and I would feel like a naughty adolescent.'

He watched her cycle down the hill and then he went back into the house. Reluctantly, hoping that she was asleep, he climbed the stairs and tapped on Melissa's door.

A whisper. 'Daddy?'

He pushed open the door. The night light showed that her eyes were red. Max groaned inwardly, but hardened his heart.

'Cécile is my friend, poppet. And she was our guest. You're to write her a note tomorrow, apologizing.'

To his surprise, she did not protest. She just looked at him, her eyes big and dark in her pale little face, her knees hunched up to her chin, cocooned in the bedclothes.

'Do you want me to go home, Daddy?'

'Of course not. Why should you think that?'

'When we were at home . . .' Her voice wobbled. 'When we were at home . . . when we were at Aunt Sarah's . . . you didn't want to be with us then.'

Max sat down on the edge of the bed, his heart thudding. Melissa's words stabbed at him. He almost said, *That's not true*, but instead he put his arm round his daughter, and sat in the half-dark, his eyes fixed on a snaking crack in the plaster on the opposite wall, appalled to realize that she had interpreted his absence as a lack of love for her. Yet why should she have thought otherwise? He had been away for so much of Melissa's young life – why should she not have seen that as a deliberate choice on his part?

He imagined trying to explain to her. First I had to go away because of my job, and then because of the war, and then because I was a bit mad. Because he recognized, looking back, that he had been pushed to a brink that he had not let himself or anyone else acknowledge, by exhaustion and despair. He knew, though, that it was too late to explain. Children understood actions, not words. Some of Melissa's difficult behaviour was because she needed to push him, to test him, to measure his love for her.

It was quite dark now. Though Melissa slept, Max did not yet go. It had occurred to him that Tilda, too, might have interpreted his distancing himself from family responsibilities as a lack of love and, though he angrily tried to push the thought away, the idea that he might, in some sense, have propelled Tilda into Daragh Canavan's arms was an unpleasant one, and could not easily be dismissed.

Tilda gave Caitlin an embarrassingly explicit lecture about the birds and the bees, and Caitlin consequently endured an anxious three weeks worrying whether she was going to have a baby. She spent a lot of time in church, praying, and made a very vague confession to Father O'Byrne. She wasn't pregnant; the relief was enormous.

She went back to her old occupation of trying to find her father. She studied the map of Ireland for hours, struggling to remember the name of the village he had told her about. Sometimes in dreams he came to her and spoke its name, but when she woke up, her face wet with tears, she had forgotten it. She knew that the village could not be far from the sea, as her father had told her that he had gathered oysters on the shore, and she knew that there had been hills and lakes. But there seemed to be no part of Ireland that was not within a couple of hours of the sea and peppered with hills and lakes. Mr Oddie, the private detective, had investigated Ireland, too, but had been unable to trace her father's relatives. Caitlin determined to do better than Mr Oddie.

Guessing most Irish villages to have a priest, she wrote letters, explaining that she was looking for her relatives, addressing the envelopes to The Priest, Ballywhatever, and the name of the county, which she gleaned from the atlas. Some of the priests wrote back to her. She learned that in Ireland, Canavan was a common surname. She did not know her grandparents' Christian names, only that she herself had been called after her father's sister, Caitlin. She persisted, confident that she would eventually succeed.

Most of the time, her prevailing emotion was one of utter boredom. She was bored at school, her position in class having sunk until it was nearer the bottom than the middle, and she was bored at Poona. She was glad she had managed to get the bedroom to herself, though sometimes, when she was really bored, she even found herself missing Melissa. She went to the cinema a great deal, envying the luxury and ease that the American films portrayed. She began to skip church, which she had attended every Sunday since she was a small child. If God had not returned her father to her, which was what she most wanted in the world, then what use was He?

Saturday mornings she spent at the stables in the village, mucking out loose boxes in exchange for a ride. Tilda had arranged the Saturday mornings after the Martin Devereux episode, and Caitlin, though she hated to enjoy anything Tilda had given her, had not been able to resist the opportunity. When she gave her horse its head, cantering across the meadow, the fast slipstream of air blanked out pain and loss and tedium.

Then she saw the notice in the window of the village shop. 'A Revue is to be performed by the Woodcott St Martin Amateur Dramatic Society. Preliminary meeting for all interested at the Memorial Hall, 7.30, Tuesday 15 February.' The notice was signed by someone called Julian Pascoe.

The Memorial Hall was ghastly: ice-cold, cavernous, with lavatories that perpetually leaked. There were about a dozen people in the room when Caitlin arrived. Mrs Cavell, who ran the post office, was calling instructions about chairs; a short, plump man with a shiny bald patch was placing rickety wooden seats in an inaccurate circle. No-one took any notice of Caitlin. Someone shouted, 'Where's Julian?' and a woman in a red skirt with lipstick that clashed said, 'Escaping Margaret, I expect,' and everyone laughed. They all seemed to know each other, and Caitlin began to think that she had made a mistake in coming. It was only an awful village thing anyway, and would probably be just as pathetic as a school play. She sidled towards the door.

The door swung open just as Caitlin reached it. A tall thin man with dark hair cut in a messy fringe almost collided with her. 'Julian, darling!' shrieked someone.

Julian, who wore coat, gloves and scarf and still looked cold, glanced at Caitlin, and said: 'Not running away, are you?'

She shook her head.

He held out his hand. 'Julian Pascoe.'

'Caitlin Canavan.'

He frowned. 'Irish. A fair colleen. "No maid I've seen, like the fair colleen, that I met in the County Down." Are you from the County Down, Caitlin Canavan?'

She shook her head. 'Cambridgeshire.'

449

He roared with laughter, as though she had said something funny. '*Cambridgeshire*. Good God. Such a delightful name, such alliteration, such an harmonious juxtaposition of syllables, and she comes from *Cambridgeshire*.' He glanced at her. 'Didn't mean to rag you, fair colleen,' he said softly. 'Now give me a nice smile – yes, that's better – and go and sit down with the others, like a good girl.'

She sat down. Her knees were shaking slightly and she was not sure whether to feel angry or flattered. The chairs made a sort of horseshoe; Julian Pascoe sat between the two arms of the horseshoe. Mrs Cavell poured him a cup of tea from a thermos flask and he beamed at her and said, 'Too sweet of you, darling.'

The woman with the red skirt said, 'Shall I light the oil heater, Ju?' but he shook his head.

'Like trying to heat the Cheddar Gorge, Patricia, and the fumes are so bad for my asthma.' Julian glanced at his pad of paper. 'We'd better start by taking names. And if you could tell me what you're interested in . . . acting, singing, props, whatever.'

He went round the circle, one by one. Mrs Cavell – 'Scenery and props. You know me, Julian, ready to muck in with anything.' The bald man – 'Bit of tap dancing', which made Caitlin giggle. A skinny young man with a prominent Adam's apple – 'Singing – my repertoire's mostly ballads and comic stuff.' He reached Caitlin.

'And the fair colleen?'

She made herself look him in the eye. 'I can act and sing and dance.'

'Dear me,' he said 'such an embarrassment of riches.' Then he glanced at his watch. 'Auditions on Sunday afternoon, people. Here, I'm afraid. Now, I shall tell you what I've sketched out so far. It's in the early stages, but . . .' Julian Pascoe shrugged his thin shoulders.

Throughout the next few days, Caitlin sometimes found herself thinking of Julian Pascoe. He was quite old – in his thirties, she guessed – and he was married. Patricia Cunningham told her about his wife.

'She's called Margaret. Frightful bitch. She makes poor Julian's life absolute hell.'

They were in the Memorial Hall's sordid kitchen, washing cups. 'Why did he marry her?' asked Caitlin. 'Is she very pretty?'

Patricia sneered. 'Horse-faced, darling. But pots of money. Nouveau riche. Poor Ju is frightfully well-connected, but there's simply no cash in the family. Before he married Margaret, he had to teach at a ghastly prep school in Oxford. Hated it, of course, and it didn't do his health much good.' Patricia shook her head. 'He is frightfully artistic, you know.'

After the auditions, Julian cast Caitlin in several sketches. She was also to sing 'Only a Bird in a Gilded Cage' entirely by herself. Some of the other women in the society had made catty remarks about that, seeing her stardom as unmerited, but Caitlin didn't care. After rehearsals, they all went to the pub. Caitlin, accompanying them, realized that they assumed that she was eighteen, so she talked about sixth form, and always wore make-up.

In the spring of 1949, Colonel Renshaw fell ill. Tilda nursed him, sitting beside his bed during the worst of the fever, putting cold compresses on his forehead while he retreated to the battlefields of Flanders.

The generator broke down again: Josh, at the weekend, took it apart, cleaned it, and reassembled it. A fox got into the hen-coop, leaving a trail of feathers and mangled corpses. Erich, a purple vein beating in his forehead, hacked a hole in the frosty ground; Tilda helped him bury the dead birds.

At half-term, Tilda took Caitlin to Cambridge. While Caitlin spent the afternoon with Kit de Paveley, Tilda met Rosi in a gloomy little basement café. Rosi was wearing a full black skirt and a tight black sweater and was smoking. Every time the door of the café swung open, she'd leap up and wave at the new arrivals.

'Charles! Maureen! Are you coming to our party tonight?' or, 'Stella! Have you seen Finn?' Then in a slightly lowered voice to Tilda, 'Finn is Irish – a poet – so talented. We read each other our work sometimes.'

Rosi, who was in the final year of her English degree, was writing a romance. Tilda suspected a great many swooning damsels, dangerous highwaymen, and hairbreadth escapes.

'How is Hanna, Rosi?'

Rosi scowled. 'Hanna is very, very dull. All the other medical students have lots of fun, but Hanna always studies. She thinks she will fail her exams.' Rosi's expression altered. 'Now, I have a favour to ask you, Tilda. I want you to make my wedding dress.'

Tilda gave a gasp of pleasure and hugged and kissed Rosi.

'I haven't a ring yet. Richard and I are to go to London next weekend and choose one.'

'And Richard's parents? Do they approve?'

'They adore me.' Rosi beamed. 'Tell me what it's like to be married, Tilda.'

Tilda looked away, remembering. It had been wonderful at first, when things like lack of money and a poky basement flat hadn't mattered. She remembered wringing the laundry in the back yard, she and Max each holding one end of the sheet. Collapsing with laughter and then tumbling into bed. Often she looked back, wondering what had happened.

'Marriage is different for everyone, Rosi. And I'm not much of an advertisement for it, am I?'

'But you still love Max, don't you?'

Only Rosi would ask such a question, bluntly, without preamble. Everyone else tiptoed round it, tactfully avoided it. Tilda rubbed her aching forehead with her fingertips. Then she said, 'Yes. Yes, I do.'

'Why don't you tell him?'

She shook her head and blew her nose. 'There's no point. He doesn't love me any more, you see.'

'Are you sure?'

She thought back to that last, terrible meeting with Max, in the street at Southam. 'Yes, I'm sure.'

They were both silent. A dozen students piled into the cramped little café, shouting and laughing.

'So will you?' said Rosi.

'Make your wedding dress?' Tilda smiled. 'Of course. If you really want me to. If you're sure that you don't want one from one of the smart London shops—'

Rosi made a dismissive gesture. 'You must sew it for me, Tilda. That is' – she looked suddenly concerned – 'if you don't mind. You do look very tired. You have a red nose.'

'It has taken me ages to get rid of this wretched cold. And the colonel still isn't well.'

'You should have a holiday.'

For what seemed the first time in months, Tilda laughed. 'A holiday? *Rosi.*'

'Well, why not? You haven't had a holiday in years.'

'Not since before the war.' The beach at Trouville, she thought, escaping an unbearably hot Paris in the baleful August of 1939. Herself and Max, building a sandcastle for baby Josh . . .

'You shall go to France,' said Rosi, as though it was settled. 'You shall go and see Melissa. Hanna and I will stay at Poona over Easter and look after everything.'

Erich worked each day in the colonel's vegetable garden and then, at half past four, he watched for Caitlin's bus. From the old beech tree, perched on one of the long, grey branches, he saw her alight from the bus and walk up the hill. Sometimes she looked tired and he would long to run down the hill and carry her bag for her, but of course he never did. He spoke to her only occasionally, at dinner-time. It did not hurt him that she rarely seemed to acknowledge his existence. He would not have expected her to. She seemed to be from a different sphere, somewhere shut off from the ugliness of the world, like the stone angel.

In the evenings, he went to The Red House and worked on the garden. From the spring flowers he had grown there he made a posy for Caitlin, twisting wire around the stems to bind them together. The wire looked ugly. Tilda had made an appointment for him to see a doctor in Oxford; she offered to accompany him, but Erich, who was now eighteen, refused. He caught the bus, stuttering over the fare, dropping his threepence to the floor while the conductor made sarcastic remarks. At the surgery he made himself smile and be cheerful in a way that he thought the doctor would like, and did not tell him about the dreams or the bits of his life that seemed, sometimes, just to be missing. When the doctor asked him about Vienna, Erich bared his broken teeth in a grin and explained that he had forgotten all that. Then he stood up and clicked his heels together and bowed, and left the surgery.

Outside, there were too many people in the streets, so he pulled his shoulders in and made himself small, trying not to touch them. In a haberdasher's shop he studied reels of ribbon, grabbing the nearest reel, a narrow scarlet, when he saw that the assistant was looking at him.

'A f-f-foot, please.'

The haberdasher cut a length and Erich paid and put the ribbon in his pocket. Then he ran for the bus, sweat sheening his forehead, the eyes of the watchers a physical sensation in the small of his back, the footsteps of his pursuers echoing in his ears.

Back at Colonel Renshaw's house, he covered the wire with a length of ribbon and tiptoed into Caitlin's room. It was scattered with stockings and petticoats and with pale talcum-powder footprints, and the air was rich with a deep, heady perfume. Erich bent to kiss one of the foot-prints, and then, leaving the posy on the window sill, he shut the door behind him and ran back to the garden.

Cécile had taken Melissa shopping in Saintes. Max had expected them back within a couple of hours, and when they had been gone over four hours he prowled around the garage forecourt, glancing from his watch to the road.

He saw them at last and gave a huge sigh of relief. Their bicycle baskets were full of bags. When they pedalled into the forecourt, Melissa leapt off her bicycle and hugged him.

'I've had the most wonderful day, Daddy! Look!' She began to take the bags out of the basket.

'In the house, Melissa,' said Cécile, as she kissed Max. 'You would not want oil on your new clothes.'

In the living room, Melissa took what seemed to Max to be an entire shopful of clothes out of various carrier bags.

Cécile said, 'Now you should hang them up in your wardrobe, darling, so they do not get creased,' and Melissa, her arms full, ran upstairs.

When she was out of earshot, Cécile said, 'They are my present to Melissa, Max. A very late birthday present.'

'Cécile, I can't possibly—'

'Melissa is my friend, Max. I hope you will not deny me the pleasure of buying a few gifts for a friend?'

He glared at her, and then realized that he must give in with grace. 'Then that's very generous of you, Cécile. And so kind of you to spare the time.'

'It was no trouble, Max. In fact, it was a pleasure. We had a delightful afternoon. And now, *chéri*, I would simply adore a glass of wine.'

She followed him into the kitchen, closing the door behind them. The kitchen was tacked on to the side of the house, somewhat separate from the rest of the building. Max poured two glasses of red wine.

Cécile said, 'I found out why Melissa does not want to go back to England.'

He spun round. 'Why?'

'I had to promise not to tell you, Max. But it is as I thought, because of a boy.'

'A *boy*?' He stared at her. 'That's ridiculous, Cécile, you must have made a mistake. Melissa's only a child.'

'Oh, Max,' she said, looking at him in the way that she sometimes did. 'So *English*.'

*   *   *

Some of the priests to whom she had written sent Caitlin addresses of Canavans in Ireland. She wrote letters to each, explaining who she was, certain that one of these Caitlin Canavans must be her father's favourite sister. Soon her father would write back to her, explaining his long absence, and then he would take her away from this horrible house and she would be happy again.

Meanwhile, she had a rehearsal with Julian Pascoe. 'Just a few chassés and poses,' Julian said vaguely, blowing his nose on a large red handkerchief. 'Nothing too complicated, the stage isn't big enough.'

Caitlin, wearing her ballet slippers and a dress with a full skirt, danced around the four chairs that were supposed to represent the gilded cage that she and Patricia were making of cardboard and gold paint. She felt rather silly, up there by herself, Julian beating time and singing the verses and sniffing because he had a cold. When she had finished, he turned away and said: 'That'll do. But cut the jumps. You haven't a ballet dancer's build, darling, and it looks rather elephantine.'

He sat down at the piano, balancing the music on the stand. Caitlin bit her lip. She had always felt rather proud of her figure, but now she saw herself through his eyes: top-heavy, short (she had stopped growing at five foot two), ridiculous.

He had begun to play. She managed to join in at the right time, but she knew that it was awful: her voice wobbled, her steps were leaden and she muddled the words of the second verse. As he played the final chord, she waited miserably for the inevitable sarcasm.

It came. Julian took his hands from the keyboard, flung back his head and closed his eyes. 'Dear God,' he said. 'This fucking cold . . . this fucking village . . .'

He spun round on the piano stool. 'I could have gone to RADA – did you know that, Caitlin Canavan? Instead of being stuck in this godforsaken hole listening to talentless little girls murder frightful music-hall songs—'

She stopped hearing what he said and walked off the stage. She tried to put on her cardigan, but the sleeves were inside out, and she could not see to disentangle them.

'Where are you going?'

She mumbled, 'Home.'

'You're crying.'

She wanted to say something sarcastic in return, but could not speak. He took her cardigan out of her hands and put it back on the chair, and turned her round to face him.

He touched her face, sweeping up the tears, licking them from his fingertip. She gave a strangled little cry.

He said, 'I've been a pig, haven't I? You mustn't mind me. I've this frightful cold and things are difficult at home.'

She managed to speak at last. 'It doesn't matter.' Yet tears rolled down her face.

This time, he stooped and kissed them with his lips. For a while she stood quite still, her eyes closed, but then she lifted up her face and let him touch her mouth with his.

Her cold refused to shift: Tilda gargled with fennel tea, but her voice was scratchy and taut. She persuaded the colonel to engage a nurse to sit with him at night, but the woman left after less than a week, refusing to occupy the same room as the products of the colonel's latest interest, taxidermy. Rosi sent a bale of material for her wedding dress, but Tilda, exhausted each evening, had not yet begun to cut it out. Neither did she write to Max, though she tried to several times, the ink from the nib of her pen spreading in a circular black blot over the blank paper.

The season shifted haltingly from winter to summer. Sleet and wind one day, blue skies and sun the next. The garden alternated between quagmire and soil so frost-hardened a spade could not pierce its surface. She was hacking away at the earth, searching for any remaining potatoes, when a voice called her name.

'Tilda?'

Looking round, she saw Archie Raphael. He pushed open the gate and picked his way across the garden towards her.

'You haven't been to the lectures for weeks.'

She dropped the spade. 'My employer's been ill. I had to look after him.'

'I thought I'd drop in and give you these.' 'These' were a huge bunch of daffodils and narcissi. 'And ask if there was anything I could do for you in Oxford.'

She wished he hadn't come. She had spoken to no-one but the colonel and family for so long that it was an effort to take the flowers and murmur thanks.

'Damned cold out here,' Archie said hopefully.

Reluctantly she took the hint, and led him into the house. In the colonel's kitchen, he looked around at the vast ceilings, the sweating pipes and groaning stove, and said, 'Dear God. Like "Gormenghast".'

She dumped the flowers in a bucket and filled the kettle. He told her about the lectures that she had missed. He had slept through one, argued through another. There was a new student who thought the United Nations was pointless because either the Soviet Union or America was bound to drop the Bomb in the next couple of years, and there was a young woman who believed that in the future all wars would be fought in outer space. 'Rather a nice idea, I thought,' said Archie cheerfully, 'lugging all those tanks and U-boats and things to the moon.' He glanced at Tilda. 'I say, are you all right? You look pretty frightful, you know.'

She said stiffly, 'I've had a cold.'

He looked around. 'A lot of work, this place, I should think.'

'I can manage.'

'Only I've a friend who's a solicitor in Oxford. I know that he's looking for someone to do secretarial work—'

'I like it here, Archie.' She began to clear up the tea things.

There was a silence. Then he said, 'Sort of *penance*, is it?'

Tilda stood at the sink, her back to him, almost too furious to speak. At last she said, 'This house gives me and my family a roof over our heads. It has given me work which I am not ashamed of. Now, I've things to do, if you don't mind.' She began to wash up, scrubbing the dishes so hard she thought the pattern might come off, but then she stopped suddenly and swung back to him.

'And what on earth do you think gives you the right to walk in here, uninvited, and criticize the way I live? We haven't all been to a smart school, you know . . . We don't all have a private income—'

He said mildly, 'I left school at fifteen, actually. My parents were tailors in the East End. The war helped me – I wasn't fit enough for active service, so I went into a unit which made stirring little films that were meant to keep up morale on the home front. You know the sort of thing – "With root vegetables, we can win the war" . . . "Make your saucepans into ack-ack guns."' Archie blinked. 'After the war, I worked for the Central Office of Information, but then I couldn't stand it any more – too patronizing – so I left to go freelance. And as for my right to come here . . . well, I thought that I was your friend.'

'I don't have friends, Archie. I haven't time for friends.' Her voice was brittle.

This time, the silence lasted longer. Then he said slowly, 'No . . . I would imagine that you keep everyone at arm's length. You're very good at that, aren't you, Tilda? It took me weeks to pluck up courage to speak to you the first time, and then – well, I hardly know any more about you now than I did six months ago. I understand that you're not attracted to me. I wasn't expecting that. But friendship would have been nice.'

He picked up his hat and gloves. She said, and the words trembled, 'Archie, you don't understand. You don't know anything about me.'

His smile was fleeting. 'That's the thing, isn't it? You made sure of that, didn't you? It's been like trying to get to know an icicle.'

He left the house and she went back to the washing-up. But one of the plates slipped from her hand on the journey from sink to draining board, and smashed on the tiled floor. Tilda stared at the shattered pieces for a moment and then she ran upstairs. In the bathroom, she splashed cold water over her face, but her reflection – red eyes, peeling nose, dark shadows – told her that Archie had been right: she looked terrible. Old and plain, with lines of bitterness and loneliness and disappointment beginning to extend from nose to mouth. She sat on the living-room sofa, her coat around her shoulders, and wondered whether Archie had been right, too, in the other things that he had said. Whether she was indeed cold and unapproachable; whether she had learned to wall herself off from other people. Whether Melissa had left because her mother had changed, had become unloving and distant.

She mopped her eyes and found pen and ink and writing paper. She began the letter, *My dear Max* . . .

CHAPTER FIFTEEN

I was wakened by my doorbell ringing repeatedly. I staggered out of bed, pulled on my dressing gown, and opened the front door an inch.

'God, Charles—' I said. 'It's *Sunday*.'

'I've had a marvellous idea,' he said. 'But first, these.' His arms were full of croissants and Sunday papers and cartons of orange juice. He squinted at me. 'You don't look well, old thing.'

'I'm fine,' I said weakly, letting him in.

'Good-oh. Then I'll make coffee.'

I was quietly sick in the bathroom while he messed around in the kitchen. 'You all right?' he said, when I came out. He was looking at me closely; his expression was unsettling. I noticed that he had spilt coffee on the work surface and floor, a trail of sticky dark grounds.

'I told you, I'm fine. *Charles*, you'll scald yourself—'

The coffee pot was overflowing. He laughed, and replaced the plunger. Then he said, 'I thought we should have a day out.'

I looked at him blankly. 'Where?'

'Cambridgeshire. Southam. We could do some preliminary research for the programme.'

'Charles,' I began. 'I'm not sure—'

'Just to see whether it would work.' He poured out two cups of coffee. 'Please, Rebecca.'

I longed to shake my head, make some excuse. I wanted a day in which I did not even have to think about Tilda Franklin and her wretched family. I hadn't much liked Southam the first time I had seen it. But I knew that I must force myself to consider Charles's offer of a job, and come to a decision about the book, and about the baby. All these things were interlinked. And I wondered, too, whether the answers to some of my questions lay in Southam. Whether I had not looked quite carefully enough on my earlier visit.

'All right,' I said.

In Charles's ancient MG Midget, we circled London on the M25, blessedly quiet for once, and then drove north up the M11. Charles drove both fast and recklessly, and all my bones rattled, and I thought nastily to myself that I'd probably be saved the trouble of arranging to terminate my unwanted foetus. As it had not rained for days, the wheels of the Midget sent up clouds of dust.

'Shall we eat in Ely?' shouted Charles, when the bulbous silhouette of the cathedral marked the skyline.

I shook my head. 'In Southam,' I yelled back. I remembered that the pub had sold food. I wanted to see the Pheasant. I wanted to know whether Jossy's private detective might have been mistaken, and whether Daragh might have huddled there unnoticed on the evening of 10 April, playing cards, drinking to forget his troubles.

The fields flattened as we drove down the slope of the Isle of Ely, and out into open country. Charles slowed a bit, glancing from side to side. 'Terrific,' he said, his eyes focusing on the rusting farm vehicles, the crooked little cottages. 'Bags of atmosphere. Imagine it in winter. Which way?'

I directed him along the fork in the road that led to Southam. I saw the landmarks that had become familiar to me from Tilda's telling: the bridge where she and Daragh had first kissed, the river where they had sailed in the stolen rowing boat. As we neared the village it seemed to be deserted, still and silent in the windless heat, a veil of black dust over the road signs and lamp posts and white-painted gates.

'Like the Midwich cuckoos,' said Charles flippantly. 'Alien seed—' he added, and then glanced at me. 'Sorry, Becca – tact's never been my strong point.'

I glared at him.

'If you don't want to talk about it, it doesn't matter,' he added. 'None of my business, more's the pity.'

'Charles—'

He brought the car to a screeching, dusty halt outside the church. Pulling on the handbrake, he said, 'Well – you are pregnant, aren't you?'

I eyed him furiously. 'How did you know?'

'Puking in the bathroom first thing in the morning is a bit of a giveaway. And you look—'

'Radiant?' I supplied sarcastically.

'Not exactly. A bit blobby, actually. Round the face.'

I blew my nose loudly and concentrated on not crying so that I wouldn't look even blobbier. After a while, Charles said, 'Just tell me it isn't the loathsome Toby's.'

I shook my head. 'Not Toby's,' I mumbled.

'A pert-bottomed bricklayer's, then, that you picked up on the way back from the shops . . .'

'Idiot.'

Then he said, 'It's Patrick Franklin's, isn't it?' and I just nodded.

I put my dark glasses back on, and we walked down the road to the pub. Inside, half a dozen people lounged at the bar or perched on stools set beside tables. I guessed that what must originally have been two small rooms had been knocked into one larger one, though even that was not of any great size. There were no alcoves or inglenooks, and it seemed improbable that Daragh Canavan could have been overlooked in the crowd.

'Have you thought about the job?' Over sandwiches, Charles twitched restlessly, fiddling with his beer glass, his cigarettes and car keys. I noticed that he hardly ate anything.

I looked out of the window. A woman was wheeling a pram up the street. The pram was battered and ancient, and she wore cheap, skimpy clothes and down-at-heel shoes. I thought of Deborah Greenlees, Tilda's mother, who had been born in this village. Deborah's punishment for bearing a child out of wedlock had been the loss of her freedom and ultimately her life; the price that such women pay nowadays is that of poverty.

'After all . . . with a baby . . . Unless you're thinking . . .' His voice trailed away.

I knew what he meant, though. To go through with this pregnancy, or to terminate it: the question haunted me. It would be much easier to keep the child, as I longed to, if I worked for Charles. And if I wrote the sort of sensational book that would sell.

I placed my hand on his, stilling his restlessly drumming fingers. 'I don't know, Charles. It's a big decision.' I watched him light another cigarette from the dog-end of the last, and I remembered his office, the chaotic heaps of paper, the garbled memos. 'Is everything all right with you, Charles?'

'Everything's great,' he said, flinging out his arms in

a gesture so expansive that he knocked over his glass. I dug tissues out of my pockets and dabbed at the trail of beer. 'I've been on the phone to simply everyone – masses of ideas – the bank'll stump up as soon as they realize how much money they'll make out of it—'

He was becoming angry, and the landlord was staring, so I said something soothing and hauled him out of the pub. We walked down the street and along the path that led beside the church. Neither of us spoke again until we reached the great field that divided us from the Hall.

Evidence of the summer's repair work still scarred the earthworks, a blackish tear in the growth that carpeted the bank. The grass had scorched in the heat, and fluffy white parachutes had escaped from the seed-heads of the thistles. The wall of the dike seemed to isolate us, sealing us away from village and countryside, encasing us in the great brassy bowl of field and sky. Heavy steel-grey clouds filled the low horizon. Our footsteps made no sound on the parched earth. I was reminded of that evening in Richmond, when I had run from Patrick's house: that same disturbing feeling of being cut off in time and space from one's surroundings. Not a blade of grass moved and, in the distance, field and sky seemed to melt together, shimmering.

When Charles took off his jacket and rolled up his shirt sleeves, I was shocked by the way his bones almost seemed to force their way through his skin. He had always been thin, but now he seemed skeletal. He gave me his hand to help me up the slope, and his fingers lingered in mine as we stood looking down into the water. The level had retreated, and a sour smell issued from the mud. Flies danced on the surface of the murky water.

'There's the Hall,' I said, looking up to the distant

building. It looked smaller today, somehow; it seemed to have lost some of its solidity.

'And that?'

I followed the direction of his outstretched arm to the dingy white house on the far perimeter of the field. 'That's the steward's house. Kit de Paveley, Jossy's cousin, lived there.'

'Was he a farmer?'

'He was a teacher and an amateur archaeologist. He was very interested in the history of the area.'

'Could have written a book or two, then. Might be useful for the programme.'

'Yes,' I said. Then I shaded my eyes with my hand, because I thought I had seen a flicker of movement behind those small black window panes.

'Rebecca?'

I realized that Charles had been speaking to me. I had to ask him to repeat what he had said. I blinked and looked back at the house, but saw nothing. A play of light, perhaps, or the reflection of a willow branch, moving in the hot, thundery breeze, caught in the glass.

'I said, you could marry me if you like.'

I turned round, startled. I thought he was joking, and I laughed. 'Oh, Charles – don't be silly—'

He muttered, 'Always the bridesmaid,' but once more I detected anger in his eyes. Unnerved, I threaded my arm through his and kissed him on the cheek, and together we headed back to the car.

The following week I went to see Tilda in hospital. This latest illness had changed her, and her frailty was written in the visible fragility of her body and in the way that she drifted sometimes randomly into the past. I could

not possibly have asked her, *Did you kill your lover?*
It would have been much too intrusive and cruel.

I reminded her about the letter she had written to
Max in 1949, asking to visit Melissa in France.

'Max wrote back by return of post,' said Tilda. 'That
was when I began to hope a little. He said that I could
visit whenever I wanted. I thought it was for Melissa's
sake, but even so, I knew that he did not hate me quite
so much.'

'So you left England . . .?' I prompted.

'As soon as Josh's Easter holidays began.'

'Just the two of you?'

'Just the two of us. Erich would not travel, of course,
and Caitlin said that she must stay at home to rehearse
the play.' She glanced at me. 'You look tired, dear. Shall
we stop?'

I knew that I looked awful. I hadn't slept properly
for weeks, and I felt far iller with this child than I had
with Toby's. Still, I couldn't help smiling. Tilda – frail,
elderly Tilda – was concerned about *my* health.

'You should have a holiday, Rebecca,' she added. 'I'm
sure Melissa would let you have the cottage for a week.
You must ask her.'

'Perhaps I will,' I said, to pacify her. 'Tell me about
France, Tilda.'

'I began to feel happy again,' she said, smiling at the
memory, 'as we travelled down through France. The
sun . . . the warmth. Max and Melissa met us at the
station. I wept when I saw Melissa, of course. I just
couldn't help myself.'

'And Max? How was Max?'

'Cold,' she said. 'Reserved. We went back to his house
to dine. He hardly spoke to me. I remember seesawing
between joy at seeing Melissa again, and despair at the

way Max distanced himself from me. Josh was to stay at the garage overnight, and I was to sleep in a little hotel in the village . . .'

*

Tilda said goodnight to Melissa and picked up her bag. Outside, the sky was ultramarine, punctured with stars. Josh and Max were on the forecourt of the garage, Max holding a torch as Joshua peered into a car engine. 'I'm leaving for the hotel now, Max,' Tilda explained. 'I'll see you tomorrow morning, Josh.'

Max said, 'I'll drive you.'

'There's no need. It's only a short walk, and I'd like the fresh air.'

'Then I'll walk with you.' Max wiped an oily hand on a cloth and took her suitcase before she could stop him.

Always the gentleman. Sometimes Tilda thought that had been part of the trouble. They had come from such different backgrounds: she from Sarah Greenlees' gypsy, hand-to-mouth sort of life, Max from a world where the way you spoke, the way you dressed, was more important than what you felt.

They set off down the twisting, narrow lane. High banks of hedge and wildflower separated them from the fields. There was still a warmth in the air, and the full moon silvered the fields and vineyards.

It was Max who spoke first. 'I was sorry to hear about Sarah. A bit late in the day for condolences, I know, but I'm sorry that I didn't come to her funeral. I should have done so. She was a remarkable woman.'

He was looking ahead, twilight flooding the hollows of his face. His words jolted Tilda out of her stupor of exhaustion, a consequence of her long train journey. She knew that she must make an effort, draw something from reserves that were almost depleted.

'Sarah was fond of you, Max. You and Josh and Erich were the only men I ever heard her have a good word for.'

He laughed, and his face momentarily lightened. He had not aged during two years in France. The threads of grey in his dark hair had not spread, the lines on his face had not deepened.

'Sarah was an original,' said Max. 'You must miss her.'

'I do. I miss her very much.'

'Rosi has sent me an invitation to her wedding. She wants me to give her away.'

She glanced at him. They had almost reached the village. It was not easy, Tilda thought, to unpick the knots of thirteen years of marriage. They remained, catching at you, tripping you up.

'You will, won't you, Max?'

'Of course.' It was too dark to make out his expression. He asked, 'And Hanna and Erich – how are they?'

'Hanna is working very hard, as usual. Too hard, perhaps. I think that as both of her parents were doctors, she feels that if she fails she'll have let them down. Erich wouldn't come with us, of course. He still can't bear crowds. He's never spoken to me about what happened in Vienna, Max. Never. Not once.' Her voice was bleak with an awareness of her failure. 'I managed to persuade him to see a psychiatrist, but it didn't work out.'

'And Caitlin? How is Caitlin? I thought you might bring her to France.'

It was the first time Max had mentioned Caitlin. Caitlin, the daughter of Tilda's half-sister and Tilda's lover.

She said, more lightly than she felt, 'Kate's in a village play and didn't want to miss any rehearsals. Hanna and Rosi are looking after her.'

They crossed the square, walking beneath lime trees whose leaves whispered in the light breeze. She did not tell Max that she had been relieved when Caitlin had refused her invitation to come with her to France. Guiltily relieved. Nor that she could not rid herself of the suspicion that Caitlin's hatred of her had a more fundamental cause than the resentment of a bereaved child for its foster parent.

They fell into a pattern: while Tilda and Melissa spent time together at the hotel or at the garage or in Saintes, Max and Josh went for long cycle rides in the countryside.

They stopped one morning at a café, where Max bought himself a beer and Josh a lemonade. Sitting outside in the shade of an old fig tree, Max thought how much Josh had altered since he had last seen him.

'How's school?' Max asked.

'It's OK.' Josh wiped away his lemonade moustache with the back of his hand. 'I'm in the rugby First Eleven.'

'And cricket?'

'Symonds Major will be captain, but I might be his second-in-command.'

'That's terrific, Josh.'

It was, Max realized, the sort of conversation he had had with his father, every six months or so in the bar of the Savoy. A few years on and he and Josh would talk about the Boat Race and Twickenham, and he would offer Josh a cheque because that was his only way of showing affection, and Josh would refuse it. He asked himself whether that was what he wanted, and knew that it was not.

'And weekly boarding? You're happy with that?'

Josh shrugged. 'We have to eat the most awful things at breakfast, Dad. They're called washers because they look like the things you put in taps. Luckhurst says they're made of blood and fat. Yuck.'

'I meant,' said Max, 'would you prefer to stay at school over the weekends? Sometimes weekly boarders feel they miss out.'

Josh shook his head. 'I have to go home at the weekends, Dad, to sort the generator out. It broke down three times in the winter. The camshaft is dodgy. And Mum gets fed up if I don't come home. I stayed once because there was a rugger match and she was really fed up, I know she was.'

'Is he . . . is he all right, this colonel?'

'He has a super collection of swords. He lets me have a go with them sometimes. And he showed me how to skin a rabbit. It was a bit disgusting, but it'll be useful when I fly round the world. And it's good when the generator breaks down because then we have oil lamps which make the house look really spooky. Though Caitlin fusses about the cold. But' – and Josh looked up at Max – 'girls always do, don't they?'

Max nodded absently. He had a mental image of Tilda slaving away in an unlit, freezing kitchen, watched over by an ex-army type who was clearly insane. What he wanted to say to Josh, but knew he should not, was, *Does he treat her like a servant?* Just the thought of that induced in him a rage that took him by surprise.

Josh added, 'I always make sure there's lots of kindling before I go back to school on Sunday. Erich sometimes forgets about the kindling.'

'You're a good boy, Josh,' Max said, and reached across the table and ruffled his son's hair. They got out the map and planned their journey home.

When they reached the garage, he dismissed the village lad who manned the petrol pump in his absence and went into the house. Tilda and Melissa were in the kitchen, surrounded by baskets of shopping. It was late afternoon and the sun shone directly through the low kitchen window. In the bright light, Max saw the threads of silver in Tilda's long hair, and the fine lines around the corners of her eyes. He saw that she was thinner than she had been, and that she looked tired. He said suddenly, 'We'll go out for dinner tonight. The restaurant in the village is very good.'

Melissa said, 'All of us, Daddy?'

'All of us,' said Max, putting the shopping away.

In the restaurant, eating and drinking, he found himself remembering Pargeter Street, picking Tilda up from the floor of the kitchen after she had fainted. How fragile she had felt; how, before she had come round, he had let himself brush back the strands of hair that had fallen over her face. He refilled their wine glasses and thought, and now she's scrubbing floors for some old nutcase – not exactly what you had in mind, was it, Max old son, when you promised to love and cherish her. You chuck in your job, disappear into London for a little *crise de nerfs*, and expect Tilda to sit at home waiting for you. And when she doesn't, when she ends up in the arms of that smooth-talking sod who's been chasing her for years, you behave as though she's committed the next worst crime to the planning of the Final Solution, and abandon her completely.

It wasn't that he didn't mind about Daragh Canavan any more. He did: he knew that he would always mind.

It was just that he had begun to see it as part of a chain of blame and parting and love and pain for which he bore a responsibility, as Tilda did.

'Dad,' said Melissa. 'Dad.'

Max looked up.

'Dad, I have asked you three times whether we can have ice-cream.'

Max mentally shook himself. 'Of course you can. We must all have ice-cream. And chocolate sauce. And those coloured things.'

'Hundreds and thousands,' said Melissa in a tone of patient superiority. 'They are called hundreds and thousands, Dad.'

Max called at Tilda's hotel at nine o'clock the next morning, and told her that he was taking them all to the beach at Royan. He had risen early and packed a picnic. The Rolls needed to be run in; he would drive them to Royan in style. They travelled through the countryside, parking at the far end of the town. On the sand, Josh hurled on his swimming trunks while Melissa changed with great decorum under a voluminous towel. Max lit a cigarette.

'Aren't you going to swim, Daddy?'

'Not yet. In a while.'

He watched the three of them run down to the sea. The tide was a long way out, so they had to tread through the swathe of sand and pebbles and shells, Josh darting ahead, Melissa skipping beside Tilda. When they reached the shallows, Josh dashed into the water: to his knees, his waist, his shoulders. Melissa doggy-paddled, shrieking in the chilly Atlantic water.

Max walked down to the sea shore. The sand was smooth and cold and rippled by the sea. He had not yet changed, and his shoes were lapped by the waves. His cigarette burned down to his fingertips, the long grey worm of ash falling onto the sand. Josh and Melissa were fifty yards or so out, ducking and cavorting in the water like seals. But Max's gaze rested on Tilda, further inland, swimming a few strokes and then standing up and looking around at the children. Her long hair had darkened, and clung to her head and back like ochre seaweed. Her bathing costume, the old-fashioned pre-war kind, outlined her slim body. Max realized in a sudden, shocking moment that he still loved her, had always loved her, would always love her. The hatred and anger that he had felt towards her had been just an aspect of love.

He heard Melissa call his name, but turned abruptly and began to walk back to where they had left the picnic basket beneath his old cricket umbrella. He scrabbled in his pocket for another cigarette, having wasted the last but then put the packet away unopened. He stood for a long while, his back to them, wanting to shut this sudden drowning realization away and return to the undemanding existence he had created for himself. But he knew that he could not. He had closed himself off from the world for a while, but then the world had reclaimed him: the curé with his chess games, Cécile with her kindness to him and her mockery of him, and most of all, Melissa. They had all drawn him back, but it had been Melissa who had reminded him of the storms and tempests of family life, Melissa who had shown him that he still had a part to play.

They ran back from the sea to the beach, Melissa shivering, wrapping herself in her towel, Josh rolling in the sand until he was covered with pale, sparkling grit, like granite, and Tilda bending and squeezing the salt water from her hair. Max poured tea from the thermos and unwrapped greaseproof paper from sandwiches, and said little. The breeze had got up, conjuring small jagged waves from the water.

After they had dressed and eaten, they went back to the car. They drove through Royan, where Max was to call briefly on a prospective customer. Royan had been bombed heavily by Allied forces before its liberation at the end of the war, and the devastation, still visible four years later, shocked him. Max saw houses that seemed to have been topped and tailed, like gooseberries, possessing neither roofs nor front doors; and walls with single floors attached, suspended eerily over chasms. The roads were pitted and cratered. A few new buildings had begun to rise from the empty heart of the town. Max drove slowly, looking around. It occurred to him that this, too, had touched them. That it had not been just he and Tilda who had been at fault, because history had played its part, tearing them asunder, showing them such savagery, such a contempt of human life, that they had for a while lost the ability to believe in better things.

On the last evening of Tilda's holiday, they cooked crêpes in the cramped kitchen of Max's house, taking turns at tossing the batter in the heavy iron pan.

'Bags I next,' said Melissa, and flicked the pancake. She missed, and it caught on the side of the stove, sliding slowly to the floor. Josh crowed with laughter.

Tilda, leaning against the dresser, held out her glass to Max, who refilled it. 'Mustn't drink too much or I'll never get up tomorrow.' She surveyed the wreckage. 'Your poor kitchen, Max.'

The following day, she and Josh were to catch the three o'clock train from Saintes. Max had insisted on booking them on the wagon-lit to lessen the exhaustion of the journey. Just as, knowing how little money Tilda had been allowed to take out of England, he had insisted on paying for everything. His courtesy towards her had, during the ten days of her stay, been unimpeachable. There had been no trace of the old, cynical, sarcastic Max. Sometimes, over the last day or two, she had found herself believing that time had lessened his anger.

Josh was tossing a pancake. It soared into the air, turned once, and landed neatly in the pan.

Tilda clapped. 'You should be a chef, Josh.'

'I'm going to be an explorer. I'm going to travel round the world.'

'You can't earn a living doing that,' Melissa said scornfully.

'Yes, you can, can't you, Dad? You travelled a lot, didn't you, Dad? So did Aunt Sarah, didn't she? And Aunt Sarah had lots of money. She buried it under the kitchen floor.'

Max looked enquiring. Tilda explained, 'Sarah left me a dozen sovereigns – one of her employers must have given them to her, I suppose. Kit de Paveley sold them for me.'

'Where did your mother live, Mum?'

Tilda felt, suddenly, as though she was standing at the edge of a morass, and asked quickly, 'Is there another pancake? I'm starving.'

Josh poured batter into the pan. Melissa said, 'Aunt Sarah and Mum's mum lived in Southam, silly. They were sisters. Didn't you know that?'

'Did your dad live there too?' Josh flipped the pancake.

And in her mind's eye she saw Edward de Paveley, driving his car, the big old Bentley in which Jossy had lied, through Southam. How the hens and small children had scattered at the imperious hooting of the horn; how the older villagers had touched their caps as he had passed. Less than twenty years ago. It seemed much longer, a world away.

'The frying pan, Josh,' said Max.

The grease on the side of the pan had caught light. Melissa shrieked as the thin orange flame curved around the cast iron. Tilda seized a jug of water and hurled it over the pan, the stove and Josh. Max, striding forward, dropped a damp tea cloth over the stove and the flames sizzled and went out. Josh, his clothes soaked, was standing in a puddle of water. 'My *pancake*.' Tilda began to giggle helplessly.

Later, after supper, Max walked her home. It was dark, the silence of the countryside absolute and resounding. She remembered walking along this road on her first night in France, and knew that since then things had changed between herself and Max. The icy politeness had thawed: he too had laughed at Josh, and for a moment they had been a family again.

They walked for a while in silence, both, she suspected, unwilling to break the fragile truce. But Max said at last: 'You'll have to tell them about your father sometime, you know. They're of an age to ask questions.'

She said angrily, 'Max, how can I?'

The stars picked out the pale, curving road and the beginnings of the village. 'They'll find out somehow,' said Max eventually. 'You did, Tilda.'

She remembered the day Aunt Sarah had told her that Edward de Paveley was her father. How she had run from Southam; the clip of the scissors as she cut her hair in the third-class carriage.

'I can't, Max,' she said flatly. 'How can I possibly

tell my children that my father raped my mother and put her in the madhouse? How can I explain that to them? And Caitlin—' Her voice shook.

They had reached the village. The lime trees in the square surrounded them, ghostly grey in the darkness. Tilda thought of the anger and hatred that lingered in Caitlin's eyes. She was Caitlin's aunt and she had made love to Caitlin's father. She hated herself for both those things.

She felt Max take her elbow and steer her to the little café at the side of the square. The metal chairs were piled on the tables on the pavement. He took down a chair and held it out for her, and she sat down. He sat beside her. 'Here,' he said, and gave her his handkerchief. She had not realized she was crying. She blew her nose and the sound echoed against the still, silent buildings.

'Cigarette?'

She hardly ever smoked, but she did so now. She said, her voice still trembling, 'Max, I resent that the past should go on hurting me. I can't escape from it. Everything I do, all that I've done – I feel that it is there, manipulating me. It just isn't fair.'

'We're all caught up to some extent in what our families have made of us, Tilda. That's how it is.'

She rubbed her eyes with the tip of her fingers. 'When Aunt Sarah told me who my father was, she cursed the de Paveleys.' She looked up at him. 'I've never forgotten that, Max. She cursed them. But she forgot, didn't she, that I was one of them.'

He frowned. 'What do you mean, Tilda?'

Elbows on the cold metal table, she voiced the fear that had haunted her for years. 'She cursed *me*, Max, don't you see? And everything that has since happened reminds me of that.'

'Tilda, you're not saying that you believe that nonsense, are you? I know that Sarah could be pretty terrifying, but some of the things she believed in were quite cracked. You know that they were just rural superstitions, the sort of thing that lingers in isolated country places.'

'But Jossy,' she whispered. 'Think of what happened to Jossy. And the land ... the house ... Caitlin has nothing, Max, nothing. And even Daragh—'

She stopped. For the first time since Max had left her, she had spoken Daragh's name. She saw his eyes narrow, yet he turned to her and touched her hand, and said: 'Tilda, you're just tired. You wouldn't be thinking like this if you weren't exhausted. It's late, you should be in bed.' He dropped his cigarette stub onto the cobbles, and ground it with his heel. 'That colonel obviously works you too hard. You shouldn't have to do that sort of thing.'

She was going to be angry with him, as she had been with Archie, but she saw, suddenly, the concern in his eyes. She thought, Max cares. Max still cares about me. She bit her lip, and heard him add: 'I can see how difficult it must be for you to talk about the past. But I think that you must give the children some sort of explanation. These things have a way of coming out at the worst possible time.' He glanced at her. 'Don't you agree, Tilda?' He touched her hand again. 'You're cold – I'm sorry – these spring nights—'

'I'm fine.' She tried to smile.

'Have my jacket.' He stood up, slipped off his jacket, and slung it round her shoulders. She wanted to hug his lapels to her face, but she did not dare.

She said slowly, 'The trouble is, Max, that I remember

how I felt when Sarah explained everything to me. How *tainted* I felt.'

He snorted. 'Sarah didn't exactly choose the right time, did she? She was never a believer in softening blows. She herself was as tough as old boots and she expected everyone else to be the same.' He frowned. 'Perhaps you could explain things in the context of the times. Perhaps you could point out that though Edward de Paveley was an evil old buffer in some respects, he had his better side. He was a damned good soldier, for instance.'

'He fought at Ypres and at the Somme,' said Tilda. Kit had told her that, when she had invited him for tea. 'He was awarded medals for gallantry.'

'Quite. So he was a mixture, as most people are. Just more extreme than most.' Max glanced at his watch. 'It's almost midnight. They'll lock you out, if we're not careful.' He rose from the table and helped Tilda out of her chair, and they walked across the square. 'I'll talk to Melissa, if you like.'

'Would you, Max?'

They had reached the hotel. He pressed the bell. She took off his jacket, gave it back to him. Soon, Tilda thought, he would shake her hand and say a polite goodnight and tomorrow she would leave France and would not see him again for months . . .

The door opened. Max said, 'Goodnight, Tilda.' Then he bent and kissed her.

She stepped inside the hallway. He had already turned, was walking away from her, his back to her. The concierge had retreated, grumbling, into her little room. Tilda leaned against the wall of the hallway and closed her eyes, unable to move. She still felt the imprint of his lips on her face, and her own overwhelming and unexpected rush of desire.

'I'll have to stay and look after Daddy,' said Melissa.

'I know, darling.' Tilda, Josh and Melissa were sitting in the small patch of garden behind the garage, in the shade of the mulberry tree. Max was out, returning the Rolls to its owner.

'He doesn't look after himself, you see. He eats bread and cheese for every meal.'

Tilda smiled. 'Your father never notices his food. I used to think that he'd eat a bowl of nuts and bolts if I put it in front of him.' She leaned back against the tree, drowsy with warmth, and with an optimism she had not felt for years.

'And his shirt collars had worn away on both sides.'

Max's shirts, bought by his mother years ago in Jermyn Street. Tilda herself had turned the collars to make them last through the war. Tilda took Melissa's hand. 'Melissa, I know that you have to stay. But you'll come and visit me very soon, won't you, for a nice long holiday?'

'In the summer. For weeks and weeks and weeks.'

'I'll teach you to shoot pigeons with the air rifle,' said Josh.

'No thank you,' said Melissa primly. 'I like pigeons.'

'There's a car.' Josh scrambled to his feet. 'I'll go and help Gaston.' He ran to the forecourt.

Melissa snuggled against Tilda. 'I can share your room when I come home, can't I, Mummy?'

Tilda stroked Melissa's fine, straight hair. 'Don't you want to share with Caitlin?'

She couldn't see Melissa's face, which was buried in her lap, only the shake of her head. Melissa's voice was muffled.

'I used to think Kate was nice because she was pretty and had lovely dresses and things, but I've thought and thought about it and I don't think she was nice at all.'

'Do you want to tell me about it?'

Another shake of the head. 'No. Not now. When I'm very old and married, then I will, because it won't matter any more.'

Tilda glanced at her watch. Max had said that he would be home by midday, yet it was already a quarter past twelve. He was to drive them to the railway station at two o'clock. She thought, for the thousandth time that day, *He kissed me*. Just a peck on the cheek, but a kiss nevertheless. The sun filtered through the heavy canopy of leaves, making thin rails of light, and she closed her eyes.

The children tied them together, a tie that not even Max, who had sought solitude, had been able to break. Max and Melissa would return to England in July to attend Rosi's wedding, and Melissa would remain in Woodcott St Martin for most of the school holidays. Perhaps Max would stay for a week or two. And perhaps if Max became her friend again, then maybe, just maybe, love could grow out of friendship. It had done so before.

The sun reached its highest point in the sky. Tilda's back was against the trunk of the mulberry tree, and Melissa's head cradled on her lap. Tilda dozed.

There was a clatter of dishes from the kitchen. Tilda opened her eyes and looked up, expecting to see Max.

A girl's voice called through the open window, 'Max, darling – I'm home! Annette is well now, and her mother-in-law came to stay, and she is such a dragon! So I thought I would come and cook you your favourite dinner.'

Melissa sat up, rubbing her eyes. 'Cécile,' she said.

* * *

The owner of the Rolls-Royce, contrary to their arrangement, was out when Max arrived. He had to wait, parked in the heat, for more than an hour. More than once he thought of giving up and going home, but he had been counting on the money, so, glancing furiously at his watch every ten minutes or so, he forced himself to wait.

He leaned against the car's gleaming bonnet, now covered with a thin film of dust, and lit himself a cigarette. Standing there, he decided that, before she went back to England, he would find a few minutes alone with Tilda and tell her that he loved her. Just that. Her response would dictate what happened next. When they had parted in Southam, she had told him that she loved him. He had disbelieved her then, but now her words came back to him, instilling in him a measure of hope. He had not been able to tell, these past ten days, how she felt about him. Edgily, he glanced at his watch again. He would give the wretched fellow another ten minutes.

The ten minutes were almost up when he saw the pale dust clouding from the road as a tractor crested the brow of the hill. The owner of the Rolls leapt from the tractor seat, and caressed his beloved car. Then he shook Max's hand and insisted they drink a glass of wine in the kitchen of the farmhouse. The money was counted out with agonizing slowness, a bundle of greasy ten-franc notes. Then Max took his bicycle out of the boot of the Rolls and pedalled furiously home.

And somehow, it all went wrong. Gaston grabbed Max the moment he rode into the forecourt; the pump had jammed again, and an irate motorist was waiting with an empty tank. By the time Max had freed the blockage, Tilda and Josh and Melissa were sitting on the bench outside the door, ready to leave for the station. Tilda had already put her cases in the back of the motor car.

Max tapped his watch. 'We've another twenty minutes before we need to go.'

'I'd like to get there early, Max.'

'But I've booked seats.'

Tilda didn't look at him. 'I'd like to buy a magazine, and Josh will want sweets.'

He said abruptly, 'Have you dined?' and she shook her head.

'I wasn't hungry. The children have eaten.'

It was as if, he thought, she could hardly bear to be near him any longer. Angrily he washed and changed and started up the car and drove to Saintes. She neither spoke to him nor looked at him; they travelled in almost complete silence. On the station, waiting for the train, Max recollected himself and said a proper goodbye to Josh, and gave him some of the farmer's francs. 'You helped with the car. It's your wages,' he said, and was touched to see Josh's face brighten.

With a heavy heart, Max watched the train draw out of the station. He gave Melissa his handkerchief because she was crying, but would have liked to have been able to howl himself. He realized, as he took Melissa's hand and walked back with her to the car, that he had waited too long, that he had left it too late, that he had lost her for ever.

When Caitlin ran up the lane that led to the Memorial Hall, she saw Julian waiting outside. The tip of his cigarette was a small orange spark in the dusk.

'Do you mind if we rehearse at my place tonight? Only I'm expecting a telephone call.'

Caitlin said, 'But Mrs Pascoe—'

Julian interrupted her. 'Margaret had to go to Eastbourne. Her mother's ill.' He threw his cigarette stub to the ground. Caitlin followed him down the path, her heart pounding rapidly. There hadn't been a rehearsal last week because Julian had had flu, and in the course of the fortnight that had passed since their last extraordinary meeting she had found herself questioning her recollections. Sometimes she was convinced that Julian loved her, that he thought she was special. He had told her that she was pretty and, most important, he had kissed her. Yet all the women in the drama group, with the possible exception of Mrs Cavell, were in love with him; and the kisses, perhaps, had been just the kisses of a friend. More pleasant, but less passionate, than Martin Devereux's kisses, for instance.

They walked along the path that led from the lane to the small estate of houses behind the post office. The houses were large and undistinguished, built between the wars. Julian opened the gate of one. Caitlin felt vaguely disappointed. The ordinariness of the house seemed to diminish him.

Then he looked back at her and said, 'Ghastly place, don't you think? Margaret's father gave the house to us as a wedding present. Along with a set of fish knives and a cocktail cabinet of such perfect vileness that I've put it in the garage and keep wax polish in it.'

Caitlin giggled. Julian fitted his key to the lock, and opened the front door. Inside, he took her coat and led her into a large room with three squashy sofas, a picture window overlooking the back lawn, and a baby grand piano.

'Drink, darling?'

'That would be lovely. Gin and it, please, Julian.'

Caitlin's momentary nervousness had gone. She felt as though she were in a play. She had made her face up carefully, she had put on her nicest dress, and the room was an acceptable backdrop. She even remembered her lines. *Gin and it, please, Julian.*

He did not yet go to the piano, but sat down on a sofa, beckoning Caitlin to sit beside him. He said, 'Sorry about last week's rehearsal, darling, but I was frightfully unwell. The strain . . . I shall be glad when this wretched little revue is finished with.'

Caitlin stared at him. She had not thought about what would happen after the revue's performance. The prospect filled her with a bleak emptiness. 'Don't you enjoy it?'

He put aside his glass. 'I enjoy parts of it,' he said, looking at her. He added, 'Things have been difficult for me lately. My father-in-law wants me to go and work for his wretched business.'

'What sort of business?'

'He imports timber.' Julian rolled his eyes. 'Can you imagine? I can hardly tell the difference between mahogany and walnut.'

He took her glass and refilled it. While his back was to her, she said, 'What would you like to do, Julian?'

'Oh – write a play . . . direct a film. Leave this place. It suffocates me.'

'It is dull,' she agreed.

He glanced at her. 'I thought you might find it so. You must long for your hills and your loughs, Caitlin Canavan.'

She did not tell him that she had seen Ireland only

in atlases and on postcards. 'I hate it here,' she said simply.

He stared out of the window, lines of discontent furrowing his forehead. 'One feels so trapped, so out of place.'

She felt a thrill of recognition. The sense of displacement she had felt ever since her mother's death remained with her, undiminished.

He did not yet sit down, but moved restlessly around the room. 'Sometimes I feel like chucking it all in ... starting again. Slinging a few things into a knapsack and walking away ...'

'But your wife?' she whispered.

'It was largely a marriage of convenience,' he said vaguely.

Caitlin imagined herself and Julian, travelling. Sleeping in hotels, working in little theatres. Riding with him, dancing with him. He would hold her to him, and kiss the top of her head. *Don't you look the little princess* ...

He was standing at the window. It had begun to rain, great drops that slithered down the glass. His posture was oddly crushed, his head bowed, his arms folded around himself. She rose from the sofa and hesitantly touched his forearm. 'Poor Julian,' she said. 'How perfectly beastly it must be for you.'

He looked up at her and smiled bleakly, and said, 'I thought that you might understand. None of the others do.' Then he held out his arms and enfolded her within them, her head against his chest. She had not felt so warm, so safe, for years. The sense of being detached from herself, that she felt most of the time, had gone. She closed her eyes, smiling, enjoying the warmth of his body. Some of the battles and confusions and ignominies of the last two years seemed to melt away, to recede to a nightmare past on which she could close a door.

For a long time, he didn't say anything, but she felt his lips touch the top of her head, and the pressure of his fingertips on her back. At last, he said, 'You've been here an hour, sweetheart. What time are your people expecting you back?'

'My guardian's away. No-one will notice if I'm late.'

'Ah.' After a pause, 'You know I want you terribly, don't you, Caitlin?'

She remembered Martin Devereux and that awful business in the back of his car, and wondered whether she could endure that again. She would have been content to stay like this, but she realized that, for men, this was not enough. It was a trade – this blissful assurance of love for that brief degradation. She looked up at him and smiled.

He took her to a bedroom on the first floor. There she began to undress herself, as she had with Martin, but he stopped her and undid buttons and zips himself, punctuating the movements with kisses and expressions of love. And then, in the bed, between linen sheets, he coaxed and caressed her so that when he touched her, she cried out with pleasure and gave herself to him.

The next time she went to Julian Pascoe's house, he opened the front door to her and led her straight up to the bedroom without saying a word. There, he made love to her with such expertise and thoroughness that afterwards she lay back on the sheets, her eyes closed, exhausted, hardly able to move her sprawled limbs.

Then he said, 'Margaret's coming home at the end of the week,' and she sat up.

'It won't make any difference, will it?'

'Of course it will make a difference,' he said irritably. He began to pull on his clothes. 'It'll make a hell of a difference.'

'But you said . . .'

'What?'

'That you would leave her.'

Julian laughed. 'One doesn't just walk out, darling. One plans a little first.' He knotted his tie.

Later, in her own bedroom, she thought about that. Her father had just walked out. Her father had not, as far as she knew, planned.

Caitlin admitted to herself that she was still unsure of Julian. He was her lover and she adored him and intended to marry him, but every now and then she was uncertain what he thought of her. When they rehearsed with the others in the Memorial Hall, he treated her exactly the same as he treated the other members of the cast, apart from the odd kiss stolen behind the wings. She realized that he had to be careful because of Margaret, but the occasional flashes of sarcasm that he still directed at her hurt her terribly. She knew that she was pretty, but his criticism of her dancing ('rather elephantine, darling,') still rang uncomfortably loud in her ears. Although he had expressed a common dislike of Woodcott St Martin and its stupefying dullness, she was not sure, when she thought about it carefully, that he had actually suggested that they go away together. When they were together, she was certain of his love; when they were apart, her certainty crumbled. The revue was to be staged in early May: sometimes she thought that was what Julian was waiting for, and that on the last night he would sweep her up and take her away. But in her most miserable, most uncertain moments, she was afraid that after the revue her life would just return to boredom and emptiness.

At Poona, Rosi wrote her novel and revised sporadically. Finals were horribly close and she suspected that she was going to do rather badly. The thought did not depress her, because she was to be married in July, and besides, her book was going very well. Her heroine, abducted by a particularly unpleasant villain, had just escaped his clutches by tying the bedsheets to a corner of a four-poster and abseiling down the wall of his castle. When she was stiff and tired from writing, Rosi cooked messily and amused the colonel. Little housework was done. Caitlin was out most of the time at the stables or rehearsing her play, Erich worked in the garden, and Hanna studied from dawn to dusk. Until she overheard the conversation in the post office, Rosi thought that everything was going very smoothly.

Tilda and Josh were due to come home the following day. Rosi went to the post office to buy envelopes for her letters to Richard. There was a rack of second-hand books among the leaflets about free cod-liver oil and the posters advertising Bring and Buy sales. Rosi slid behind the rack and began to look through it, searching for titles she had not yet read. The post office's door opened as another customer came in. The woman's voice filled the tiny shop.

'Have you the evening free, Dorothy? Only I simply must finish those flats tonight, or Julian will be furious.'

'I thought Miss Canavan was supposed to be help-ing you.' This was said rather slyly. Rosi, listening, hidden by the rack, replaced a book and took out another one.

'She did promise, but she never turns up. These young girls . . . so unreliable.'

'I believe that Julian is giving her a lot of extra rehearsals.'

A silence. Then, 'Dorothy . . . you don't mean . . .?'

'Didn't you know, Patricia? Nigel saw them in the Memorial Hall kitchen in a clinch. The whole village is talking about it.'

'But she's just a schoolgirl!' Patricia's voice quivered. 'And poor Margaret—'

The doorbell clanged as another customer entered the shop. Mrs Cavell said, 'Oh, she'll forgive and forget, she always does,' and Rosi stuffed the book, a romance called *Love's Young Dream*, back in the rack upside down and ran out of the shop.

Cleaning out cupboards that afternoon, she decided not to say anything to Hanna yet. Hanna worried too much and besides, it might only be village gossip. Yet the more she thought about it, the more Rosi was concerned. Caitlin had had a rehearsal almost every evening this week. Rosi had noticed that she left the house plastered with make-up and wearing her fanciest clothes – furs and silks that Rosi assumed had once belonged to her mother. Caitlin was an inveterate flirt: when Richard, Rosi's fiancé, had visited Poona earlier in the year she had even made eyes at him, to his consternation and embarrassment. As far as Rosi was concerned, Caitlin could go to the devil, but she knew that Tilda would not feel the same way. She considered her options. She could confront Caitlin, but she suspected that Caitlin would lie to her. Or she could try to find out the truth.

After supper that night, Caitlin emerged from her bedroom wreathed in clouds of cheap perfume. 'Another rehearsal?' enquired Rosi sweetly, and Caitlin nodded.

'I may be rather late. Julian wants to run through the whole thing.'

Rosi waited until she had heard the front door slam before grabbing her jacket and running downstairs. She followed Caitlin down the road that led to the path beside the Memorial Hall. She felt like a spy, ready to duck behind a tree if Caitlin turned round, but Caitlin never once looked back. Eventually they reached a large house, its gardens bordered by a privet hedge. Sheltered by the privet, Rosi saw Caitlin ring the doorbell. The door opened and Caitlin slipped inside. Rosi slid the gate off the latch and walked up the gravel drive, trying not to make any noise. Then she skirted round to the back of the house. No rooms were lit downstairs, but there was a light in an upstairs window. 'Stupid, stupid little girl,' muttered Rosi to herself, as she ran back to the front door. There, she pressed her finger on the bell, and did not take it away until she heard the thunder of footsteps and saw that the hall light had been switched on.

A man flung open the door and stared at Rosi furiously.

'What the hell . . .?'

She assumed him to be Julian Pascoe. 'I've come to take my sister home,' she said, and pushed past him, making for the stairs.

CHAPTER SIXTEEN

I worked in the library, surrounded by reference books, on a time-line of the events that had surrounded Daragh Canavan's death. The flood, Daragh's encounter with Tom Kenny and his henchmen, his brief affair with Tilda, and Jossy's realization of her husband's betrayal and her pathetic attempt to hold on to him, an attempt which had ultimately cost her her life. A few days later, Max's fleeting and disastrous return to Southam, followed by Daragh's disappearance the same night. I had tried to map out how Daragh had spent his last day. He had been drinking. He had suggested to Caitlin that they go riding the next morning. They had packed the picnic and, at sunset, Caitlin had watched her father leave the house and walk across the fields. It had been April, which would have meant, I estimated, that Daragh had left the Hall between six and seven o'clock in the evening. Caitlin, watching from the garden, seemed to have been the last person to see Daragh Canavan alive – apart from his murderer, of course. Though Daragh had taken the footpath to Southam, none of the villagers had recalled seeing him that evening. His body had been found forty-eight years later, in the wilderness between Hall and village.

But no sudden inspiration, no answer to an old

mystery came to me, sitting there between the shelves of encyclopedias. I could not distinguish, as both Tilda and Caitlin had told me to, the truth. I had begun to think that the task I had set myself was hopeless. I could not tell whether Tilda was the angel the newspaper articles had proclaimed her to be, or the murderous hypocrite of Caitlin's recollection. I thought once more of the cut-glass chandelier in The Red House's garden room, moving in the draught, sunlight catching the facets so that they reflected different lights, no two colours quite the same. Though I wanted to believe Tilda's version of events, I found myself leaning to Caitlin's. That Tilda had turned the fifteen-year-old Caitlin out of her home seemed to be borne out by the diaries. Caitlin had been promiscuous and deceitful – but that was understandable, surely, in the light of the bereavements she had suffered. She had been cruel to Melissa, but then many adolescent girls are unkind to each other. Tilda's abandonment of Caitlin seemed unjustifiably harsh.

I thought once more of my flight through London, running from Patrick's house to Charles's offices. I felt now as I had done then, coming at the familiar from a strange route, unable to recognize it. I stared at my notes, rubbing my aching forehead with my fingertips.

And my thoughts drifted, as they so often did, to Patrick. Had we parted because of a distrust engendered by our equally unhappy past experiences, or because I would not bend to his will? Was Patrick capable of loving me, as I had once believed, or did he pose a physical threat to me, as Charles had unnervingly suggested? Everything we had done, everything he had said to me, could be seen in two lights. Those crystal beads again, always turning, amber and turquoise and pink.

* * *

It was dusk by the time I reached home that night. My next door neighbour was having a party, and I had to park some distance from the house. Walking home, my skin prickled with the awareness that I was being watched. I glanced around, but could see no-one.

I let myself into my flat, and felt safe again. It was too hot and too late to cook, so I cut bread and cheese and opened a packet of olives. Sitting at my desk, I rewound my tape recorder. Tilda's voice, describing her holiday in France in 1949, echoed round the room. I began to take notes, but my eyelids were growing heavy and my head still ached. I switched off the tape-player, kicked off my shoes, and curled up on the bed.

I dreamed that I was cleaning fireplaces in a large old house. Sweeping out the ash, blackening the hearth, laying the fire. It took ages to clean up all the ash, because no matter how conscientiously I brushed, little runnels of soot trickled from the flue, gathering around the metal firedogs and behind the ornamental grate. I worked on my hands and knees, possessed by a feverish anxiety. I was wearing a long black high-collared dress, a white apron and button boots. My hair was swept up into a bun. The house was dark and silent at first, but after a while I became aware of a sound. A rattling and clicking, as though someone was trying to open a door. My anxiety to finish the grate increased, but soot still whistled down the chimney, dirtying the gleaming tiles. I heard the door handle turn once more, and knew that soon, when I looked round, I would see the face of my employer, Edward de Paveley. And if the grate was not clean, then I would feel his body against mine, the weight of him crushing the air out of my lungs. The door rattled.

I woke up, gasping for breath. There was, as before, that overwhelming relief when I remembered that this was 1995, and not 1913. It was pitch dark, and when I glanced at my clock I saw that it was eleven o'clock. Then I heard the sound again. A rattle: the sound from my dream.

I couldn't move; I was paralysed with fear. I had begun sternly to tell myself that I was imagining things again when I heard a dull thud. Someone had jumped from the kitchen draining board to the floor. I pressed my knuckles against my mouth. That was no old ghost: that was neither Edward de Paveley nor Daragh Canavan. Someone was in the kitchen.

I managed to kneel up. My fumbling fingers groped around the bedside table, but found nothing more than the lamp and alarm clock. I remembered that I had returned the hefty book about the Fens to the library. I heard footsteps crossing the kitchen floor. *Actually, I wondered whether you felt physically threatened.* I tried to call out Patrick's name, but could not speak.

The door opened and light flooded the room, burning my eyes. 'Charles,' I said.

My first reaction was one of overwhelming relief. My dear old friend Charles. Safe, reliable, unthreatening Charles. Yet, when I looked at him properly, my relief faltered. Something about his eyes; something about his grubby, unkempt clothing.

'Charles,' I said again. 'What on earth are you doing here?'

'You should get your window fixed, Rebecca.'

'For heaven's sake—' I was becoming angry. 'It's eleven o'clock at night—'

'I said, you should get your window fixed. Anyone could walk in. Though perhaps that's what you want.'

His gait was unsteady as he walked into the room, and I thought that he was drunk. As he neared my bed, I stood, but he reached out a hand and pushed me back onto the sheets.

'No,' he said. 'Stay there. I want you to stay there.'

I said quickly, 'We can talk in the kitchen, Charles. Let me make you a cup of tea.'

'Don't want to talk,' he muttered. ''S not what I've come for.'

Charles is slightly built, but I am five foot two and he is six foot. My fear was fast returning.

'I waited *years*,' he said suddenly. 'But I'm not going to wait any more.'

I whispered, 'Waited for what?'

'For you.'

He was neither ill nor drunk. There was an absence in his eyes. Something missing.

'I waited for you, Rebecca,' he repeated. His hand still rested on my chest; slowly, it slid down, caressing my breast. 'When you were screwing that prick, Toby Carne, I waited. When you lost the baby and he chucked you, I waited.'

'You've been a good friend, Charles,' I said. Though I tried to sound reassuring, my voice faltered. I could hear the sound of the next door party: music and screams of laughter. I knew that if I too screamed, no-one would hear me.

'And things were going better,' he added as though I had not spoken, 'and I began to hope again. And then you jumped into Patrick Franklin's bed. I couldn't believe it. All those years I'd waited. You are so faithless, aren't you? I kept an eye on you, though, Rebecca.'

He withdrew his hand and looked at me, and when I saw the cunning in his pale green eyes,

I understood. 'You were watching me, Charles. It was you.'

'Course it was. I like to watch you sleep, Rebecca – did you know that? Sometimes you leave the curtains open a little, and I can look down at you. If Patrick Franklin had slept here, I would have killed him.'

He said that in such a matter of fact way that my mind, racing for an escape, seemed to still, unable to even think any more. Then I gasped and said, 'Charles, you're not well. Let me phone your doctor. Or Lucy—'

'No.' He looked down at me. There was in his face an expression of such mingled desire and pain that just then I hated myself. I had never taken seriously Charles's avowals of love. I had not considered him a person capable of being deeply hurt.

'And then you quarrelled with Patrick,' he went on. 'You let me hold you that night – you cried on my shoulder. Do you remember, Rebecca? I was so happy.'

I remembered weeping down the phone, and Charles coming round, laden with wine and roses. Now he bent his head, laying it on my breast. I stroked his fine, tangled hair, trying to calm him.

But when he straightened, his expression had altered. 'I thought that you loved me then. I'd waited and waited and you needed someone, and I was there. So I offered to marry you. Even though you were carrying that man's child, I offered to marry you. I had a ring, Rebecca – did you know that?'

I shook my head, unable to speak. I remembered Southam, and the glassy, unreal stillness of the landscape.

'And you laughed,' he said wonderingly. 'You laughed.'

I saw that the love in his eyes had been replaced by anger. Very slowly, almost imperceptibly, I began to raise myself upright, so that I could run for the door if I had to.

'I didn't mean to laugh, Charles,' I said gently. 'I shouldn't have laughed. It was wrong of me.'

He turned suddenly, seizing my shoulder, shaking me. 'Why aren't I good enough for you, Rebecca?'

'It isn't that.' His bony fingers dug into my shoulders, hurting me. 'You know that I'm very fond of you, Charles. You're my oldest friend—' I could hear my panic in my voice.

'I only wanted what everyone else has had. And then, after we went to the Fens, I realized that you weren't going to give it to me. Everyone else, but not me. So I thought, why shouldn't I take it?'

There was a sound – just the wind blowing the open window shut, I thought – but enough to make Charles turn his head. I saw my chance and wriggled out of his grasp, running across the room. But as I seized the door handle, he flung himself against me so that my head ricocheted against the door. My knees buckled, and I slid to the floor. The artexed ceiling of the room was studded with stars. I heard a voice call out my name, and I said weakly, 'Patrick,' and then thought how stupid I was, imagining that Patrick had come to save me. Charles's body was pressed against mine, and his hands clawed at me, making real all my worst nightmares.

And then, quite suddenly, the weight was gone, and I was free. I opened my eyes, and as my vision cleared I saw Patrick dragging Charles across the room. Charles swung his fist at Patrick, and Patrick collapsed against my desk. My laptop, the box of disks and heaps of paper spilled to the floor. Charles hurled himself on top of Patrick, who somehow managed to push him aside. I knew that I should do something – call the police, or hit Charles on the head with a vase the way heroines do in films, but I simply could not move. The fight wasn't like in films, anyway. It was messy, scrappy, their fists more often missing than finding their mark. Eventually Charles, struggling to his feet, struck his head on the underside of my desk and fell back to the floor, stunned. When Patrick drew back his fist to hit him again, I cried out, 'Oh, for God's sake, Patrick – stop it! That's enough!'

Patrick looked at Charles, who was not moving, and then he staggered back to the bed and sat down, his head in his hands, gasping for breath. Then he said, 'Are you all right?'

I nodded. I wasn't sure, actually. There was a moment's silence, and then the awful noise began. Charles was crying. Beneath the desk, he hunched his knees up to his chin, and wept. My battered room was filled with his despair.

I sent Patrick into the kitchen to find ice to put on his cut eye, and I crawled across the room and gently coaxed Charles out from under the table. I sat on the bed, Charles's head cradled in my lap, as he wept and told me that he had not meant to hurt me. My entire body felt bruised, but much more painful was the guilt I felt. Charles had loved me, and I had made light of his love. If nothing else, Tilda's story should have taught me love's capacity to wound the lover. Now, I believed Charles when he said that he had not meant to hurt me. When Patrick picked up the telephone to call the police, I stopped him.

'Rebecca. For God's sake. He tried to rape you. I heard him.'

'He's ill, Patrick.' I tried to think what to do. 'I'll call his sister – perhaps his mother can get him to go into a clinic or something.'

He argued a bit more, but I insisted. A night in a police cell would finish poor Charles off. We tracked down Charles's mother and then everything seemed to happen very quickly. Rattled out of her usual cold detachment, Charles's mother arrived with a Harley Street doctor, protesting at being hauled out of bed at such an hour. Charles was more or less catatonic by that time, and went with them quietly. And then Patrick and I were alone in the ruins of my living room. It was past three in the morning.

I said, 'Thank you, Patrick.' My voice shook. 'How did you know . . .?'

'I didn't. I'd something to tell you. I've been trying to contact you for weeks – I left several messages on your answering machine, but you didn't get in touch.'

'I erased them,' I said, shamed, 'without listening to them.'

'Oh.' He glanced at me. His good looks were marred by a ragged cut above his eyebrow. 'Just as well, perhaps, or I wouldn't have called tonight. Anyway, I was working late, so I thought I'd drive back this way and call in if there were any lights on. I was about to knock at the door when I heard the shouting. So I went round the back to see whether the door was still open. It wasn't, but I managed to climb through the window.'

'You are going to have a splendid black eye, Patrick. What did you want to tell me?'

'The results of the DNA test came through. The body is Daragh Canavan's.'

I had never doubted that. We sat for a while in silence. Then he said, 'Rebecca, I overheard Charles say something. He said that you were expecting my child. Is it true?'

My head in my hands, I nodded.

'Good God.' He stared at me. 'But that must be – how long—'

I could see him struggling with arithmetic, so I said quickly, 'It must have been in Cumbria. I'm almost three months' pregnant, I think.'

'You think?' Always the lawyer, he pounced on the significant word.

I blinked. For the first time in that long, dreadful evening, I wanted to cry. 'I haven't seen a doctor yet. There's no point. I haven't decided what to do.'

'Oh.' He seemed to shut himself off from me. The single syllable was flat, noncommittal.

'It's not easy,' I said angrily. 'I'd love to have the baby, of course I would, but you can see how small my flat is, and I don't earn very much, and I'm just not sure I could give it a decent life. If my writing doesn't work out I'll have to teach or do secretarial work or something, so it'd be a latchkey child, and—'

'Stop.' He put his arm round me and held me to him and I wept onto the shoulder of his expensively tailored white shirt.

Patrick insisted on taking me to the nearest A and E department for a check-up. There, waiting among the broken arms and cracked heads and scalds, he said, 'Why didn't you tell me before?'

Wearily, I thought back through the missed opportunities and misunderstandings of the past weeks. 'It never seemed to be the right time. And I thought you hated me. And that you were still in love with Jennifer.'

'I saw you, that evening. I ran after you, but I lost you in the crowds.'

I felt foolish, as well as exhausted. My pursuer, the ghost that had followed me that night in Richmond, had been Patrick. I saw too that I might have misinterpreted a friendly hug, the sort of greeting a man might give to the mother of his child.

'We have to keep on reasonably good terms,' he explained, echoing my thoughts. 'I don't want Ellie to grow up with her parents continually sniping at each other. If we can remain friends, it'll be better for her.'

Three youths staggered in, two supporting their injured friend, who had a broken nose. There were blots of blood on the floor.

I closed my eyes and took a deep breath. 'Patrick, there's something I've been meaning to say to you for weeks. I don't want to hurt Tilda. I like Tilda – I love her, I suppose. I've no intention of harming her in order to further my career. I'm not that ambitious.'

He looked away from me. 'That wasn't what Toby Carne implied to me.'

'Toby?' I remembered Patrick saying, just before we had quarrelled in the wine bar, *I ran into a friend of yours the other day*. Old lovers' ghosts again, haunting me.

'If Toby told you that, then he was miffed because I didn't run back to him as soon as he realized he missed me. It's over between us, Patrick – utterly and completely over. When I needed him, he let me down. Toby just can't accept that I'm not interested. He likes to win.'

Fleetingly, Patrick smiled. 'I know. I've been up against him in court.'

'Who won?'

'Me.'

Then I asked him the question that had haunted me for some time. I said, 'You knew that Daragh was dead, didn't you, Patrick?'

He did not answer. 'Didn't you?' I persisted. 'That was why you didn't want Tilda's biography written.' And when he still did not reply, I said, 'Patrick. Please.'

He stretched his long legs out in front of him. The boy with the broken nose collapsed on the floor, and two nurses rushed to pick him up.

'I didn't *know* he was dead – how could I? But I thought it likely – and if he was dead, he'd obviously died in suspicious circumstances. From what I'd heard of him, he didn't sound the suicidal type.'

'You told me that you thought he'd run away.'

'Yes. Well.' He looked slightly ashamed. 'That was possible, of course.'

'But not what you believed?'

He sighed. 'It just always seemed far more probable that someone had clocked him over the head and dumped him in a convenient ditch. Tilda thought the same.'

I remembered Tilda, standing at the window, looking out at the garden. *He would not have left his daughter.*

'I never thought Tilda had anything to do with it, of course,' said Patrick touchily.

'Did Caitlin ever talk to you about her father?'

'A little. To Caitlin, he was a god. But if you read between the lines, he'd spoiled her rotten and then left her without a penny. But it wasn't just because of Daragh that I thought the book a lousy idea.'

I glanced at him. 'Why, then?'

'I could see how the business about Caitlin and Erich

might look. Melissa, even, going off to live in France with my grandfather. It was all . . . messy. But I suppose families are messy.'

I thought of my own family, and resolved to phone my father the next day.

Patrick added, 'I was afraid that it would hurt Tilda more than she had anticipated. She's so innocent in some ways. Frankly, I don't particularly care who killed the wretched man. Daragh Canavan was a shit, by all accounts. And Tilda's suffered enough.'

'I know,' I said gently. 'I know.'

'Come to Cumbria with me,' he said suddenly. His eyes, that light, lucid blue, focused on me. 'I've bought the house. I had to hassle like mad, but I exchanged contracts a couple of days ago.'

I was bewildered. 'I thought it was a weekend place.'

'God, no. I've been trying to get out of London for years. Only Jen wouldn't settle.'

'You're *farming*?' I couldn't imagine him in an old Barbour, rounding up sheep.

He roared with laughter. 'Farming? Dear Lord, no. I've bought a practice in Penrith. They need lawyers in Cumbria too, you know, Rebecca. It'll be a bit more routine, that's all.'

Jealousy resurfaced. 'You'll be near Jennifer.'

'I'll be near *Ellie*. She starts school in September. She'll stay with me alternate weekends.'

His eyes pleaded with me. Part of me longed to say yes, yet I knew that I could not. I was not ready for that sort of commitment. So much was unresolved, and there were still too many loose ends. I turned aside.

'*Rebecca*. I know I've made a mess of it before, but—'

'It's not that. It's me.'

'Oh,' he said again. He sounded flat, defeated. 'Love. That elusive little thing that everyone's chasing.'

I thought of Tilda. It had taken me a long time to realize that Max had been the great love of Tilda's life, and not Daragh.

'I think I love you.' He spoke quickly, almost as if he was afraid that if he thought about it, he would hold back and spare himself from the vulnerability that such a declaration entails. 'I think I fell in love with you when you turned up at the hospital to see Tilda with that bunch of wilting daffodils and you were all pink and your hair was all over the place—'

'I'd got lost,' I said defensively. 'Hospitals are such mazes.'

'—and you gave Matty the money for her wretched can of Coke. There was just something about you.'

The unreason of love, I thought. A nurse called out my name. I looked at Patrick.

'Not yet,' I whispered to him, as I stood up. 'Some day, perhaps, but not yet. Give me time, Patrick. I've things to do. Things to understand.'

I have to know, I might have said, the end of the story. As I kissed the crown of his head and walked away from him, I realized that I was impatient to see Melissa again. Everything was unfinished. I had left Tilda travelling back from France in the spring of 1949, convinced that Max no longer loved her . . .

CHAPTER SEVENTEEN

Max had been kind to her, but not because he still loved her. Max, civilized Max, would be courteous to the mother of his children, but would give his heart to that pretty blonde Frenchwoman who had dashed into a kitchen she obviously knew well and offered to cook his favourite dinner. Tilda knew now that Max had kissed her because he pitied her. Max himself had pointed out how tired she had looked. He had been too gentlemanly to say, *how old*. Max was still, after all, attractive. Men, Tilda acknowledged bitterly as she studied her face in the tiny mirror in the ladies' room on the ferry, aged better than women.

Later, on the deck, watching the dark swell of the waves, Tilda wept tears of humiliation and bitterness. The ferry docked in the early evening, and they caught the train to Oxford. It was dark by the time they reached Oxford station, and rain lashed the rickety bus shelter. As they lurched along the winding roads, Tilda longed to see her other children again, and longed to curl up in bed and sleep.

In the house, she hugged Rosi and Hanna and Erich and gave them presents and letters from Max and Melissa, and looked around. 'Where's Caitlin?'

Rosi said, 'In her room.'

Tilda took off her wet mackintosh. 'I'll go to her.'

'Tilda.' Rosi drew her aside. 'Tilda, I must speak to you first.'

Erich was looking at his present, a book about flowers, and Hanna had run upstairs to try on the blouse that Tilda had bought her. Josh had begun to eat his supper.

She followed Rosi into the kitchen. Rosi shut the door behind them. Tilda's heart began to pound with fear.

'Rosi, is Caitlin all right? Is she ill?'

'No, no. Caitlin is well. She's sulking, that's all. But Tilda, something happened when you were away. I have to tell you about it. Sit down, please.'

By the time Rosi had finished telling her story Tilda was glad that she had sat down, because her legs were shaking too much to hold her. When Rosi paused for breath, Tilda looked up and said, 'Perhaps it hasn't gone very far ... perhaps it was just a flirtation—'

'She was in bed,' said Rosi grimly. 'I went upstairs and dragged her out of his bed. She howled and made a fuss and scratched my face.'

Caitlin, Daragh's precious only daughter, who was not yet sixteen, was having an affair with a married man. 'This man—'

'Julian Pascoe.'

'What is he like?'

'Thirtyish. Good-looking, I suppose, in a petulant sort of way. I can see that he might appeal to Caitlin.'

'Does he love her?'

Rosi shook her head. 'He seemed to be more concerned about whether the neighbours would hear. Caitlin made a lot of noise when I took her home.'

'Dear God,' said Tilda softly. She stood up. 'Tell me where he lives, Rosi.'

Rosi looked worried. 'You should have your supper first, Tilda. You look tired. It can wait, surely.'

She said, 'No, I don't think it can,' and put her wet raincoat back on. Rosi gave her directions and she left the house. She felt, as she walked, a fury that threatened to choke her. Thirtyish. Married. *Good-looking . . . I can see that he might appeal to Caitlin*. She took the path that led to Julian Pascoe's house, splashing through the mud, kicking aside nettles and brambles, hurling open the wrought iron gate and running down the drive to ring the doorbell.

'Yes?' A woman opened the door. Mrs Pascoe was well-dressed, with neatly permed dark hair and a haughty expression.

'I'd like to speak to Mr Pascoe.'

'Julian? A person wishes to speak to you.' Mrs Pascoe did not ask Tilda in.

She knew, as soon as she saw Julian Pascoe, why Caitlin had been attracted to him. Tall, wiry and dark-haired: there was a superficial resemblance to Daragh, to the father Caitlin had loved and lost.

Tilda said, 'My name is Tilda Franklin. I've come to speak to you about Caitlin.'

Julian Pascoe glanced furtively over one shoulder. 'Not here,' he muttered. Raising his voice, he called, 'I've a rehearsal, darling!' and then he took a jacket from the peg and stepped out of the house, closing the door behind him.

She said, 'Your wife doesn't know about Caitlin, then?'

He darted a look at her. 'No. And I'd prefer to keep it that way. Shall we walk?'

They went down the drive, back towards the road. He said suddenly, 'Are you her mother?'

She realized that he knew nothing at all about Caitlin. 'Caitlin's parents are both dead,' she said icily. 'I have looked after her since her mother's death.'

'Ah.' They had paused in the road. He took a cigarette case from his pocket. 'I didn't seduce her, you know,' he said, looking up. 'She was willing.'

Tilda felt a rush of anger so intense she could hardly speak. 'You took advantage of her, Mr Pascoe. You were in a position of power, and you took advantage of a silly, confused girl.'

'She knew exactly what she was doing.' He struck a match.

'You are – how old?'

'Thirty-one.' He blinked.

'Caitlin is fifteen. Did she tell you that, Mr Pascoe?' For the first time, he looked shaken. 'Fifteen?'

'Yes. Statutory rape, I believe it's called.'

'Good God. I had no idea . . . she told me she was eighteen. I'm sure that she told me she was eighteen.' He gave a weak little laugh, and pushed back the lock of hair that had fallen over his face in a gesture that Tilda suspected he practised at the mirror. 'If I'd known, obviously I wouldn't have touched her. I prefer older women anyway.' His eyes, open and appealing, rested on Tilda, and he grinned boyishly. 'You won't tell my wife, will you?'

For a moment she said nothing. Then she whispered, 'Mr Pascoe, if you attempt even to speak to Caitlin again, I will tell your entire family. I will tell your friends, your colleagues, your neighbours. And I will tell the police. Do you understand?'

'Yes.' There was sweat on his upper lip; he wiped it away with the back of his hand. 'Yes.'

She turned on her heel and began to walk away. From behind her, she heard him say, 'She wasn't a virgin, you know!' and she spun round, and struck his face hard with the flat of her hand.

Walking back to the colonel's house, her palm stung. At Poona she went directly to Caitlin's room. Caitlin was curled up on the bed. Seeing Tilda, she sat up.

Tilda said, 'Rosi told me about Julian Pascoe.'

'The bitch ... poking her nose in ... she had no right—'

'Rosi had every right, Caitlin. She was responsible for you in my absence.'

'I can look after myself.'

'Until you are twenty-one, Caitlin, you are my responsibility. And at present you are only fifteen. Mr Pascoe knows that now.'

Caitlin gasped. 'You've spoken to Julian?'

'Yes.' Tilda sat down on the edge of the bed. The brief rush of energy that her anger had given her had dissipated, and all her muscles ached with exhaustion. 'I told him to leave you alone.'

Caitlin's pretty face creased with fury. 'How dare you? Julian *loves* me.'

No, he doesn't, Tilda thought, but knew how cruel it would be to say that. 'Mr Pascoe is married,' she said, more gently.

'Julian's going to leave his wife.'

Tilda looked down at her hands, knowing how carefully she must choose her words. 'I don't think that he will, Kate. And besides, you are not old enough to marry anyone.' She took a deep breath. She felt old and tired and hopeless. She knew that she had failed Caitlin utterly. 'Kate, I can see how unhappy you are here. What would you prefer? A boarding school, perhaps?'

'Boarding school?' Caitlin laughed. 'That'd be a convenient solution for you, wouldn't it, Tilda?'

Her breath caught in her throat. She looked up. 'What do you mean?'

Their eyes met just for a moment, and then Caitlin shook her head, and said sullenly, 'Nothing.'

There was a small silence. Tilda sighed. 'Kate, if you go on as you are doing, then you'll end up in trouble. I cannot keep you under lock and key. You'll find yourself with a baby and without a husband. Is that what you want?'

Caitlin looked away. Tilda persisted. 'Do you think that's what your father and mother would have wanted for you?'

'What do you know about what my father would have wanted? You know *nothing*!' Caitlin went to her dressing table, and began to drag a comb through her hair. Her hand shook. She pulled on a coat.

'Where are you going?'

'Out. I've a rehearsal. I missed last night's because of that stupid Rosi. I'm not missing another one.'

'Mr Pascoe understands that you cannot be in the play.'

'Can't be in the play?' Caitlin's eyes were black with fury. 'Of course I'm going to be in the play! You try and spoil everything that belongs to me, don't you?' She flung open the door. 'I hate you! I hate you, Tilda Franklin, and I'm going to pay you back!'

At the Memorial Hall, Caitlin pushed open the door and ran inside. It was a dress rehearsal: in their garish make-up and shoddy costumes they all stared at her.

Julian said, 'Excuse me a moment,' and jumped down from the stage. There was a ripple of laughter.

He seized Caitlin by the wrist, steering her out of the hall and into the cramped little kitchen. 'Why the hell have you come here?'

'To see you, Julian. Tilda told me that she'd spoken to you.'

'Ah yes. The beautiful Mrs Franklin.' He smiled grimly. 'Barged into my house, actually. I'm going to have a hell of a lot of explaining to do to Margaret.'

She wailed, 'But she says that I mustn't see you any more!'

'Of course you mustn't. And sweetheart, if I'd known you were just a kid, then I wouldn't have looked at you in the first place. There are limits, you know.'

She said quickly, 'I'm sixteen in October. You'll wait, won't you, Julian?'

His expression altered, from distaste to amused contempt. 'Wait? For you? Don't be ridiculous, Caitlin.'

'But I love you!'

He glanced at his watch. 'You have a crush on me, that's all. It's something little girls often have for older men. You'll grow out of it.'

'Julian.' She seized the sleeve of his jacket, pulling him towards her. 'I love you. I really do. And you love me, I know that you do.'

'No,' he said, very deliberately. 'No, I never told you that. I may be a complete bastard, but I would never have said that. You were an amusement for me, Caitlin. A diversion. You are reasonably attractive, and you were willing and I was bored. That's all.'

Her hand slipped from his arm. She whispered, 'But the play—' and he said, 'I've told Veronica she can do your song.' He smiled at her. 'She hit me, you know,

515

your guardian. Slapped my face.' He added, 'Do you know, I rather enjoyed it,' and then he went back into the hall.

Caitlin went back to Poona only because she could think of nowhere else to go. Had she ten shillings in her pocket then she would have walked away, left the village, never come back. In her bedroom, she sat wrapped in her eiderdown, her knuckles pressed against her mouth, her gaze fixed on the small posy of flowers in the jam jar on her window sill.

The following day Caitlin found Erich in the garden, netting the fruit bushes. 'Erich,' she said, 'the chain has come off my bicycle. Do you think that you could put it back on for me?'

He blushed and stumbled to his feet, and followed her from the garden to the shed. There was something repulsive about his gangling arms, his lank hair, his crooked, broken teeth. But she showed him her bicycle. 'Can you mend it?'

He said nothing, but stooped and fiddled with the oily chain. While his back was to her, she said curiously, 'You give me those bunches of flowers, don't you?'

The chain fell from his clumsy hands. 'I'm s-s-sorry,' he muttered.

'There's nothing to be sorry for, Erich. They are beautiful flowers.'

He looked back at her. She saw the disbelief in his eyes. 'You like them, Caitlin?'

'Of course I do.' She smiled at him.

His expression changed from doubt to joy, and she knew that she could do it. She could make Erich Wirmer love her. It was the best revenge she could think of. She would make Erich love her because Tilda had taken

Julian from her. Tilda had taken both her father and her lover and, in return, Caitlin intended to take something of hers.

Max was walking back from seeing Melissa to the school bus when he heard a voice call his name. He spun round.

'Cécile!'

'Max, *chéri*.' She kissed him.

'I wasn't expecting you until next week.'

She frowned. 'Didn't Melissa tell you that I came back early?' Her frown became deeper, and she pressed the palms of her hands together, touching her fingertips to her mouth.

Max felt confused. 'Melissa didn't mention . . . when did you call?'

'It must have slipped her mind.' Cécile seized his hand. 'Buy me coffee, *chéri*, won't you?'

They went to the café in the square. Max ordered black coffee. Cécile said, 'I called at your house when I came home a few days ago. I was going to cook you dinner. I did not realize that your wife would be there.'

He glanced at her sharply. '*Tilda?*'

She nodded. 'I just walked in, I'm afraid. I saw Melissa in the garden and called out to her. I did not see Mathilde at first, they were in the shadow of the tree.'

He said urgently, 'Which day was this, Cécile?'

She thought back. 'Wednesday. At midday, or perhaps a little later.'

Max swore. Wednesday had been the last day of Tilda's holiday. At midday on Wednesday he had been delivering the Rolls to that wretchedly tardy farmer.

She touched his hand. 'Max, I did not know that your wife was visiting, or I would not have called.'

517

'Not your fault,' he said absently. 'The arrangements were rather last minute. Tilda wrote, asking to visit at Easter. You had already left for your cousin's.' He groaned, realizing how it must have seemed to Tilda. Cécile, coming into an obviously familiar house and starting to cook. No wonder Tilda had been cold, distant, that last afternoon.

Cécile said, 'I spoiled things for you, didn't I?'

He shrugged. 'I'm not sure.'

There was a silence. Cécile stirred her coffee, watching him. 'And you,' she said slowly, 'you are still in love with her, aren't you, Max?'

He looked away to the square, with its trees that dappled the cobbles with shadow.

'Tell me!' she said.

He turned back to her. 'Yes. It's taken me an age to realize it, but I still love her.'

It was her turn to look away. 'Then you will go back to England.'

'I don't know.' He had, over the past three days, veered between concluding that Tilda was lost to him for ever, and wanting to leap on the next train to Calais.

'Of course you will. You must.'

'Perhaps.'

'And me?' she said.

He took her hand. 'Cécile, I owe you so much. You have been such a good friend.'

'But you do not love me.' Her voice was harsh.

'You are my dear, dear friend.'

'I love you, Max.'

He stared at her. She laughed. 'Didn't you know, Max?'

'Cécile.' He hated himself. 'I never meant—'

518

'I know that. So now you must choose, Max. Who is it to be?'

He didn't answer. After a while, she said gently, 'Don't worry, I know that there is no choice. You will go back to Tilda.' But he saw that there were tears in her eyes.

'Cécile,' he said. 'I am so sorry. I have been such an idiot. Such a selfish swine.'

'Oh, Max,' she said, and laughed again. 'So *English*.'

Hanna was certain that she was going to fail her exams. She had made a revision timetable and she had started work in plenty of time, but this morning she had glanced at her notes on the liver, which she had revised weeks ago, and had not been able to remember it at all. All the long words had muddled up in her head. She was afraid that when it came to the exams she would write nonsense, or she would forget all her English and scribble every answer in German.

She had a headache most of the time and found it hard to fall asleep at night. When she did sleep, she had awful dreams about Holland and Germany, arousing memories that she had tried to put out of her head. She heard her parents' and her sisters' voices calling out to her and, when she woke, often with tears pouring down her face, she would feel overwhelmed with guilt.

She spoke to Tilda one day after dinner. 'I think I shall go back to college early, Tilda. I need to work in the library.'

Tilda was making tea. She poured Hanna a cup. 'You look tired, Hanna.'

Hanna said fretfully, 'I have so much work to do. And my brain is like that colander – I put things in and they just fall out.'

Tilda passed her the sugar. 'Perhaps,' she said gently, 'you are working *too* hard, Hanna.'

Hanna said nothing, but scowled and stirred sugar into her tea.

'Aunt Sarah used to say to me that each day I should do something with my head, something with my feet, and something with my soul. It was good advice.'

'I haven't time for all that.'

'I just meant . . . go for a walk. Or feed the ducks. Or sit in the church for half an hour. It's nice and cool there and your head might ache less. Then you'll come back refreshed and be able to work better.'

Hanna was suspicious. Her tutor at Cambridge had said much the same: that she should work for no more than a couple of hours at a time.

'Just a little walk,' said Tilda coaxingly. 'Please, Hanna.'

Hanna scowled, but put on her jacket. Outside, it had rained and the air smelt fresh and sweet. April and May were her favourite months, but this year she had hardly noticed the changing of the seasons. She wandered through the garden and onto the main road. The breeze was cool and pleasant on her aching forehead. She tried mentally to list the bones of the foot, but found herself instead admiring the bluebells in the woods and the delicate nodding heads of the windflowers. She dug her hands into her pockets and ambled aimlessly. She would return to Cambridge tomorrow, she decided. Rosi, unable to bear her separation from her fiancé, had already gone back.

She found herself in the road that led to The Red House. Looking up, she saw in the distance two figures. She recognized Erich instantly, but had to look twice to convince herself that the girl beside him was Caitlin.

Hanna watched, frowning, as Erich opened the gate. She remembered the garden of The Red House, its wild beauty, and the patterns and blossoms that Erich had coaxed from the wilderness.

Then she glanced at her watch. She realized with a feeling of panic that she had been walking for forty minutes. She turned round, and headed back to Poona and her books.

Erich showed Caitlin the box trees, the lawn with the copper beech, the orchard and the shrubbery. Lastly, he took her to the garden behind the house. He led her along the curling paths, beneath the rambling roses. Erich explained how he had discovered the garden, how he had uncovered the paths, cleaned the pond and released the flowers from their imprisonment of weeds and dead leaves. He had never been able to talk so easily to a girl before. He hardly stuttered at all. When she smiled, he could not have been happier, and when she stood in the little clearing that he had made, and he looked from Caitlin to the marble girl who was her twin, he could hardly breathe for delight.

He picked her a bunch of flowers. Bluebells, roses, long strands of honeysuckle. She pressed her face in the bouquet to smell their scent, and looked up and smiled. 'They are heavenly, Erich,' she said, and he was part of the world again. No longer excluded, trapped by his gaucheness, his memories, his history.

Tilda felt as though everything was dissolving into chaos. Hanna was working too hard and Rosi wasn't working at all, and Josh had gone back to school and she missed him dreadfully. She wept each night for Melissa, in France. She had been a rotten mother to Daragh's child and she had lost Max. Only Erich, oddly, seemed happy. Erich's happiness disturbed her most of all. She wanted to rejoice in it but could not. His happiness, like his misery, was extreme: a euphoria that seemed causeless, that emphasized the brittleness of his fragile body, and of his more fragile mind. He picked at his dinner, rose early and went to bed late. He never sat still and was constantly restless. She touched his forehead one evening, suspecting a fever, yet it was cool. He said, when she enquired, 'I have a secret, Tilda, a very good secret,' and laughed. She went guiltily into his room when he was out, and looked in his little suitcase, but there was none of the food that he tended to hoard there when he was deeply unhappy, only his few mementoes: his father's broken watch, his mother's photograph. From the telephone box in the village, Tilda called the psychiatrist in Oxford and made an appointment.

She went through her daily routine with a mechanical dullness that even the colonel noticed. '*France*,' he said scathingly. 'Damnable place. I was there from '14 to '17, y'know. You'd have better holidayed in Weymouth, m'dear.'

She worried about Caitlin constantly. The anger and resentment had eased off, replaced by cold politeness. Yet she remembered the way that Caitlin had looked at her. The undiluted hatred in her eyes. The sense that they lurched on the edge of something dangerous, a threatening truth that was only just hidden. Tilda made enquiries about boarding schools. A new school would give Caitlin a new start. She wondered how on earth she would afford it. Kit would help, perhaps.

She was afraid that Caitlin might be pregnant, and was overwhelmed with relief when Caitlin told her that she was not. She tried to talk to Caitlin again, to warn her once more of the dangers of the road she travelled, but Caitlin just said stonily, 'Julian doesn't want to see me any more. So you've got what you wanted, haven't you?' Tilda knew that there would be other Julians, other men who would exploit Caitlin's carelessness and vulnerability.

At night, unable to sleep, she thought of Max. She wrote to him a stiff little letter thanking him for her pleasant holiday. She knew that she must let him go, that she must allow him to begin a new life.

They sat on the terrace that looked out over the secret garden. Erich said, 'The box trees in front of the house will be like the pieces on a chess board. The Black Queen, the White Knight.'

Caitlin glanced at the tall hedges, which Erich had begun to sculpt into shape. 'Are there enough?'

'There are eight. I'll plant more around the lawn for the pawns.'

Caitlin had a bar of chocolate in her pocket. She gave Erich a piece. It was evening, and the late sun touched the winding paths and flowering shrubs with gold. 'They'll take ages to grow, won't they?'

'Many, many years. But only a short t-t-time compared to the life of this garden,' he explained. 'Whoever planted this would have known that he would not see it finished. That's the thing about gardens.'

Caitlin liked things to be complete, to know the end of them. They sat for a while in silence, and Caitlin realized that she had for a while forgotten her purpose in seeking Erich's company. She fidgeted uncomfortably, reminding herself that what she had meant to do was to make him love her, and not Tilda. She was good at making men love her. Sometimes she thought that was all she was good at.

She said curiously, looking at him, 'What happened to your teeth, Erich?' One tooth was missing, another was a broken stump.

'A soldier hit me.'

'In Vienna?'

He nodded. 'When they killed my father.'

She stared at him. 'Did you *see* them kill him?'

'Yes. They came one evening. I hid from them.' He began to chew the ragged skin at the edges of his fingernails.

For a moment, she felt sorry for him. She said suddenly, 'My father's in Ireland, you know. I'm going to find him.' She explained about the priests she had written to, and the three Caitlin Canavans whose addresses she had subsequently obtained. Erich listened attentively and asked sensible questions, and she realized that he was not as stupid as she had always assumed him to be.

'I've had two replies and they were no good, and I'm waiting for the third. I'm sure she's the one. She lives in County Wicklow and I can remember my daddy talking about County Wicklow.'

'What will you do if you find your father?'

She imagined a grand house, with pillars and a wide front lawn. Herself and her father, riding through the hills.

'I shall go and live with him, of course.'

Erich stood up and began to pull weeds from the stone urns at the top of the terrace. Caitlin remained sitting on the steps. She felt unusually peaceful, looking out over the garden in the warm early evening, with the scent of the flowers perfuming the air. Some of the perpetual restless unhappiness that was always with her began to slide away. She did not mind being with Erich because he asked nothing of her. She had thought that with men you always had to give something – smiles or kisses or sex – but Erich asked for nothing. Erich seemed to like her without expecting anything of her, anything at all. Her arms wrapped round her knees, Caitlin watched a bee nuzzle the golden trumpets of the honeysuckle.

Then Erich, behind her, said, 'I have made the garden for Tilda. It will be a wonderful surprise for her, won't it?' and Caitlin stood up, kicking at the crumbling stone steps with the tip of her shoe.

When Hanna remembered to eat, she ate each meal with an open text book beside her. In the bath, she propped *Gray's Anatomy* on the taps, but the wretched book tumbled into the water and she had to spend ages drying it. She lost her temper with Rosi when she played her record-player too loud, and refused an invitation from Richard to go punting. She had decided to work each day until midnight, yet she found herself waking earlier and earlier, the short hours between going to bed and waking interrupted by nightmares.

One night, a few days after she had gone back to Cambridge, Hanna fell into a brief, uneasy sleep and then woke again, shivering and miserable. She thumped her pillow into shape and pulled on socks because her feet were cold, and tried again. This time, her dream was vivid. She was in Vienna, walking with her mother and sisters in a park. She did not recognize the park; the winding paths and overhanging trees were menacing and unfamiliar. They seemed to reach out to her, drawing her into the dark undergrowth. At length they came to a clearing, where she saw a statue made of white, polished stone. 'Isn't it lovely?' said Hanna to her mother, but even as she spoke flakes of stone began to fall from the statue. The beautiful face was eroding away. Hanna turned to her mother, but she had gone. Her sisters too had gone, their footsteps barely audible as they ran through the park, which had metamorphosed into a forest of pendulous black branches and coiling creepers. Hanna thought that she was alone, and then a hand gripped her shoulder, shaking her, trying to drag her away—

'Hanna, *liebling*, don't cry.'

She opened her eyes and sat up, staring wildly around the room. Her face was wet with tears. Rosi, in her nightdress and with curlers in her hair, leaned over her bed.

Rosi said gently, 'It was a dream, that's all,' and hugged her.

'Put the light on.'

Rosi switched on the lamp. 'That's better, isn't it? Was it your usual dream?'

Hanna shook her head. 'It was different, this time.' She sat up in bed, her knees hunched up to her forehead, almost overwhelmed by her sense of dread.

'Tell me about it. Ah, it's cold in here. Just a moment, I shall get my cigarettes.' Rosi scrabbled around in a drawer and then snuggled into bed beside Hanna.

'There was a statue—' Hanna struggled to remember where she had seen the statue before. 'I remember. I saw it in the garden of The Red House.'

'The Red House?'

'It's an empty house at home. Near the river. Erich is making a garden there. He showed me, ages ago, he said it was a secret. He had found a statue.'

A statue of a nymph. Small, perfect features and tumbling curls.

'So?' said Rosi. There was a hiss as she struck a match and lit her cigarette. 'A statue?'

'Erich thought it looked like Caitlin.' Remembering, Hanna's unease deepened. 'Rosi, Erich is in love with Caitlin.'

'No,' said Rosi, very definitely. 'How could he be? She hardly ever speaks to him.'

'Someone like Erich,' said Hanna, 'might fall in love with someone who never spoke to him. Erich doesn't expect people to be nice to him, does he?'

'Even if he is in love with Caitlin, she would never pay any attention to him. Erich is not handsome enough for her.'

'But I saw them, Rosi,' said Hanna. Her voice shook. 'I saw them going into the garden of The Red House.'

'Then they are friends, perhaps.' Rosi fell silent.

Hanna glanced at her. 'What is it, Rosi? Rosi? You are dropping ash everywhere. You will set my bed on fire.'

'Tilda told me that she was worried about Erich.' Rosi scowled. 'You don't think . . . you don't think that Caitlin would tease Erich a little, just to annoy Tilda?'

Hanna was bewildered. 'Why should she want to annoy Tilda?'

'Because she blames Tilda for having ended her love affair with that horrible Julian Pascoe. And because she hates Tilda.'

Hanna remembered the day her foster parents in Amsterdam had introduced her to Erich Wirmer. Erich had been nine years old. His little suitcase had been full of hoarded bread and cheese, much of it green with mould. He had not spoken to any of his adoptive family for almost a month. He had slept beneath the bed rather than on top of it.

'If Caitlin teases him,' said Hanna slowly, 'and leads him to think that she likes him, and then hurts his feelings, then I do not think that he will be able to bear it.'

They were both silent for a few minutes. 'Perhaps,' said Rosi as she stubbed her cigarette out in a discarded teacup, 'perhaps we should write to Tilda.'

Tilda caught the nine o'clock bus. In Oxford, the psychiatrist, a tall, handsome man called Dr Marriott, showed her into his office.

'You said on the telephone that you wanted to talk to me about your son, Mrs Franklin.' Dr Marriott glanced at his notes. 'Erich. I saw him once, a couple of months ago.'

'I had hoped that Erich would consult you on a regular basis, Dr Marriott.'

He indicated a chair and Tilda sat down. 'Erich denied that anything was wrong with him,' he said. 'I cannot persuade a patient to speak to me if he does not want to.'

'Yes. Of course. I do see that.' She fell silent, her mind whirring in anxious circles.

'You are worried about him?'

She tried to put her fears into words. 'He's changed, recently. He is euphoric . . . elated. He won't tell me why. He says that he has a secret.'

'A secret?'

Tilda shook her head. 'I have no idea.'

'A girl, perhaps?'

'You saw him, Dr Marriott. Is it likely?' Yet the thought made her uneasy. 'If he has met a girl, then I shouldn't intrude. After all, he's nineteen, almost an adult. It's just that he still seems to me a little boy, sometimes. A frightened little boy.' She looked up. 'I thought that if he would not come to you, then perhaps you would come to him.'

'A house call, you mean?'

She nodded, eyes fixed on his chiselled face. She wanted to cross her fingers, to mutter her good-luck charm. *Grant that no hobgoblins bite me, no hungry devils rise up and fright me.*

But Dr Marriott said, 'I rarely make house calls, I'm afraid, Mrs Franklin. I find that it's better to see patients on neutral ground.'

She swallowed her disappointment, and rose and held out her hand. 'And there is the possibility,' he added, as he saw her to the door, 'that Erich would be an unsuitable candidate for psychoanalysis. That to confront his hidden memories would be too great an ordeal for him. That to do so would destroy him.'

The letter came by the second post. Caitlin's heart began to pound when she saw the Irish postmark. She ran out through the garden to the copse where the pig and the hens pecked at acorns and beechmast. Sitting on the silvery bole that bulged from the trunk of the beech tree, she tore open the envelope. The letter was signed, 'Caitlin Kinsella, née Canavan.'

She read the first sentence. 'My dear Caitlin, I cannot tell you how pleased I was to receive your letter. To know that I have a niece the age of my eldest daughter is a joy indeed.'

Caitlin had read in cheap romances the phrase, *The blood coursed through her veins*, but it was not a phenomenon she had previously encountered. Now, as she realized that her search was nearing its end, her body seemed to become suddenly alive, to slough off in one glorious moment the dullness and detachment of the years since her father's disappearance. It was as though she had touched a live wire, or pressed a switch that had returned her to what she once had been.

Aunt Caitlin went on, 'It was wonderful to have news of Daragh and to know that he has done so well for himself. A big house and horses and a farm – it is good to hear that my brother has fulfilled all his ambitions.'

Caitlin turned over the page. 'I do not quite understand,' wrote her Aunt Caitlin, her father's favourite sister, 'why you believe your father may have returned to Ireland. With such a fine house and lands of his own, why should he wish to come here? Brendan inherited Granda's farm, and Da sold the shop years ago, after Ma died. There is nothing for Daragh here.' The pig snuffled at Caitlin's sandal; frowning, she kicked it away.

'Daragh would never come back to Ireland, my dear. I am afraid that he *could not* (underlined heavily) come back. I still miss my brother very much, but I have to tell you that he would not be welcome here. He borrowed money from our neighbours and did not repay it. I have neither seen nor heard from Daragh for seventeen years.'

There was some more – family news, an invitation to Caitlin herself to visit – but Caitlin hardly glanced at it. She re-read the second paragraph, examining each word minutely.

I have neither seen nor heard from Daragh for seventeen years.

Her mind flailed desperately, looking for an explanation that would give her comfort. The letter dropped out of Caitlin's hand. For a while, there was just the familiar emptiness as hope crumbled and the last of her illusions faltered. Sitting there, she acknowledged for the first time that either her father was dead, or he had chosen to leave her. Though neither of these options was bearable, there were no other possibilities. If he were dead, then she did not know how to live with such a loss. If he had chosen to leave her, then it had been because she was not worthy of him. He had seen through her and had known that she was bad. Why else would he go? She was, after all, a bad girl. Caitlin, who rarely looked at herself, did so, and acknowledged that she was deceitful and selfish and promiscuous. In order to have the bedroom to herself, she had made Melissa's life so miserable that Melissa had gone to stay with her father in France. Though she was not yet sixteen, she had already slept with two men. She remembered herself in the back of Martin Devereux's car, her knickers around her ankles, her skirt pulled up to her waist. Or lying in Julian Pascoe's bed. The things he had done to her. Men only did those things to bad girls. Good girls said no. Good girls waited for marriage.

A voice said her name, but she did not look up. A cautious hand touched her shoulder. 'Caitlin – don't c-c-cry.'

She sprang up, as though he had hit her. 'Don't touch me!'

'I'm s-s-sorry.' Erich stepped back.

The emptiness had returned, and she knew that it would never leave her. Caitlin stared at Erich, with his hunched shoulders and missing front tooth, and recalled that she had tried to make him – even him – love her. The thought sickened her.

He took a handkerchief from his pocket. 'Here,' he said, holding it out. 'T-t-take it.'

'Leave me *alone*.'

Yet he did not go. He stood there, lolloping and clumsy, clad in dirty trousers and a handknitted jumper with holes in the elbows, staring at her with that mournful, devoted expression. She wanted to push him away, to beat at him with her clenched fists, but instead she said softly: 'Why don't you go away, Erich? I don't want you. No-one wants you. Not even Tilda. She only feels sorry for you.'

When she saw him wince, she was aware of a fleeting exhilaration. 'Go back to your stupid garden,' she hissed. 'It's not yours anyway – someone else will buy the house and dig up the garden and you won't be allowed there any more.'

'No,' Erich said. His face was white.

'Of course they will. It's not your house, Erich. It's not your garden. Tilda will never see it because some awful people will buy it and make it how they like it. They'll cut down your silly box trees and dig up your stupid flowers and build garages and tennis courts and things like that. That's what people do. Didn't you know?'

The expression on his face was so odd that she began to laugh. She gasped, 'Don't you know how stupid it all is, Erich? That's what I thought when you showed it to me – stupid, stupid, stupid. That's what Tilda will think, too. What a stupid surprise – to give someone something that isn't even theirs! Oh, she'll say how nice it is, because she pretends to you like she pretends to everyone, but inside she'll think, how *stupid*—'

Sliding down the tree trunk to sit on the beechmast, Caitlin laughed and could not stop laughing. She drew her knees up to her chin, rocking backwards and forwards as her laughter turned to tears. When both her laughter and her tears were exhausted, she looked up and Erich had gone.

Hanna had not been able to go back to sleep after her dream about the statue. The suspicion that something was terribly wrong had intensified rather than diminished. She cursed the colonel for not having a telephone, and knew that she could not say what she needed to say within the fractured phrases of a telegram. A letter would take a day or two to reach Woodcott St Martin, and she was seized by a sense of urgency she could not shake off. She rose early, but could not eat any breakfast. She tried to work, but found herself staring out of the window and thinking of Erich and the expression on his face when he had shown her that wretched statue. Her head ached dreadfully, and when she tried to read the letters danced in front of her eyes. Angrily she threw a textbook and her toothbrush into her bag, and cycled to the railway station.

On the train, fighting her headache, she reflected guiltily that she had been too absorbed in her work to be a good sister to Erich. She should have spoken to him after she had seen him with Caitlin; she should have made sure that he was all right. She knew Caitlin to be capable of hurting him; Caitlin was careless of everyone's feelings but her own. Her book open and unread on her lap, Hanna stared out of the window as the trees and fields, clad in their early summer brightness, trailed past with irritating slowness.

Erich went to The Red House. As he pushed open the gate and entered the garden, he knew that Caitlin had told him the truth. The garden was not his, and someone would take it away from him. People could take your house, he knew that, they could just walk in and smash windows and pictures and crockery, and laugh, and no-one would try to stop them.

The sound of Caitlin's laughter still echoed in his ears, mingling with the soldiers' laughter from long ago. Since then, since the day when they had walked, heavy-booted, into the house in which he and his father lived, he had known that the world was random, predictable only in its casual cruelty. Since then, he had never been sure what people were thinking or how they felt. Though he might begin to trust them, they could always change, become different.

Erich walked through the box hedges. Their high, dark walls reminded him of the tall buildings in Vienna. After the soldiers had come to his house, he had lived alone in the streets for almost three months. Like a rat, a creature of the dark, scavenging, scurrying behind walls or into sewers when he saw the brown uniforms, or heard the strident voices. Then one day a woman had caught him searching through her dustbin for food, and a few weeks later he had found himself on the train with hundreds of other children, travelling through Germany. The fear he had felt during that journey was still vivid. When the Gestapo had walked through the carriages at the border with Holland, he had crouched over his case, trying to make himself invisible.

In Holland, there had been Hanna and, later, Tilda. He remembered the drive to Ijmuiden, where they had been too late for the ship and he had curled up, wanting to die. If you were dead it was all over and you weren't afraid or guilty any more. He remembered sitting in the car next to Tilda, and the Nazi paratrooper stepping in front of them. He remembered how bubbles had risen to the surface of the dike as the soldier's body had slid into the water. Then the boat – Felix adjusting the sails, Tilda working the tiller. The planes that had swooped down towards the tiny craft, and the glitter of tracer-fire in the sky. And much later, lying on the deck in the half-dark of dawn, the sea empty of ships, the sky free of aeroplanes. The silence. The charcoal-grey peace of it all. Like dying.

Erich crossed the terrace and stood on the steps, looking down to his secret garden. He imagined how they would hack at the paths with pickaxes, and how they would uproot the flowers. How they would topple the statue from its plinth, breaking it in half. He knew that the good bits of his life were over. His mother, holding him in her arms; his father teaching him to ride his bicycle. Tilda: sometimes he had felt safe with Tilda.

And Caitlin. He had sat beside Caitlin on these steps, and longed to touch her black, cloudy hair, longed to press his lips on her soft skin. He knew that he would never do these things, because the past had marked him out, had made him different. The things that he had seen were written in his eyes. They were things other people did not wish to be reminded of.

He collected the trowel and fork from where he had left them the previous evening, knowing that he would not use them again. He said his farewells to The Red House, and walked back to the colonel's garden. There, he opened the door of the shed, and hung the tools from the hooks on the shelf. He had always liked to be tidy. He looked around the little shed at the terracotta pots, the petrol can, the jars of nails and lengths of rope. He took what he wanted. Standing there, he made himself remember the night his father had died.

They had been eating their evening meal when the *Sturmabteilung* had come to the house. Fish and potatoes and beans. The wireless had been on, playing selections from operettas. Erich's father had loved operetta, and had taken Erich to see *The Merry Widow* when he was only six years old. Erich remembered the knock at the door, the maid's brief outrage, her screams. Erich had felt surprised rather than frightened, and he had put down his knife and fork and looked at his father. The wireless had played its happy music. The door had opened and the soldiers had come into the dining room. They had thrown the crystal glasses against the wall, and they had upended the sideboard. In the distance, from the other rooms, Erich had heard the chime of breaking glass mixed with heavy boots and loud laughter. One of the soldiers had begun to take plates from the dresser and to drop them onto the slab of marble in front of the fire, and Erich had looked at him and had said, before his father could stop him, 'Why are you doing that?' The soldier's blow had knocked his face into the polished mahogany table. Through the taste of blood, through his hurt and bewilderment and his father's roar of fury, he had felt, for the first time, frightened.

The order of things muddled up after that. Seeing the soldiers kicking his father. Sliding under the table, creeping out through the door when they were not looking. Wanting to go to his father, yet being afraid to. Spitting into the palm of his hand and seeing the little, bloodied, hard pieces of tooth. The sound of steel-tipped boots on soft flesh. *Dirty Jew. Dirty Jew.* Knowing he should help his father, but being too frightened to do so. Running into the cupboard below the stairs. His father's screams, then his pleas. Peeping out of the tiny crack between the ill-fitting cupboard doors. In that long, thin line, with darkness on either side, glimpsing the soldier with the length of washing line in his hands. 'We'll use this. It'll be easier.' Realizing that he had wet himself, like a baby. The shame of that. The shame of doing nothing.

They had hanged his father from the balcony that looked down over the hall. The knot had been tied to the balustrade, and the noose placed around his throat. If Erich had been able to look up, he would have seen his father kick and jerk and then go limp. From the cupboard he had heard the rattle of air in his father's lungs and the soldiers' laughter. And the wireless, playing the catchy little tune. Boots echoing in the hallway as they left the house. After a long time, he had opened the cupboard door and come out. Looking up, he had seen his father. He had crawled upstairs and sat beside the balustrade, as near to the gently swaying body as he could get. He had not been strong enough to haul his father back over the wooden rails. The battery of the wireless had run down at last, but Erich had remained on the landing, one arm pushed through the balustrade, touching the top of his father's head, singing the tune to himself, the catchy, happy little tune.

When Erich, who was usually very punctual, did not appear for lunch, Tilda asked Caitlin whether she had seen him that morning. Caitlin shook her head, and said nothing. Her eyes, Tilda noticed, were very red.

She enquired about Erich as she served the colonel his lunch. 'That Hun? Saw him leave the place an hour or so ago. Damned nuisance. Wanted a hand tethering the goat. Damned thing's in the asparagus bed.'

Tilda caught the goat, and washed up, but there was still no sign of Erich. She thought that he might have taken the spare eggs to sell at the shop. Once or twice in the past she had found him outside the shop, basket in hand, unable to pluck up the courage to go in.

Erich was not in the shop, and had not, she discovered when she enquired, called there that day. Tilda glanced in the post office and looked up the road. The Oxford bus was pulling up beside the village green. Tilda watched absently, wondering whether Erich might have decided to go to Oxford, dismissing the idea almost immediately. The passengers alighted from the bus: an old man with a walking stick, two women with small children tugging at their hands, and a girl who looked like Hanna. Tilda stared at the girl, and then she began to run.

She called out, as she reached the bus stop, 'Hanna, why didn't you tell me you were coming home? You're not ill, are you? You look so pale—'

'I'm fine,' said Hanna. 'I'm very, very fine.' Her English still occasionally deserted her in moments of stress. 'I was just worried.'

'About your work?'

'About Erich,' she whispered.

'Erich? Hanna, do you know where he is?'

'Isn't he here?'

'He had breakfast with me this morning, but he didn't come home for lunch. You know that's not like Erich. I've been looking for him.'

Hanna's face crumpled. Tilda said gently, 'Hanna, tell me why you have come home.'

Sitting on the bench beside the duck pond, Hanna swallowed her tears and explained about her dream, and her fear that Erich loved Caitlin. And Rosi's suspicion that Caitlin might use Erich to hurt Tilda.

And then, grabbing Tilda's sleeve, Hanna pulled her from the bench, and said, 'I think I know where he might be.'

Hanna ran ahead, her long plait beating against her back with the rhythm of her stride. Through the village, out towards the river, and then she flung open a gate and began to run down a path. Tilda followed her. The garden was wild and vast and beautiful, the house weathered and old. Hanna turned back to her and called, 'Erich made it. He was making the garden for you, Tilda.'

She told herself that he must be here, in this sanctuary that he had made. Each time she ran down a path or ducked the overhanging branches of a tree, Tilda thought she might glimpse him sitting on the lawn, or lying on his stomach beside the pond, watching the tadpoles. Through her fear, another emotion surfaced: an awe at what he had done. This huge garden, tamed by an ailing boy. This wilderness, made into something exquisite. Her poor, damaged Erich, whom she had plucked out of danger and transplanted to a sort of safety, had made this.

But the garden was deserted. Tilda went back through the ranks of box hedges, Hanna following after her. Hanna was crying, Hanna who had hardly wept a tear on that long, dangerous voyage across the North Sea. 'He'll be all right, won't he, Tilda?' Hanna wailed. 'It is my fault! It's all my fault!'

As she closed the gate of The Red House behind her, Tilda remembered Erich's euphoric happiness of the last couple of weeks. And Caitlin screaming at her, '*I hate you! I hate you, and I'm going to pay you back!*' At Poona she began methodically to search the garden. The vegetable patch, the orchard, the pigsties. The sheds and summer house, with their dusty, spidery clutter. The outside privy, and then the woods that separated Poona's vast garden from the fields beyond.

The leaves of the beech trees were like lime-green lace against an azure sky. Looking up, she thought she saw a black sack, caught up in the branches by the wind. Or a coat, discarded by Josh while climbing the tree. Then she saw the rope.

CHAPTER EIGHTEEN

Melissa was crying. I had to swallow hard to keep the tears from my own eyes.

She said, 'I was in France when he died. There was a telegram. We left for England the next day.' Her tears made rivulets through her make-up, but she did not yet dab them away. 'I didn't know about Caitlin's part in it at first. Rosi told me, after the funeral. Caitlin had gone by then and Hanna was ill, and my mother . . . I'd never seen her like that before. She seemed so *beaten.*'

She looked up. 'I've a photograph of Erich. Would you like to see it?'

As she went to fetch it, I looked out of the window to her back garden. A week had passed since the episode with Charles. The hospital had kept me in overnight, but my body had clung to this unplanned, unexpected child. Charles was now in a private nursing home, recovering from a nervous breakdown. His sister had told me that his production company had gone bankrupt. From the events of that night I still endured a lingering sense of shame, combined with a guilty relief that Charles was still considered too ill for visitors. Tall trees surrounded the velvety lawn in Melissa's garden, but I was afraid to look at them in case I saw a dark shadow in their branches.

'There.' Coming back into the room, Melissa handed me the snapshot. 'That's Erich.'

His face looked back at me, thin and dark with haunted eyes. The black and white image reminded me of those photographs one sees in the newspaper of other lost boys: runaways, and rent boys, and the residents of remand homes. I asked Melissa if I could borrow the photograph.

She agreed and, in the distance, I heard the front door slam. A voice called out, 'Mum!'

'Matty!' cried Melissa, and leapt from the sofa, darting out of the room. As I gathered my belongings, I couldn't help overhearing the conversation.

'Matty, I expected you yesterday.'

'I missed the ferry, Mum.'

'And you are so brown – and so thin – you have been eating properly, haven't you?'

'Mum, don't fuss—'

'I don't want you to catch anorexia—'

'You can't catch anorexia, Mum, it's not contagious. And I'm fine – starving actually—'

Matty wore the familiar Doc Martens and layers of black T-shirts. Her hair was a furze bush of snaking dreadlocks, and the nose-ring had been augmented by a little loop of silver in her eyebrow.

I thanked Melissa and took my leave, and drove home carefully. The events of the last week, and Melissa's story, had made me aware of the fragility of life. At home, after I had eaten, I typed up my notes. No wonder Tilda had found it difficult to talk to me about the postwar years. Her husband and her daughter had left her, the child whom she had, at great risk to herself, saved from he terrors of occupied Holland had killed himself. Her lover's daughter – her own niece – had been, if not responsible for Erich's death, bound up in it in a disturbingly unpleasant way.

When I switched off my laptop, I glanced at my watch and saw that it was midnight. I stared at the photographs on my pinboard. Daragh, Caitlin, poor doomed Erich, and Tilda herself, sitting in the garden of The Red House, surrounded by children.

A few days later, I received cards from the library, telling me that the books I had ordered had come in at last. When I arrived home after collecting them, a message was waiting on the answering machine. I switched it on, and there was a pause and a mumble, and a familiar voice cried, 'God, I detest these damned things!'

Caitlin Canavan. I listened carefully.

'Let me buy you a drink, Rebecca. We could have a nice old chat. Umm . . . give me a ring. I've left the Savoy, the service isn't what it once was. Oh, my address . . .' She gave the name of a hotel in south London.

I glanced at my watch; it was three o'clock. I dialled directory enquiries, who gave me the phone number of the hotel, but when I rang no-one answered. I hastily washed my face and combed my hair, and went out.

It took me over an hour to cross London, another half-hour to pick out the hotel from the warren of seedy buildings that lined the narrow streets. Caitlin's hotel, the Blenheim, did not live up to the grandeur of its name. Paint peeled from doors and windows, and when I rang the bell and was eventually admitted, the stale smells of cooking wafted into the hall.

I was about to ask the number of Caitlin's room when I caught sight of her through a doorway. She was sitting at a window table in the small bar room. The bar was formica-topped, backed by rows of bottle and optics. A bored young man rubbed a dirty cloth over the formica as Caitlin's voice penetrated above the low buzz of a radio.

'—simply must come to Dublin, darling. You'd love it. I could introduce you to simply masses of divine people.'

I went into the bar. 'Caitlin?'

She looked up. 'Darling! How lovely to see you.' She lunged inaccurate kisses at me. 'You'll join me, won' you, Rebecca?' She gestured to the barman. 'Barry?'

I realized that she was already quite drunk, and that, i she was staying in this hole, she must be short of money 'Let me buy the drinks, Caitlin.'

'Too sweet of you. A G and T, darling.'

I bought a gin and tonic and an orange juice, and sa down opposite her. The window beside us was open and the rumble of the traffic made the table shake Caitlin's hand trembled slightly when she raised the glass. Though her face was heavily made up, she had been unable to disguise the redness of her eyelids.

'I thought,' she said, 'that you might want to attend my father's burial.'

I stared at her. 'The body's been released?'

She nodded, and then she rummaged in her bag for a tissue as tears began to slide from her eyes. 'There's to be a private Requiem Mass in Cambridge, but he's to be buried next to my mother in Southam. I insisted on it.' She told me the day and the time.

'Caitlin, I'm so sorry.'

'I'm not,' she said fiercely, blowing her nose. 'I'm glad. I've found him at last.'

There was a silence, which I expected her to fill with

544

wild accusations about Tilda. Instead she said, 'All these years, I never stopped searching for him. Every street I walked down, every time I entered a room, I would look for his face. I even went to America once – did you know that? And all the time' – and she laughed unsteadily – 'he was in Southam. So now I don't have to look any more.'

It occurred to me that Caitlin had looked for Daragh in other ways too. In the succession of lovers, in the unsuccessful marriages that Patrick had mentioned. In her imitation of the way her father had lived – the drinking, the extravagance, the reckless bonhomie.

I said, 'I've been talking to Melissa. She told me about Erich.'

I expected scornful denials, and for her to contradict Melissa's version of events, so that I'd have to pick through the sad remains of another death, trying to salvage the truth. But she scrabbled in her bag again, this time taking out her cigarettes and lighter, and asked warily, 'What did Melissa say?'

'That Erich hanged himself.'

'I suppose she told you that it was my fault?' A flash of her old spirit. 'He was unstable, you know. Unhinged.'

'Melissa said that Erich was always haunted by what had happened to him in Austria.'

Caitlin lit her cigarette. 'He was odd. Different. Rather peculiar and unattractive. He almost *smelt* of fear and defeat. I used to try to avoid him. He gave me the creeps.'

'Erich showed you the garden of The Red House, didn't he?'

She paused, the cigarette between her first two fingers. 'Yes.' Her voice, just then, was barely audible. 'It was beautiful. You've seen it, of course?'

I nodded. 'Melissa said that you left home after Erich died. Where did you go?'

'I went to London. Tilda was going to send me to boarding school, so I ran away. We'd had the most frightful quarrel, you see. I found a job in a bar, and then some film work.'

'You were an actress?'

She blinked. 'It wasn't quite what I was hoping for. A bit . . . *blue*, if you understand what I mean, darling. But it paid the rent, and then I met a lovely man who was so sweet to me. But he got into a teeny bit of trouble with the police, and quite soon after that I went to Ireland.'

'To look for your father?'

'I thought that even if Daddy hadn't been able to go to my Aunt Caitlin, he must have had friends. My daddy always had simply masses of friends. Everyone loved him.'

Not quite everyone, I thought. Someone had hated Daragh Canavan enough to bind him hand and foot and bury him alive in the wall of a dike. A death of deliberate barbarism.

'But I couldn't find him, so I went back to England. I was working in a little club – quite chic, darling – when I met Graham. We married a fortnight later. Terribly romantic. A register office, I'm afraid – Graham had been married before, so we couldn't wed in church. It was lovely at first. We had a sweet little house and Graham treated me like a princess.' She sighed. 'But he was dull, darling, and that's the truth of it. Terribly dull. Especially about money.'

I imagined that, for Caitlin, the role of housewife had quickly palled. 'Did you have any children?'

She shook her head. She was looking into her empty glass. 'Couldn't, darling. I'd got myself into a bit of a pickle when I first went to London. I sorted it out, but I must have botched it a bit.'

I shuddered. A knitting needle, perhaps, or an alcoholic doctor who'd years before been struck off the medical register.

'You'll come, won't you?' she said suddenly. She had gripped my hand; her eyes pleaded.

'To your father's burial? Of course I will.'

I slipped my notebook back into my bag. As I rose to go, she said, 'I didn't mean to hurt him. At the end, I quite liked him.' The words were slightly slurred, and it took me a few moments to realize that Caitlin was speaking of Erich. 'I didn't know that he would do *that*.' The pain and regret of decades echoed in her voice. 'I didn't mean to hurt him.'

It was two months since I had visited The Red House. In that time, the garden had faded from the bright lushness of June to the dusty pallor of the end of August. The lawns were parched and yellowed, and the skeletons of the plants that had gone to seed cast lacy silhouettes against the walls. Plump greyish clouds intermittently blocked out the face of the sun, but it did not yet rain.

I had telephoned that morning to check that Tilda was well enough to talk to me. I found her sitting in the solar, a blanket, in spite of the lingering heat, folded over her legs. There was a photograph album open on the table in front of her.

'My Red House children.' She indicated the album. 'Here's Joan.' A dark-haired girl in a cotton dress: Joan was now, of course, Tilda's housekeeper. 'Joan was one of the first,' she explained. 'And Luke and Tom, the twins. There's Brian, and Annie, and . . .'

She turned the pages of the album, naming the children.

I listened for a while, but I could not stop myself saying: 'Didn't it frighten you? Didn't you fear for them? Didn't you want to turn away, do something different?'

She looked up. 'After Erich? Of course. When he died, a part of me died. A cliché, but it's true. I wanted to hide away. I could hardly bear to face the world again.'

'Then why did you?'

'Max made me.' She closed the album. 'It has always haunted me, though. Not— I don't mean why he hanged himself. I understood that he could not bear to live. But my part in it. The part of the de Paveleys.'

'The de Paveleys?' I did not understand her. 'What have they to do with it? They're all dead, aren't they?' The de Paveleys, in the chapters of the biography I had already written, had neatly epitomized the twentieth-century decline of the aristocracy.

'Not quite,' Tilda chided me. 'There is Caitlin, of course. And I myself am half de Paveley, so my children and grandchildren have de Paveley blood. And you appear to have forgotten Kit.'

Kit de Paveley, that reclusive, unattractive bachelor, had been easy to overlook.

'He still sends me flowers on my birthday,' Tilda said, and I stared at her, shocked.

'Kit's alive?'

'Of course.' She seemed surprised that I had assumed otherwise. 'He's a year or so younger than me, you know. He never left Southam.'

I remembered standing on the dike with Charles, on the day he had proposed to me, and looking down to that distant, shabby white house and seeing a flicker of movement behind a dusty window.

'I haven't seen him for years,' Tilda added. 'I wonder whether Caitlin keeps in touch with him? Probably not. They were never close.' She paused for a moment, and then she said sadly, 'I meant, Rebecca, that the de Paveleys have haunted me and my family. Even poor Erich's fate was bound up with theirs. Caitlin knew about me and Daragh, you see. That was why she hated me so much.'

I remembered the private detective's report, now in my desk drawer in London.

'If Sarah had not wanted to punish the de Paveleys for what they had done to her sister, then Daragh would not have married Jossy. And Caitlin would not have, years later, also wanted to punish me.'

I rose and went to the window. Clouds bobbed in the sky, but it was not yet raining. The shadows cast on the topiaried box trees were pasted black on the faded lawn.

'Chess pieces,' I said, suddenly, looking down. I understood the box trees now: bishop, queen, king, and, half hidden by a copper beech, the flaring mane of the knight.

'Of course. Didn't you realize?'

'I hadn't looked at them properly from here. And from the path you can't make them out.' The trees were bunched up, crowded, so that you had to look carefully to distinguish their shapes. I was beginning to guess why, at the close of her life, Tilda had chosen to have her biography written. Not for the reason she had first given me – to tell her mother's forgotten story – and not, as I had more recently assumed, to leave a bland official version for posterity.

'Erich and I used to play chess quite often,' said Tilda. 'Max taught me the game.'

The sun re-emerged from behind the cloud. 'It's a puzzle, isn't it, Tilda?' I said. 'You wanted me to solve a puzzle.'

Her grey eyes, calm and steady, met mine. 'You're good at solving puzzles, aren't you, Rebecca? I realized that when I watched *Sisters of the Moon*.'

Researching the programme, it had taken me four months to track down Ivy Lunn's child, taken from her mother at her birth in the workhouse in 1920. She herself had tried to find her natural mother a few years earlier, but had failed to do so. She had been adopted, and her adopted parents had changed her name. She had subsequently married twice. Tracing her had not been easy, but I had enjoyed it. It had been interesting yet uninvolving. It had allowed me to study the joys and griefs of others without suffering them myself. Yes, I liked solving puzzles.

'You chose me,' I said slowly, 'because you thought that I might find out what had happened to Daragh?'

'If he had not died, then Erich might have lived!' The fleeting passion blazed and then faded, and Tilda said quietly, 'I want to know before I die. Or I do not see how I shall rest easy. I didn't foresee, of course, that Daragh's body would be found. That was a great shock to me, but it was meant to be, don't you think, Rebecca? It was meant to be.'

'And your family . . .' I remembered Patrick's hostility. 'What did they think?'

'Melissa and the girls understand. And Max would have understood, of course. Josh has his own concerns, as always. Patrick tried to dissuade me from going through with it. I think that he was anxious about my health. I tried to explain to him how important it was to me, but he can be stubborn sometimes.' She smiled.

'Patrick often reminds me of Max. You're fond of him, aren't you, Rebecca?'

She looked at me, and I felt myself redden.

'He got into such a tangle with that wretched Jennifer,' she added. 'Ellie was the only good thing to come out of that marriage. Jennifer had expensive tastes, and Patrick worked long hours to satisfy them. They were rarely together, and the marriage fell apart. But Patrick is deeply attached to Ellie.'

I remembered Patrick running down the path of The Red House, his dark-haired daughter clasped in his arms.

'I've been hoping for some time,' Tilda said meaningfully, 'that Patrick would meet a nice girl. A sensible, kind, intelligent girl.' Again, she looked at me. 'It worries me, Rebecca, to think of him alone in that house in Cumbria. He showed me a photograph. It seems terribly bleak. What did you think? He told me that he'd taken you there.'

I had to go to the window again, and fiddle with the tassels on the curtains and make some noncommittal answer. The old questions still haunted me, but I found that I was looking at them in a different way.

Even if Tilda had killed Daragh, even if her explanation that she had engaged me to solve the mystery for her was only an elaborate red herring, did that negate the good that she had done in her life? The children she had cared for – the *Kindertransporte* children, the evacuees, the Red House children. The causes that she had later fought for – UNICEF and the Red Cross, and the psychiatric clinics that she had founded to help traumatized children. If she had, in a moment of anguish and fury, killed Daragh Canavan, did she deserve that I should expose her?

I didn't think so. As for the book – as for the baby

– I could feel myself coming to a conclusion. But not yet. Not quite yet.

From behind me, Tilda said, 'Patrick telephoned me yesterday. Apparently Daragh's body has been released for burial.'

'Caitlin told me.'

Her lids flickered. 'You've spoken to her?'

'Yesterday.'

'How was she?'

'Unhappy. Lonely.'

She said, 'Poor Caitlin.'

'She asked me to go to her father's interment. I said that I would.'

'I'm glad. I'd send flowers, but Caitlin would not welcome it.'

She was silent then for a such a long time that I wondered whether she had fallen asleep, but then she looked up suddenly and said, 'You'll stay for supper, won't you, Rebecca? Joan could make up a bed for you. It seems such a long time since you stayed the night.'

She seemed lonely, like Caitlin, but I had to refuse. I bent and kissed her.

'Next week, Tilda, I hope. I'll telephone.'

Tilda closed the album. Her heart ached with remembering. She would have liked Rebecca's company that evening; it would have distracted her for a while from the memories that would rush in as soon as she was alone. She had needed the past unravelled; she had needed Rebecca, the uninvolved outsider, to do that untangling for her. Yet she had not fully anticipated the depths of the pain that the past could still inflict on her: it had taken almost more from her than she had felt able to give. Recently, she had feared that she was running out of time.

The disjointedness, the bright horror of the days that had followed Erich's death, she had never forgotten. The inquest; the terrible scene with Caitlin. *You were my father's lover!* The tormenting knowledge, from that moment, that she too had played a part in Erich's death.

Max had come home. Tilda smiled fleetingly. Max and Melissa had come home, and Max had taken over all the tasks she had no longer been able to do. She had forgotten how to peel a potato; to scrub a floor exhausted her. Max had telephoned Hanna's college tutor to tell her that Hanna would not return to university until the autumn; Max had engaged a woman to cook and clean for the colonel, and Max had gone to the police station in Oxford, to persuade them to attempt to trace the runaway Caitlin.

Max had arranged the funeral. Tilda remembered sitting in the front pew, looking up at the bright, fractured lights of the rose window. Unable to say the prayers or to join in the hymns. Unable sometimes even to stand. If Max had not been been there, she could not have endured it. Afterwards she had looked around the sea of familiar faces. The van de Criendts had travelled from Holland, and with them had come the elderly couple who had looked after Erich in the months before the invasion. Anna had been there, and Professor Hastings, and Michael. And Harold Sykes and his wife and daughters. And Archie Raphael, and their old neighbours from Southam. She had not realized that so many people cared.

It was becoming dark. When she looked out of the window, she saw that the box trees cast a purplish shadow on the gravel. Tilda remembered the first time she had taken Max to The Red House. It had been a week or two after the funeral – long, dark days, all jumbling exhaustingly together. She had found the courage, at last, to sort out Erich's things, and had discovered his plans for the garden rolled up in a drawer. She had taken Max to The Red House that evening and had shown him what Erich had made, and what he would have done if he had had more time. And there, sitting on the steps of the terrace, looking down at the winding paths and drooping roses, she had sensed Erich's peaceful presence. The rustle of a lilac bough. A footstep, almost heard. Free of fear at last, he had haunted his garden.

To write a book is to make a pattern, and yet, of course, in real lives, there is no pattern. People are not coherent, they are not programmed as a computer is programmed, to react in the same way to similar events.

Many people had known Tilda better than I ever would, and yet even they, perhaps, had not fully understood her. The events that had made her – her brutal conception, the pathos of her birth, the infancy spent in an institution, had no doubt spurred her to help all those other neglected and abandoned children, but they had also cut her off from the rest of us. The more extreme our experience, the less others are able to identify with it. This is why people avoid the bereaved. Because they do not, until it happens to them, know what to say or what to do. Their incomprehension, their dumbness, causes them to retreat.

I worked for hours that evening, concentrating on the latter half of Tilda's life, writing about the Fifties, Sixties, and Seventies, the years when the difficulties of Tilda's private life had retreated, and had taken second place to her work. I had photographs: Tilda being presented with a bouquet outside the newly opened Erich Wirmer

Clinic; Tilda receiving her CBE. I put in order my taped interviews and letters from adopted and fostered Red House children; I went through the list of grandchildren, ticking off those to whom I had spoken.

Though I did not finish work until almost one o'clock in the morning, I could not sleep. I lay in bed, memories reeling through my head like a fastforwarding film. The box hedges in Tilda's garden, the expression on her face as she had shown me her photograph album. Patrick, at the hospital. *Come to Cumbria with me*. I wondered whether I could. The thought terrified me. I had lived in London for seven years – could I uproot myself and start again in that bleak, beautiful place? Though my home was small and inconvenient, though I was often lonely, there was a safety in my present life, the safety of the familiar. To live in Cumbria with Patrick would take such a leap of trust, of commitment, that my heart shrank at the thought of it.

My thoughts exhausted me, yet I remained wakeful. I selected the biggest and oldest and dullest of the library books on my desk, and began to read. The book's publication date was 1926; the first chapter dealt with the history of the Fens: a sure cure for insomnia. Curled up in the duvet I began to read about the Romans, their colonization of East Anglia, their attempts to drain a hostile land, their eventual decline and replacement by a less organized people. Then the Anglo-Saxons – St Guthlac complaining of mires and miasmas – and Hereward the Wake.

By the time I began the section on the medieval history of the Fens, my eyelids were growing heavy. I almost put the book aside but, flicking forward, I saw that there was only a couple of pages to the end of the chapter. I made myself continue. When I came to the paragraph describing the medieval punishment for landowners who had neglected their sea defences, I had to read it twice. My heart began to beat very quickly, and I was suddenly wide awake again.

I sat up in bed. I knew now who had killed Daragh Canavan.

These days, she woke about four in the morning, just before the first birds began to sing. Max was with her then: when she turned in bed and reached out to him, she was always surprised that he was not there.

Often she managed to doze again; today she could not. The conversation with Rebecca remained with her, the memories that it had stirred lingered, so that the events of forty years ago were more vivid than the misty grey of a late summer's morning. Tilda rose from the bed and left the room. She walked quietly through the house, careful not to disturb Joan's sleep.

Each room had its memories, yet he was closest to her, of course, in the solar. Voices whispered as she stood in the great bay window.

'I assume it's for that door.' He pointed to the peeling, rotting entrance to the house.

Tilda looked at the key Max had given her.

'I collected it from the estate agent this afternoon. I'm buying The Red House, Tilda. It'll take six weeks or so, but they gave me the key so that we could look round.'

She whispered, 'Buying the house?'

'For you. I know that you love it. For us, if you choose, Tilda.'

She did not move, did not fit the key to the lock. She said only, 'What about Cécile, Max?'

'Cécile? Cécile was a friend, a dear friend.'

He was lying. 'Cécile was your lover,' she said.

When he bent his head in acknowledgement, she said angrily, 'You should go back to her, Max. You don't have to stay here just because you feel sorry for me.'

He took the key from her palm and fitted it into the lock. The door creaked, and was freed from its spider-web chains. There was a swirl of dead leaves in the hall. Max held out his hand. 'Come on.'

She hesitated only momentarily, then she followed him inside. The rooms were just as she had imagined them, faded and beautiful, with fireplaces of golden stone, and worn, paved floors.

'Cécile's selling the garage for me,' said Max. 'And I went to see my father this morning, and he's lent me enough cash to put down a deposit on The Red House. The price is reasonable – it's been empty for years, and no-one wants houses of this size these days. It'll need a lot of work, but I'm sure we can make it habitable. And when it's ready, we can fill it with children.'

'Max,' she said.

They were in a room overlooking the front garden. The wide stone bay window was almost smothered by creepers. 'Our own children, or your waifs and strays. It doesn't matter. You'll find them, Tilda, I know you will. It's what you're good at.'

She shook her head violently. 'But I'm not, am I, Max? I failed Erich. I failed Caitlin. Even Hanna—'

'Hanna will recover,' he said. 'Hanna is strong. As for Erich and Caitlin, you did your best, Tilda. No-one could have done more.'

'I've always remembered what you said to me, years ago, in London. It was your birthday. The snow had begun. Do you remember? You said that I was fooling myself. That I was trying to put sticking plaster on wounds that were too deep. You were right, Max, I know that now. I thought I could help Erich, but I couldn't.'

He said, 'I remember that I was patronizing and arrogant. I remember believing that no-one could understand grief as I did.'

She whispered, 'I am afraid.'

Standing beside her, he put his arms around her. 'Loving someone is about taking risks. Love is dangerous.'

Then he kissed her. When, at last, she looked up, she saw that the setting sun had painted the garden with wild pinks and gold. She thought they had come home at last.

Slowly, they had come to her. The damaged, the bruised, the neglected. The children that no-one wanted.

Joan had been the first. Joan had come to live in The Red House in the July of 1949, a few days before Rosi and Richard had married. Archie had found Joan, at twelve years old already the casualty of half a dozen children's homes, stealing food from a market stall. Tilda had wanted to say no, to shake her head, to explain that it was too soon, but something about the child had stopped her. *I'll try*, she had said, in the end, and a fidgeting, shuffling Joan had stood beside her in church as Rosi and Richard had made their vows.

Luke and Tom, the twins, had been discovered locked in a room with their retarded, dying mother. They had spoken no language except one of their own invention, and when Tilda had first heard of them they had been destined for a mental institution. The vast gardens and big, airy rooms of The Red House had at first terrified them, and they had made a cave of sheets and blankets in the corner of the bedroom in which they had huddled for the first fortnight of their stay.

Other children had followed. Teenage girls, far too young to be mothers to the babies they were expecting; boys with police records for burglary and vandalism. The money Max had earned from freelance journalism had at first been barely enough to feed them all.

Yet that other baby, the second daughter she had longed for, she had been denied. In her late forties, when she had given up hope, she had sat beside Erich's grave and wept both for the son she had lost and the daughter she had never had. Then she had picked herself up, and walked back to The Red House, and her children.

The sky clouded over on the afternoon of Daragh Canavan's burial, and the fidgety breeze marked the shifting of the seasons from summer to autumn. Less than half a dozen mourners attended the brief ceremony in Southam churchyard. I knew Caitlin, of course, and guessed the elderly woman beside her to be Jossy's cook's daughter. I wondered whether the two suits standing back beneath the yews were policemen. I saw, looking around, that *he* had not come.

As the earth was sprinkled onto the coffin, I slipped out and walked to where the path led from the church to the dike. The boughs of the trees, their leaves just beginning to turn, met overhead to form a tunnel. When I emerged in the open field, I remembered how I had felt when I had walked here with Charles: cut off from the village, separated from my surroundings by both place and time.

The field had already been ploughed. Clouds, heavy

and swollen, rolled in from the east. Black dust adhered to my shoes as I crossed the furrows, heading for the old steward's house. The latch was broken, and the breeze flicked the gate open and shut as I walked down the path to the front door. There were small heaps of cement and stone in the grass, where pebbledash had fallen from the walls of the house. The window panes were dull and unreflecting, and the blistered paint on the frames was so tarnished by the weather that I could no longer tell what colour it once had been.

I knocked on the door. The sound of my knuckles on the wood was hollow, echoeless. I stood for a moment, listening to the wind shaking the leaves of the willow trees. When I glanced back to the dike, I saw that grass had covered the scarred earth that had once marked Daragh Canavan's lonely grave. I knocked again and, stooping at the letter box, called out Kit de Paveley's name. I heard shuffling footsteps, and the clink of metal as the chain slid from the door.

'Yes?'

I suppose one expects to see in the face of a murderer evil, or guilt. But I saw only, through the inches between door and jamb, a very old, very sick man. The sound of Kit de Paveley's wheezing, that Tilda herself had described to me, was painful to listen to.

'My name's Rebecca Bennett,' I bawled, assuming, as one patronizingly tends to with the elderly, that he was deaf. 'I'm writing a biography about Tilda Franklin, and I'd like to speak to you, if I may.'

'Tilda?' he said. Pale eyes, the whites yellowed, glared at me.

I took a deep breath. 'I came to Southam to attend Mr Canavan's burial, and I'd like to talk to you about him.'

For a moment, Kit de Paveley neither moved nor spoke. But at last he opened the door and said, 'Then you'd better come in.'

I followed him into the house. The smell made my stomach, still delicate, turn. Must and mould and damp and unwashed clothes. I followed Kit de Paveley along a corridor of greys and browns, of peeling wallpaper and ancient, dingy distemper. Heaps of damp-spotted books stood against the wainscoting, and a stack of broken umbrellas and cracked, mud-encrusted galoshes were abandoned in a corner. It was the sort of house where a lonely old pensioner lies dead for a month before a passer-by catches the scent of death and we all feel a collective shame. Both the house and its owner were decaying.

He led me into a room at the back of the house. More books, and piles of yellowing newspapers and magazines. There was a tray with a milk bottle and a sliced white loaf and a jar of Marmite. He had just had his tea, I supposed.

'Sit down, Miss Bennett.'

I sat, though I would have preferred not to. It wasn't a house you wanted to touch: as though sickness and old age and old crimes were themselves contagious.

Kit de Paveley sat opposite me. He wore baggy tweed trousers and a shirt without a tie, and a cardigan of some indeterminate mustardy colour. The frayed collar of the shirt was greyish-white. His face was a similar colour, greyish and translucent, as though letting through the colour of the bones beneath. I wondered whether he was afraid.

He said, 'Daragh Canavan's interment . . . doubtless an edifying event. Were there many mourners?'

I shook my head. 'Very few.'

He laughed, and then he began to cough, a horrible, racking noise that filled the dark room. My mouth was dry. I said, 'I thought that you might come, Mr de Paveley.'

'Now why' – and he smiled – 'would I wish to do that?'

'Guilt, I suppose. You killed Daragh, didn't you, Mr de Paveley?'

'Dear me,' he said. 'Such an imagination.' Yet he seemed neither offended nor concerned.

I glanced around the room. Such a lot of books. I said, 'You're a historian, aren't you, Mr de Paveley?'

'I don't recall' – again, that small smile – 'that being an historian is considered a criminal offence. Even in these uncultured times.'

'I borrowed a book from the library.' I delved in my bag and took it out. 'I expect you've read it, Mr de Paveley. In fact, I'm sure you have. There's probably a copy of it somewhere in this house. After all, you've always been interested in the history of the Fens, haven't you?' I found my marker, and opened the page. I said, 'This section discusses the medieval penalty for those who neglected the banks and drains on their land. "Bound hand and foot, the miscreant was staked down in the breach in the bank and there buried alive. In death, he thus became part of the Fens' sea defences."' I looked up. 'That's what you did to Daragh, wasn't it, Mr de Paveley? You tied him hand and foot and buried him in the breach of the dike.'

He began to cough again. When the spasm was over, I said, 'I don't understand *why* you killed him. I don't understand why you hated him. As far as I can see, you didn't have much to do with each other.'

There was a long silence. A fly crawled around the rim

of the Marmite jar. I heard Kit de Paveley say softly, 'The assumptions of the young are always so preposterous. Assuming that I was responsible for Mr Canavan's death, why on earth, after so many years of silence, should I choose to tell *you* about it?'

'Not me,' I said. 'Tilda.'

The supercilious mask shifted slightly. 'Tilda?'

'Tilda's old and frail, Mr de Paveley. She wants to know the truth before she dies.'

'She was well rid of him!' he hissed suddenly. 'He would have destroyed her!'

He still sends me flowers on my birthday. I thought I understood. 'You loved her?'

'Of course I loved her. She was beautiful. And she was kind to me. She was nothing, a housemaid's bastard daughter, but she was a *lady*.'

When he smiled, I saw the similarities between them, Kit de Paveley and Tilda Franklin, and recognition made the breath catch in my throat. Both had the same long, straight nose, high forehead and light grey eyes. In Tilda, beauty was informed even now by energy and compassion, but in Kit de Paveley the same features had been dulled by bitterness and apathy.

'What is it?' he said suddenly. 'Why do you stare at me like that?'

I had not meant to stare. I turned my face away, and wondered whether I should tell him that Tilda Franklin was his cousin, his blood relative. The impulse died, lost as suddenly as it had been born.

He rose, and shooed the fly from the Marmite jar, and screwed on the lid. Then he stood beside me, his shadow over me, and for the first time I felt afraid.

'For Tilda? Well then, I will tell you. After all, I've nothing left to lose.'

In the brief pause that followed, I heard the first raindrops strike the window pane.

'I killed him because he laughed at me.'

I licked my lips. Suddenly, he reminded me of Charles. 'About Tilda?'

'Not at first.' He remained standing beside me, one mottled purple hand resting on the frayed arm of the sofa, just a few inches away from me. 'I'd spent the day trying to rediscover the site I'd been working on before the flood. It was evening. I was about to pack up, and go home. It had been hopeless, of course. Layers of silt covering everything, artefacts washed away. Anyway, Daragh Canavan appeared just as I was packing away my things. He was drunk. He was disgusting. Swaggering.' Kit de Paveley's voice lowered, and as he leaned towards me, sharing his secrets, I tried not to shudder. 'Shall I tell you what he said to me?'

I nodded mutely. He was mad, I thought. Isolation and disappointment and bitterness had turned his mind.

'He said, *Did the water wash away your mud pies, then?*'

'So you hit him?'

'Not yet. He was bigger than me, remember. Stronger. Like an animal. He rutted like an animal – I saw him once, lying in a field with some tart from the village. He thought that I was a weakling. He used to make fun of me in the Home Guard, in front of the other men. And in the flood, he sent me to the church, with the women.'

I had to look away then, unable to bear the intensity of those eyes. The room had darkened as the clouds swelled, and heavy drops of rain battered against the dusty panes, sliding down to the sills.

'Would you like to know how I killed him, Miss Bennett? So that you can write it in your book?'

Again I nodded, and sighed silently with relief as he moved away and sat down again.

'He said, *Did the water wash away your mud pies?* but I didn't rise to it, I just kept on working. He was drinking from a hip flask. He offered me the flask, and I said no, alcohol didn't agree with me. He said that it agreed with him very well, that it improved his performance. He said he could keep going for hours if he'd had a drink or two, which would make the lady he was going to see very happy.'

He began to cough again. The sound was so dreadful that I thought his frail old lungs would burst. I left the room, and opened one door after another until I found the kitchen. I filled a teacup with water, and brought it back to him.

The redness induced by the coughing fit was succeeded by pallor. He was not only mad, I thought, but close to death. I should have left the house, perhaps, gone to find a doctor, but my curiosity persisted. I said, 'Did you know that Daragh was going to see Tilda?'

'He'd been sniffing after her for years. Wouldn't leave her alone. I asked him. He told me. And that was when' – Kit de Paveley's forehead was damp with sweat; he dabbed at it with a handkerchief – 'that was when he guessed that I loved her. And he laughed at me. So I hit him with the shovel. The first time I hit him, he was stunned, and fell to the ground. And then I hit him again, while he lay there.'

He began to smile. The smile was worse than anything. 'It was easy,' he said. 'He was drunk, and he never thought I'd do it. He thought I was a cissy, a weakling. But I've strong arms, Miss Bennett. All that digging.'

'You hit him with the spade and killed him?'

He stifled a cough. The rain still drummed against the windows. Water oozed through the leaky frames.

'Not – just – then.' He sipped the water. 'I couldn't think what to do at first. I almost ran to get help, and then I realized that we'd all be better off without him. Tilda – Jossy – me – everyone. He was a harlot and a wastrel. I'd a lantern with me, and I remember looking up and seeing the repair work to the dike. And I thought, how appropriate, how perfect. Of course I've read that book. Daragh Canavan hadn't looked after the land as he should have done. I'd tried to tell him, years before, that the Fens are different. He hadn't listened, of course. I bound his hands and feet with my bootlaces, while he was still unconscious. They were good leather laces – I bought the boots for a dig in Crete in '36 – he'd not have been able to break them. Then I lugged him to the gap in the bank. I wasn't sure then whether he was dead or not. It's not as easy to tell as you might think. But when I began to shovel the earth on him, I saw him move. His foot twitched. But I kept on shovelling.'

He went quiet. I felt sick. My fear had gone: he was just a mad, pathetic old man. I wanted to leave this dirty, airless little house, with its old hatreds, old jealousies.

But he was still talking. After so long, he welcomed the release of the confessional, perhaps.

'I thought they'd find him. All the next day I waited for the knock on the door. For weeks, months, I thought they'd find him. I'd dream about bones pressing up through the grass. I'd dream about opening a trench, and finding myself looking down at a skull. I couldn't *dig* any more.' He laughed. 'Well, I couldn't, could I? At night, when I was alone – and I was always alone – I'd imagine a knock at the door, opening it, and seeing him standing there, brushing the earth from his clothes.'

I had to get up and go to the window, though the dust and the rain kept out the light. 'Did you regret it?'

'Of course not! Think of the harm that he'd done. Think of poor Jossy.'

'Jossy *loved* Daragh. And what about Caitlin? Didn't you realize how much Daragh's death would hurt her?'

He mumbled something inaudible. The silence was filled only by the fly's buzzing, the rain's tattoo.

He said, 'What will you do now, Miss Bennett? Will you go to the police? They came here, you know. I lied to them – pretended that I knew nothing. What will you do?'

I shook my head. 'I don't know.'

'You shouldn't count on a dramatic trial. Your name in all the newspapers. I am dying, Miss Bennett, which is why I have told you this. I would not have done so otherwise. I have cancer. The lungs rotting from within. They say that I could have another six months, but I don't think I will live that long. I don't intend to see another New Year.' He looked around the shabby room. 'I have outlived my time. The world has become unfamiliar to me.'

He stood up. 'How many mourners attended Daragh Canavan's burial, Miss Bennett?'

'Five,' I said.

'Do you think I will have as many?'

His words followed me as I walked down the corridor. As I opened the front door, he said, 'Give my regards to Tilda, Miss Bennett. Remember me to her.'

I left the house, and walked across the field to the dike. The rain soaked through my thin dress and jacket, but I welcomed its falling. It cleansed me. I climbed the bank and stood on the summit in the wet grass. In the dike the raindrops made concentric circles on the black surface of the water. I looked up to the distant Hall, square against the grey sky, and I knew what I must do. I began to pick the last wild flowers that bloomed on the bank: purple loosestrife, oxeye daisies, tormentil. The bunch of flowers in my hand, I walked back to the village. In the churchyard, I knelt by Jossy Canavan's grave, and arranged the flowers in the metal container. Though I am not a believer, I said a prayer for Jossy, who had passed her childhood in terror of one man, and had endured through her adult life a tormenting love for another. I prayed that now her lost love lay beside her, she would rest in peace. I stood up, my hands protectively clutched over my flat belly. I knew that I would keep my baby, that there had been too many lost children in this story for me to abandon this one. I glanced for a last time at Tilda's sister and Tilda's lover, and then I walked to my car.

CHAPTER NINETEEN

Her ghosts remained with her, kindly companions for the most part. One night, she dreamt, as she had not done in years, of Daragh. They were riding across the Fens, and she was sitting on the horse's bare back behind him, her arms around his waist. She could feel the wind in her hair, and the warmth of his shoulder against her face.

Waking, she sat up too quickly and pain jabbed at her chest. 'Max,' she whispered feebly, and crouched for a moment, waiting for the beast to abandon its sport. When she was able to, she got out of bed and walked slowly to the bathroom. The indignities of old age – stiff limbs, weak bladder, forgetfulness – irked her more than usually. Inside, she was still the young girl galloping across the fields with her lover, yet the light grew dimmer, the body too frail a receptacle. When, washing her hands, she looked into the mirror, she could not remember what she once had been, and why they had once loved her. Daragh's face, seen in her dream, was fading too, yet the man she had loved, she thought, had died long before that fateful night in 1947, ruined by his own weakness. *You have got what you deserve*, Aunt Sarah's voice whispered. Daragh's greed had destroyed him years before he had walked across the field to Southam, and had encountered Kit de Paveley.

Kit, too, was dead, had died the previous October. The last of those to bear the de Paveley name had gone. *I curse the de Paveleys and all their issue* – Aunt Sarah's voice again. Sarah might have triumphed at the extinguishing of a line; she, Tilda, could not.

She washed and dressed, and went, as usual, to the solar. A first draft of the earlier chapters of Rebecca's book lay on the table. She had smiled to herself when she had read the title that Rebecca had scrawled in pencil on the topmost page: *Some Old Lover's Ghost: A Life of Dame Tilda Franklin.* When she looked out of the curved stone window, she saw that the frost had silvered the lawns and greyed the box trees, and that the pale wintry light showed that it was not quite dawn. She felt very alone. February was such a dead, silent month. 'Max,' she whispered again, but he was not there. The pain gathered ominously in her chest, and she fisted her hand against her ribs and leaned her forehead on the glass pane. So long since he had gone: almost fifteen years. You did not get over such a loss, you only grew accustomed to it.

Often she sensed him here, but today that was not enough. All she had ever wanted, she thought, was to be with her family. She had never yearned after wealth or fame or position. Yet her life had been one of repeated separations from those she had loved, each tearing away more painful than the last. A series of failures. Erich had taken his own life, and Caitlin had wasted hers. At seventeen, Josh had run away from school for the last time, and had wandered the world ever since.

The pain intensified, and she fumbled in the pocket of her cardigan for her tablets. She must not be ill. Melissa and Matty were to visit today. Melissa had promised her a surprise guest. One of The Red House extra children, perhaps, and she smiled, wondering which one.

Yet her sense of failure persisted. Tilda sat down on the sofa, and closed her eyes and dozed. She was walking through London during the Blitz. Fires burned in the East End, brightening the night sky in a horrible mockery of daylight. Rubble was tumbled across the road, but she carried on, scrambling over it, tearing her stockings on the broken mortar. She could smell the brick dust, hear the water from the firemen's hoses sizzling on the burning wood. She entered a street where the front walls of the houses had fallen away, so that the rooms, now three-sided, could be seen from the pavement. It reminded her of a dolls' house: open it up and see the patterned wallpaper, the three piece suite, the kitchen sink. The emptiness frightened her, but she kept on walking, skirting around the fallen beams and the shattered sticks of furniture and the iron bath tumbled like an upturned turtle in the centre of the road. Max was standing at the end of the road. She went to him, and he embraced her, and said, 'I was waiting for you.'

When she awoke, she felt better. The sense of failure, of futility, had eased. She was, after all, only a small part of history. She had had no more control over what had happened to her than she had had over the events that had led up to her birth. Her sufferings were not unique: they were symptomatic only of the sufferings of many in the troubled first half of the century. The ill-starred love affair that had led eventually to Daragh's death had not been the real tragedy of her life. The greatest tragedy had been that of war. War had deprived Rosi and Hanna of their families, war had robbed the child Erich of all hope for the future. It had taken Max away from her, and it had shown him such sights that he had been afraid to love again, because with love came the possibility of loss. Tilda sat for while, feeling more at peace with herself and with her past than she had felt for a long time. Forgiving herself. Then, in the distance, she heard a car door slam.

The sun had broken through the mist. Footsteps on the gravel. Tilda rose, but could not yet see her visitors: they were hidden by the box trees. She heard Melissa's voice, Matty's laughter. A child's high-pitched squeal, and then a deeper voice. Her heart beat faster, and she pressed her face against the glass. They emerged from the tall column of trees. Melissa and Matty first. Then Max. No, not Max. He was tall and lean and had a spring in his step, like Max, but his hair was fair, not dark. Patrick. And beside him, Ellie and Rebecca. Rebecca, whom she had chosen for her detachment, had become a part of the family. In her arms, Rebecca carried Tilda's newest great-granddaughter. *Sarah*, whispered Tilda, looking down at the child, and did not feel alone any more.

She went downstairs to greet them.

THE END

THE WINTER HOUSE
by Judith Lennox

For three girls growing up in the Fens in the tumultuous years between two world wars, the Winter House was a special place of refuge and friendship. Winter or summer, they would meet secretly at the old wooden house by the waterside to confide all the secrets and heartaches of childhood and adolescence. There was Robin, idealistic and clever, destined for Cambridge; Maia, the most beautiful and ambitious of the three, looking for a rich husband; and quiet Helen, living under the seemingly benevolent tyranny of her widower father, the local vicar. Adulthood separates the three girls, and Robin, abandoning ideas of university, goes to London to work amongst the poor, meeting there her first great love, the handsome but brittle Francis. Maia's ideal marriage to a wealthy man ends in tragedy and Helen, meanwhile, kept in near-imprisonment by her obsessively protective father, has her very sanity threatened.

Hugely satisfying, dramatic and romantic, *The Winter House* tells how these women find their way through a world changed for ever, through political and social upheaval, through the Spanish civil war and to the brink of the Second World War. Set against a backdrop of London, Paris and the unchanging English countryside, it is a novel of rare warmth and beauty.

0 552 14332 4

THE SECRET YEARS
by Judith Lennox

During that last, shimmeringly hot summer of 1914, four young people played with seeming innocence in the gardens of Drakesden Abbey. Nicholas and Lally were the children of the great house, set in the bleak and magical Fen country and the home of the Blythe family for generations; Thomasine was the unconventional niece of two genteel maiden aunts in the village. And Daniel – Daniel was the son of the local blacksmith, a fiercely independent, ambitious boy who longed to break away from the stifling confines of his East Anglian upbringing. As the drums of war sounded in the distance, the Firedrake, a mysterious and ancient Blythe family heirloom disappeared, setting off a chain of events which they were powerless to control.

The Great War changed everything, and both Nicholas and Daniel returned from the front damaged by their experiences. Thomasine, freed from the narrow disciplines of her childhood, and enjoying the new hedonism which the twenties brought, thought that she could escape from the ties of childhood which bound her to both Nicholas and Daniel. But the passions and enmities of their shared youth had itensified in the passing years, and Nicholas, Thomasine, Lally and Daniel all had to experience tragedy and betrayal before the Firedrake made its reappearance and, with it, a new hope for the future.

0 552 14331 6

APPLE BLOSSOM TIME
by Kathryn Haig

'There are ghosts. The air is buzzing with them and I have to sit and listen while they whisper to me . . .'

Edwin Anstey died a hero's death in France in 1918. Of that his daughter, Laura, had been assured – by her grandmother, the formidable Lady Anstey, by her mother, by her stepfather Tom, her father's old comrade-in-arms, and by the old people in the village of Anstey Parva. But they were all strangely reluctant to talk about this hero; his name did not appear on the village war memorial, and in the picture gallery at Anstey House his portrait had not joined those other men of the family who had served King and Country with distinction over the centuries. Was there some terrible secret? Why was Laura not allowed to know about her father, whom she had never seen?

A child of the Great War, Laura was twenty when the Second World War broke out, and as an Anstey she had to do her bit. In the ATS she was posted to Egypt and learned at first hand about war and what it means. She found love – or thought she had – but realised, almost too late, that her heart belonged much nearer home. And always, haunting her, was her father – handsome (she believed), brave (she hoped) but always, mysteriously, absent.

0 552 14537 8

A SELECTED LIST OF FINE NOVELS
AVAILABLE FROM CORGI BOOKS

14049 X	THE JERICHO YEARS	Aileen Armitage	£4.99
14514 9	BLONDE WITH ATTITUDE	Virginia Blackburn	£5.99
14309 X	THE KERRY DANCE	Louise Brindley	£5.99
12887 2	SHAKE DOWN THE STARS	Frances Donnelly	£5.99
13830 4	THE MASTER STROKE	Elizabeth Gage	£4.99
14442 8	JUST LIKE A WOMAN	Jill Gascoine	£5.99
14382 0	THE TREACHERY OF TIME	Anna Gilbert	£4.99
14097 X	SEA MISTRESS	Iris Gower	£5.99
14537 8	APPLE BLOSSOM TIME	Kathryn Haig	£5.99
14385 5	THE BELLS OF SCOTLAND ROAD	Ruth Hamilton	£5.99
14529 7	LEAVES FROM THE VALLEY	Caroline Harvey	£5.99
14297 2	ROSY SMITH	Janet Haslam	£4.99
14465 X	MARSH LIGHT	Kate Hatfield	£6.99
14220 4	CAPEL BELLS	Joan Hessayon	£4.99
14207 7	DADDY'S GIRL	Janet Inglis	£5.99
14390 1	THE SPLENDOUR CALLS	Susanna Kearsley	£4.99
14397 9	THE BLACK BOOK	Sara Keays	£5.99
14045 7	THE SUGAR PAVILION	Rosalind Laker	£5.99
14331 6	THE SECRET YEARS	Judith Lennox	£4.99
14332 4	THE WINTER HOUSE	Judith Lennox	£5.99
14002 3	FOOL'S CURTAIN	Claire Lorrimer	£4.99
13737 5	EMERALD	Elisabeth Luard	£5.99
13910 6	BLUEBIRDS	Margaret Mayhew	£5.99
14498 3	MORE INNOCENT TIMES	Imogen Parker	£5.99
10375 6	CSARDAS	Diane Pearson	£5.99
14123 2	THE LONDONERS	Margaret Pemberton	£4.99
14400 2	THE MOUNTAIN	Elvi Rhodes	£5.99
14466 5	TOUCHED BY ANGELS	Susan Sallis	£5.99
14513 0	THE LAST SUMMER	Mary Jane Staples	£4.99
14296 4	THE LAND OF NIGHTINGALES	Sally Stewart	£4.99
14118 6	THE HUNGRY TIDE	Valerie Wood	£4.99